'A swashbuckling thriller – *Pirates of the Caribbean* meets *Fire-*

'Reynolds makes the human story compelling in a narrative that, spiced with bizarre characters aplenty and propelled by vengeanc   Robert Louis Ste   *Nature*

Also by Alastair Reynolds from Gollancz:

Novels

Revelation Space
Redemption Ark
Absolution Gap
Chasm City
Century Rain
Pushing Ice
The Prefect
House of Suns
Terminal World
Blue Remembered Earth
On the Steel Breeze
Poseidon's Wake
The Medusa Chronicles (with Stephen Baxter)

Short Story Collections:

Diamond Dogs, Turquoise Days
Galactic North
Zima Blue
Beyond the Aquila Rift
Slow Bullets

REVENGER

Alastair Reynolds

First published in Great Britain in 2016 by Gollancz
an imprint of the Orion Publishing Group Ltd
Carmelite House, 50 Victoria Embankment
London EC4Y 0DZ

An Hachette UK Company

10 9 8 7 6 5

A CIP catalogue record for this book is
available from the British Library.

ISBN 978 0 575 09055 2

Typeset by Input Data Services Ltd, Somerset

Printed and bound by CPI Group (UK), Croydon, CR0 4YY

www.alastairreynolds.com
www.orionbooks.co.uk
www.gollancz.co.uk

ONE

RACKAMORE

1

Adrana had always hated Doctor Morcenx. He'd been the family physician since our parents landed on Mazarile, before we were born. He'd been there as Adrana and I grew up, and he'd been there when the plague took our mother. The plague was what turned my father against men like Captain Rackamore, because he reckoned they were meddling in things that were better off being locked up, but as far as I know no one ever proved the plague came out of a bauble.

None of that stopped him from being talked into a stupid investment in exactly the thing he disapproved of.

He was like that: easily persuaded against his own judgement. And it came to a head in the Hall of History one Forgeday evening in spring 1799. Father had gone to see what had come of his investment, and because he wanted to make a good showing among all the monied bigwigs in the Mazarile chamber of commerce, he'd brought both of us along for the evening. We were meant to be on our best behaviour. Prim and proper educated young ladies.

Adrana wasn't having any of it.

'Doctor Morcenx,' called Father, noticing the family physician a few tables away. 'Come and join us. It's been too long since you've seen Adrana and Arafura. Look how much they've grown.'

Doctor Morcenx limped over. He was a pepperpot-shaped man who always wore black, and too many layers of it. 'Always a pleasure, Mr Ness,' he said, in his gruff, greasy voice, touching a hand to his forehead. Then he started humming a little tune. Doctor Morcenx was always humming little tunes, as if his own thoughts needed blacking out, the way one skull can smother the signal from another. 'Your daughters are a credit to you,' he said, buttering his words until they were soggy. 'They must be a great consolation, given the disappointments of Captain Lar's expedition. Your investment wasn't too burdensome, I presume?'

'We'll weather it,' Father said, putting a brave face on things.

'You always do, Mister Ness, and it's to your credit. As are your daughters. Fine specimens, both. It's been my pleasure and my privilege to have seen them through their development.' He carried on with the humming, and started digging his short, fat fingers into his pocket. 'Would you like a . . .'

'We're a bit old for sweets now,' Adrana said. 'I'm eighteen and Fura's not far off it.'

'It's all right,' I said, allowing the doctor to take out his bag of sweets and pop a crystallised ginger into my palm.

'I've been meaning to visit,' Doctor Morcenx said to our father. 'I wanted to talk to you about something that might be of interest . . . especially in Arafura's case. These childhood years are so precious . . .'

'She's not a child,' Adrana said. 'And I know what you've got in mind. It's that drug, isn't it? The one that slows things down? Well, you can—'

'There's no need for that tone,' Father said, cutting across her. 'The doctor's been very good to you and Fura, over the years.'

'Oh yes,' Adrana said. 'And not that there's ever been anything odd about him skulking around the house like he lives there. It's no good now, Doctor Moonface.' She had a way of slipping that out as if it was his actual name, so casually that sometimes you barely noticed it at all. 'I'm old enough to know better, and Fura soon will be.'

'Apologise to the doctor right now,' Father said.

'I won't,' Adrana answered. 'You can't make me, just as you can't make me enjoy this stupid evening with the stupid captain and all your stupid friends, trying to pretend they haven't blown half their fortunes.'

'I can have Paladin take you home,' Father said in a warning tone.

Our old red robot swivelled its glass dome of a head, trying to follow the conversation. Lights flashed on and off in the dome. Paladin often got confused when its name was mentioned, unless it was given simple, direct orders.

'I'll be in touch,' Doctor Morcenx said, tucking his sweets back into his pocket.

'I'm sorry for my daughter's rudeness,' Father said.

'Think nothing of it, Mr Ness. The emotional lability of the young is nothing new to me.'

We watched him turn and waddle back to his table. He had a roll of flesh on the back of his neck like an inflated tube. He was still humming.

'There was no call for that,' Father said. 'I've never been so—'

'Humiliated?' Adrana finished for him. 'You know what the real humiliation is? Being a Ness, that's what. Grovelling our way up the Mazarile social ladder, trying to pretend we're something we're not.'

In a way, I was glad when a drunkard started shouting obscenities from the audience. Up on the podium, Captain Malang Lar kept talking, and then someone from the chamber of commerce stood up and tried to shout down the drunk man, but by then it was too late. Constables in pillbox hats and flashing blue epaulettes came bursting through the audience from the back of the room and started wrestling the drunkard away from the proceedings. But he was determined to put up a fight, brawling with the constables and staggering into a table, sending it toppling.

Paladin swivelled around. 'Disturbance detected,' it kept saying. 'Disturbance detected.'

Father started rolling up his sleeves. 'I suppose I'd better . . .' he was saying, making a show of letting everyone know he was at least considering getting involved, even though he was happier behind a desk than wrestling with drunks.

Then we both realised that Adrana had slipped away from the table.

'Find her!' Father snapped at Paladin.

The robot swivelled its head and rolled away from the table, picking a path through the brawl. Someone gave Paladin a kick, just for the fun of kicking a sentient machine. Paladin was used to that sort of thing. It wobbled a lot, but managed to stay upright.

'It should have kept a better eye on her,' Father said, fuming as he tugged his sleeves back down again.

'Paladin can't help it,' I said. 'It's just an old robot trying its best. Look, I'll go and see if I can find her. They were only letting people in through the north entrance, weren't they?'

'No,' Father said, wiping a hand across a sweat-glistened brow. 'They were using both entrances, and you can bet your sister's headed for one of them.'

Paladin was still sweeping the room, its dome spinning around, lights flashing agitatedly behind the glass.

'All right,' I said. 'You go back to the cloakroom, where we came in. I'll go to the south entrance.'

'Can I trust you to come back?' Father asked.

'Of course.'

I meant it, too. I had no intention of disobeying him. I wanted all of us to get back on the tram and ride along Jauncery Road to the house, away from the drunken chaos that had started out as a polite civic function. I wanted to be back in my room on the third floor, next to the parlour with all our books and maps and games.

'Then be quick about it,' Father said.

I left the table, skirting around the brawl – which was quietening down now, as more constables arrived – and began to make my way along the length of the Hall of History.

A clammy cold hand closed on my wrist.

'That sister of yours is a disruptive influence. The sooner she's out of your life, the better. Shall we look for her together?'

'I'm all right, Doctor,' I said, slipping from his grasp as if his fingers were coated in slime. 'You keep a watch on this room. The robot's trying to find her, but its vision system isn't very effective.'

'You're a good girl, Arafura. At least one of you's turning out the right way; a fitting memorial to your mother.'

'Thank you, Doctor Moon . . . Morcenx.' The insult had slipped out accidentally, almost as if Adrana was inside me, stirring up mischief. I flashed an awkward smile and broke away from him, knowing that with his limp he could never keep up with me. We had our best dresses and boots on, Adrana and I, but we could hitch up our hems and run in them if we needed to.

The Hall was much longer than it was wide. It needed to be, with so much history to cover. To begin with, before I knew what it was all about, I liked the fact that the Hall of History was pretty, with that long black wall running the height and length of the room, and the coloured bars that were lit up along its length, like irregularly spaced fence posts. It was easy to be impressed by the glowing colours and the writing in them. I was fixated on what was known.

It was years later before I stopped to think about the black intervals between the bars, and what they meant.

Soon I was at the south door. It was open and the warm evening was pushing in from outside. Constables were trying to impose order and stopping people from coming back in. A man was insisting that he needed to get back to the cloakroom where his wife was waiting, and an argument was brewing as they told him to go around the front of the building, which he felt was too much trouble.

A hand closed around mine.

I twisted it away, half expecting to see Doctor Morcenx again. But it was Adrana.

'Good,' she said. 'Now we can have some fun.'

Adrana started dragging me to the door. 'I'm supposed to take you back to Father,' I said.

'Oh, come on, Fura.' Her eyes were wide with anticipation. I knew she'd had a glass of wine when we came in but there was nothing foggy or reddened about them. 'We're a stone's throw from Neural Alley. I've got some quoins. Let's go and live a little.'

'I'm not interested in Neural Alley.'

'How can you know, if you've never been there?'

'And you have?'

But we were through the door now, into the evening, and there was no chance of the constables letting us back in through the south door. I glanced back in time to catch a glimpse of Paladin, still sweeping the room, working its way gradually to the open door.

'C'mon,' Adrana said. 'They won't blame you. I'm always the one setting a bad example, aren't I?'

We went down the steps at the entrance, followed a line of lanterns through the museum gardens, then crossed the tram tracks at Jauncery Road. The Dragon Gate was a neon portal before us, with the narrow winding passage of Neural Alley extending beyond it, curling its way south in the general direction of Hadramaw Station. I stared a bit at the Dragon Gate, just as I always stared at flickerboxes and screens when I caught them in the public spaces. It was a burst of brightness and colour like nothing we had at home.

'You weren't very nice to Moonface,' I said. Adrana had a hand around my sleeve and was dragging me towards the Dragon Gate.

'And you have no idea what a creep he really is. I know what he wants to do to you. They've come up with this medicine now. It slows down biological growth, allows adults to stop their children from ever growing up.'

'Why would anyone want that?'

She looked back at me with an exasperated expression. 'You're so naïve, Fura.'

'And you're only a bit older than me.'

We ducked through Dragon Gate, into the glow and swelter of Neural Alley. Adrana grinned back at me. 'We're in! Look at us, Fura – dressed up to the nines and out on the town! Here.' And she dug out her purse and passed me a two-bar quoin. 'That's half of what I've got on me, so make it count.'

I stared down at the heavy metal disc of the quoin, not sure what to make of this gift. 'Thanks,' I said doubtfully. 'But I've caught up with you, haven't I? We should go back. You can still say you've seen Neural Alley.'

But Adrana was moving forward, confident as if she already knew the place.

'Watch out for pickpockets and gropers now,' Adrana said, as if my words counted for nothing. 'We'll go all the way along, then come out at Cat Gate.'

'Then we go home?'

'Of course.' She grinned back at me. 'Where else?'

*

A fortune teller studied a man's palm. A barefoot girl with mad eyes and a glow coming from her skin begged on a corner. Two rheumy-eyed men slouched past wearing drab brown space-suits – everything except the helmets, which they held under their arms. Behind the men came someone dressed as a Crawly, shuffling upright on too many limbs, wearing a sash in the col-ours of the Bank of Hadramaw, with a big goggle-eyed mask on their head. Then I saw that it was a real Crawly, not fancy dress, and the alien was with the men in spacesuits.

I stared and stared, until I caught my slack-jawed expression in the opposite window.

'Yes, aliens,' Adrana said, like it was old news. 'They come here. It's close enough to the dock that they can do business, especially those of them in the banking line. Speaking of aliens, aren't these clothes beautiful?'

I tore myself away from the Crawly as it shuffled past, trying not to stare at the little whiskery appendages that came in and out of its proboscis. Adrana, unimpressed by the alien, was standing at a shopfront. Behind the glass were mannequins done up in glittery dresses and skirts made of tiny shimmering facets. 'That's Rattler skin,' Adrana said. 'They discard it. *Used* to discard it, anyway. Turns up in baubles, sometimes enough of it to make a dress out of. It's illegal on some worlds – they don't want to offend the Rattlers if they ever come back.'

'I don't think the Rattlers are coming back,' I said, remembering the bar in the Hall of History. The Rattlers had come and gone during the Fourth Occupation, about nine million years ago, and nothing had been heard of them since.

'Probably fake anyway,' Adrana said, with a knowing sniff, as if she had plenty of experience in this area. 'C'mon. Don't want to dawdle, not when there's so much to see. The next one's a Limb Broker.'

'A what?'

She raced ahead of me. 'You'll see.'

The window of the next shop was full of hands and arms and legs, stuck on velvet plinths or glass brackets or kept in bubbling vats. Some of them were alive and some of them were artificial, made of metal and motors and circuitry.

'That's horrible,' I said, watching as a tin hand opened and closed its fist in slow motion, like it was catching an invisible ball.

'You wouldn't say that if you needed a hand. Out on the ships people are always having accidents. More so in the baubles, when doors close on them or something, and they can't get out quickly enough. They can buy a new one here, if they need one – metal or flesh, doesn't matter. They can fix them all on.' Adrana eyed me with lingering disappointment. 'Doesn't take much to make you wilt.'

'Why is it called a broker?'

'Because that's what it is. You can sell a limb here too, if you need some quoins in a hurry. Then buy it back at a loss, or let the shop take the profit from a sale.' But then Adrana stiffened and planted her hand on my sleeve. 'Paladin.'

'What?'

'I just saw Paladin, coming through Dragon Gate.'

'All right,' I said, with a shaming relief. 'We've had our fun, haven't we?'

'We've barely started. Let's go and hide in that stall. The robot'll never look in there.'

It was a blue-and-white tent, squeezed between two built-up shopfronts. There was no writing or sign on the front, and only an open gash in the fabric serving as an entrance.

Adrana pushed me through, glancing over her shoulder as she did so.

'Someone on your trail?' asked a woman seated at the back of the tent.

'Just a robot,' I said.

Adrana lingered outside, then came through herself, drawing the gash tighter.

'Oh, the pretty dark-haired one,' the woman said. 'The girl from the nice end of town. Thought you'd be back, sooner or later. And who've you brought with you?'

'What?' I asked, frowning.

The woman rose from her desk at the back of the tent, scuffing her chair back over the flagstones. All her shop contained were plain wooden shelves that had been pushed against the fabric and draped in the bright glow of healthy lightvine. The shelves were all full of bits of bone, all the bony colours you could think of – some bits as small as fingernails, others big enough to use as clubs.

Next to each bit of bone was a small card tag with a description and a price.

'Your sister didn't clue you in, then,' said the woman. 'Seeing as you clearly *is* sisters.'

'How do you know each other?'

'Because she's been here before,' said the woman. 'Haven't you, Adrana? A few weeks back, wasn't it? And what's your sister's name, while we're at it?'

11

'This is Arafura,' Adrana said levelly. 'Fura. You should test her as well, Madame Granity.'

'Test what?' I asked.

'Aptitudes,' the woman said, sidling up and putting a finger under my chin. She elevated my face, peering into my eyes and frowning slightly as she did so. She had spectacles pinched onto her nose, huge circular ones with heavy brass frames, the lenses making her eyes swell up like a pair of worlds. She had a pinafore on over a gown, pockets stuffed with a glittery assortment of metallic devices. She had thimbles on all her fingers and thumbs, with fine wires running back up her sleeves. 'The sort of aptitudes that interest the ships.'

Adrana risked a glance through the opening of the tent. 'Paladin's nearly here,' she called. 'It's scanning the other booths.'

Madame Granity still had her finger under my chin. She stroked the other hand against the side of my face, up to the cheekbone, onto the temple. It wasn't just the coldness of her thimbles I felt, or the sharpness of their tips.

Something else was coming through: a shivery tingle just beneath the skin.

'If it's loitering, it knows you're near,' Madame Granity said. 'Do you want it to find you? Both of you?'

'No, we don't,' Adrana said.

'I'd like a say.'

'You'll get one. Look, we'll give Paladin the slip for now. Then we'll have some more fun and find our own way home. I'll cover for you.'

'You'd better come into the back,' Madame Granity said. 'The robot won't follow you in there.'

'How do you know?' I asked.

'Mr Quindar'll see that it doesn't.'

Behind the desk was a gap in the fabric, cinched loosely shut. Madame Granity undid it and led us through another partition. There was a big chair, with a padded back and a high headrest, tilted back on a sturdy-looking frame. A man was lying in the chair, a hat jammed low over his face, snoring, a newspaper spread across his chest. Madame Granity did up the cinch in the fabric then went over and gave the man a shove.

'Eh, eh?' the man said, dropping the newspaper.

'Wake up and earn your commission. I've got the Ness sisters here and there's a robot on its way to take them home.'

'A robot?'

Adrana was lingering, one eye up to the gap in the fabric. 'Yes, and it's coming inside.'

I didn't need to be able to see Paladin to hear the crunch of its wheels, the hum it put out, the buzzy whine as it moved its arms.

'Get off the throne, Mr Quindar. And you,' Madame Granity said, pointing to me, '*you* get on it. I know your sister's got the gift, and it often runs in siblings, however I'd still like to see it for myself.'

'What gift?'

'Just get in the chair,' Adrana said.

'What do you want me to do about the robot?' Mr Quindar asked, bending himself off the throne.

'Stop it coming in here for starters,' Madame Granity said.

Now that he wasn't lying down, it was clear that the man was very tall and thin. He wore a long black coat, and the hem of it should have covered most of his legs, but they seemed to stick out more than was right, like black stilts. His feet didn't quite seem to brush the ground, like a puppet that wasn't being operated very well. He reached into the coat with his right hand and came out with a stubby black stick, gave it a flick, and it popped out to six times its original length.

'"Stop it," she says. Vidin'll stop it. Stopping things is what Vidin does, most of the time.'

Without any great urgency, the man walked to the other side of the chamber, raised the stick, and began to smash it against the dividing curtain. After a few blows he stepped up his attack, reaching with his other hand to undo the cinch. The curtain dropped open, Paladin now fully exposed.

'Come on. Show old Vidin what you've got, you wheely devil.'

The robot whirred forward, or tried to. Mr Quindar – if that was his name – blocked its approach with a boot, jamming it against one of the leading wheels, and carried on smashing the casing. Paladin tried to defend itself with its arms, but its deep programming stopped it doing anything that might hurt Mr Quindar back.

'Go on,' Adrana said, encouraging the assault. 'Hit the dome. Smash the stupid thing to bits!'

'No,' I said, struck by some lingering affection for the machine. 'It's just doing its job.'

'Just get on there, Fura,' Adrana snapped back. 'I've got the talent, the aptitude. I found out weeks ago. Don't you want to know if you've got it as well?'

I hesitated, caught between curiosity and a sick horror at what was happening to the robot. But curiosity was the stronger of those two. I climbed on, thinking I'd regret whatever I was about to get myself into, and going ahead anyway, the way you do sometimes.

'What do you mean, weeks?'

'I sneaked out here on my own. That time I was supposed to go and get fitted for new boots. Well, I did that as well, but there was time to dodge down Neural Alley and I had to know. I've had an inkling, you see . . .'

There was a plate at the bottom of the throne where I placed my boots, padded rests at the side where I settled my arms, and the plump embrace of the headrest. The more I relaxed into it, the more it seemed to enclose my skull.

'What inkling?'

'That I might be able to read the bones.'

Madame Granity went to another device, some sort of apparatus hanging over the chair. It was like a lampshade, with a flexible neck. She stooped to touch some switches and the thing gave off a smell like burning toast.

Lights glimmered around the base of the shade and the object leaned in over me.

'I have been charged with locating Arafura and Adrana Ness,'

Paladin's voice boomed out. 'If you have knowledge of their whereabouts, please inform me.'

'The only thing I'm informin' you,' Mister Quindar said, 'is that you're getting' your tin head stoved in if you come any further into this shop.'

'Make him stop!' I called.

'Stay still,' Adrana said. 'It's mapping your brain. Working out how likely you are to be able to mesh with a bone.'

'Reading a bone is a skill,' Madame Granity said, speaking calmly despite the commotion beyond the partition. 'But it only works if your brain is still forming and breaking connections. Still learning how to be a brain, in other words. Children can do it, but they haven't got the wits to work out what the bones are whispering to them, so they're no use to a captain. Adults are no good, once their brains harden up. Teenage boys and girls work well. You can push it into your twenties, but it's a downward slope.' She made a ruminative sound. 'This is very good. *Very* good.'

The scanner lowered itself as close to my head as it could reach. Again I felt that tingle, but this time it was coming from the machine, not Madame Granity's thimbles. And it was beneath my scalp now, as if some small itchy thing were crawling around inside my skull.

'Is she up to it?' Adrana asked.

'On the way,' Madame Granity said. 'Maybe not as sharp as you, but then she's a little younger, isn't she? You've both got the talent, and the fact that you come as a pair makes you *very* marketable.'

'You are damaging me,' Paladin said. 'I must ask you to desist before I suffer irreparable damage.'

I twisted around, clanging the lampshade aside. Through the gap in the partition I saw Mr Quindar swinging the rod at Paladin, raising it high and bringing it down hard, the end of the rod gripped double-handed.

'Desist,' Paladin said, and some fault in its coordination made the rear wheel jam, as it was prone to, and now the robot could only spin around, no retreat possible even if the man had permitted it. But he had no intention of giving in now.

He tossed the rod aside, reached for one of the larger skulls on Madame Granity's shelves, and began using it as a bludgeoning instrument, smashing it down hard on the dome.

'Stop,' I shouted. 'Leave him alone!'

'Him?' Madame Granity asked, her eyes huge behind her spectacles. 'It's just a robot — one you were very keen to avoid only a while ago.'

Paladin was gyring around frantically. The arms flailed. They caught against the shelves, scattering bones. Vidin kept bludgeoning. He'd begun to crack the dome. Finally, and it was a kind of mercy, Paladin's rear wheel jammed against the base of a shelf. The jolt made the whole robot keel over, clanging against the ground. The forward wheels kept turning for a few seconds and the spindly arms on Paladin's side whacked against the stones.

The mechanisms inside the dome buzzed and clicked. Lights went out.

Paladin was still.

Vidin tossed aside the bone. He reached for the discarded rod, contracted it to its former length and tucked it back into his coat.

'I hate robots. Smug machines living longer than the rest of us, acting like they own the place.' He dusted his palms. 'Did you get a read on the girl, Madame Gee?'

'A partial, before you distracted her with all that clattering. She's got potential, that's plain. You think you can find employment for them?'

He scratched at his scalp. He had a very bald head, a lantern jaw, deeply sunken eyes, a pale scar running all the way from one eye to the edge of his mouth. 'According to the newspaper I was so earnestly scrutinising before you disturbed me, Rack's been docked at Hadramaw for a few days.'

'Rack?' I asked.

Mr Quindar pulled a chair from behind one of the shelves

and eased his lengthy frame into it. The flaps of his coat hung down to either side, stiff and ragged like the drying wings of some enormous bird. 'Rackamore, properly. Captain. Not the best of 'em, but not the worst you'll meet, either. Word is Rack's in the market for a new Sympathetic. That's Bone Reader to you and me. He'd sign up one of you like that. Sign up two even quicker.'

'Sign up for what?' I asked.

'Are you slow in the grey, girlie? For his crew. For his ship. For expeditions and so on. All above board. You sails out for an agreed term. Six months, maybe less. See some worlds. See some sights. I've seen a hundred worlds and that's barely scratching what's out there. More than just sphereworlds like this. Wheelworlds, spindleworlds, brittleworlds, laceworlds . . . more worlds than we've got names for 'em. You want to drink in some of that? Crack a bauble or two on the way, you'll be golden.' He cupped his fist, shook it as if it held a stack of quoins. 'More than you'll ever earn on this dungheap. Sign on a bit longer, you can retire on it.'

'We couldn't,' I said.

'Father's almost beggared us,' Adrana answered. 'That's why he got talked into that stupid investment, thinking it'd turn around our fortunes. Now we're even worse off than we were before.' She placed her hands on my shoulders, looking me square in the eye. 'But we can change that. Go out, just for a while. A few months. Then come back home, and share what we've made with Father. Do something for *him*, for a change. Oh, he wouldn't agree to it — I know that. But people don't always know what's good for them.'

'Truer words,' Mr Quindar said, 'was never uttered.'

'You know where to find Rack?' Madame Granity asked him.

'Near enough.'

'Then take them there. They can still change their minds, can't they? But you make sure Rack understands that he owes us both a finder's fee, if they pass his tests.'

'They will,' Mr Quindar said. 'Got a nose for these things, I 'ave. And these sisters ain't slipping through my fingers.'

I stepped back into the front part of the tent, where Paladin remained on the floor, silent and still, its dome partly smashed. Adrana, Madame Granity and Mr Quindar followed me.

I knelt down by the ruined robot, gently touching the broken dome, then looked back at Quindar.

'You didn't need to smash it up like that.'

'If he hadn't,' Madame Granity said, 'the robot would be dragging you home by now.'

'It wasn't Paladin's fault. It was just doing what it was told.'

'That's all it ever can do,' Adrana said. 'There's nothing in that head except lists of instructions. We're not like that, Fura. We've got something Paladin never had and never will have – free will. You go home now, it won't be long before Father brings Moonface round. He'll give you that medicine, the one that stops you growing older. And then you'll never get this opportunity again, not for years and years. This is it, here and now. Our one and only chance to *do* something.'

I looked at my sister, then at Madame Granity, then at Vidin Quindar.

'We just talk to Captain Rackamore,' I said. 'That's all. And when he tells us we aren't suitable, which he will, we come home and never say another word about any of this. Is that a deal?'

'Deal,' Adrana said.

2

Rackamore rented an office on the side of Hadramaw Dock, so high that the elevator had taken long minutes to crawl its way up there. The office was small, sheeted over in grey metal, with one large window looking back out over Mazarile, and because we were above the skyshell now there was nothing beyond that window but vacuum. It seemed wrong that anyone could be comfortable in such a place. There was a desk in the room and three people around it. Two were seated on one side of it, facing us with their backs to the window, the third one was standing on our side of it, leaning over papers and still in low conversation with the other two.

Vidin Quindar, who'd brought us from Neural Alley, coughed at the door.

'Ah, Quindar,' said the older of the two seated men. 'These are the girls, are they?'

'These is the lovelies, Cap'n Rack.'

'Then show them in. I'll take it from here. You can wait outside.'

Vidin Quindar made a humble, grovelling motion with his fingers. 'Usual percentages, usual terms, is it?'

'Ever the cut-throat, Mr Quindar. Rest assured that if the girls satisfy – and it'll be Cazaray who delivers the verdict on that, not I – then you'll have your quoins.'

We took our positions next to the standing man. It was pretty clear that some business was being concluded. The standing man gathered the papers on the desk, rolling them tight. Despite myself I couldn't pass up a squint. They were drawings, white ink on a blue backing; complex diagrams full of scratchy lines and geometric shapes. 'I can expect your word tomorrow, Captain? I cannot make you a better offer than this.'

'Thank you, Mister Gar,' the older man answered. 'You'll hear from us.'

When the man with the papers had left, the older man looked at us and said: 'We lost a hundred acres of sail out by Trevenza Reach. Have you any idea of the cost of sail? No one *makes* it now, despite what you may have heard. The wholesalers – men like Gar – gather up scraps, measure the shapes, sew the lot back together into useful acreages. Then they sell it back to us – the poor beggars who owned it in the first place – at about ten times what we made on the original deal.' A cautionary note entered his voice. 'But we cannot function without sails, and a poor sail is worse than no sail at all, because it inspires false confidence. Gar has a reputation.'

'So, unfortunately, do his prices,' said the other seated man.

'Was there trouble by Trevenza Reach?' I asked.

Captain Rackamore looked at me with mild interest. 'You've heard of the world?'

'Read about it. It's in one of the highest orbits, and it's very eccentric. It must have swung out of the Congregation a long time ago – a collision or something, sending it out into the Empty.'

'Right enough,' Rackamore said. 'No, there wasn't trouble – not the kind you're thinking of. We just ran into some debris, and it peppered our foresail pretty badly. Had to limp back on ions. No weapons, no pirates. Does that disappoint you?'

'Debris still sounds pretty dangerous,' Adrana said.

'It can be,' Rackamore said, nodding at my sister. 'Speed is our principal ally, and if we carried more armour we'd be too slow to be economical. So we take that chance. But I wouldn't overstate the danger: we're much more likely to lose a sail than to take a direct hit on the hull.'

He was handsome, in a slightly too obvious way, like a picture of a prince in a children's book. Square-jawed, piercing eyes, a distinguished nose. Fine cheekbones. Arched, aristocratic eyebrows. A cruel curl to his lips. His hair was long, but tied back neatly. He was tall, even in the chair, at least as long and thin as Vidin Quindar, but there was a refinement about him that wouldn't have been out of place anywhere on Mazarile. The white of his shirt was spotless, the leather of his waistcoat polished up like a mirror, creaking as he leaned forward in his chair.

In one hand he held a multi-bar quoin, tapping it against the desk.

'See for yourselves,' he said, moving aside some of the remaining papers to expose a handwritten sheet. 'This is a breakdown of my losses over the last ten years – the crew who died, were injured, who never came back; set against capital earnings. Cazaray will vouch for it.'

The younger man sitting next to him nodded at the ledger.

'I've lost two Scanners, three Openers, one Assessor, one Integrator,' Rackamore went on. 'That's a normal rate of attrition for the kinds of target we go after. We've hauled in to seventeen baubles in that time, and cracked thirteen of them. I lost the Integrator when a piece of Fifth Occupation technology turned on her.'

I swallowed.

'That's rare, though,' he went on. 'Integrators normally stay on-ship when my teams are working a bauble, and on-ship is always the safest place to be. There's no reason for a Sympathetic – a Bone Reader – to leave the ship.' Rackamore drew a clean, manicured nail down one of the columns on the ledger. 'See for yourselves. I've never lost a Bone Reader.'

'Then why do you need a new one?' Adrana asked.

Rackamore looked surprised. 'Didn't Mr Quindar outline our situation while he was bringing you to the docks?'

'Getting anything straight out of that grinning spider was more of a challenge than it was worth,' Adrana said.

'Mm.' Rackamore set his features in a troubled grimace. 'Tell them, Cazaray.'

The younger man was dressed as well as Rackamore, and his voice, although higher, was also that of an educated man. His face was scrubbed and pink, his hair blond, raffishly tousled. 'Even the best of us don't last for ever in the position, Miss . . .?'

'Adrana,' she answered levelly, meeting his gaze.

'And I'm Arafura,' I put in.

Cazaray nodded and looked at us in turn, a touch bashfully, before settling his attention on Adrana. 'We start young – the sooner the better, generally speaking. As our brain circuits harden into place, it becomes knottier to maintain coherence with the skull, or to adjust to changes within the skull itself. And almost impossible to learn to work with a completely *new* skull.' He leaned back in his seat. 'There's no tragedy in it. I've had a good run, and I don't mind saying that I've been well rewarded for it.'

'What are you going to do next?' I asked.

'Train up my successor first – no small business. After that, I should be very content to retire. I've earned enough.' I noticed now that there was a distance in his eyes, the same one people said they saw in ours. 'Under someone like Captain Rackamore, on a good ship like the *Monetta's Mourn*, ten years is enough to set you up. Provided you don't have exorbitant tastes.'

'We're not looking to sign on for ten years,' Adrana said.

Rackamore moderated the curl of his lips with a smile. 'I'm not looking to sign a pair of green unknowns on a ten-year contract either. Quindar should have mentioned a six-month term? Shorter than that, and it's not worth Cazaray training you up. But in six months, you'll have time to prove your worth, as well as decide whether the shipboard life's one that suits you. It's not just about being able to pick up the whispers. A good Bone Reader needs a fair hand, too, to set down transcripts quickly and neatly, and they've also got to be able to send as well as receive. The question is, do you want to take your chances in space?'

'We're not afraid,' Adrana said.

'Quindar wouldn't have brought you here if he didn't believe you had potential. What do you think, Cazaray? Could you work with them?'

'We've not exactly been spoiled for choice with candidates,' Cazaray said. 'And they've got to be better than Garval, at least . . .' But then he clamped his lips tight.

'I've heard of siblings working the bones on other ships,' Rackamore said, looking at us thoughtfully, stroking the quoin as he spoke. 'If these two can work together to pull some sense out of that skull, they might give us an edge.'

I drew the ledger closer to our side of the table. 'These numbers,' I said, tapping a finger against one of the columns. 'Is this what you'd pay one of your crew members?'

'Per year, and assuming a certain level of success with baubles, yes.'

'It's a lot of money.'

Adrana pulled the ledger nearer to her. 'Divide that number by two, for six months, and then double it again because there are two of us. You don't get a discount because we're sisters. That's already eighty bars worth of quoins. I'm not saying that would undo all our losses, but . . .'

'Losses?' Rackamore enquired gently.

'Our father made some bad investments,' I said. 'Sunk money into Malang Lar's expedition.'

Rackamore's expression was one of muted sympathy. 'Yes, a regrettable business all round. We're cautious – I won't deny that. But Lar took caution to unheard-of depths, keeping to the shallow processionals, the Sunwards, the well-studied baubles. The trouble is, those are the ones most likely to have given up their prizes already.' He gave a non-committal shrug. 'So it proved. Was it really bad for your family?'

'Our parents came to Mazarile before we were born,' I said.

'They'd escaped one economic slump and thought to better their fortunes on Mazarile.'

'Just as Mazarile was entering a slump of its own,' Adrana said. 'The crash of 1781.'

'Their timing wasn't very good,' I said. 'But they did the best they could. Arrived with a few belongings, some credit, an old robot. After the recession, they had to take us out of school. The fees were too expensive. So now we study at home, under the robot. Father hoped the Lar expedition would dig us out of that hole.'

'We shouldn't downplay Malang Lar's accomplishment,' Rackamore said, with a touch of forced charity. 'Every sliver of history we recover is a little less ignorance. A beacon in the darkness.'

'But it's not worth anything,' Adrana said. 'And when you open a bauble and bring back relics, proper relics that are actually worth something, you usually bring back some history as well.'

'It tends to happen,' Rackamore said.

'But not to Lar,' Adrana said. 'Which is why Adrana and I have to join your ship. We'll sign on, and Cazaray will train us. And we'll earn your pay.'

'And then after six months you'll leave us?'

'A lot can happen in six months, Captain,' Adrana said. 'Perhaps you'll be glad to see the back of us. Or perhaps we'll take to the life . . .'

'Cazaray?'

He leaned in confidentially, while still looking at us. 'I say we sign them, Captain. Standard six-month trial. Usual terms.'

Rackamore tapped the quoin against the desk, like a judge delivering a verdict. 'All right, we'll get the paperwork drawn up. Subject to concluding my business with the sailmaker, we'll be looking to break orbit in a day. Are there affairs you wish to settle, either of you?'

There was a knock at the door, and a long, pale face pushed through the crack.

'Quindar,' said Rackamore, irritated. 'I asked you to remain outside. We're not finished here yet.'

'Beggin' your pardon, Cap'n, but you might want a little chin-wag with the cove who's just shown up. Calls himself Mr Ness, says he's the father of the lovelies, and he ain't too thrilled about developments. Oh, and there's constables too.'

Rackamore gave a sigh. 'Show the fellow in.'

Father pushed past Vidin Quindar, and two constables loomed behind him, epaulettes still flashing. Father had loosened his collar, and his hair was dishevelled with worry, as if he had pushed his hand through it too many times. He looked grey.

'You ran away,' Father said, shaking his head at the words, as if they had no business coming out of his mouth. 'You *ran* from me. *Both* of you. The constables found what was left of Paladin! That robot was worth half the cost of our house, and now it's in pieces. The shame you've brought on me, on your mother's good memory . . .'

'Mr Ness,' Rackamore said, with a calming tone. 'I'm sure we can resolve this. I am impressed with your daughters, and I wish to sign them on to my ship. They'll be well looked after, and they'll have every option to return home in six months.'

'They aren't of age.'

'I am,' Adrana said. And after glancing at me, she went on: 'And if Arafura wants to assign herself into my guardianship, she's free to do so. That's all legal. You can't stop it.'

Father touched a hand to his chest. His heart was weak, we both knew that, some defect that the Mazarile physicians weren't confident enough to repair, but he'd developed a habit of playing on that weakness at moments like this.

'You wouldn't,' he said.

'Captain,' Adrana said. 'May I examine that quoin?'

Rackamore handed Adrana the fat metallic disc. She turned it this way and that in her hand, staring down into the shifting lattice of patterns that seemed to play beneath its surface, as if the quoin's disc were an aperture into some higher, multi-dimensional realm.

'You were using this as a paperweight, Captain,' Adrana said. 'I was.'

'It's a valuable quoin, isn't it?'

'One hundred bars.'

Adrana looked at Father. 'That's almost what you sunk into the Lar expedition. Fura and I could go out and earn eighty bars in six months – more if we're lucky. Couldn't we, Captain?'

Rackamore took the quoin back from Adrana and slipped it into a pocket in his waistcoat, where it made a circular bulge. 'I can see you care for your daughters, Mr Ness,' he said, directing his attention at Father. 'I understand also that you find yourself in hardened circumstances. Let me make matters plain. The moment your daughters commit to my crew, I will place a bond of twenty bars in the Bank of Hadramaw, assigned solely to the Ness family. In six months, regardless of what happens in space – regardless of how your daughters fare, or however many prizes we do or don't find – that bond transfers to you.'

'While you shoot off into space with my daughters,' Father said, drawing a finger along the clammy edge of his collar.

'Let me clarify my position,' Rackamore said, leaning forward slightly – just the faintest degree, but enough to suggest an authority, even a menace, that I hadn't picked up on until that moment. 'I am Captain Pol Rackamore of the sunjammer *Monetta's Mourn*. I run a tight ship, and I expect both excellence and unswerving loyalty from my crew. I do not promise them wealth. No captain can make such a promise, if the truth matters to them. But I will say this: while there is blood in my veins, marrow in my bones, and fire in my grey, you may trust your daughters with me. I have lost crew members, I have even lost a ship. But I have never lost a Bone Reader, and I do not intend to change my habits.'

'It's just six months,' Adrana said.

The captain was looking at me now. 'Assuming that the law – the Mazarile law – does allow for this assignment of guardianship, which we'll know before we leave this dock, do you still wish to go through with this?'

I glanced at Adrana, at Father, at the bulge of the quoin in Rackamore's pocket, then back to Father. He looked like he was about to faint, or worse. He wasn't just grey now, he was starting to look see-through, like something drawn on paper and left out in the rain. I think he was still hoping to wake up and find this was all the result of too much strong drink and food.

'I do,' I said.

'Her mind seems set,' Rackamore told my father.

Father took a step back, almost like he was going to slump to the floor. One of the constables took him by the arm, and Father looked at the man with something between gratitude and resentment.

His voice was strained. 'Where are you and your ship going, Captain?'

Rackamore gave a little grimace of regret. 'I'm afraid I can't tell you, Mr Ness. Of course we have an idea of our itinerary. But the baubles we've chosen to visit are commercial secrets. There are other ships out there, other crews, and some of them would stop at nothing to jump our claims. I'm afraid it also won't be possible for your daughters to send you much in the way of news until we complete this circuit.'

'How long?' Father asked, desperation clawing lines down his face.

'A few months. I can't be more specific than that.' Rackamore looked pained. 'I make no guarantees. But depending on our fortunes there is a fair chance we will stop at Trevenza Reach before we return to Mazarile. If that is the case, your daughters will have every opportunity to send a message home.'

'Arafura,' he said. 'I beg you. I can't make your sister change her mind. But don't do this. Come back home.'

There was a future stretching out before, a safe and predictable one, familiar and comfortable as an old chair, and in that moment I nearly gave in and submitted to it. But I thought of the house, of the cupola up on the roof, of the nights I'd spent peering out into space, of the glimpsed worlds, and the fantasies and desires I'd projected onto them. I thought of the magic and the mystery of their names, from Vispero to Dargaunt to Trevenza Reach. And beyond them, to the worlds without number, the tens of thousands of places where people lived, and the sunjammers that chased the photon winds between their orbits, and all the fortune and glory that awaited their crews.

'I'm sorry, Father,' I said. 'I love you. You know that. But I've got to go with Adrana.'

'I won't rest,' Father said, and when he spoke those words it wasn't clear who they were meant for: us or Rackamore. 'I'm not a wealthy or influential man. But I'll move the worlds to bring my daughters home. You can count on that.' And he held his finger out, but his hand was shaking more than he must have wanted.

'Wait for word from Trevenza Reach,' I said. 'And if that doesn't come, you'll hear from us when we return to Mazarile.'

And then I took Adrana's hand and turned from him, because I couldn't bear to keep looking.

*

There was a rumble as the rockets gained power, a lurch as the dock's restraining clamps let go, and then we were free, climbing away from Mazarile.

The launch had four rows of seats, one on each side, with a gangway between them. Each seat had its own porthole. Near the front, where the hull closed into its bullet-shaped end, Captain Rackamore had a control seat of his own, set before an arc of rounded windows. He worked levers and sticks, while dials twitched and readouts flickered across the curve of the console before him.

If we'd experienced a loss of weight in Hadramaw Dock, it quickly built up again.

'We'll notch up to three gees on our way to the *Monetta's Mourn*,' Rackamore said, twisting around to speak to us. 'That's more than you're used to, but if you're fit and well, you shouldn't find it uncomfortable.' But seeing our blank expressions must have given him pause. 'You understand what I mean by a gee?'

'You'd better assume we don't,' I said.

He smiled, patiently enough. 'Tell them, Cazaray. I need to lay in our vector.'

'A gee is the standard unit of acceleration in the Congregation,' Cazaray said. Adrana and I were sitting on opposed seats, Cazaray one row in front of us, just behind Rackamore. 'It's how it felt to stand on Earth, before the Shatterday – that's the story, anyway. The gravity on Mazarile, in the streets of Hadramaw, wasn't far off a gee. But that's only because they made sure the swallower at the heart of Mazarile was a certain mass, so that you feel a natural weight on the surface. If they'd made the swallower larger – or Mazarile smaller – you'd have felt much heavier. It's like that on many worlds, whether they have swallowers or not. The ones that spin – wheelworlds or shellworlds or whatever else – it's often close to a gee. And that's not because we've made them that way recently. They've been like that down through all the aeons, because it suits people. Sometimes the tenants came in and altered worlds for their own tastes, sped them up or down, added swallowers or took them away, but the majority never got changed.'

'What sort of world are you from, Mister Cazaray?' I asked, all proper and polite.

He grinned back at me. 'It's all right, Cazaray is fine. My first name is Perro, but I never liked that much – it's a very low name. And I'm from Esperity. Have you heard of it?'

I might have remembered the name from the *Book of Worlds*, but I couldn't swear on it.

'I don't think so.'

'Not many have. Esperity's not a bad place by any means. It's a tubeworld, a long can full of atmosphere, like a lungstuff tank, with windows to the outside to let the Old Sun in. They say the tubeworlds are some of the oldest in the Congregation, but they're fragile, so not many have lasted until now. The historians think there was a war, a bad one, between the Second and Third Occupations. Anyway, Esperity was all right, but unless you want to become a banker or stockbroker there isn't much to do there. I thought I might have the talent, but there's no one like Madame Granity on Esperity. I had to go all the way to Zarathrast just to have the most basic aptitude test.'

Then he turned to face the front, because our weight was going up and it must have been a strain even for Cazaray. My seat, comfy when I'd got into it, now felt hammered together out of knives. I wasn't in danger of blacking out, but even drawing breath was getting hard, and when I tried holding my hand above the armrest, my muscles went all quivery. I couldn't think of speaking.

That didn't bother me at all, though, because there was more than enough to be taking in.

The little porthole on my left wasn't quite as big as a dinner plate, but I could already see more of Mazarile than I had at any other point in my existence. It was the same for Adrana, looking out the porthole on her right. The line of her face, the way her jaw was hanging down, told me the view was knocking her sideways.

I knew how she felt.

Mazarile had been our world, our universe, all we'd ever known. We'd read of other places in the *Book of Worlds*, caught glints of them in the night, seen pictures and moving scenes thrown onto our walls by Paladin, heard Father mutter their names as he read the financial pages, but none of it was preparation for this.

Mazarile was tiny.

We'd seen the curve of its horizon from Hadramaw Dock, but now that arc had grown into a good portion of a circle. The lights of Hadramaw were like a glowing wound under the lacy scar tissue of the skyshell. I clapped eyes on Bacramal, Kasper, Amlis – smaller cities, each under their own quilt of skyshell. The curve kept on sharpening, and the dayside started coming into view – along with the cities of Incer, Jauncery and Mavarasp.

There was Tesseler, the crater that folk said had once held a city twice as large as Hadramaw. Smaller towns were strung out between these settlements, and hamlets that were built out onto the surface, without the cover of skyshell. I couldn't have named one of them.

All this on a world a bit more than eight leagues across, and none of those cities extending more than a single league across the surface.

Now I also understood properly how the docks – one at Hadramaw and a second at its counterpart at Incer – were like a pair of horns jutting out from our world on either side, as tall again as Mazarile's own radius, so that the distance from the swallower to the tip of either dock was more than sixteen leagues.

'Impressed?' Rackamore asked.

'I don't know,' I said, and it was the honest truth. It was impressive to see our entire world in one glimpse. But it also made me feel small and insignificant and a bit stupid for ever thinking Mazarile was anything special.

It wasn't.

'A world the size of Mazarile could manage very well with only one dock,' Rackamore said, sounding all effortless, despite the crush from the launch's rockets. 'But then it would be out of balance, and that would do awkward things to your day and night cycle. So they built two, exactly opposite each other, and we can take our pick of where we land. Mostly we prefer Hadramaw – the customs officials are friendlier.'

Rackamore worked the levers on the console and I felt the pressure of the chair ease against my bones. The rumble of the rockets became a murmur, like a dinner party going on next door.

'All right,' he said. 'We have the speed we need to match the *Monetta's Mourn*. It won't be long now.'

Soon we were weightless, the rockets silent. Adrana and I were still strapped into our seats, but I felt the missing weight in my belly, like the endless plummeting fall of a bad dream.

Rackamore said we'd be better off not undoing our buckles for now. We'd need time to adjust to weightlessness, and there'd be plenty of that later.

Mazarile had shrunk to a two-horned ball. The cities of night still glowed, but now Hadramaw was turning to the Old Sun and it was Bacramal's turn to slide into purple twilight.

'Here she is,' Rackamore announced, making the rockets fire again, but this time with less ferocity.

Adrana strained to peer through her window. 'It's tiny!'

'Everything looks small in space,' Rackamore said. 'It's just the way of things. No lungstuff to fuzzy up the view.'

'Lungstuff's got nothing to do with it,' Adrana countered. 'That ship's just small.'

The launch veered, bringing the orbiting *Monetta* to my side of the windows. Adrana hadn't been exaggerating. It did look tiny. Worse, we'd be putting our lives in the care of that fragile-seeming thing. The thought put an extra twist in my belly.

What we were looking at was just the hull of the ship, as the sails and rigging hadn't yet been run out. It was just a dark little husk, pointy at one end, flared at the other, lodged against the twinkly background of the Congregation like a paper cut-out in a lantern show.

Put a crossbow to my head and force me into describing it, and I'd say Rackamore's ship was fish-shaped. The hull was longer than it was wide, and all curvy along its length, with hardly any angles in the thing at all. There were ridges and flanges all along it, just as if it had been made from planks, curved and joined neat as you could ask. But like a fish – like some bony, poison-ous, bad-tempered fish – it also had all manner of fins and barbs and stingers and spines jutting out this way and that. Some of them I could guess had something to do with her rigging. And like a fish, it had a big gapey jaw at one end, and a pair of bulgy eyes near the jaw – they were big windows – and at the other end of the hull was a thing like a lady's fan, stiffened with ribs, that couldn't help but look like a tail.

We sidled in closer. Rackamore used the rockets like a miser, quickly tapping them on and off to cut our speed almost to zero.

'See? She seems bigger now. As she should. Four hundred spans, prow to stern. Seventy-five spans across at the widest point. She could swallow twenty of these launches and still have room in her belly. Prow is the open mouth where we're about to dock. Stern is the other end, where the ion exhaust fans out. She moves both ways, and up and down, and sideways if need be, but we have to agree on *something* – you never know when your life might depend on it. Do you like her?'

'Still doesn't look big to me,' Adrana said.

It didn't look big to me either, even up close, but now that she'd stated her mind I saw a chance to get one over on my sister.

'It's big enough. What were you expecting, a palace?'

Adrana glared at me.

'She's a good ship,' Cazaray said. 'Whatever you make of her now, she'll feel like home before you know it.'

Someone on the *Monetta's Mourn* must have been alerted to our arrival, for the jaw gaped wider, cranking open to reveal a red-lit mouth, a red-lit gullet, into which we slid like a fat morsel, no quicker than a walking pace, until the launch clanged against some restraint or cradle and all was still.

We stayed weightless. Rackamore and Cazaray came out of their chairs and indicated that we could unbuckle, but that we should move with caution until we were confident. 'One kick in the wrong direction,' the captain said, 'and you'll be nursing a bruise until Mournday week.'

Through my porthole, I watched the jaw close up again, squeezing out the last glimmer of the Congregation. Now all I saw were the red walls around us, ribbed with metal and strung with guts of pipes and tubes. Figures moved around outside, just beyond the launch. They wore brassy spacesuits with armoured parts and complicated hinged joints, their faces hidden under metal helmets with grilled-over faceplates.

'We can pressurise the launch hold,' Rackamore said. 'But most of the time it isn't worth the trouble. Easier to suit up.'

There was another clang, then some metal scraping and scuffing noises, conducted through the fabric of the hull, and then a squeal as the lock was opened from outside.

A small, wiry woman, not wearing a suit, popped her head into the launch.

'Welcome back, Cap'n.' Then a nod to the younger man. 'Cazaray. These the recruits, is they?'

'The Ness sisters,' Rackamore said. 'Treat them well, for they may turn our fortunes.'

'We thought that about the last one.'

'This is Adrana, this is Arafura,' Rackamore went on. 'And this is . . . well, why don't you introduce yourself?'

'Prozor,' she said.

Her face had a hard, feral look to it. The name was one I'd already seen in the ledger. Rackamore had lost two Bauble Readers in the last ten years, but Prozor had been in that position for long enough that her name had gone all the way down the bottom half of the ledger, year by year.

'Get them aboard, show them their quarters, make sure they're given something to eat and drink. Oh – and Prozor?'

'Cap'n?'

'This is new to them. Every part of it, from weightlessness to living with vacuum only a scratch away.'

Prozor shrugged. 'I'll make allowance.'

'Good. And now I need to talk to Hirtshal about the new sail we've just brought from Mazarile. We'll break orbit shortly, on ions if the sails aren't ready. I've a mind to put some leagues between us and Hadramaw Dock.'

'Something up?'

Rackamore nodded, his jaw set tight. 'Family business.'

*

They never told us exactly how old the ship was, or who had owned it before Rackamore, much less who'd put down the quoins to have her made. But if the long-dead coves who'd designed the *Monetta's Mourn* had set out to make her insides as confusing and twisty as possible, they couldn't have bettered the job they'd done. It was a mad maze of passages and rooms and cupboards and doors. Four hundred spans doesn't seem like much, and maybe it isn't when you're speaking of a row of houses or a stroll through Mavarasp Park. But it's surprising how many little rooms you can stuff into the fat belly of a four-hundred-span ship, and surprising how many different ways you can come up with of linking them together, especially when there's no up or down and no good reason not to put a door in a ceiling or a window in a floor. Passages twisted, forked, doubled back on themselves for no sound argument. Ladders and stair-ways threaded between decks, while bone-scraping crawlways linked compartments. There were hatches and ducts, elevators and winches. Pipes and wires went everywhere, and the ship gurgled, hissed and hummed to itself like a thing that was al-ready half alive. Lightvine had been strung along the pipes and wires, encouraged to grow into all the inhabited spaces of the ship. Where the lightvine couldn't be coaxed, other artificial lighting sources had been used.

'This is where you'll get your squint-time,' Prozor said, when we reached what seemed to be a set of cupboards. 'Ain't large, but you won't need much space when we're under way. More beddin' if you need it – you probably will.'

'We sleep here?' Adrana asked.

'No, girlie, you play skittles here.' Prozor opened the doors to show us what we were facing.

'Does it get cold?' I risked asking.

'Truer to say it sometimes gets warm. Not afraid of a little cold, is you?'

'I'm not,' I said.

'We'll manage,' Adrana said, casting me a glance.

The space was a compartment about the size of the smallest room either of us had ever slept in, and this was meant for two. At the back of it were two hammocks, one above the other, and a curtain that you could tug across the hammocks for privacy.

Prozor showed us the hatches that held more bedding, as well as space for personal effects – not that we'd brought anything with us.

'Sumptuous,' I said.

'Used to better, is you?'

'I thought the captain told you to be nice to us,' Adrana said.

'You were getting the nasty side of me, you'd know it.' But after a heavy sigh Prozor said: 'Ain't as bad as it looks. A cove gets used to things soon enough, and you'll only spend as much time here as you want to. We nosh together. You'll be the new cooks now – it's always the Bone Reader what cooks, 'cause them being so precious and delicate they ain't got much *else* to do. Other than that, you'll be in the galley with the rest of us, singin' songs, tellin' stories, puttin' on plays, readin' fortunes, whatever passes the hours.' She gave us a forbidding look. 'Plenty of things scarce on a ship. Hours ain't one of them.'

'Are there books?' I asked.

'Books your thing, are they?'

'Yes. It's called reading.'

Prozor sniffed, wrinkling her nose. She had sharp features: sharp nose, sharp chin, sharp dark eyes under jagged brows. She had a face that would look angry no matter her mood – all vees and angles, as if she had been sketched in a hurry, with hard strokes. Her hair was as sharp-looking as the rest of her, bristling out at all angles and stiffened into spikes and barbs by some kind of glue or lacquer.

'Talk to Cap'n Rack. He's always pleased to show off his library. More books in there than you'll know how to read.'

'I doubt that,' I said.

Prozor led us back through the ship. It might have been the way we had come, or some completely different route. It was hard to tell. She was pointing out different things all the while, grumpily unconcerned with how much we could take in at a time.

'Near the middle now,' she said, as we squeezed around an elbow in the passageway, still weightless. Adrana and I were moving by our fingertips and careful use of our feet, while Prozor darted forward with reckless speed, only to keep stopping and looking back at us as we caught up. She slid open a panel, ushered us through it.

'Are you lost yet?'

I nodded. 'Yes.'

'Good. Way we like it. Someone else comes aboard this ship, we don't want 'em stumblin' on the bones too easy.'

We were at a grey door, armoured like an airlock, with a wheel-shaped locking mechanism. We'd passed a dozen similar doors already. 'Put it here for other reasons, not just to make it hard to find,' Prozor went on. 'Needs to be somewhere quiet, not too close to the bridge or the galley or any of that stuff. Can't be too close to the sail-control gear or the engine room, either. This is the prime spot, and you're welcome to it.'

'Do you ever go inside?' Adrana asked.

'Couldn't pay me enough, girlie. I read baubles. That's what I'm good at.'

'You're forgetting your talent for charm and hospitality,' I said.

'You think this is funny, what you're getting into? Let me tell you about baubles. Readin' baubles will drive you mad, but that's only because it's knotty and a lot depends on making the right interpretation. Lives. Quoins. Reputation. Readin' skulls . . .' Prozor trailed off with a sadistic little shudder, before adding: 'I like my head as it is. Don't need no alien ghosts rattling around inside it, givin' me shivery dreams.'

With the bone room dealt with, Prozor took us to a compartment full of clothing: cupboards, drawers and hoppers full of trousers, tunics, belts, gloves, all of it jumbled up with no rhyme or reason with regards to size or fit. 'Find what suits you. Long dresses might look fancy on Mazarile, but here they'll only trip you up.'

Prozor wore trousers, leather slippers and a black blouse, with various items of tarnished jewellery rattling around her throat in the weightlessness.

Adrana sifted through the musty, mould-spotted contents of one drawer. She pulled out a glove, jutting her finger through a hole.

'Did a bullet do that?'

Prozor examined it thoughtfully.

'No, girlie, that'd be a rat.'

'We'll keep our dresses,' Adrana said.

*

The galley was up front, between the bridge and Captain Rackamore's quarters. By the time we arrived, the other crew had gathered there to welcome us. Even though we were still weightless, they were all managing to sit on chairs around a large circular table that was patterned with black and white hexagons, with items of food and drink fixed onto it by some means. Two windows of similar size bulged out into space on either side of the room – Mazarile was visible through one of them, turning slowly as we orbited it. There was a console in one corner, a few screens and readouts lit up, and some smaller controls and displays dotted elsewhere around the place, glowing like little flickerboxes, but mainly it appeared to be somewhere for the crew to eat, relax and discuss plans, and none of them seemed to be paying any heed to the equipment.

'Come on in,' said a burly, bearded man, indicating two vacant spaces either side of him at the table. He had an open, friendly face. 'We don't bite. If you've already met Prozor, then you'll find the rest of us a distinct improvement.' He slid a tankard across the table, from a black hexagon to a white, lifted it, then pinched his lips around the drinking nozzle in its lid. 'Mattice,' he added, after a sip. 'Opener to his imperial majesty Captain Rack. And a damn fine one if I say so myself.'

'You do,' said the woman next to him. 'All the time.'

'Whereas you've never been known to brag about your touch with the gubbins, Jusquerel.'

'That's not bragging, Mattice. You think this ships runs on

moonbeams and puppies?' She nodded at us. 'Jusquerel. Integrator. Did Prozor show you the bridge?'

'Not yet,' I said.

'I'll show you later. I put the main sweeper in, and the squawk, and that secondary console over there. My job is getting one box of gubbins to talk to another, even when they weren't even made by the same species. Anything on this ship works the way it was meant to, you can thank me for it.'

Jusquerel was an older woman with a strong jaw, a small upcurved nose, and very long hair, which she wore in a complicated braid, slung back over her shoulder so that it hung – or floated – down her chest, cutting diagonally across it. The braid was all threaded shades of silver-grey and bluish-white, as if it were spun from extremely fine metals. There was a poise to Jusquerel, an elegance to her posture that set her apart from the others.

'Come and sit with us,' Mattice repeated, patting one of the vacant chairs. 'Here. Beer. Bread. Are they all so skinny in Hadramaw?' He directed a reproachful look at Prozor. 'I hope you haven't scared the wits out of them.'

'Someone needs to,' Prozor said, unconcerned, taking her own seat at the table. She slid a metal box across the table, black hexagon to black hexagon, and eased open the lid, fishing around until she came out with a loaf of bread. 'Any greener, they'd be foetuses.'

'We were all green once,' said a third member of the crew, as we took our places, one either side of Mattice. 'None of us were born on a ship, out in space.' He coughed, touched a hand to his throat. 'Triglav. Ion systems. I'm the poor bastard who has to move this ship around when the sails won't flap.'

Triglav was small, bald and unassuming. He had the sort of downcast face that was bound to look worried about something regardless of what kind of day he was having. 'Cazaray thinks you might be our new Bone Readers. If Cazaray says it, it's good enough for me.'

'You said that last time, Trig,' said the woman next to him, who was as small as the ion engineer, but tough-looking instead, with her arms bared on the table before her, all messed over with tattoos and bulging with muscles. She had her hair shaved on one side of her scalp, long on the other, and her eyebrows looked like they'd been drawn on with ink, which maybe they had.

'Trysil,' she said, in her broken rasp of her voice. 'Assessor.' She reached out a hand, shaking with us in turn. Her grip was firm, and her palm was rough.

'What happened last time?' I asked.

'There wasn't a last time,' said Mattice, smiling fiercely.

'They may as well find out about the screamer now,' Prozor said, biting into her loaf. 'Because they soon will, whatever happens.'

'Screamer?' I asked.

Just then there was a creak, a groan, as if the ship itself were suffering some spasm of indigestion. I tensed, as did Adrana, but only for as long as it took for us to realise that none of the others were concerned. In fact, the sound drew a murmur of celebration from them, with even Prozor lifting a tankard.

'That didn't take long,' Trysil said, clenching a fist so that the muscles popped out along her arm.

'You know the captain. When he wants to leave, we leave.'

'Are we on sails now?' Adrana asked.

'Ions,' Triglav said. 'We'll run the sails out when we've put some distance twixt us and Mazarile, but this close in there's too much risk of puncturing them with space debris.' He wiped a hand across his mouth. 'Best go and earn my fee, hadn't I? I don't want that engine overheating before Hirtshal's ready with the new sail.' Then he nodded at Adrana and me. 'Welcome aboard.'

'Thank you,' I said.

They cleared away from the table, one after the other, until it was only Jusquerel left with Adrana and me. She kept on eating and drinking for at least a minute before saying anything. That was just her unhurried way, though, and I didn't think there was anything in her manner meant to unsettle us.

'You needn't mind Prozor.'

'She doesn't seem to like us very much,' Adrana said.

'It's not you. It's what you are.' Her jaw worked as she chewed. 'Here. Have some more bread. Mattice was right: you both need feeding up.'

'I don't have much of an appetite,' I said.

'Space sickness,' Jusquerel said. 'If this is your first time up, it's no wonder. We don't run with a doctor on this ship, so if anyone fits that bill, I suppose it's me.' She fished into a pocket and came out with a little metal tin. She clacked it onto the magnetic table, slid it over to us like a deck of cards. 'One a day should see you straight, but take two if you need to. My guess is you'll be fine by the time we hit the bauble.'

I took the tin. It was pretty, with a machine-engraved pattern of interlocking birds, and I wondered if it had come from one of the earlier Occupations.

It was often difficult to tell if things were a hundred years old, or a hundred thousand.

'Do we owe you anything?' Adrana asked.

'Do well by the bones,' Jusquerel said, 'and that'll be payment enough for me.'

'Thank you,' I said. 'How long will it be, until we get to the bauble?'

'I can't tell you,' she answered, drawling out her answer as if some mainspring or regulator in her head ran a little off synchronisation with the rest of us.

'Can't or won't?' I asked.

'Can't. None of us know, except Cap'n Rack and maybe Cazaray. That's how it works. If one of us knew which bauble we were headed to and squawked that information to another crew . . . or even just blabbed about it without thinking – that could ruin us. So the Cap'n tells us to expect a voyage of at least a certain number of weeks or months, and we make sure we've provisions for that sort of trip. Hirtshal sets the sails, but even

Hirtshal doesn't know how far out or for how long we're going – not until the Cap'n gives another order, and we steer or haul in.'

'You said Cazaray,' I replied.

'Yes.'

'Why would he know?'

'The only way secrets come in and off this ship – other than sealed papers in the Cap'n's pocket – is through the Bone Reader. There's no way for the Bone Reader *not* to know anything important about a sunjammer – and if you try to hide it from them, they'll find out anyway.'

'So Bone Reader's quite an important position,' Adrana said. 'But they also have to be someone quite young, or they can't work with the bones.'

'Yes,' Jusquerel. 'Young. Often the youngest of any of us. But gifted with the Cap'n's secrets and the Cap'n's ear.' She gave a barely interested shrug. 'You can see how that might sit badly with some people.'

'I suppose it might,' Adrana said.

3

We were on ship's time from then on. It'd been night in Hadramaw when we left, but it was mid-afternoon here, and that gathering in the galley hadn't been more than a light meal between duties. The next six hours were our own, and then we were to gather again in the evening. Rackamore said we should explore as much of the *Monetta* as we liked, provided we took care. Adrana and I went back to our quarters and we spent an hour sewing up our dresses so that they were less cumbersome in weightless or near-weightless conditions. 'I don't mind blending in,' Adrana said, speaking with a needle between her lips. 'But I draw the line at wearing rat-eaten clothes.'

'I haven't seen any rats yet,' I said, trying to inject an optimistic note. 'How would rats get on a ship like this anyway?'

'How do rats get anywhere? How did rats end up in the Congregation?'

I shrugged, unwilling to follow that line of thought too far. 'How did anyone?'

When the dresses were ready we set off again. We went from room to room, up and down levels (not that 'up' and 'down' had much meaning now), slowly building a map in our heads.

The ion engine wasn't exactly powerful. It put out five-hundredth of a gee, and you had to work hard to notice that. For a long while it didn't seem possible that we'd ever get anywhere.

But the sly thing about it was that it was continuous, and over hours and hours, while we were busy doing other things, it was easy to forget that the ion engine was still giving out its push. When Adrana and I came across a window on the side of the ship facing Mazarile, it was jarring to see how small our world had become. We'd already travelled tens of thousands of leagues, turning Mazarile into a barely significant speck, a double-horned dot slowly losing itself against the greater mass of the Congregation.

We were heading out, into the Empty.

'I don't like not knowing where we're headed,' Adrana said, in a low whisper, as we watched our world turn tiny.

'Bit late for misgivings now.' I put a hand on hers, wondering why it had fallen on me to comfort her, not the other way around. 'You wanted adventure, Adrana. Don't be too sorry when it happens. I'm actually starting to enjoy this.'

'You've gone soft for Rackamore. Or maybe Cazaray.'

'I'm going soft for what we've got ahead of us. Baubles. Prizes. Quoins. We'll come back from this richer than we ever thought possible. Even Father'll realise we did the right thing. And we'll have adventures, Adrana. We'll see things no one on Mazarile ever saw.'

That was when we heard the screaming.

Adrana and I looked at each other. Neither of us had imagined it. It was muffled, but it couldn't be coming from far away. Despite ourselves, we began to work towards the source of the noise. There were doors all along the corridor, marked for stores, equipment and so on, but we'd given them no thought until now. The final door, before the corridor bent around, had a grille cut into it, and a kind of sliding partition, large enough to shove a hand through.

The sound was coming from behind this door.

It was a woman's whimpering, interspersed with chokes and gurgles and odd little fragments of half-language.

I tried the door. It was on hinges, like an ordinary door, and after I'd clicked the latch it pushed open easily enough.

I peered through the gap while Adrana hovered next to me.

'What is it?' my sister asked.

'There's someone in there. On a bed. Not a hammock, a proper bed.'

I saw a figure, lying on their back. She was fully clothed, on top of bedsheets. Straps bound her to the bed, criss-crossed over her chest, with more securing her arms and legs, and another strap doing the same for her head.

Despite these restraints, the figure was doing her best to struggle free.

Adrana pushed me aside, taking in her view of the bound sleeper. 'What are they doing with her?' she asked, as if I had all the answers.

I grimaced my irritation back at my sister. 'Maybe we should ask her.'

I went through the doorway and into the room, more fearlessly than I felt. The woman couldn't move much but she twisted her head as far as she was able and tracked me with her eyes, so wide open they were mostly white. A tongue moved across her lips. She was struggling a bit less, as if sudden curiosity had taken her mind off whatever was troubling her.

'You're new to them,' she said, rasping out the words the way someone sounds when they've been punched in the throat. 'New voices. I heard you scuttling around. Sisters, aren't you?'

'We might be,' I said guardedly.

'Brought you in to snoop on the bones, did they?'

'And if they did?' Adrana asked.

'You want some advice, you get off this ship as soon as you can. And don't let the bones get into you. You don't want their whispering inside your dreams. You think you're strong enough to keep the whispers where they belong? I thought I was strong, too.'

'Ah,' said a voice, startling us from the door. 'You've saved me the trouble.'

'The trouble of what?' I asked, trying not to look all guilty and furtive.

Cazaray pushed a hand through the disorder of his blond locks. 'There was never going to be an easy way to bring it up. You've probably heard that the last recruit didn't quite work out.'

'This is . . . what was her name?' Adrana asked.

'Garval.' Cazaray came alongside us, speaking of the woman on the bed as if she were somewhere else entirely, not listening in and understanding every word. 'She came from Prevomar – it's a spindleworld, not a bad one, in the eighth processional. The other side of the Old Sun from us right now, but after we've cracked a bauble or two, stopped at Trevenza Reach . . .'

'You'll take her home? In that state?' Adrana asked.

Cazaray looked diffident. 'Given time, she may heal.'

'May?' I said.

'She was never right for us, Arafura. She was caught up in something . . . some bad business with her family over a marriage. She wanted to leave Prevomar so badly that she bribed someone to make it seem she was a better talent than she was. I thought she was strong enough to take full engagement at the very first attempt . . .' He shook his head, and if ever I was certain of anything it was that his remorse was genuine. 'She lied to us,' he carried on. 'But I don't hold that against her. We've all bent the truth once or twice, and she had every reason to leave Prevomar.'

'I didn't lie,' Garval said. But the words came out more weakly than before, as if she had nearly used up whatever energies she'd pent up for conversation. 'Didn't lie.' Some wave of exhaustion passed through her and I sensed a sort of easing, the first since we'd set eyes on her.

'Whether she lied or not,' Adrana said, 'what guarantee do we have that we won't end up the same as her?'

'None,' Cazaray said. 'And that's the sharp end of it. We're speaking of an alien technology none of us properly understand. Just because we use it doesn't mean we *know* it.'

Cazaray went to a fixture in the wall. He dampened a cloth, and dabbed it over the woman's brow and cheeks.

He turned to us. 'She has bad hours and good hours. If she seemed lucid then you caught her at a good time. The exposure she received was relatively short, so I'm optimistic – hopeful, at least – that her neural wiring will eventually find other pathways.'

'Good luck to whoever was going to marry her,' Adrana said.

'I doubt that marriage will be uppermost in anyone's thoughts,' Cazaray answered, returning the cloth to the wall, and then leaving the room.

Adrana was rattled, I knew. So was I, a bit. But I wanted to make Cazaray think I was feeling bold and fearless and ready for what was ahead.

'I'd like to see the bones.'

'Not now,' Cazaray replied, smiling at my enquiry. 'It's good that you're keen, but we're on ions, and that interferes with the equipment. Hirtshal's going to run out the sails tomorrow, and we'll travel quieter then.' Cazaray gave a last look at Garval before closing the door. 'The skull likes it that way.'

*

That evening the galley was full of smells and steam, the table crowded with cages of fruit, lidded tureens of cooked vegetables and various spiced meats, as well as tankards and metal-wired bottles, all held down with magnetism.

The lungstuff had a blu-ish haze, with the screens and displays flickering unwatched. The crew were rowdy when we arrived: Mattice finishing off the end of a story, something about another ship called the *Murderess*, and what had happened to her captain, a man called Rhinn, Trysil coughing because she'd been laughing too much, Cazaray trying to get a word in, Rackamore sitting back slightly like he was content just to observe, happy enough that his crew were happy. And they seemed to be, most of them. Prozor was still scowly whenever she caught either of us by the eye, Triglav still looked sad and worried, but that was just how his face was put together. There was one man we hadn't seen before, though, and he was as serious-looking a cove as ever you'll meet. This was Hirtshal. He was an older man with fine features, a moustache, a crescent of white hair growing thin on the scalp. When we were introduced to him, he nodded distantly, as if it wasn't really worth his bother to remember our names, knowing we wouldn't be sticking around.

'Hirtshal,' he said, before dragging his attention back to the tankard before him.

'Hirtshal is our master of sail,' Rackamore said, as if it was his job to fill in for the other man. 'If there's a person on this ship we all need to respect, this is the one. Without Prozor and Mattice we don't open baubles; without Trysil we wouldn't know what to take away with us. But without Hirtshal we don't go home. Be nice to Hirtshal. Be *especially* nice to Hirtshal when he's had a busy day.'

'Were you always a master of sail?' I asked, feeling it was expected of us to make conversation.

Hirtshal looked at me for longer than was comfortable.

'No.'

'You did something before?' Adrana put in.

He took so long answering that one it was as if she'd asked him to multiply two long numbers in his head, and then find the cube root.

'Yes.'

He drank from the tankard, sucking contemplatively on its spigot so that we were tempted to think there might be some continuation of his statement.

But that was it. His name, and a no, and a yes, and that was all we'd got from him.

'A man of few words, our Hirtshal,' Rackamore said, narrowing an eye at us. 'But always honest ones. I'd rather have an honest and reliable man, if a taciturn one, than someone I can't depend on.'

'Cazaray says we'll be running out the sail soon,' I offered.

'Yes.' Hirtshal gave a nod.

'And when would that be?' Adrana asked.

He made a face, as if just squeezing out another word cost him a tremendous and painful effort, like he was passing a stone.

'Tomorrow.'

'Can we see it happening?' Adrana asked.

Hirtshal thought about this for so long I was starting to think this was all a big joke on the two of us.

'Yes.'

'You *should* see the sails run out,' Rackamore said, opening the cage to extract a fistful of fruit. 'It's an important moment in any expedition, and it'll give you a better idea of how the ship functions.'

'Once we're trimmed,' Cazaray said, 'I'm planning to show them the bone room.'

'Will you bridge them up?'

Cazaray skewered meat from one of the lidded tureens. There was no cutlery, just skewers. 'I don't see why not.'

'Good. Little sense in delaying the inevitable.'

After a moment Cazaray said: 'They know about Garval.'

Rackamore cocked an eye. 'Do they, now.'

'I . . . might have preferred a little more time to prepare them.'

'So might we all.' Rackamore bit into a piece of fruit. 'Did you tell them that she came to us under false pretences?'

'I did, yes.'

'That we ran the tests that we were able, and still she kept her true nature from us?'

'They understand the fault was hers, not ours.'

'Then that's an end to it.' Rackamore chewed thoughtfully. 'Garval isn't a secret and we've no reason to be ashamed of her – or for Adrana and Arafura to worry that they'll end up the same way.'

'May I ask something, Captain?' I said.

He dabbed at his mouth with a napkin. 'Most certainly.'

'Garval seems quite ill. I know she's from – what was the name of the place, Cazaray?'

He drew the skewer from his mouth, speaking with his lips nearly sealed. 'Prevomar.'

'Prevomar,' I repeated. 'Well, I hadn't heard of it. But Mazarile has hospitals and hospices, and I know we can treat diseases of the mind.'

'Maybe not *this* disease,' Rackamore countered.

'All the same, are they any better equipped on Prevomar? I just wonder why you didn't set her off the ship while you were docked at Hadramaw. I mean, with the launch. You could have brought her down in that, couldn't you?'

Spelled out like that, I suppose it was a bit insolent of me, questioning him that way. I knew it and so did Rackamore.

But I'd had to ask.

'I'll tell you why,' he said, pausing to help himself to the vegetables. 'Not because we're cruel, or indifferent to her predicament. But because I *must* hold the reputation of this ship paramount. Our competitors watch us. They may well know that Garval was our last recruit.'

'And you wouldn't want them to know that she had failed,' I said.

Rackamore aimed the tip of his skewer at me. 'You have the crux of it. News like that would get around quickly. The *Monetta's Mourn* is in trouble. Well, I won't have that. So Garval will remain with us until we are confident that we have new – and righteous – recruits.'

'Perhaps now we do,' Mattice said, picking a crumb out of his beard.

'You think so, Mattice?' asked Triglav.

'I do. And I wouldn't rip the guts of anyone who agreed with me.'

'We'll swing by Prevomar soon enough,' Rackamore said. 'In the meantime, she's well cared for. You say you hadn't heard of the place, Arafura.'

'There's an awful lot of worlds, Captain.'

He conceded my point with a dip of his skewer. 'Too many for all the grey in one head, and that's the truth.'

'Girlie says she's bookish,' Prozor said.

'You should try reading a book sometime, Proz,' Rackamore

said, smiling at her. 'See if you can do it without moving your lips, and you'll really impress us.' This got him an extra scowly scowl from Prozor, a laugh from some of the others. But his attention was still fixed on me. 'You must have seen the *Book of Worlds* at some point.'

'Our family had a copy,' I said, before adding: 'But not a recent edition.'

'I have a copy . . . actually several. Different editions. Among other books. When you're done with Cazaray and his bones, drop by my quarters. You too, Adrana, if this sort of thing spurs you.'

'It might,' Adrana said.

Rackamore lifted his tankard in a kind of salute. 'It ought to. The past is all we have left. The least we can do is make the most of it.'

*

If you've ever tried to sleep in a grumbly old house with pipes that hiss and clank, floors that creak, walls that groan, windows that rattle, you've maybe a tenth of an idea what it's like to try sleeping on a ship like the *Monetta's Mourn*. If it wasn't the restless noises of the ship it was someone barking out an instruction, someone calling the hour of a watch, or a mad woman screaming while bound to a bed.

Just when I might have managed to sleep for half an hour, there was a soft knock, and then Mattice drew aside the curtain that shielded our quarters, making enough of a gap for his big beardy face to loom into my vision and say: 'Morning watch. There's hot tea in the galley, hot water in the washroom. You'll feel like death now but we've all had our first night on a ship and it gets better.'

'How many nights does it take?' Adrana asked.

'Oh, not many. Sometimes as few as twenty.'

'Thank you, Mattice,' I said, shivering despite all the layers I'd pulled around myself in the night.

'Take your time. But not too much of it if you want to see the sails run out. Hirtshal's already begun.'

Running out the sails got everyone twitchy. Hirtshal was the master of sail, the man in charge of them, but if something went badly wrong at this stage, half the crew would need to go out in suits to untangle the mess.

'We run a tight crew,' Rackamore told me, while we were gathered at the hemispherical window, watching the sail-control gear swing out from the hull. 'That's not just because a light ship is a fast ship. It means we don't have to split our profits too many ways.'

'I want to learn what I can,' I said.

He nodded. 'That's a fine attitude. And you will – within reason. Knowing how to wear a suit, operate an airlock, find your way around the outside of the ship – that's basic survival abilities. And some knowledge of the other areas of expertise is always useful. You'll want to know a little about baubles, a little about relics, and so on, if only because it'll give you a healthy respect for what you *don't* know.' His jaw tensed. 'But I have to draw a different line with my Bone Readers. You're scarce . . . too scarce to expose to the risks that the other crew members naturally accept.'

Prozor, next to us, said: 'What he means is, girlies, you're goin' to be pampered, so get used to it.'

Beyond the glass, the barbs that had been folded along the *Monetta*'s hull were angling out, just as if that bad-tempered fish were stiffening its spines in some defensive reaction. These were the anchor points for the rigging, the whiskery filaments that linked the ship to her sails. Under Hirtshal's supervision, they'd be tugged and released all the while, making up for tiny shifts in the solar flux and accommodating the changes in our course that Rackamore had in mind.

'We don't run out the main sails all in one go,' he was saying. 'They'd snag and rip. Hirtshal uses the drogue sails first. Do you see them, unfurling about a league away from us? They'll take up the slack in the lines, get them handsomely taut and aligned, and then we run out the main sails, a thousand square leagues of reflective area.'

He had a way of saying 'main sails' that sounded as if the two words were running together.

'It might seem simple,' he went on. 'It's anything but. The sails are as tricky as they're delicate.'

Hirtshal was already outside, standing with magnetic boots on the back of the *Monetta*, using controls that came out through her hull for exactly this sort of operation. If something jammed or tangled, he could sort it out before it got too bad. The launch was ready as well, just in case something got snarled up tens of leagues beyond the ship.

But all was going well. The drogues snapped open, blossoming like sudden chrome flowers, and they in turn helped the unfolding of the main sails, intricate, interlaced arrays of them. I don't mind saying: it was properly marvellous, the way they gradually opened out, planing apart along seams we'd never have known were there, layer after layer of them, snapping wider all the time. It was like a conjuring trick, something a cove would do in Neural Alley, with cards and a sly gleam in his eye. The sails blazed back at us, each glittering facet silver tinged with red and purple, reflecting the world-filtered light of the Old Sun. The rigging was invisible, but already it was straining to move the ship. In response, *Monetta*'s creaks and groans had a different sort of music to them. An eagerness, now. The ship was straining, wanting to catch the photon winds.

And so we sailed. *Monetta's Mourn* no longer had to slink around on ion thrust, or cower from the gravity well of a swallower. She'd become the thing she was always meant to be: a vessel of the deep void, a creature of the Empty.

That ship of ours was a sunjammer.

*

Cazaray spun the wheel that opened the door to the bone room.

'Go in,' he said quietly. 'Just don't touch anything – for now.'

Adrana went in first. I followed on her heels, taking care never to lose my hold on the wall. Cazaray came after us, then closed the door, turning the inner wheel so that it latched itself tight against the frame.

It was quiet in there. I couldn't hear anything of the life-support system, nothing of the sail-control gear – the occasional whirr and whine of its winches and pulleys had become familiar since the sails were run out – nothing of the usual clamour and chatter of the crew.

The room was a sphere, about fifteen spans across, and the skull was floating in the middle of it like the main exhibit in an art gallery. It was trussed up in a kind of bridle, a frame made up of metal bars and struts, and this bridle was fixed onto the walls by dozens of springs.

'Quieter and stiller we hold her, the better,' Cazaray said. 'Trig's damped the ions, and that helps, but it would only take a jolt to rattle something loose.'

From end to end the skull was about as long as my sister was tall – about eight spans. It was the colour of a bad tooth, rotten to the root. It wasn't anything like a monkey skull. It was stretched out, all snout and jaw, more as if it had belonged to some giant horse than a person. It was made up of lots of parts, joined together like a sort of puzzle. A dark fissure ran across it, stitched together with a ladder of little metal sutures. Whoever had done that had worked a long time ago, and with care.

The skull had also been drilled and tapped in many places. Slender probes and wires had been pushed through the bone into the not-quite-emptiness within.

'Tell me what you know,' Cazaray said, never raising his voice above a murmur.

'It's old,' I answered.

'How old?'

'No one knows,' Adrana said.

'Good answer. And it's the truth, too. They were finding skulls in the Sixth and Seventh Occupations, but whoever left them must have been through these parts a lot earlier than that. They don't fit the morphology of any of the aliens we know about today, not the Crawlies or the Stingtails or the Tuskers. Some people who ought to know better think they come from dead Bonies or Bug-Eyes, but I've seen enough of them to know that can't be true. My guess is that the coves who used to own these bones died long before people got going. It was some other aliens who left the skulls here, and they used them just the way we do, like a kind of squawk.'

From opposite sides we peered into its mysteries.

'It's not empty,' Adrana said. 'There are little lights, flickering on and off.'

'Whatever mind was in that skull,' Cazaray said, 'it's long gone. There's no grey, no brain tissue. If ever there was. But the machinery that was in that brain, it's still there. That twinkly stuff still twinkles. Still doing *something*. What, we don't know. Trying to regain contact with others of its kind? Trying to send signals back home, to whatever part of the Swirly they came from? Singing an endless song of death? No idea, and best not to dwell on it. What matters is what we can do with those patterns. We can imprint our own messages on them, treat them like carrier signals.' He nodded at the equipment racked around the walls, all neat and clean and organised. 'That's what all this hardware is for. And it's a Bone Reader's job to send and receive those imprinted messages. The skull won't work for everyone. Doesn't even work for me some days. But you have the lamps for it, I think. Ready to try?'

I was about to answer, but Adrana said the word first. 'Yes.'

'Behind you. That apparatus hooked onto the wall. Slip it over your head.'

It was a bony metal contraption, halfway between a crown and a torture device. She settled it over her scalp, pushing hair out of the way. A pair of metal muffs folded down over her ears, and there was also a kind of visor that could be pulled down over her eyes.

'You too, Arafura,' Cazaray said.

I unhooked my own apparatus and fiddled it onto my head, not as prettily as Adrana had done.

'That's the neural bridge. None of this works without the bridge. To speak to the skull you have to mesh with its expectations. The messages come through almost subliminally – it's like catching a whisper on the wind. The bridge is the focusing device, the amplifier.'

'I don't feel anything,' I said.

'You're not plugged in yet. Draw the contact wire from the bridge. Reel it out, all the way.'

The wire was an insulated spool, running into the left side of the bridge. It ended in a little nub.

'You can hook the wire into any of those probes on the skull, or you can splice onto one of those wires. Gently does it. Normally one connection is sufficient, but you can hook into multiple contact sites if you're chasing a weak signal. There's a splitter on the wall.'

Adrana was bolder than I, but even she hesitated to make the final connection. I shared her misgivings. I could not help but feel there was going to be some kind of psychic jolt, like an electric shock, as soon as the contact was made.

I thought of Garval, tied to her bed.

'It's all right,' Cazaray said gently. 'Just do it. No one gets the full rush the first time. What happened with Garval . . .' He shook his head, clearing the thought. 'You'll be lucky to pick up anything, even if you've got the talent.'

I picked a probe near the open eye socket and clicked the wire home. Not caring to be second, Adrana made her own connection almost simultaneously. The skull bounced lightly on its springs for a few seconds, before the motion ebbed away.

We looked at each other across the skull, daring each to feel the first twinge of contact.

'When we've had a little more experience, when you know where the probes lie, you'll prefer to work in darkness. Now, empty your minds. Let your senses drift. I'll be silent.'

There was nothing.

I guessed there wouldn't be any sense in holding my breath – I couldn't have kept that up for long – but still I tried to become quiet in my head, ridding my mind of everything, becoming a room with an open door.

I did the only thing I could think of, which was to wait.

Adrana was waiting as well. Our eyes were averted, looking down, but every now and then one of us couldn't resist glancing at the other, to see how they were doing. Once or twice our eyes met, and the silliness of that moment made us glance quickly away, until the impulse to look built up again and we ended up doing exactly the same thing.

After a couple of minutes of that, I resolved to jam shut my eyes, and not care whether Adrana followed suit.

Cazaray was present, but he made no sound, no observation. Still there was nothing, no whisper on the wind, not even a hint of that wind. Just silence, and the absurd, slowly forming idea that this could and would never work.

I do not know how long it was before Cazaray spoke.

'Disconnect. Try different probes, a little closer to the base.'

We did as he suggested, this time disturbing the skull much less as the probes went out and in.

I still felt nothing. But for the sake of showing my determination, I floated with my eyes closed, willing something – anything – to enter my head.

'I think . . .' Adrana began.

But she fell silent.

'You felt a contact?' Cazaray asked.

'I don't know. Maybe it wasn't anything. It came and went, like someone standing behind me for a second. A cold presence.'

'It's best not to read too much into the first session. The more you want that contact, the more you're likely to imagine it.'

Despondent, I eased the neural bridge from my scalp, messing my hair back into shape where it had been pressed down. 'Maybe she was wrong about us, Cazaray.'

'When I began, I was in here three weeks before I got so much as a twitch out of it. The skull has its moods. It had to get used to me before it was willing to talk.'

Adrana relieved herself of the neural bridge. We uncoupled from the skull and hooked the bridges back onto the wall.

'Better luck next time, I suppose,' I said.

'Luck has nothing to do with it,' Cazaray answered. 'What you have is in your lamps, and there's no mistaking that. You'll come through, and those bones *will* talk.' Then he moved to the wall and retrieved one of the bridges for himself. 'Normally it's best to work alone. But you can watch, if you like.'

'I thought it was getting harder for you,' Adrana said.

'It is.'

Cazaray put on the bridge, adjusting it until it was a tight fit over his blond locks, then spooled out the contact wire and slipped it into several probes in succession, concentration making a mask of his face until something eased and he gave the slightest of nods, followed by a half-voiced: 'I have it. It's faint today, so you shouldn't worry about not feeling anything.' Then he started babbling. His eyes were open, but they had begun to roll up under his lids. We caught words, phrases, but never the whole of it. 'Down to the Sunward processionals . . . two orbits beyond the Dargan Gap. Opening auguries for the Jewel of Sundabar. *Fire Witch*, dropping sail at Auzar – assistance required. Wedza's Eye will close in eight days, eight hours.'

More of that. He stayed in that babbling state for two or three minutes, before his eyes snapped back into focus and, like a man waking from a restful sleep, he at last moved his hands to the neural bridge.

'Did you hear me?'

'Yes,' we answered.

'I don't always remember all of it. And a lot of it isn't worth remembering – it's just noise, certainly nothing Captain Rackamore needs to hear.'

'And this time?' I asked.

'Did you hear me speak of auguries? That's useful knowledge. Intelligence. Someone else's idea of where and when baubles will open, and for how long. Knowledge like that can make or break an expedition.'

'Then why would anyone share it?' Adrana asked.

'They don't mean to.' Cazaray unplugged from the skull and hung up the neural bridge. 'We operate alone, for the most part, but there are other ships that we'll occasionally help out, if they've done the captain a favour in the past. Some of the other ships, though, operate together all the time. They're run by governments, or the private combines. And they have to communicate, to coordinate their efforts. Squawking's all right – but it's slow, easily intercepted, and signals don't always get all the way through the Congregation, especially if the Old Sun's putting out a storm. The superloom – that's what we call the system of the skulls – is much, much faster, it's hard to jam it, and there's not much signal attenuation.'

'But you've just listened in,' I said.

'They take matched skulls, matched pairs of readers, and put them on different ships. But if you're good – if you're experienced, and you've got a skull that's especially sensitive in its own right – like this one – then you can catch a rumour of a rumour.' Cazaray gave a self-deprecating shrug. 'I make it sound easy.'

I smiled. 'You don't.'

'You said it was hard to jam,' Adrana said. 'But you didn't say it was impossible. What would it take to do that to a skull?'

Her question had been innocent enough. But something clouded his face when Cazaray answered us.

'Nothing you'll ever need worry about.'

4

I'd been in bigger and grander libraries than Rackamore's, but I could safely say I'd never been in a library on a ship, or one laid out in such curvy, swoopy lines, or one that was full of such strange and old books. It was up near the front of the *Monetta*, built into a room that connected through to both his galley and the quarters, and I got the impression Rackamore liked it the most of any of the places on his ship.

'You'll find things easier now we're under sail,' he said, standing up, one booted foot resting on the rail beneath the lowest shelf. He still had his white shirt and leather waistcoat on, but he'd undone his hair so that it spilled out in a black fan across his neck and shoulders. 'We pull twice as hard as when we're on ion thrust, so your inner ear has even less reason to feel confused. I confess I'm never entirely at ease until the sails are out.'

'Will the sails carry us all the way to the bauble, Captain?'

'More or less.' He studied me shrewdly. 'Do you have some idea of how we sail?'

'The solar wind blows on the sails, Captain. The sails move the ship. Just like a boat on water.'

He smiled. 'Well, not *quite*. Some of the worlds have small seas, and people sail on them, I know. But it's not the same as solar sailing. A boat can sail into the wind, but we can't – there's no other medium for us to push against, the way a boat's keel works against the water. So we can't tack, in the nautical sense. But we *can* use orbital mechanics to our advantage. We're in a gravity well, you see, and that means we have angular momentum to play with. The sails can add or subtract from our motion around the Old Sun, if we tilt them – and that means we can move between orbits, provided we're patient. Which we are, most of the time. And if we're in a hurry, there's the ion engine. The sails can serve as energy collectors as well – they have both a reflective surface and an absorbent one, and Hirtshal can flex one or other to face the Sun. There's no part of the Congregation we can't reach in under two years of sail, and many worlds are only weeks or months apart – some even closer.'

'How many of those worlds have you seen, Captain?'

'You can drop the formality, Fura. I invited you here, didn't I?' But he still gave some consideration to what I'd asked. 'It must be fewer than a hundred. Which means that for every world I've stood on, there are at least two hundred I've yet to see. And that's just a tiny fraction of all the worlds – just the few to which we've given names, and found a way to live on.' He beckoned me nearer. 'Here. We spoke of the *Book of Worlds* before. I think these might be of interest.'

It was a bit awkward, being alone with him. Adrana never cared for books as much as I did, so she'd turned her nose up when I mentioned visiting his library. I wasn't sweet on him either, no matter what Adrana might have cooked up in her head. He was handsome enough, but he was a lot older than me and there was something stiff and serious about him that made him seem more like an uncle or a teacher. It wasn't that I had anything against him, although I don't suppose at that point I'd had much chance to really know him. But he was the captain and I was the newcomer, and it was the right and proper way of it that I should be timid and respectful around him.

The truth was, though, whatever I thought of Rackamore, I *was* sweet on his books.

'These can't be real,' I said. 'There can't be this many of them, all different from each other, all in one place . . .'

I caught the pride in his answer.

'They're real. All of them.'

I counted the black spines, read the fine silver lettering, took in the gradual alteration in the style of the script, from curving to blocky and back to curving again. He had twenty editions of the *Book of Worlds*, going back much earlier than any I'd ever seen before.

I reached out a hand – then pulled it back like I'd been about to reach for the wrong knife at the table.

Rackamore smiled. 'Go ahead.'

I took out the earliest one, the worn binding feeling leathery and fragile under my fingertips. It was still a heavy volume, but there were far fewer pages in it than in the edition at home. I turned the thin pages carefully, scared that I might tear them from the binding. The lettering was old-fashioned, the words sometimes unfamiliar, the phrasing archaic where I could make sense of it at all. I also fancied that there were fewer entries in the whole book, and that the space given to each was more generous than in our own volume.

I searched for Mazarile, but it wasn't in there.

'That book is nine hundred years old,' Rackamore said, in a low and reverent tone, as if some ghost or spirit hiding in the book might be roused if he spoke too harshly. 'There are only five thousand entries. The number of worlds occupied by people was about a quarter as many as there are today. Supposedly there are even earlier editions, each rarer than the last, although I've never chanced upon one of them. These books trace our expansion from a single starting point – the gradual spread from world to world, slow and difficult at first. Then we got better at it, and more confident, and the number of occupied worlds swelled far beyond ten thousand.' He took the old edition back from me, slotted it back onto the shelf, and ran his finger halfway along the row of spines. 'Here. A 1384 edition. Four hundred and fifteen years ago.' He drew out the volume, blew dust off it, stroked his finger against the binding, then offered it to me. 'Many more pages, and fewer lines per entry.

There were seventeen thousand occupied worlds at that point and the rate of expansion was slowing down. There might be fifty million potential worlds in the Congregation, but we can only live on about twenty thousand of them. The rest are cracked wide open – no lungstuff, no water, and too knotty to seal them off and bring in those things even if we had the will. Or they're already totally bottled in, with no way in or out that we know. Or in some other way inimical to settlement – haunted by bad things left over from earlier Occupations. Wrapped in bauble fields that we can't break through and that don't show any sign of opening any time soon. That's the wonder and frustration of it, Arafura – fifty million prizes, and we'll never know most of them before our time is done.'

I found Mazarile:

Prosperous sphereworld in the thirty-fifth processional, with a diameter of eight and one third leagues. A swallower sits at its core. Seven principal settlements, of which Hadramaw and Incer are the two largest. Opposing spacedocks, amenable to improvement. Population at last census, two and four fifths million . . .

'Our time,' I said, with a little shiver. 'You think it will end?'

'Most assuredly. You've seen the Hall of History on Mazarile – there are similar institutions on most worlds. Each of those coloured bars represents an empire, a dominion, a parliament of worlds, much like our own. Earlier Occupations, earlier phases of expansion, settlement and stagnation. They passed. So, eventually, will we.'

'But not today.'

'And not tomorrow, hopefully, since I still have some rather onerous debts to settle.' He took the book from me – I'd done no more than leaf through the pages, unable to take any of it in – and moved me along the shelves. 'Understand this library and you're halfway to understanding me. Sunjammers don't put the spur into me. Nor baubles, especially. But I *am* spurred by what baubles contain, especially if they offer us some illumination on the past.' He snatched out a book and opened the covers. Instead of pages there was only a milky rectangle, like an opaque slab of crystal. 'Whatever this was, it doesn't work for us now. Sometimes something flickers across it. We were caught in a solar storm once, ghost-fire lighting the rigging, and half the mute books in this room lit up and started showing pictures and words. But none of them were in languages I knew, and before I had a chance to scribble down more than a few fragments, the storm abated.'

'Are all the old books like that?'

He shook his head. 'No. Some of them are in a written form, and occasionally the scholars have made some small headway with the languages. Only the monkey languages, though – never the alien ones.'

'I saw a Crawly in Hadramaw,' I felt obliged to say, remembering the alien shuffling along behind the spacesuited men in Neural Alley. 'We know their language, don't we?'

'Only because it's worth their while to share it. But I'll say this: there's nothing we know about the Crawlies that the Crawlies don't want us to know.'

'They help us, don't they?'

'In their fashion. They put mirrors in the high orbits, so we can use solar pressure more efficiently. They understand swallowers better than we do, and they can stop worlds crashing into each other when their orbits start drifting. I don't say that they haven't been of benefit to us. But of all the other places in the Swirly, what brings them here?'

'Perhaps there's no one else out there that they like being around as much as us.'

'I suppose,' Rackamore said.

'It's good of them to run the banks for us, isn't it? We made a mess of it, my father said. The crash of 1566 proved that? Hundreds of worlds went bankrupt because people aren't honest enough to handle money on that scale. People were starving, actually starving and dying, because of the greed and incompetence of bankers. But the aliens don't need money for anything, not *our* money, anyway, so there's no reason for them not to be trusted with it.'

'There's truth in that,' Rackamore said. 'But some might point out that the Crawlies hadn't been in the Congregation for very long before the crash. Fifty years. Maybe less. They were newcomers, just like the Hardshells or Clackers today. A coincidence, I suppose.'

'What?'

Rackamore gave a shrug, as if none of this was worth dwelling on. 'I mull on things overmuch. Search for patterns, and you'll find them, as surely as sailors see old lovers in the billowing of photon sails. But I suppose it gives me a reason to keep looking for things, and sometimes what you turn up isn't the thing you had in mind, but something better. Who knows what we'll find, in this bauble or the one after?'

I didn't ask him how far we still had to sail. I supposed I'd get my answer sooner or later. But I couldn't stop thinking of the Crawly, of the whiskerlike appendage poking in and out of its proboscis, drawing molecules out of the lungstuff, catching the chemical stink of wealth.

*

Cazaray kept on with us in the bone room. There were two sessions per day, one in the morning watch, the other in the afternoon. The routine was always the same. We'd put on the neural bridges, plug in, flush our minds out, and try to snatch a whisper from the wind. The first day had been a failure, the two sessions of the second not much better. Even Adrana didn't dare claim that she'd picked up anything, even when Cazaray told her that the skull was indeed receiving something.

On the second session of the third day, though, after trying five or six different input points, Adrana tensed up. I was watching her by then, certain that my own efforts weren't getting anywhere.

'Something . . .' she whispered. 'A voice. A word, really clear. As if someone just spoke it into my head.'

'Which was?' Cazaray asked.

'Daxian.'

After a moment he said: 'Have you heard this name before?'

'No,' Adrana answered.

'It's a world, I think. One of the settled ones. A wheelworld, pretty deep down.'

'Maybe she read it in the *Book of Worlds*, and the name jammed in her memory,' I said.

'And maybe she didn't,' Adrana shot back.

Cazaray got her to try several other inputs, but nothing came through on them. When he stuck the neural bridge on himself, the only contact he found was on the same input where Adrana had heard Daxian. It was faint today, he said, looking at her with something between doubt and awe. 'If you dragged some sense out of that, after only three days in the bone room . . .'

'Let me try again,' she said.

'No – we can't rush this. Your brain is adjusting to the skull, just as the skull's coming to terms with you. Tomorrow we go again. You too, Arafura. If your sister's able to tune in this quickly, you may not be far behind.'

I checked on that world, too. Looked it up in one of the *Book of Worlds*, the same edition we had back home. I turned to the page where Daxian should have been, had it existed.

Dastrogar

Daxperil

Dazazoth

But no Daxian. I slid the book back, certain now that my sister couldn't have picked up on the name from that edition. I ran my finger along the spines of the other editions until I got to Rackamore's most recent copy, and fumbled my way to the entry for Daxian. There it was:

Wheelworld in the third processional. Settled less than a century ago by venture-expansionists from the Conjugate

Worlds of Thrisp and Trenniger. Diameter: sixty-six leagues.
Spin-generated gravity at inner surface: nine tenths of a gee.
Population one million, three hundred thousand at last
census . . .

Later, when we were alone, I asked her what it had been like.

'It wasn't like a voice,' she said, after thinking about it for a few seconds. 'I know I said it was, but that was the best I could come up with. It was something different. If a voice is raised lettering, something that stands out, this was the opposite. Like a word pushed into silence, the way you can make a word into clay. Silence shouldn't be able to do that.' She paused – I knew she was trying to do her best to put into language something not easily explicable in anything but its own alien terms. 'There was a mind behind that word. A monkey mind, someone like you and me, in a bone room somewhere, plugged into an alien skull. But do you remember what Cazaray said about carrier signals – that all we're doing is imprinting our own messages on something else? There was another mind underneath the transmission. Something dead, cold and very, very alien. And yet still thinking, or still trying to think.'

'There's no thought going on,' I said. 'No neural material. Cazaray said it!'

'He lied.' She gave a yawn and a shrug at the same time. 'Or he doesn't really understand it, or he doesn't think we'd understand it. But there's something there, and I got a little glimpse of it, just for one fierce moment. I lied as well.'

'About the word?'

'No. About wanting to go back and listen again. I didn't, Fura. It was as if someone opened a cold window at the bottom of my skull, in a room I didn't know about, and it let something in, and whatever it is is still whistling around in the basement of my brain.'

'But you will go back,' I said.

'Yes,' she said, after a moment. 'Of course.'

67

I lingered at the open door to the bridge. Rackamore was in there, late in that evening watch, with his back to the door and two booted feet up on the console. All the gubbins looked thrown into place, tangled up in knots of cable and wiring, like an animal's nest made out of shiny bits of monkey and alien scrap. There were flickerboxes, flickering with views of the ship and the scratchy signals of long-range broadcasts. The green globe of the sweeper sat before him, a yellow bar cycling round and round like a demented clock hand. A yellow smudge sat in the depths of the display, barely fading between cycles.

'You wanted to see me, sir?'

'Come in.' His voice was low, tired. 'Prozor showed you this room when you came aboard, didn't she?'

'Not really, sir. To be honest, Prozor couldn't wait to see the back of us.'

The captain had a little metal apparatus in his hand. He worked his fingers back and forth against springs, strengthening his grip. It was a habit I had noticed among other members of the crew.

'You shouldn't read too much into that. Prozor's a good sort, deep down. After what happened at the Fang . . .' But he silenced himself quickly. 'Never mind. A message came through on the squawk a little while ago, from Vidin Quindar.' He gave the kind of grimace you do when you've bitten into something sour. 'Quindar's a man easily swayed by money, Fura. I deal with his sort only because the alternatives are generally worse.'

'What about Mr Quindar, sir?'

'He's asked me to convey to you . . . and your sister . . . that he is now acting in the interests of your father.'

I blinked. I got the words, but not the sense of them. 'I don't follow, sir.'

'Quindar has been hired by your father to expedite your return to Mazarile.' Rackamore pushed a finger into his brow, like he was testing a bruise to see how painful it was. 'We were entirely too hasty in accepting the legality of Adrana's guardianship, it seems. On paper it appeared lungstuff-tight, but Quindar has found all sorts of qualifiers that Cazaray either missed or did not believe relevant to your case. Now it appears that they were.'

'Hang on, sir. Father's got no money left as it is. He can't afford to hire anyone, let alone Quindar.'

'Where there are ways, Fura, there are generally means. Unfortunately I now find myself on the wrong side of the law, at least as far as the matter of guardianship is concerned.'

'It wasn't your fault, sir.'

'Fault is not the issue at hand. I intend no ill by your father, and I certainly never meant to tangle myself up in Mazarile family law. There's promise in both of you – tremendous promise. But now I wonder if I'd be better divesting myself of you before I deepen my troubles.'

I swallowed. 'Me, sir . . . or both of us?'

'I wouldn't separate you. Ordinarily – given that we're under full sail, with an itinerary ahead of us – it would be quite beyond my ability to return you home.' He nodded at the sweeper. 'Do you see that return?'

'That big shape, sir?'

'No, that's our own shadow. The sweeper projects from the hull, and it can't see beyond our own sails. That's a quarter of the sky lost to us, but it doesn't really matter when most of the things we'd need to worry about would come from behind, not ahead.' The springs squeaked under his fingers, making the muscles jump out along the line of his arm.

'Things, sir?'

He touched a finger to the edge of the scope. 'That distant smudge is a long-range echo from the *Iron Courtesan*.'

'Is that trouble?'

'Hardly. I know Jastrabarsk well enough, and stealing another crew's prize isn't the way he does business. Still, being polite, he'll come no closer than that. But there's an opportunity here. The *Courtesan*'s just completed a sweep of baubles, and she'll be on her way back to Trevenza Reach much sooner than us. It'd cost us both time, but if I felt it were the right thing to do, I could arrange for a rendezvous so you could be transferred to the other vessel. From Trevenza Reach you wouldn't have long to wait for another ship back to Mazarile, and I'd make sure you had the funds to cover the passage.'

'But we've only just joined the crew. We were just starting to settle in . . .'

He looked at me with a touch of scepticism. 'Really?'

'Well enough, sir. I know it's early days.'

'It is. And as a rule they won't start warming to you until you start cooking for them. Even Prozor generally comes round in the end, once she's got something in her belly. We're not monsters, as I hope you'll have decided by now.'

'I never thought you were monsters, sir.'

'I hear a but.'

'It's true that you have to make some hard decisions now and then, isn't it? Like with Garval, and not taking her home, even though she's so unwell?'

'I suppose you think me indifferent to her.'

I bit my tongue, deciding I'd already said more than I should have. 'It's not my position to say, sir.'

'But I see it plainly in your face. It's all right, Fura – you can speak your mind. Look, you have my word that we'll get her home eventually.'

'But she won't be the same, will she?'

'No, but then none of us are the same as the day we set foot on this ship. The skull drove her mad, but there's no one it doesn't leave some sort of mark on. Understand this, though: do well by the *Monetta*, do well by me, and you'll never have a more loyal crew around you.' He sighed, as if something needed to be said and he'd been bottling it in long enough. 'May I speak candidly?'

'Isn't that what we're already doing?'

He smiled at that, but it was a sad sort of smile. 'I had a daughter once, and she was very dear to me. She sailed with me everywhere, knew every part of the ship, from sails to squawk. She was about your age when I lost her, and I'm afraid you remind me more than a little of her.'

I was careful in my choice of words, but I couldn't think of any kind way of putting things. 'What happened, Captain?'

Rackamore looked back to the sweeper. 'A stern-chase. The only one I ever lost.'

'She died?'

'Yes. Yes, she did. And in you I see something of Illyria, and that makes me take more than the usual interest in your welfare.'

'I don't want to go back to Mazarile, Captain. Not yet. And I know Adrana'd feel the same. You shouldn't worry about Vidin Quindar, whatever he says. I knew exactly what I was doing when I agreed to join your crew, and by the time six months are out I'll be able to decide my own fate.'

'Your father might disagree.'

'He's a good man, sir. But after Mother died he made one bad decision after another. This is just the latest of them, and now it makes me even more determined to stay and earn our prize money. You won't signal the other ship, will you?'

There were creaking noises from the metal thing in his hand as he worked it in and out. 'We could see how things lie after the first bauble, I suppose. If I know Jastrabarsk, he'll mean to have the crumbs we leave behind.' His face set as he made his decision. 'We'll speak no more of it. I'll squawk Quindar and tell him that you remain under my authority. In the meantime . . . do you wish a word or two to be relayed back to your father?'

'I thought you said there wouldn't be any messages, sir.'

'I am making an exception, Fura.'

I thought about it for a few seconds. I didn't mean to be hard or callous about it. But if he knew we were alive, and not coming to any harm, that was enough.

'Tell him nothing's changed,' I said.

*

71

It was the sixth day before something came through the bones again. Adrana got more than a fragment this time. She was hearing a dialogue, two parties whispering to each other, and she babbled out as much of it as she could get her tongue around.

'. . . hauling in to Mulgracen and needing yardage. Damage to fore- and mid-sun-gallants, possibly repairable . . . advise on costs . . .' She shook herself out of it, like someone discarding the last tatters of a nightmare. 'Yardage. What the chaff is yardage?'

'What the likes of Hirtshal call rigging, when they're speaking to their own profession,' Cazaray said. 'And sun-gallants are a type of sail. Unless you picked that up since you came aboard, you could only have heard it from the skull.' He shook his head, equal parts wonder, admiration and – I suppose – relief. 'I never doubted you,' he said. 'But I wondered how long it might take. You're weeks ahead of me!'

'Let me try, on the same node,' I said.

Nothing came through that day for me, or the next. But on the eighth day of our instruction, during the morning session, that cold window opened in my head as well. I didn't get a conversation, not even one word I could sing back to Cazaray. But I'd felt something creep inside my head, something shivery and wrong that didn't have any business being there, and it wasn't any kind of feeling I'd ever had before in my life.

I told Cazaray. He closed his eyes, as if a prayer had been granted.

'There's much still to be done,' he said. 'But I don't doubt that the captain's found his new Bone Readers. You're going to change the fortunes of this ship, both of you.'

'Do they need changing?' Adrana asked, hanging the bridges back up on the wall.

'Lately they haven't been at all bad, it's fair to say. But they can always be bettered.'

'There's something I wanted to ask,' I said, fussing my hair back into shape. 'I heard the captain mention something about the Fang, and then he told me that he used to have a daughter, only he lost her in a stern-chase. Were they the same thing?'

Cazaray took a moment to answer. It was like we were asking him to speak of something against his nature and better judgement, some dark business that was better off not being mentioned.

'No,' he said carefully, in a low voice. 'The Fang was one thing and the stern-chase another. The Fang's a bauble. It's where we lost Githlow . . .'

I slid a pin into my hair.

'Githlow?'

He tightened his lips so that they creased. 'You want the truth of it, you'll have to wait for Prozor to share it. She's the one who came off the worst of us.' He let out a sigh. 'The stern-chase . . . It happened before I came aboard. I never saw her.'

'Rackamore's daughter?' I asked.

'Bosa Sennen,' he corrected me. 'The one who took her from Rack.' He turned from us to attend the skull. 'And if you're wise, you'll never mention that name in Rackamore's presence.'

*

Day by day we adjusted to the routines to the ship. We started taking over the cooking duties from Cazaray, and that helped break more of the ice with the crew. And we got better at the bones, both of us. Adrana could pull messages from the skull with more and more ease, and once or twice she was even able to tune in when Cazaray found the signal too weak. And I came on, as well. On the thirteenth day I pulled three whole words from the skull, and on the fifteenth a complete sentence. It wasn't anything that was going to bring quoins, but it was proof that I had the aptitude as well. Satisfied that we had the basics sorted out, Cazaray started moving on to the finer aspects of Bone Reading, which included being able to send as well as receive. He had us bouncing test messages to friendly ships, and then had them verifying that the messages had come through clean. We also had to show that we could write down complex messages as they were coming in, which was harder than it sounded, sort of like rubbing your belly at the same time as patting your head.

Throughout all this it was only ever a case of sending messages between ships, never between ships and worlds. Skulls were particular, it turned out, and they didn't work too well near swallowers or all the hustle and bustle of people and their goings-on. When a world needed to send something secret to another world, the message had to hop and skip its way from world to ship and ship to world, with people doing the errands at either end.

I was realising that you could spend a lifetime working with the bones and not get to the bottom of all their quirks. But a lifetime was the one thing none of us could ever count on.

Slowly word got around that we weren't so bad. To help myself blend in a bit more, I found a very sharp knife – what they called a yard-knife, because it could cut through any sort of rigging – and had Adrana hack away half the length of my hair. I surprised myself when I next caught my reflection. There were angles in my face I hadn't seen before, a sort of hardness pushing through from underneath. I hadn't got any uglier, but I certainly hadn't got prettier either. And I liked it. Afterwards, grudgingly-like, Adrana had me do the same to her hair as well. But I knew she liked how it had changed me, and wanted a part of that for herself. We also stopped insisting on wearing our dresses and boots all the time, and started trying on some of the less grubby items left for general use. Also, I may as well admit, we stopped being so particular about washing. Whatever it was we did – one of these things, or all of them, or just some slow adjustment, the crew now seemed more willing to invite us into their confidences, to share their work and its difficulties, to occasionally drop an unguarded remark about Rackamore.

'If we can tear him away from his books . . .'

'When the captain's finished ironing his shirts, perhaps he'll be able . . .'

'Even his nibs wouldn't turn his nose up at that . . .'

And so on. It wasn't ever anything damning, and probably

no worse than what any captain must face from their crew, and under it all was a respect and fondness. They liked him, even if he sometimes got under their skin with his high manners, educated way of speaking and the time he spent with his nose jammed into books.

Not that they were an unlearned lot. We already knew that Cazaray had come from a good background. Mattice, the Opener, had picked up his craft from books, not word of mouth. He showed me these journals – their handwritten pages a mad scribble of facts and lore relating to all the doors, locks and countermeasures one might encounter within a bauble.

'Most of these pages aren't in my hand,' he said, as I flicked through the arcane contents. 'When I was young – yes, I was young once, as miraculous as that will seem – an old Opener called Lautaro entrusted these books to me. They were all the cleverness he'd stored up over a life of opening baubles – and the books weren't even new when Lautaro began. You see how the hand changes twice? He had 'em from an even older Opener. Going back a hundred, hundred and fifty years now. If I'm one of the best in the business – and I wouldn't gouge the lamps out of anyone who made that claim – then it's only because of those who went before me.'

'Do you mind going inside those things?' I asked.

'Mind?' A smile split his beard. 'It's what I live for, girlie. Everything else – all this chaff about sailing from one bauble to another – that's the rubbish I put up with!'

'Captain Rackamore says Adrana and I won't ever go into a bauble.'

'His imperial cleverness knows which side his bread's buttered. Other than the sails – and maybe the skull itself – you two are about the most valuable items on this ship.' He touched a finger to his stub of a nose. Every part of Mattice was rounded, worn down, like a very old rock that had seen aeons of time and weather. 'You're safe. You'll earn your quoins fair and square, and if anyone resents you for it, you can tell them Mattice fancies a word.'

But my finger had stopped on one of Mattice's pages. There was a drawing of a circular object with a long narrow section cutting all the way into it from the outside. Notes and details crowded the diagram. They were in the recent hand, Mattice's.

And a name:

The Fang.

'That's the place,' I said quietly. 'Something went wrong there, didn't it?'

'Aye,' Mattice said, his voice as low as my own. 'That it did.'

5

The photon winds had taken us twenty million leagues beyond the Congregation by the time we dropped sail. I suppose the bauble ought to have been the thing that most caught my eye, but it wasn't like that. Baubles aren't much to look at, generally – it's what's inside them that puts a fever on the brow. But I'd never seen the Congregation from outside, and that *was* something worth a gawp or two. It was one thing to know that we were far from home; quite another to see and feel it.

If I tried to put it into nice and pretty words, all proper and ladylike, the way I was taught by Paladin, I'd say that it was a hazy circle of shimmering, scintillating light, with the Old Sun at its focus, masked and gauzed by all the intervening worlds, so that the Old Sun's weary light was filtered by its passage through the skyshells of sphereworlds, the glassy windows of tubeworlds, the photon-shifting fields of baubles themselves, sometimes pushing that light from red to blue, sometimes from blue to red. And I'd go on to say that the cumulative effect of all those worlds floating between us and the Old Sun was to create a constant twinkling granularity, an unending dance of glints, from ruby-red to white, from white to indigo, and an almost impossibly deep purple-blue.

I wouldn't stop there, though, because even then I wouldn't

have got you seeing it exactly the way it was. So I'd carry on and mention how the light stabbed at us, withdrew, stabbed again – each flare the moment a single world tricked the Old Sun's light in exactly the right fashion to send it spearing into our eyes, before its orbit or angle bent the light elsewhere. You couldn't point to a single glint and say that was a certain world, but in your head, knowing what you did, you knew each must have had its instant. Even your own little world.

It was a lovely thing, what people had made of the Congregation. We couldn't take credit for the worlds, no. It wasn't us who'd done the Sundering, or put all the pieces back together again. People, yes, but not us. But we could take credit for spreading back through the worlds, finding places to live again, and doing so in something close to peace and harmony for more than eighteen centuries.

And yet, moved as I was by all this – struck through by a powerful, wrenching homesickness – I couldn't shake the words of Cap'n Rack in his library.

That all the Occupations end up being temporary, and ours wasn't going to be any different.

*

'Brabazul's Ruin,' he said. 'And no, it won't be *our* ruin – not if I've any say in it. Some of you will have heard of it – Loftling's crew scored here pretty well, back in 1754. But they were late hauling in and they didn't have time to go very deep before it was time to back out. Vaspery came out here again in '81, but the bauble didn't open. It's held to a fairly predictable cycle since then, but in eighteen years no one's chanced another expedition. Prozor – you can disregard the auguries in your book. Cazaray pulled updated numbers through the skull just before we reached Mazarile.'

'Nice of him to say so,' she said.

'Nice of him to keep a commercial secret, you mean, so that we can all divide the quoins when it pays off?' Rackamore didn't wait for her answer. 'If the auguries are righteous, by my reading she'll open for us in two and a bit days, a whisker over fifty hours from now.'

It was the start of evening watch. Fifty hours would take us to just after midnight.

If you looked through the opposite window to one that was facing the Congregation, then the bauble took up the same amount of sky as all the worlds, but the difference was it was only a few leagues away. It was a sphere, about as wide as Mazarile, and it glowed all sullen and red. Pressed on that radiance, and shifting all the time, were patterns: complicated geometric forms, like carvings or embroidery. The patterns flickered from one form to the next, and now and then you caught a squint of something lurking underneath them.

'Do we know what's inside?' I asked, trying to sound like a member of the crew.

'Loftling's account's still the best we have,' Mattice said. 'It's a rocky world, and there's a swallower, which is why we're in orbit. Gravity gets through the field, you see, even if nothing else does. Once it opens for us, there are doors on the surface. We have Loftling's maps, and they're pretty detailed. The doors, and the countermeasures, go back to the late Fifth, and we've enough experience of those times not to run into anything we can't handle.'

'The Commonwealth of the Throne of Ice,' Jusquerel said. 'A brutal dictatorship, by all accounts. They say the screams of their victims echoed for a hundred thousand years.' She rubbed her hands. 'But they left some glorious loot.'

Little needs to be said about the next fifty hours. We went through the usual watches, did our time in the bone room, cooked for the crew. Adrana and I slept as best we could. One late hour, when Garval's screaming seemed to cut through the whole ship like a cold cruel wind, I untangled myself from my hammock and went to her room. The door was unlocked, as it had been before. Rackamore must have reckoned his crew a tolerant lot, I thought, or else it had never occurred to him that someone might wish to smother Garval for the sake of a quiet night's sleep.

I had no intention of smothering her, but I won't pretend that my thoughts were entirely charitable. I suppose I'd been thinking of shaking her out of her phantasms, forcing her to stop acting like a mewling child.

But once I was at her side, my anger dissolved.

'Oh, Garval,' I said, softly as if I whispered a lullaby. 'You can't help this, can you?'

Within the limits imposed by her restraints, Garval thrashed and convulsed. Her head snapped from side to side, the strap that should have bound her having worked loose. Her hands were fists, the nails digging into her palms, the tendons standing out like ridges. She moaned out a torrent of agonies.

I found the cloth Cazaray had used to moisten her brow, and went to the water dispenser in the wall. I returned to Garval, stationing myself at her side, and tried to open her fingers enough to slip my hand into hers.

'You asked if we were the new ones. I'm Fura, and my sister's Adrana. You were right about us: we've come aboard to do the same thing you did – to read the skull. I know it didn't work out well for you, but that's not your fault. You had to find a way off your world, and you did. Adrana and I were the same.'

I dabbed the wettened cloth against her brow and lips, while she twitched and jerked as violently as when I had entered the room.

'Well, maybe not the same,' I went on. 'We didn't have it that bad. It's just that things hadn't gone very well for the family. Mainly, I think Adrana wanted adventure – earning quoins was just an excuse, a way to justify what she did. She tricked me, in a way, but by the time I realised what she'd done, I think I liked the idea of escaping just as much as she did.'

Whether it was my words, my presence, or just a change in the weather in her head, but Garval's distress seemed to lessen by some small degree. I administered the cloth again. I had no fear of waking the others with my talking: if they could sleep through Garval, they could sleep through the Sundering.

'Velgen,' she said, just that one word.

'Someone close to you?' I asked, chancing that it was the name of a person rather than a world.

'Brother,' she answered, her voice roughened from all the moaning. 'Good brother. Good Velgen. I should have looked after him better. You look after each other, don't you?'

'We do,' I answered. But it was the sort of thing you say, whether you mean it or not.

'Where are we?'

'At the bauble now, orbiting it. It's going to open soon and they're going inside it. I don't think it's a dangerous place, really. They have charts and the crew seem to know what they're doing. Rackamore seems confident . . .'

She cut across my words with a thin, knowing smile on her lips. 'Don't always believe what your captain says.'

'I think he wants the best for us.'

'The best for himself. If the rest of 'em do all right out of it, that's a bonus.'

I looked to the door, making certain it was shut. It was just a conversation, but all of a sudden it had a mutinous edge that made my skin prickle.

'I don't think he's a bad man.'

'Didn't say he was. But whatever Rackamore is, a captain's part of it, and what drives the likes of them isn't what drives the rest of us.'

'So what does drive him?'

She drew a laboured breath. 'They tell you about his daughter?'

I brought the water and cloth to her bedside. 'Not much.'

'Good. All things considered, maybe it's better that way.'

*

Gradually it became clear who was and who wasn't going down to the bauble. A few hours before the field was supposed to drop, they all gathered in the galley, half in and half out of their spacesuits, with their helmets on the magnetic table like trophies. Cazaray – he'd been with us in the bone room until the last minute – was the least prepared, and he was being helped into his suit by Prozor and Triglav, while Hirtshal helped the others check that their connections and lungstuff seals were all secure.

The suits were familiar to me now, and we had been shown how to use them in an emergency. Every part of them was brown, or some metallic shade that contained or reflected that hue: brown fabric, brown alloy seals, brown concertina joints, brown helmet, brown glass on the little porthole of the faceplate, brown bars across the front of that faceplate. Only a few smears of colour on the helmets and shoulders identified one suit from the others.

'They're old,' Rackamore said. 'And there's not much in them that you wouldn't have found a thousand years ago. Old isn't always bad, though. It's what we can afford, which is one thing, but it's also what we know we can trust and repair easily.' He knuckled the white crown of his own helmet. 'Short-wave squawk. That's all that you can bank on. No in built sensors or navigation overlays. No power amplification for the rest of the suit. If you have it, you'll soon come to depend on it and you'll lose the strength you need to get out of a jam when the suit goes limp on you. No energy weapons or cutting gear. Nothing that relies on power works well in a bauble, and you're better off not counting on it. Gas torches work, most of the time. Electrical pumps and supply valves for the life support, hard to avoid those, but if they seize up – and sooner or later they will – you can run on pressure alone for a few hours. Can't rely on a heater, either.' He had dredged up a smile. 'There's a reason we like to get in and out quickly. Saves on the frostbite.'

Trysil was working her fingers in the glove, easing some movement into the stiff articulation of the joints. The gloves squeaked as if they needed oiling. I remembered Rackamore exercising his fingers and understood why.

'The bauble's following the expected pattern,' the captain said now. 'Field drop should follow in . . . Proz?'

'Ninety-seven minutes,' she said.

I'd seen the gradual change in the bauble for myself. It was hard not to be captivated by it whenever I happened to pass a window facing the right way. The dance of patterns on the dark red surface had quickened, hastening towards a conclusion. More and more of the world was showing through the surface. Underneath that skin of energy was a ball of rock, not so different from Mazarile.

When they were ready there was time for a quick toast to the success of the party, handshakes and pats on backs, and then the expedition gathered their helmets and made their way to the front of the ship. The rest of us tagged behind. Rackamore, Cazaray and Mattice went inside the launch and the airlock was closed. Trysil and Jusquerel put on their helmets, double-checked seals and lungstuff supply, and went through another lock into the launch's storage bay, where they worked to un-couple it from its cradle.

The mouth opened. Trysil and Jusquerel jammed levers against the hull of the launch and heaved it on its way. It backed slowly out, tail first, Rackamore using puffs of gas to control its flight. Once it was clear of the *Monetta*, Trysil and Jusquerel used gas-guns of their own to cross over to the launch and get aboard. It all happened in silence, like some complicated ballet that was going through a rehearsal without the orchestra.

They left. We watched the launch fall away from the *Monetta*, remaining below us as we orbited, carving out a spiral course like a watch spring. It was a silver bullet, then a silver hyphen, then it wasn't anything more than a bright mark against the bauble's surface.

'Fifty minutes,' Prozor said.

'What happens if they hit the bauble before it opens?' I asked Triglav, one of the five of us (besides Garval) who'd stayed back on the ship.

'From the bauble's point of view?' The little man rubbed at

his hairless scalp as if it needed polishing. 'Not much. Might jinx Prozor's calculations a little, but it won't make a shred of difference to the auguries.'

'And from their point of view?'

'They say it's painless.'

'Do you mind Trysil going in there?' Adrana asked. By then we'd worked out the that the two of them were together, the only couple on the ship that we knew about.

'Oh, I'd sooner not have her out of my sight. But the truth is I know ion systems and that's enough for this little bone-box. In a bauble I'd just get in everyone's way. No, Trysil's welcome to her line of work and provided I get her back in one piece at the end of an expedition, I'm happy enough. Do you know your history?'

'A little,' I said.

Triglav scratched behind one bendy ear and said: 'When Mattice opens a door, Trysil can walk into a room full of million-year-old loot, give it no more than a glance, and tell instantly whether it's worth our while. Trysil says time builds up in old things like steam in a kettle, needing to get out. Old things – properly old things – are bursting at the seams with time. And what she knows isn't from books or museums. Talk to Trysil about the Eleventh Occupation, she'd give you a blank look. Ask her about the Council of Clouds or the Empire of the Ever Breaking Wave, then she'd hold you down and tell you a thousand stories, none of which you'll ever find in the Hall of History.'

'What's the most valuable thing you've ever found in a bauble?' I asked.

'Found, or pulled out?' Triglav asked.

'There's a difference?' Adrana put in.

'Tell her about the engine,' Prozor said, as if she was cutting off a line of conversation she didn't care for.

'It was about the size of a tea urn, a bronze-green thing with all sorts of pipes all over it,' Triglav said. 'Not a monkey trinket. Tusker or Bug-Eye, perhaps. We didn't even try to make it work.'

'Did someone?' I asked.

'Yes, on a sphereworld called Prosperal, somewhere down in the mid-processionals. And they got a hole drilled through their world for their trouble – all the way out from the inside.' Triglav bent his sad features into half a smile. It was like someone wearing clown make-up, trying to form the opposite expression to the one painted on. 'The lesson there is it's not our business to fiddle around with things. Provided we've found 'em, and been paid for 'em . . . that's enough for me.'

'I'd have thought you'd be more curious,' Adrana said.

'Curiosity's for coves that don't know when they've got a good thing,' Triglav said, scratching under his jaw. 'I'm happy with my lot. Plenty worse things than being a bald little ion engineer on a sunjammer, even one that's never going to make anyone's fortune.'

'Good,' said Prozor. 'Because that's what you're stuck with.'

We were still talking about baubles and trinkets when Hirtshal came into the room. The master of sail had a way of ending any conversation without a word. He cocked his bearded chin at the window, not even bothering with a question.

'Five minutes,' Prozor said. 'You want a ringside seat, Hirtshal?'

Hirtshal stood with his arms folded, his eyes all cold and flinty like nothing could have interested him less.

'No.'

The launch was now very close to the bauble's surface, but with telescopes and binoculars we could still track it, a little grain of silver sliding over the flickering ruby-red of the surface. Prozor had consulted her books once or twice in the last few hours, but nothing had given her cause to alter her figures. The bauble's changes were happening so quickly now it made me dizzy to look at them.

'Rack'll have his hand on the rockets,' Triglav said in a low whisper. 'If that bauble doesn't pop on cue, he'll turn around sharpish, put about five gees on the launch, and damn the rivets.'

'I hope he has enough fuel,' I said.

'Plenty. Remember, it's not just the crew he's hoping to bring back to us.'

I had been expecting something spectacular when the bauble opened, but the truth was that it was a bit anti-climactic. The view of the underlying world had been growing sharper and more prolonged by the minute . . . and then suddenly it held, and the ruby-red surface didn't return.

It was just like Mazarile, only less interesting to look at. A face of rock, craters, ridges and clefts, without even the compensation of areas of skyshell and the cities beneath.

'Start the clock,' Triglav said.

'Already have,' Prozor answered. 'Two hundred and fifty-eight hours and counting.'

The launch continued its descent. It passed the point where the artificial surface had been and carried on to the true one beneath. Even though it was just a dot of silver, it gave off a smudge of light whenever Rackamore touched the steering jets. The swallower gave Brabazul's Ruin the same surface gravity as Mazarile, so the launch needed to use its rockets to achieve a landing.

'You see that line of craters?' Triglav asked. 'They're on Loftling's charts. There's a way in near the rim of the rightmost crater. The captain'll put down as close to that point as possible – no sense in walking further than you have to.'

The bauble had opened on schedule, so we could bank on it closing just as promptly. Rackamore's party had two hundred and fifty-eight hours until they'd need to be back in space, above the level where the bauble's surface had formed. That was more than ten days, and Loftling had only needed one day to make a round trip.

'They're down,' Prozor said. It was only a minute or two later that Rackamore squawked back to confirm that they were safe and beginning to leave the launch.

'Keep a watch on the sweeper,' he said. 'And if the sisters aren't in the bone room, they should be.'

We waited just long enough for the party to step out onto the surface, although even with the telescopes there was nothing we could see of that. After a few minutes Rackamore said that they'd found Loftling's entrance, and that Mattice was already following Loftling's guidelines on opening the lock.

At the door to the bone room, before we spun the wheel, we experienced a moment of collective hesitation, a silent exchange of looks, both of us knowing that we had to push aside our doubts and rise to the moment. My throat was dry, my hands clammy.

I spun the wheel and we went inside.

Without Cazaray to squeeze some of the space out of the room, the skull seemed larger. I moved around it as if seeing it for the first time, picking my way through the loom of supporting strings, wondering again at the long-dead creature that had once owned these bones.

'I'll start at one end,' Adrana said, taking the two sets of neural bridges from the wall. 'You the other. If we meet in the middle without getting anything, we'll know no one's sending.'

I took the pins from my hair so that I could flatten it close to my scalp, and put on the neural bridge, jamming it down as tight as possible. I plugged in, closed my eyes, and emptied my thoughts. There was nothing from the peripheral input. I gave it long enough to be sure, then moved along to the next location. The skull quivered in its springs. Adrana moved her input at the same time as mine, disturbing the skull no more than necessary.

Nothing on the second nodes, for either of us.

We opened our eyes, met each other's gaze, nodded, carried on.

On the third I felt a prickle.

'Something . . .' I whispered.

'What?'

'Quiet.' I should have kept my trap shut – Cazaray would have chastised me for that – but the prickle was still there. Something was sending, or trying to send. But the signal was weak.

'I'm moving to the next input. It might be stronger.'

'All right,' Adrana said doubtfully.

I uncoupled, plugged in again. The contact was clearer this time. I shivered a little.

'Better?'

'Yes.'

'Then tell me what you're getting.'

'It's not clear yet.' I was speaking and trying to hold my mind empty at the same time. 'Let me work on it.'

'Is it near or far?'

'I can't tell. Chaff it – let me concentrate.'

I moved to the next node. Nothing coming through on that one. I returned to the previous site. The signal was still there, but I was pretty sure it had got fainter.

'Well?' my sister demanded.

'I don't know. It's not as strong.'

'Let me try.'

'Because you're always better than me?'

'In this case – yes.'

Pride nearly got the better of me, and I don't mind admitting it. But I rose above it and allowed Adrana to couple onto the node. I backed away from the skull, eased the bridge from my head.

'Show me how it's done.'

Adrana ignored my goad and plugged in. Her face went all placid and doll-like, as if she'd been doing this since we were in nappies. For a good minute she showed no reaction, but then there was a twitch at the edge of her eyelid, and a faint crease dug itself into her forehead.

She unplugged and went back to the node where I'd first detected the presence. Then back to the other node. Her lower lip pulled back from the top one.

'Well?' I asked.

'I thought there was something. On the first input, just for a moment. Then it was gone.'

'I didn't imagine it, then.'

'Sometimes there's noise on these inputs. Static charges building up in the skull. You know that.'

'That's not what it was.'

'All right,' she said, jerking the neural bridge off her scalp. 'So what are you suggesting we do about this ghost signal? Take it to Triglav, or Prozor, or Hirtshal, and tell them to call back the party because we *might* have picked up a send from anywhere in the Congregation?'

'No, of course not!'

'Then what?'

'I'm just saying there was something there. Something that didn't feel *right*. I don't know where it was sending from, or to whom. That's all.'

Adrana took my neural bridge and hung it back up with hers on the wall.

'We're jumpy,' she said, taking a conciliatory tone. 'It's our first time alone.'

I put one pin between my teeth while I fiddled another into my hair.

'I didn't imagine it,' I said, gritting out the words.

*

'Mattice got the door open,' Triglav said, scratching behind an ear. 'No surprise there – Mattice is *almost* as good as he thinks he is, and Loftling's instructions can't have been too wide of the mark. They were in contact until that point, but now they've begun to descend into the world we won't hear too much from them again.'

'Isn't that a risk?' I asked.

'Cap'n's way,' Prozor said. 'Settin' up repeaters, runnin' wires through doors, that all takes time. All goes well, they'll hit the loot in about six, eight hours. Gives 'em time to scope it out, sort the loot from the chaff, get some of it back to the launch, check in with us, and maybe think about going deep again.'

'Say eighteen hours round trip,' Triglav stated. 'But they still need to rest and sleep. Maybe a round trip a day, if they push it.

Room for ten of those before the bauble blinks on us, but Rack won't push it anywhere near that close.'

'They'd already have been awake for much more than a day,' I said.

Triglav nodded vigorously. 'But nothing'll put a spring in your step quicker than a room full of loot. Believe me, they don't all share his caution.' He took a swig from his tankard – it was never very far from him – looking like a man drowning a multitude of sorrows. 'But caution's what's kept them alive until now. Isn't it, Hirtshal?'

The master of sail glanced up from a puzzle of knotted strings. He ruminated on the question for some moments.

'Yes.'

'There: a resounding show of support from the ever-loquacious Hirtshal.'

'Too much caution, I say,' Prozor mumbled. 'Weeks to get out here, why not use all the time we have?'

'You know why,' Triglav answered. 'Sometimes you can push things too far. If anyone knows that, it's you.'

Hirtshal placed a hand on Triglav's wrist. 'Enough.'

But Triglav wriggled out from under the master of sail and helped himself to more bread and beer. 'Why not? We all know what happened. If the Ness sisters are going to be part of this crew, they'll end up knowing sooner or later. Why not now?'

'Are you talking about the Fang?' I asked.

'Mattice wasn't always our Opener,' Triglav said. 'That was Prozor. And do you know our dark secret? Proz was the best of them all. Until Captain Rackamore overreached himself, and our old Bauble Reader wasn't as reliable as Proz is now—'

'Shut up,' Prozor said.

Triglav took another swig. 'They've a right to know what can happen.'

'Not now,' Hirtshal said.

'Never will be a good time for it, will there? But it's part of what we are, and none of it was Proz's fault. *That* you can blame on the Bauble Reader we had back then.' Triglav rubbed a hand across his scalp, as if reassuring himself that it was still hair-less. 'And don't worry – I wouldn't stain the ship with his name. Enough to know that the estimate was wrong, the auguries all cockeyed. You tell 'em, Proz.'

She scowled at him – or made more of the scowl that was her normal expression – but now that the story had been dredged half into the light I could tell she needed to finish it off, the way you needed to finish lancing a boil once you had started.

'You were right,' she said, nodding at me. 'It was the Fang. Just a name for a bauble. It's still out there, somewhere, although I don't care to remember the orbit it was on. Ordinary enough place, to begin with. Nothing shivery about it. Bone-coloured rock, all smoothed over with no craters. Been cracked a few times, some loot, but no one had ever gone really deep.'

'Until we hauled in,' Triglav said. He passed Prozor a beer.

'Rack wanted to see what was in it, though. Meant going down further than anyone else. We made four trips in, and each time we reached a deeper set of vaults. On the fourth . . . well, we found somethin'. More than a league and a quarter down. Rooms. Lots of rooms. And a different kind of loot than any of us had seen before. Stuff I ain't heard of before or since.'

'Such as?' I asked.

'Nasty stuff. Gold boxes. Like cases of treasure, except en-graved with skulls and bones, done like corpses with the meat comin' off them. Crouching lions, with fizzogs half gone. All grinny and sockety. Monkey faces, too. Put the deep shivers in us all. Something about those boxes said *keep away*. Got worse, the closer you got to 'em. But Rack had the spur in him then. Had to know what was in those boxes. So he cranked one open. Cove was shaking just to be that near, but credit to 'im, he did it. Wasn't no lock on it or anything, just a hinge. And inside . . .'

'What?'

'Ghostie stuff,' Prozor said. 'More of it than you or me or anyone else has ever seen in one place. And there wasn't just that one box. There were dozens of 'em. We opened a few, when we could stomach it. Wasn't easy.'

'Ghostie stuff?' I said.

'The Ghosties go back a long way. First or Second Occupation, maybe earlier. They were people . . . maybe. But not like us. They did things we can't do or even think of doin'. Wrong things. Things against the common laws of nature. Mostly they didn't leave much behind, just a shivery reputation. Some coves say the whole reason for baubles is to keep Ghostie stuff from spilling back out into the worlds again, except now the baubles ain't doing such a peachy job of it. You ever seen Ghostie stuff, Fura?'

'I don't think so.'

'Queer thing is you don't really see it. Ghostie stuff's sly. When you stare at it right on, it ain't there. You only catch a glimpse of it side on, when you're not trying.'

'Is there Ghostie stuff on the ship?'

'Jusquerel wouldn't touch it if there was. It's powerful. Useful, sometimes. Weapons and armour we can't even dream of now. Some coves'll take a chance on it. But it ain't to be trusted.'

'But you brought some of it back.'

'No. Wasn't time. Rack thought there was, but the auguries was off. We were still down in those vaults when the field started thickenin' up again. Whatever fear that Ghostie stuff put into us, it was nothin' compared to the fear of being locked in a bauble.'

'But you had time,' I said. 'To get out. Even if you didn't have time to bring out the loot, you could still save yourselves.'

Prozor met my eyes. 'Most of us.'

'A surface can snap back like an eyelid, quicker than a blink,' Triglav said. 'That happens, there's no chance of getting out. But it can be slower too. In this case, they had about an hour to get off the world.' He glanced at the other man. 'You feel like chipping in, oh loose-tongued one, don't hold back.'

'No,' Hirtshal said.

Prozor sank more beer. 'Fang was always a difficult bauble to crack. Half the reason Rack's never returned to it, even though he's the only captain knows what's really down there, and what it might be worth.'

'Tell them the other half of the reason,' Triglav said.

'I made Rack promise we'd never go back. He wants to, I know. Cove's got unfinished business there. But he can leave it unfinished while I'm on the crew. I ain't reading the patterns for him on that one, not after what it did to us the first time.'

'What was so bad?' I asked.

'Everything. Wasn't a staircase on it like this one, just a shaft. Maybe there were stairs once, but they got worn away, and all that's left are the walls of that shaft. Straight down, all the way to the swallower. Cap'n rigged up a winch, braced it off the top of the shaft. Now, a winch is a nice thing, but you can't always use one. Bulky, for a start, and if you've got doors to get through before you hit the shaft – like they have here – then a winch is just too big to carry with you. But the Fang was easier, with the shaft open to space, so all we had to do was slide the winch in over the top and get it anchored good and solid. Had a bucket on it, so we could go up and down, and bring back the loot. But there wasn't room in that bucket for more than one of us at a time. When word came in that the bauble was closing ahead of schedule . . .' Prozor gave a little shivery shake of her head, as if the horror of that experience were coming back anew.

'And the rest,' Triglav said.

'Six of us had to go back up that shaft. Cap'n insisted on being the last one out. I went up on the first trip – that was Rack's order. He needed to save his Opener. I was golden.' She paused, swallowed hard. 'But there was a disagreement. Githlow was supposed to come up next.'

'Tell them who Githlow was.'

'My husband,' Prozor said.

'Githlow was an Assessor,' Triglav said. 'Damned good, too. Even Trysil'll tell you that, and getting praise of out Trysil's like trying to warm your toes by starlight.'

Hirtshal lowered his puzzle. 'Githlow. Good man.'

'Githlow was already in the bucket, ready to go back up the shaft, when Sheveril spooked.'

Sheveril was another new name to us.

'Who was that?' Adrana asked.

'Mattice's apprentice Opener,' Triglav said. 'Rack ran to a bigger crew then, and some of us were training up apprentices. Sheveril was green . . . too green as it happened. Got the shivers in the blood, and it did rum things to her. Hell, we've all known the shivery. That's no admission. We're all cowardly deep down. But it's how you act on it, that's what separates one bastard from another.' He dragged a hand across his lip. 'Sheveril tried to jump into the same bucket Githlow was already in. It tipped, and they both went down. No easy way to end that fall. One saving grace.'

'Which was?' I asked.

'No lungstuff in that shaft. They went down fast.'

'Why was that a mercy?' Adrana asked.

'Because once we were out of squawk range,' Prozor said, 'I didn't have to hear my husband's screams as he carried on down.'

*

They'd been in the bauble for eighteen hours when we heard back from them. They were tired, but very pleased with what they had found.

'Tell Hirtshal he can ruin another set of sails,' Trysil said, her voice coming out of the secondary console in the galley. 'And another, if he fancies it. Loftling's charts paid off well enough, but Mattice got us into two vaults Loftling never even cracked. There's a lot here, more than we can ever bring back, but what we've already brought to the surface ought to bring us a thousand quoins, maybe more.'

Triglav cocked an eyebrow by way of appreciation. 'What sort of prizes, Trys?'

'Mostly from the last five Occupations, maybe one or two earlier than that. Thirty sheets of Prismatic Ironglass – tougher than any we've seen. A pretty jade box with a pair of duelling pistols, Empire of the Atom. A space helmet, done up with horns. A sword that teaches you how to swing it. Half a robot. A skull or two – Cazaray thinks he might be able to squeeze something out of 'em. Oh, and . . . well, you'd better wait. Cap'n wants a word.'

'Hello, Captain,' Triglav said.

'Do we still have the bauble to ourselves?' Rackamore asked.

'Nothing close on the sweeper, and we've been checking it like you said,' Triglav said. 'It gives Hirtshal something to do.'

'What about Jastrabarsk?'

'Keeping his distance, like the good fellow he is. Looks as if he'll be content to pick over our scraps, once we've left the table.'

'We haven't left it yet,' Rackamore said. 'Maintain the watch. Thirty-minute intervals.'

Hirtshal glanced at Prozor, but said nothing. I didn't think they had been bothering to check the sweeper more than once or twice a watch.

'Well, of course,' Prozor said.

'I'm glad to hear it,' Rackamore said. 'If the sweeper's clear, I see no reason not to chance another trip into the rock, once we've rested a little.'

'Whatever you think best,' Triglav said.

'Oh, and one other thing. Our new Bone Readers – the estimable Ness sisters. Cazaray is most anxious to hear from them. Have there been any developments?'

I glanced at Adrana, and Adrana glanced at me. 'Everything's all right, Captain,' I answered.

But there was a strain in my voice that I could not quite disguise.

'Really?' Rackamore asked. 'No new messages coming in?'

'We haven't picked up anything,' Adrana said, sounding much more sure of herself than I was.

'No news is good news. But Cazaray says to keep on listening. I know it's a burden of responsibility, but if there's anything you're not sure of, I'd sooner know it.' He made a sniffing sound. 'Well, we've work enough to do here. I'm sure I leave the *Monetta's Mourn* in capable hands.'

'Be careful, Captain,' I said.

'We shall.'

When Rackamore had closed the connection, Triglav set down his tankard with a sharp clack against the magnetic table. 'You sounded a little unsure of yourself there, Arafura. Or was it my imagination?'

'We'd best go to the bones,' I said, before he pushed us again.

Once we were in the room I tightened the wheel on the door, then took the bridges off their hooks. My hands were shaking, and I didn't mind Adrana seeing it.

'You're making too much of it,' she pleaded at me. 'It was there and gone and it didn't come back. Cazaray said that sort of thing happens all the time.'

'I don't care what he says. Whatever it was felt wrong.'

'Yes – wrong, but out there, somewhere in the Congregation. Not necessarily right on our doorstep. Did you hear what they said? The sweeper's clear.'

'We have to be sure,' I said, tossing Adrana her neural bridge while already pushing mine into place. 'We won't waste time with the peripherals. We'll hook in on the same node, at the same time.'

'Cazaray said that wasn't a good idea.'

'He isn't here. If we don't show some initiative, no one else is going to do it for us.'

I took the end of my input line, took the end of Adrana's, and jacked them into the same node on the skull.

Adrana gave me a long, level look. 'All right. We try it. But we both have to agree about the signal.'

'Fine,' I answered, meeting her gaze.

Without a further word we closed our eyes and waited for the skull to speak to us.

There wasn't anything. The old bones were silent. After an interval, we agreed to try some of the surrounding nodes, just in case the focus had wandered. But they were as dead as the first.

A long silence passed, before I dared pipe up.

'Something's not right.'

'I know.'

'We should try separate inputs, just in case there's a problem with using the same node. Maybe there's more to it than Cazaray told us.'

'Perhaps . . .' Adrana said doubtfully.

But it was worth trying anyway. We went back to the old method, connecting at adjacent sites.

'It's still dead,' Adrana said, after a while.

'Yes.'

'I mean *really* dead.' She was bending over to look into the skull through the eyeholes. I watched her expression cloud. 'Something's wrong, Fura. Those little lights . . . the twinkly alien stuff . . . you can hardly see any of it. We can't have broken it, can we?'

'Cazaray warned us against it, he didn't *forbid* us. He said we weren't quite ready – not that we could never do it.' I took both neural bridges and placed them back on the wall. 'If it's our fault, it's only because we were trying to help the ship. No one'll hold that against us.'

We left the bone room, tightening the wheel on the other side of the door as Cazaray had instructed. When we got back to the galley Triglav and Prozor were using tankards as game pieces, shifting them around the magnetic hexagons of the table. It looked like the kind of game children play for a season before the novelty wears off. Hirtshal was coming in from the bridge where the sweeper was cycling around. He still had his fingers webbed in the knotty puzzle.

'We'd like to speak to Cazaray,' Adrana said. 'Get him on the squawk.'

Triglav abandoned the game, leaned over to the galley's squawk console, worked the heavy switches and dials. Static crackled out of the speaker grille. 'Captain Rackamore? Triglav here. Yes, all's well. It's just that your shiny new Bone Readers would like a chinwag with Master Cazaray, if that isn't too much trouble.'

Cazaray sounded agreeable enough. 'Hello. Is there something I need to know?'

Triglav invited me to speak into the console.

'This is Arafura, Cazaray. I'm here with Adrana. We've just come back from the bone room.'

'And – is there something I ought to know?'

'We're not sure. There wasn't anything wrong with the skull the last time, but now it seems to be . . . dead.'

'Dead,' Cazaray repeated. 'And by dead you mean . . .'

'We thought there might be something wrong with the connections,' Adrana said. 'I'm going to be honest: we tried connecting in on the same node. We wanted to see if we could amplify a faint signal . . .'

I heard an edge in Cazaray's voice, but it was not the recrimination I might have feared. 'No . . . that wouldn't have done anything to damage the skull. There might be something wrong with the input, or the lines to the bridges, or the bridges themselves . . . but it's hard to see why. Did you try the spare bridge, the one I used?'

'No,' I answered. It was an obvious thing to suggest, and I chided the both of us for not thinking of it.

'Well, be quick about it. Try some of the other nodes. Only one of you needs to go – the other one can stay here.'

Adrana looked at me. Neither one of us relished being in the bone room alone, but if there was one of us who stood a chance of picking up a faint signal, it was my sister.

'Adrana's gone back.'

'Good,' Cazaray said, that edge still in his voice. 'All right. There's more than likely nothing wrong, just a loose connection somewhere. But let's backtrack. You mentioned a faint signal . . . was that something you picked up now, since we spoke the last time?'

'No, sir.' I swallowed. 'Whatever it was, it was there before.'

'But you distinctly said that you hadn't picked up anything.'

'We hadn't, sir.' All of a sudden I felt as if I had only just joined the crew; that all the weeks that had passed since Mazarile counted for nothing. 'It wasn't anything clear. Not a message, not even a word. It was just . . . *there*. And then it wasn't. And now most of the lights have gone out inside the skull . . .'

'What did you say?'

'Adrana looked inside it, when we knew it wasn't working. The lights had gone dead, lots of them anyway.'

Cazaray broke off. I could hear him talking to Rackamore, Rackamore answering, but not what either of them were saying. My hands were damp, a line of ice running all the way down my spine. I didn't know if I'd made some terrible gaffe, or acted just in time. I glanced to the door, wishing Adrana would hurry up.

'This is the captain,' Rackamore said. 'Triglav: can you hear me?'

'Aye, Captain.'

'I do not wish to snap to rash conclusions. But the fact that we have just arrived at this bauble, and just had our skull go silent . . . I cannot dismiss the coincidence.'

'The sweeper's clear,' Triglav said.

'I'm aware of that,' Rackamore answered urbanely. 'Nonetheless, we may still need ions and sail at very short notice. Coordinate with Hirtshal to make the necessary arrangements.'

'What is it?' I asked Prozor.

She whispered: 'Captain's shivery we might be about to be jumped.'

'Jumped?'

She kept her voice low. 'Someone waits for us to do the hard work, emptying the loot from a bauble. Then pounces on us and steals our prize. Or tries.'

'But there's no one else out here,' I said.

Prozor looked back at me. 'Best you pray there ain't.'

6

I must have passed those black boxes a hundred times without giving them a second glance. If I'd stopped to consider, which I hadn't, I'd have assumed they held water, compressed lungstuff, spacesuit parts . . .

'Cap'n's philosophy is to run light, and that includes armament,' Prozor said, as she undid straps and slid the topmost box free of the others. 'But that don't mean we just lie back and take it.'

She undid catches and creaked open the lid. Inside the box, contained with packing, was a framework, straps, something like a mask.

Prozor dragged the thing out of the box and set it to one side.

'The Gunner's Girdle,' she said. 'Put it on.'

Prozor opened another three boxes. She took out more girdles and started putting one on herself, doing up a leather strap that went around her waist and then two more that crossed diagonally over her chest. The mask was on a hinged piece, ready to swing down over her head.

She folded down two metal struts like the rests of a chair, with a kind of pistol grip at the end of each strut.

I copied what she was doing. 'Which part is the gun?'

'The part that stays outside. This is the part that points and fires. Open those boxes and bring me two more of these.' Prozor reached over and lowered the mask over my eyes. It was a blank metal plate, curved so that it obscured my vision to the left and right. Prozor touched a stud on the left arm of my harness and the mask seemed to swell to blank out everything around me.

Blackness filled the mask, and then stars peppered that blackness.

'Now look around. Move your head, your whole body.'

I twitched one way and there was the bauble world, with part of the *Monetta* looming into view beneath it. I turned some more, and there was the purple-blue shimmer of the Congregation. Swinging out from the hull, exactly following my line of sight, were the muzzles of guns.

'You feel this trigger?' Prozor forced my index finger onto a hard metal stud in the pistol grip. 'One squeeze, that's all it takes. Works anywhere inside the ship, within reason. Shoots magnetic slugs, five leagues per second. Use 'em sparingly, or you'll cook the coils before we run out of slugs.'

'Maybe it would have been an idea to have the firing lesson weeks ago.'

'Not my problem, girlie. This is what happens when you make Cap'n Rack twitchy.'

'Fura.'

I lifted up the mask. It was Adrana, working her way back from the bone room. From her expression I could tell the news wasn't any better than before.

'No change?'

If she had questions about the harness I was wearing, she put them aside. 'Cazaray's bridge didn't make any difference. I tried all the inputs. It's like it was never alive in the first place.'

'Perhaps I should try . . .' I started saying.

'I said it was gone,' Adrana said, and I nodded, accepting that the bones were beyond any use we could make of them.

Prozor was gathering up the girdles. 'Never mind the skull. Help me with these. You can each carry one.'

When we got back to the galley, Triglav was just coming back in from the bridge. 'Still nothing on the scope,' he said, before setting his gaze on me. 'I see we've just recruited our new gunner.'

Prozor moved to the console and worked the controls. 'Cap'n?'

'I'm still here. Do you have encouraging news for us?'

'Triglav says the sweeper's clear. But the bones are still dead.'

'Are you certain?' Rackamore asked.

Adrana leaned in. 'Definitely. I tried everything I could think of. What're you going to do now?'

'We're returning. Cazaray is concerned, and that's reason enough for me.'

'Hirtshal and I'll put on suits,' Prozor said. 'We can get you in and out quicker.'

She snapped a switch and turned from the console. 'Better hope this isn't something simple, both of you, or you'll have cost the Cap'n good hours in that bauble.'

'What's Cazaray so worried about?' I asked, sensing more was at hand than anyone was willing to discuss.

'Something like this has happened before,' Triglav said, squinting a cautious eye at his colleagues. 'A skull, a powerful skull – with a powerful Bone Reader – can freeze out another one that's nearby. Jam it, if we were talking about squawking. Or kill it completely, like a bolt of lightning hitting circuitry.'

'You think that's what might be going on?' Adrana asked.

'My job's to act, not think. Captain wants ions, I'll give him ions.'

'But the sweeper,' I said. 'It's clear. There can't be anyone near us, can there?'

No one answered.

Hirtshal pushed himself off from the table, the threads slipping from his fingers as if they'd never been knotted. Prozor patted him on the back, the first nice thing I'd seen between them. We remained in the galley, just us and Triglav for the moment. A little while later we made out the flash of fire as the launch fired its chemical rockets and began its ascent.

Triglav took us through to the bridge and showed Adrana

how to use the sweeper controls, including the power-boost. 'The instant you see so much as a twitch on the scope, give it everything. That'll give us a hard fix with range and angular size. Doesn't matter if we burn out Jusquerel's wiring, so long as we get some warning and a clear idea where to shoot.'

'What about me?' I asked.

'Drop that visor over your lamps and start looking for anything out there that shouldn't be.' Triglav began to shrug himself into one of the same gun harnesses, grunting as he tightened the belly strap under his paunch. 'Look for a milky haze in the opposite direction from the Old Sun – all the leftovers that didn't get made into worlds after the forging. If there's a ship, it'll stand out against that.'

He scooped down the visor and settled his hands on the pistol grips, ready for action.

'Triglav? I think I'm frightened.'

I'd become used to the sad-faced man, but the lower half of that face, all that showed beneath the visor, didn't seem to belong to the same person at all. The set of the mouth was hard, humourless, fierce.

'Good. Not being frightened, now *that* would worry me.'

I lowered the visor, then pivoted slowly around.

A grid of lines and little numbers. Ship under me. Congregation at my back. Its shifting purple-blue-red radiance played across the *Monetta*'s hull, making it squirm and dance like a living thing. The bauble, and the nearing metal bullet of the launch.

Away from that, looking out into the Empty, only two things: stars and blackness, and a lot more of the latter than the former. The stars were impossible little pinpricks, and the black was a cruel, cold slap against the idea of light.

'Launch is twenty leagues out,' Adrana called out. 'Can't see anything closer than the *Iron Courtesan*, and she's too far out to matter. If you see anything nearer, Fura, or *think* you see anything . . .'

'Triglav.'

My breath slowed. I had turned my point of view very slightly, sweeping an area that I thought I had already ruled out. I saw a knot of darkness, like a very black rose. I blinked, swung my vision off it, tried to find it again.

'What?'

'Nothing. I thought something was there, just for a second . . . but it wasn't.'

'Sweep the area again, Arafura.'

'Wait.' That knot of darkness against darkness, a black rose on a black field, was back again. It seemed to float both in front of and beneath the plane of the sky. It was there and then it wasn't.

Its petals were tattered sails, emanating from a central focus.

'Triglav, I . . .'

'Where?'

'Quadrant fifty-five, twelve.'

'Yes. I see it.'

I heard a click as Triglva worked a trigger. Then, more distantly, the discharge of the magnetic coil-guns. It was like a drum roll, played very fast and hard, cutting off as sharply as it began.

Now I saw a sequence of flashes, clustered very tightly, and lasting about as long as our scatterfire volley.

'Fire, sir, from the other ship!'

Between the time I registered the flashes, and the time I finished speaking, they were on us.

The *Monetta* shook again, but this time the shaking was a hundred times as violent.

I lifted the visor, certain I'd done all that I could for now. The drum roll came again, our own guns returning fire. Then another impact, dull-sounding, like a huge bell being struck by a hammer. Feeling a deeper dread than anything I'd known, I went to the window, making out the tiny speck of the launch, willing it closer.

'We've already been hit, haven't we?'

'Just softening us up,' Triglav said. 'She meant to kill us, we'd know it by now.'

Rackamore's voice sounded over the squawk. 'We're lined up. I see Prozor and Hirtshal inside the bay. Get those nets tight as you can – I'm going to burn off some of this speed at the last moment, but this still isn't going to be a soft docking. Cazaray wants to know . . .'

He was speaking and then the only thing coming across the squawk was a scream of static, so loud that reflex got me lunging for the console until some circuit or overload broke the connection without any help from me.

'They've been hit,' Triglav said, flipping up the visor and making his way to the console. He worked the controls, switching through channels. 'Captain – are you reading us? Prozor! Hirtshal!'

Prozor's voice came through, ragged and distant. 'We see 'em. Launch is tumbling pretty bad. Venting gas. They're veering.'

'Enough to miss us?'

'Not sure. Angle's changing.' Then her tone altered. 'Oh, hell. It doesn't look good, Trig. Got a hole in her side big enough to drive a barge through. Bleedin' out like a stuck pig.'

In the window the launch was a slowly cartwheeling cylinder, gushing out a glittery spiral of escaping gas. I thought of the people aboard it, the five members of the party, and wondered if a single one of them remained alive. Rackamore, Cazaray, Mattice, Jusquerel, Trysil . . . not exactly friends, yet, but people I'd come to think of as friends-in-waiting.

They couldn't be dead.

The launch had been lined up for the *Monetta*'s mouth-like docking bay, but now it was drifting off-course, threatening to do at least as much harm as one of the enemy's slugs if it struck our unprotected hull. Gas was still squirting out, the angle of drift steepening.

But a figure was emerging into view around the curve of the hull, stomping across the hull plates on magnetic soles. The helmet, with its grilled-over faceplate, caught the light for a moment. I saw a sternly impassive face, cut across by a white moustache.

The figure stomped on, coming nearer to the window. It bent down to a piece of low, heavy equipment mounted on the outside of the hull. It had a powerful, compact look to it, like some iron beast squatting before a pounce. I wondered for a second if it might have been one of the guns, then recognised it as part of the sail-control gear.

'Hirtshal!' Prozor called. 'There isn't time!'

'Yes,' he answered.

Hirtshal curled a fist around a handle and tugged so hard on it that the recoil severed the magnetic bond between his boots and the hull. The equipment sprang away from the hull on a coil-driven hinge, swinging high and wide like a catapult.

From its end spilled an inky mass of tightly packed rigging, furling out into a ragged, billowing net.

Hirtshal regained his hold on the hull plating and ducked, raising one arm over his helmet in self-preservation. Still tumbling, still putting out gas, the launch passed the front of the *Monetta*. The rigging was unpacking itself, magically unknotting. The launch was already starting to drift into that smoky confusion, faint threads of rigging cloying their way around the tumbling hull, offering the beginnings of resistance . . .

'He's done it,' I said. 'Hirtshal caught the launch!'

The threads tightened, and then we felt the jerk as the momentum of the launch was transferred to the *Monetta*. The sail-control gear strained under the load, and the launch began to move in an arc, until it clanged against the hull, drifted off, and stopped. It was lashed to us, but safe.

Hirtshal began to pick his way through the tangle he had made. Prozor was clanging into view in her own set of magnetic boots.

Triglav tried the console again, flipping between different channels. There was still only static. The flow of gas from the hole in the launch had begun to taper off.

A door popped open in the side of the launch. Lungstuff blasted out and a fist appeared, then a forearm, then a brown-suited form clambered out of the wreck, almost immediately tangling themselves in the rigging. Another figure.

Triglav was next to me, still with his visor pushed up.

'Shouldn't you be firing the guns?' I asked.

'Coils heat up pretty fast if you sustain fire.' He settled his sad eyes onto mine. 'We're not a battleship, girlie. This ain't what we do for a living.'

Prozor and Hirtshal had pulled knives out of their belts and were hacking through the rigging, helping to untangle the survivors of the launch party. Two were outside now, and a third was coming out of the lock. That one had a white patch on the crown of their helmet, just as Rackamore's had done.

Adrana said: 'Something new on the sweeper, Triglav.'

'Multiple contacts, between us and the other ship?'

'I think so.'

'She's putting out her own boarding party. Ceased fire 'cos she don't want to cut 'em to ribbons with her own scatterfire.' Triglav jammed down the visor. 'But doesn't stop us giving some of it back. I'll see if the coils have cooled down enough.'

A rain of blows began to sound against the hull, concentrated on the side of the *Monetta* facing the enemy. It was lighter this time, not the same as the earlier scatterfire volleys.

'That's the boarding party's own guns, not the ones on the ship,' Triglav said, just his mouth visible. 'Can you still see Prozor and Hirtshal?'

'They've got three of them,' I said. 'They've cut their way through the rigging and I think they're working their way back to the front of the ship, or an airlock.'

All we could do was watch while the five suited figures made their slow, stomping progress back to the bow, moving in rocking lock-step like clockwork figures that had nearly wound down to stillness.

'Prozor and Hirtshal are going out of sight,' I said. 'The other three are still behind them.'

Our guns stopped. Triglav squeaked up his visor.

'That's us done. Barrels are cooked, or we're out of slugs, or both. Can you see Trysil?'

'I'm not sure. Could that be Trysil bringing up the rear?'

He looked through the window. 'Yes, that's her. Rack and Jusquerel just ahead.'

The one I was sure was Hirtshal stopped mid-stride, and for a stupid instant I cursed him for hesitating. But then I saw something had gone right through him. It was a thin gleaming line, entering by his right shoulder, exiting by the left hip, the end of it skewered into the hull, pinning him into place like a specimen.

A harpoon.

The weapon must have had a piercing head, and the entry and exit wounds it had punctured through his suit were wider than the diameter of the shaft. Lungstuff was geysering out of those two holes, and with the lungstuff came something else – a cargo of sparkling pink glitter.

Prozor was trying to help Hirtshal. Trying to staunch the flow of lungstuff and blood, one hand on his shoulder, the other on his thigh, pressing her faceplate against his. The outgassing made a mockery of her efforts, laughing its way between her fingers.

'Prozor!' Triglav shouted. 'It's over – leave him! Get inside before one of those things takes out someone else.'

But there weren't words enough in the universe to make Prozor turn her back on him. And it wasn't words that decided it, in the end. The harpoon exploded, turning into a line of sun-bright fire that burned right through Hirtshal, its vicious energy finding every join, every seam, in the armour of his suit. Light fanned from his wrists, from his elbows, from his knees and waist and neck. His faceplate became a dark-fretted searchlight.

Hirtshal came apart. His helmet drifted away, then his arms and torso, and the upper parts of his legs. Only his magnetic boots remained, still fixed to the hull.

'Hirtshal . . .'

Triglav settled a hand over my wrist. 'Mourn him later – it's for the best.'

'Why didn't it explode straight away?'

'Because this was crueller,' Triglav said.

Rackamore urged Prozor on. I'd nearly lost sight of them around the curve of the hull when another harpoon caught Trysil, pinning its way through her lower leg, between knee and ankle. Trysil reached down, trying to drag the harpoon out of her leg. Rackamore and Jusquerel turned back, while Prozor waved at them to continue. They returned to Trysil and tried to heave the harpoon out of her suit. It was jammed firmly into the hull.

'No,' I said.

I saw them look at each other. Trysil motioned them away with both her hands. Rackamore took a hesitant step backward, then reached out a hand. His fist closed around Trysil's, and then he bowed his whole body, and I knew that this wasn't some final attempt at rescue, but a captain's farewell.

Rackamore let go, but even as he stepped back he never turned his gaze from his colleague. Then the harpoon flared, and the brightness of it seemed to eat all the way through Trysil's boot and the lower leg. She flailed her arms and her pinned-down leg came apart just beneath the knee, truncated in a furious molten glow.

Rackamore reached out to try and grab her hands, but it was too late. Trysil fell away from the *Monetta*, the stump of her leg still smouldering.

'Triglav, I'm sorry,' I said.

'Trysil,' he said. 'Trysil. My Trysil.'

I felt a gust of lungstuff, and started in panic. Somewhere we had been holed. But without even looking at me Triglav raised a calming hand. His voice was surprisingly even and composed, given what he had just witnessed.

'Just the lock opening for the bauble party. Normally we get the pressure nice and equalised first.'

They weren't long in making their way to us. Rackamore was tugging off his white-crowned helmet even as he entered the galley. Then came Prozor, cradling her helmet, and behind Prozor was Jusquerel, carrying a large wooden box.

'Cazaray and Mattice are gone,' Rackamore said, before any of us'd had a chance to fire off a question. 'They died when the launch was hit.'

I wanted to believe he'd made a mistake; that both of those men were still breathing, but deep down I knew Rackamore wasn't in error. And I thought of both of them, the way they'd been good-hearted to Adrana and I, and of Cazaray in particular, who I'd come to regard a decent man who wanted the best for everyone around him, and now they were gone and the speed at which it had happened was almost too shocking to take in. I don't suppose I'd really known grief until then, because when mother died we were both small, and there are some emotions you can't really feel until you're older. But it wasn't just grief. I was angry, too, and a little part of that anger was turned back at myself for not voicing my fears early enough.

'Did they suffer?' I asked.

'No,' Rackamore said. 'The one mercy was that it was quick.' But his jaw tensed and he needed to gather himself before continuing. 'I'm afraid we also lost Hirtshal and Trysil out there, and they didn't have that mercy. You saw all that, I think. Triglav: I'm sorry. We did what we could.'

'You did more than you had to,' Triglav replied.

'You think it's her?'

'If it's not the *Nightjammer*, Cap'n, it's her vicious bitch of a twin. She's close enough for the eyes now. Take a look for yourself.'

Triglav meant one of the screens, which was showing a view through one of the cameras outside the ship. To begin with it was hard to know what I was looking at, as if someone had made a collage out of different kinds of black fabric, so nearly similar that you couldn't say where one piece ended and another began. But slowly my eyes got the shape of it.

'It's like us,' I said.

It was a sunjammer, turned bow on so that we were looking at its gaping mouth. Larger or smaller than the *Monetta*, I couldn't say. But the shape wasn't so very different. A bony, fishy hull, with ribs and spines and spikes and the angled arms of sail-control gear. Blacker than us, though – blacker and bonier still, and somehow uglier and more fierce. Something else, too. The *Monetta* came to a blunt nose above its jaw, but the nose of this other ship was sharp, tapering out to a kind of lance, and fixed to that lance – under or above it, depending on which way you agreed was up – was something I didn't care to recognise, but did all the same. A monkey form. I just knew, there and then, that it wasn't a carving or a sculpture, but an actual body, pulled into some agony of contortion with their knees up to their chest, their arms squeezed into their ribs, their head angled back to look forward along the line of the harpoon, and their hands knotted together like they'd been praying that the next breath would be their last, and by some thin mercy maybe it had.

'It's her,' Rackamore said. 'The better part of me hoped we'd never meet again. But there's another part that was counting on a reckoning. If I can just draw her out of that ship . . .'

'Does it have a name?' I asked.

Jusquerel set the box on the table and opened it. Inside, tucked tightly together in opposing directions, were about a dozen crossbows. Rackamore took one out, ratcheted the bow and slid a bolt into the groove, then turned to us with a hard, hungry gleam in his eyes. '*Dame Scarlet* is the name she was given,' he said. 'But to call her that would be to give her some kind of legitimacy. She's the *Nightjammer* to us, and that's all the name I care to give her.'

'Who?' I asked.

'Bosa Sennen,' Triglav said, as if the name was an oath. 'And she's got us over a barrel. We could send a crew out to fix the guns, but it'd be quicker and kinder to slit their throats now.'

'It's the way she wanted us,' Rackamore answered, holding his crossbow in one hand, levelling the other on Triglav's shoulder. 'She forced a sustained rate of fire on us, knowing we couldn't keep it up.' He managed a smile. 'I'm sure you bloodied a few noses, Trig.'

The others started preparing their crossbows. None of them needed any tuition from Prozor, readying the weapons with as much ceremony as if they were cleaning cutlery. Triglav dished out two to us, then gave us a quick, cursory lesson in how to load and fire them. 'Aiming's the easy bit,' he said. 'On a ship, especially. Hard thing is *not* hitting someone.'

'Just make sure it's the right someone,' Rackamore said.

I was thinking back to the one time I'd heard the name Bosa Sennen. Cazaray had mentioned her, just after talking about the stern-chase that had cost Rackamore his daughter, Illyria.

'It's going to be bad, isn't it?' I said.

'I don't know,' Rackamore said. 'We'll fight, and we'll give her something to remember us by. But if we're driven back, and we fail, and if she means to take you, and you happen to have the means to *stop* her doing that – any means – you do it.'

I understood Rackamore. There were knives on the ship. There were power lines and doors that opened to vacuum. Explosives to crack open the doors inside baubles. Crossbows you could turn on yourself. A hundred other ways to deprive Bosa Sennen of a living prize.

But I wondered if I'd have the spine, if it came to that.

Something thumped against us.

Then something else. These were soft thuds, and they came in quick pairs.

Footfalls.

'They're on us,' Triglav said.

Rackamore slung his crossbow over his shoulder and went to the console, working the switches and dials with a hasty ease. He bent his lips towards the grille.

'This is Rackamore of the *Monetta's Mourn*. I presume I am addressing Bosa Sennen? You want something, that is plain. So do I. State your terms, and you shall have my response.'

Rackamore snapped a switch.

The console buzzed, and a voice crackled out of it.

Maybe it had been a woman's voice, once, but it was hard to be sure. The voice had been shredded, rubbed raw, forced through circuits, looped back on itself, mangled into a parody of itself, and then cut through by static and random bursts of electronic noise.

'There are no terms, Pol, except your immediate and unconditional surrender. Open your locks and prepare to be boarded.'

'Why in all the worlds would I do that?'

'The fruit of your loins, Pol. That's why. I never killed her, you know. She was too juicy a prize for that. Bosa's taken fine care of your Illyria. She's well and she remembers you, and if you want to keep her alive, you'll stop stalling and start opening locks.'

I watched his face, trying to gauge how much of a shock this was to him. Maybe less than I'd expected.

He swallowed, but kept his voice composed.

'I want to see her.'

'When you've been a good host and acceded to Bosa's requests, then you'll have your wish. Open your locks, or we'll start cutting.'

His fingers clenched and unclenched over the console. Adrana was working her crossbow action over and over, as if she stood a chance of it becoming automatic in the time available to us.

'You know we'll fight,' Rackamore said.

'If it makes you feel better. But don't put too much spirit into it. You do want Illyria back, don't you?'

'Give me a moment to prepare for boarding. You've damaged quite a few of our systems, so I can't just open the locks at the snap of your fingers.'

Rackamore locked her out of the circuit before she had a chance to reply, then turned to us. 'You have one task, if I might request it. I know the bones aren't working, but if you can squeeze anything out of that skull, any kind of outbound transmission, you owe it to the other ships. Put out that we're under attack, and that it's Bosa Sennen. Warn them to keep clear. I don't want Jastrabarsk or anyone else getting mixed up in our trouble when there's so little they could do.'

'He could help us,' I said. 'Couldn't he?'

'You could throw six ships against the *Nightjammer*,' Triglav said, 'and it'd still be uneven.'

Rackamore turned back to the console and threw a switch. 'I'm opening the locks, Bosa. Be ready for a fight.'

*

Crossbows in hand, we made our way through the twisty dark maze of the *Monetta's Mourn*. I led the way, noises and shouts chasing us from the front of the ship.

'I couldn't do it,' Adrana said.

'What?'

'What Rackamore was saying. Kill myself to avoid being taken by Bosa Sennen, or whatever her name is.'

'He wouldn't have said it if he didn't mean it.'

'But it's different for them. They've all done all sorts of things with their lives. Seen and lived more than we have. Probably been closer to death more times than we know.'

'I'm not sure how that changes it,' I said.

'We haven't had our lives yet, Fura. And I'm not ready to end mine just because Rack says it's for the best. How the hell does he know? Maybe Bosa'll take us and we'll like working for her.'

'Yes, she seems the caring, compassionate type.'

'Or we'll escape. She's obviously just some thug with a ship. Probably a bit stupid. But we're smart. We're the Ness sisters.'

'Yes, and look at how smart the Ness sisters are.' I pushed my hair out of my eyes. 'If the Ness sisters had a brain cell between them, they'd be back in Mazarile, taking needlecraft lessons from a robot.'

We squeezed around one of the narrow bends. Rightly or wrongly we'd have felt safer in suits, but with all that bulky armour on there'd have been no hope of making it through to the bone room.

'We got to see the whole Congregation,' Adrana said. 'And a bauble. We saw a bauble open. And a pirate ship. We saw a space battle. We saw scatterfire. Don't tell me you'd rather we stayed at home.'

'I'd rather not die,' I said. 'That's all.'

But there was something in what she said. I'd seen a sight that few others would ever know, and the moment had changed me. I'd seen the fifty million worlds of the Congregation in one glance, seen the shifting, shimmering purple twilight that was all that remained of the Old Sun's energies, after those tired old photons had fought their way to the great void of the Empty. I'd seen the glimmer of the rubble left over from the forging.

I pushed on ahead of Adrana. She was dawdling, always looking back the way we had come. My ears popped and I drew a sharp fearful breath.

'What was that?' Adrana asked.

'Rackamore must have opened the locks.'

'He gives in easily.'

'I don't think he has much choice. Hurry? We're nearly at the bone room.'

'It won't do any good, Fura. You know that, don't you? He's just giving us something to do, to take our minds off what's ahead.' She rattled her crossbow against the wall. 'You think these little toys are going to help us?'

'I'd rather have these than nothing at all.'

We were squeezing through a narrowing in the corridor when an alarm sounded. Where the corridor narrowed was a bulkhead door. It was sliding shut, grinding its way from one side of the corridor to the other, and I was on one side of it and Adrana on the other. There was an instant, no more than that, when one of us might have had time to squeeze through that narrowing gap. But we were too shocked to respond.

I twisted back and my eyes met Adrana's.

'Stop it!' she called out, hammering her fist at a bank of controls on her side of the bulkhead.

'I'm trying.' There was a similar bank on my side but the controls were not responsive. 'No good!' I was shouting at her through the gap, over the metallic squeal of the closing door.

'The ship won't allow it! Must be an emergency override!'

Adrana jammed her crossbow into the gap, by now much too tight for one of us to have squeezed through. The door continued until it met the crossbow, at which point it gave a screech and began to shudder in its runners. I smelled burning.

'It's holding,' Adrana said.

But the barrel of her crossbow was already beginning to buckle under the door's force. Wooden splinters crunched away from the stock. The door lurched tighter.

'It's going to close. You'll have to find another way to the bone room. If you go all the way to the stern . . .'

'What if the doors are shut there as well?'

'I don't know. Try it. I think I can get there easily enough from here.'

Adrana pushed her hand through the gap. I closed my fingers around hers.

'I don't want to let go.'

'You have to.'

'I'm sorry, Fura. I did this. I brought this on us.'

'No, you didn't. I signed up to it as well. It's not your fault. Whatever happens, you remember that. This is not your fault.'

Her crossbow was useless by now. On an impulse I unshouldered mine and slipped it through the gap, just as the door lurched tighter and brushed my arm hairs. I was still holding Adrana by the other hand, but I released at the last instant, just as her crossbow gave way and the door sped down to close the gap.

There was a tiny window in the bulkhead. Adrana was on the other side of it. Her eyes were wide and frightened. Not my older sister now, but just someone alone and scared in an unfamiliar place.

I knew how she felt.

I mouthed and pointed for her to go back. I knew there was another way to the bone room, and perhaps by the time she got to another bulkhead, the manual controls would be operable again.

Perhaps.

Through that little window I saw Adrana spin round. There was movement at the far end of the corridor – a dark confusion of arms and legs and faces, coming nearer.

Part of me knew it wouldn't do any good, but I hammered my fists on the glass and when that achieved nothing I tried to budge the door with my muscles. But it might as well have been welded in place for all the difference it made. Watching was all I could do.

Adrana raised my crossbow. She got off one bolt, silent through the glass, and then the mass of figures surged forward. They had suits on, but they were better than ours, tighter around their forms, and quicker for moving through a ship. They were shiny black, throwing back reflections and glints so that it was hard to tell which arm or leg belonged to which body, and where the suits ended and the weapons started. There was no time for Adrana to ratchet back the crossbow and slide in another bolt. The mass was on her like a sudden rising tide. She pushed a hand against the glass, palm flattened, and I pressed mine against it from the other side, and then something pulled her hand from the glass, leaving only a moist imprint, and I turned and fled.

I reached the bone room, sealed the door behind me, turned the locking wheel until it was as tight as I could make it. My breath was like a saw cutting wood.

A voice buzzed from the wall.

'Listen, all of you. This is Bosa speaking. It's all over. Bosa's got your ship, Bosa's got your loot, Bosa's about to have the pick of your crew.' The voice was the one I had already heard: distorted, gashed over with static and feedback, looped over itself in strange echoes and stutters, just barely recognisable as the product of a female larynx. 'But Bosa doesn't need this ship, not when she already has something faster and better and stronger. She doesn't even need most of the crew, so some of you can walk – if you do right by Bosa. And that means helping her with a new Bone Reader.'

Another voice cut across the first, but it was only Bosa Sennen's voice that was clear.

'Something to contribute, Captain Rackamore? Speak up now. Yes, you had a Reader in Mister Cazarary, I know. But Mister Caz is dead now, as you rightly stated. There's just a tiny, tiny complication.'

Rackamore said something else. There was a pleading, futile tone to his voice, as if he knew that there could be no bargaining with Bosa Sennen, no reasonable outcome to her demands.

'Yes, Captain, but here's the thing. It's known to Bosa that you've been on the look-out for a new Reader recently. Been very active in that line of recruitment, haven't you? Rushing around like there was no tomorrow. And the word is your efforts have been rewarded. Not just one new Reader, but two! Yes, two minds come through very clearly, so Bosa's assured.'

Rackamore said something else. Now the pleading had given way to a kind of abject despair.

'What's that, Pol? You say they wouldn't work for Bosa?' She gave a horrid, cackling laugh. 'You don't know much about Bosa, in that case. No; they'll suffice, if they have the skill. The only question to be settled is which of you are the Readers. You'll help with that, won't you, Pol?'

Rackamore screamed.

I've heard some sorry sounds in my life, but that was the worst thing I ever caught coming out of another person.

'Oh, Pol – where's your cooperative spirit? You know that Bosa doesn't like to ask twice. What of the tall girl? Green enough, by the squint of her, and although she hides it well, it's plain that she doesn't yet have her space legs. What's your name, my pretty?'

I heard my sister answer. Her voice was strong, clear and defiant, and it made me proud and frightened all in the same moment.

'Ness.'

'Ness what?'

She hissed out the whole of it like a curse. 'Adrana Ness.'

'And can you read a bone or two, Adrana Ness? Oh, don't look so timid. You're frightened of me, frightened of what will become of you – and who'd blame you? You're being addressed by Bosa Sennen, after all, and that's enough to put a twist in anyone's guts. But don't believe all you hear. I'll ask you again. Are you a Bone Reader? No? But you *seem* the sort. Doesn't she, Pol?'

Rackamore didn't give her the answer she wanted. She made him scream again.

'You,' she said, her focus shifting. 'Sad-faced little man. What do you have to say about the girl? Is she the one?'

I heard Triglav answer this time.

'No? What would she be then? Master of sail? Those hands of hers haven't done an honest day's work in their lives. Squint your lamps at them!'

I remembered Adrana's hand in mine, and the imprint she'd left on the glass.

'Admit it, sad-faced man.'

Triglav said something.

I heard a sound like a whipcrack, then a man's scream. But the scream didn't last long. It guttered out, became a kind of gurgling, and then the gurgling turned to silence.

I knew she'd killed Triglav.

'Now that was rude of him, wasn't it, Pol? Bosa asked a fair question and Bosa expected a fair answer. What about you, sharp-faced lady? Are you going to be so reticent?'

I heard a shriek, a woman's shriek, and of those who remained I knew it belonged to Prozor rather than Jusquerel. Then Prozor let out a curse. There was no whipcrack this time, but a thud and a groan and then another thud, and then a kind of wet crunching sound, as if a skull had just been smashed in.

Then a terrible silence.

'Stop,' Adrana said, her voice breaking as she spoke up. 'Stop. It's me. I'm the one you're after. I'm the Bone Reader.'

Again I got that shiver of admiration and terror, all mixed together. The fact that she didn't sound brave and sure of herself only made me think more of her. She was scared and still she'd spoken.

'Good,' Bosa Sennen said. 'But think of the trouble you'd have saved, if we'd got here sooner. Come here, girl. I was right, wasn't I? You have the look for it. Can't mistake a Sympathetic, and the more time you spend with the bones, the more it shows. Now – who's the other one?'

'There isn't anyone else,' Adrana said.

'But Bosa had it on good authority that there were two minds sending through the *Monetta*'s bones.'

'It was him . . . Cazaray. Plugging in at the same time, teaching me how it works.'

'Teaching you how it works. So what you're telling Bosa is, no one else came aboard with you at Mazarile? You were the only recruit?'

'Yes,' Adrana said. 'Yes. Just me.'

'But when we found you, they said there was someone on the other side of that glass. Another girl, somewhere else on this ship.'

'There's no one else,' Jusquerel said, in her slow, calm way. 'There never was. Your idiots saw her reflection in the glass, that's all.'

I heard the whipcrack sound again. I waited for the screams, but Jusquerel didn't give her that satisfaction.

'You killed her for nothing,' Adrana said.

'Bosa was just making a point, that's all. There's a bone room on this ship and we'll find it sooner or later. And if there's another on board who so much as smells of Mazarile, we'll have them as well.' There was a slurping sound, like something being pulled from a pudding, then a kind of mechanical ratcheting, like a clock being wound up. 'That's Bosa's promise, you see. And Pol knows that Bosa keeps her promises. Don't I, Captain?'

Rackamore mumbled something. I had taken him to be dead by then, but it was clear that she had kept him alive, even as she butchered the rest of them.

'Oh, Pol. What's wrong? Don't you want to look Bosa in

the eye? Does it trouble you too much?' And she let out a sick cackle. 'Here. Let me help you. Fix your lamps on me, and tell me you like what you see.'

Rackamore let out a shriek, then. There was pain in it, certainly, and I didn't doubt that she'd hurt him badly. But something more than pain. Something I didn't care to dwell on too much, because it sounded too much like grief or despair.

Someone tried the door.

The wheel began to turn, the lock being worked from the outside. I moved to the wheel and braced my hands against it, planting my feet against the wall. I had no plan, beyond resisting the turning of that wheel for as long as I was able. For a second or two, it almost felt like I had a chance. The wheel held, and I began to force it back in the other direction, tightening the lock. I only managed a quarter turn before it jerked in my hand and began to turn hard the other way, far too strongly for me to resist.

Garval pushed her head through the widening gap.

'Come with me,' she said.

'How . . .'

'Just come.' Garval reached in and pulled me out of the bone room. Then she closed the door and spun the wheel again, tightening it until the tendons popped out on her forearms. 'Make them think there's someone in there – give them a reason to waste their time.'

'How did you get out?'

'Your sister,' Garval said matter-of-factly. 'She came and she undid my straps. She said if something bad was going to happen, she didn't want me tied up in there.'

It must have been when Rackamore sent Adrana back to make one last check on the bones, while I was being shown the Gunner's Girdle.

'I'm glad she did. But I'm afraid it hasn't helped us much. Did you hear Bosa Sennen just now?'

'I heard.'

'She's killed most of them. Cazaray and Mattice outside,

in the launch. Hirtshal and Trysil on the hull, Prozor, Triglav and Jusquerel just now. I don't know about Rack. But she's got Adrana, and she knows I'm somewhere else on the ship.' I drew a heavy breath, and my eyes stung as if I were about to start crying. I thought about the ones who were already dead, and how close I'd come to accepting my own fate, and now this woman I hardly knew was here to help me. 'Oh, Garval. I'm so glad to see you. But we're still in trouble – I am, anyway. She's going to keep looking until she finds me.'

'She won't,' Garval said. 'Bosa Sennen knows there's another Reader. But she doesn't know it's you.'

I wiped a tear from my eye, wondering what I was expected to make of that pretty distinction.

'The automatic door closed between us,' I said. 'Sealed me down here, Adrana on the other side. Bosa's people got her. But I'd already given her my crossbow, not that it would have made much difference.'

'You won't need a crossbow,' Garval said.

'My sister fought them. I'll do the same.'

'No. You'll hide.'

She took me away from the bone room in the opposite direction from that I had come, making our way in a general sense towards the stern rather than the bow. Before very long we'd come to one of the sealed bulkhead doors. Garval hammered the controls, but the door stayed shut.

'I knew we'd be blocked.'

'No.'

Garval dug her nails into a slit in the walling next to the door and levered away a whole panel, revealing an opening into a dingy, echoey recess. A person could just about squeeze through the opening before they met a secondary wall clotted with pipes, tubes, cables and wires, some of which glowed with a sickly radiance. I wondered if it was the work of Jusquerel, at some point in her career as Integrator. Some of it ran through the corridors on the other side of the panels, but just as much of it was hidden.

'Get in.'

'I'm not getting in there! My sister's up front with Bosa Senne—'

'She's dead,' Garval said bluntly. 'Your sister. Or might as well be. Bosa'll use her up and spit her out. You think they didn't tell me what Bosa's capable of? You need to stop thinking about your sister. She was kind to me, but I can't help her, and I *can* help you. You hide. Sit tight and quiet. Bosa doesn't want this ship, she wants two readers. Once she's got them, she'll leave.'

'She said she'd tear the ship apart until she finds me.'

'Only if she thinks she hasn't already got you.'

'I don't understand.'

'You were kind to me as well, Fura. I'm sorry about all the screaming.'

Some inkling of what she meant to do formed in my mind. 'No!'

'Quiet. You get in that hole before it's too late. I'll seal you in good and tight. You wait a day at least, two if you can stand it, then you get out. Bosa'll be gone by then.'

'No,' I said again, but softer this time. 'You don't have to do this, Garval. You can still go home.'

'There's no home for me, Fura. The skull cracked me open like an egg. What's broken can't be put right. Even Rackamore knew that. He was just making the right noises, saying they'd get me back eventually. It was never going to do me any good.'

I edged my way into the hole, trembling at the thought of being sealed in, and of how long I might have to remain there.

'I won't forget this.'

'It's not about forgetting me. It's about remembering Bosa Sennen. If the chance ever comes for me to slip a knife into her throat, I'll do it. But it probably won't. You, though . . .' She paused, measuring me up, as if at the last instant she'd called her own judgement into question. 'You'll remember. I know you will.'

I was in the hole. There was space to either side of me, stretching away into darkness. I had to draw my knees up high to fit into the gap. It was already uncomfortable, and I'd only been inside for seconds.

Garval reached out and took my hand.

'Move,' she said, before allowing our fingers to slip apart. 'I'm sealing you in. Good luck, Fura.'

'Good luck, Garval. When you find my sister . . . you'll tell her I'm all right, won't you?'

'Of course.'

'And that I won't forget her. I'll find a way to get her back.'

'I will.'

Garval slid the panel back into place. There was an outline of light, Garval's fingertips on the edges of the panel, then darkness.

TWO

JASTRABARSK

7

Voices came and went. Boots and fists hammered on metal. I heard shouts, calls, once or twice a broken-off scream of fury or anguish. It was uncomfortable where I was, and more so by the hour, but the ship was always a creaky, grumbly thing and if I'd stirred I might easily have made a sound that gave away my position. I didn't stir, though. It wasn't because I had the willpower to keep myself still, but because the fear was running through my blood and it locked me into place just as if Doctor Morcenx had slipped some paralysing agent into me. My chin trembled and my heart sped, but the rest of me was like rock. Hours and hours passed like that, with the pain of being squeezed into that spot getting louder and sharper, but the fear of moving always beating it, like the two were playing a game to see which could get ahead of the other.

I say hours, but without a watch it was a knotty thing to know how much time was passing, and my own heartbeat was about as useful as an over-wound clock. I thought back to the boredom of long, dreary lessons and afternoons of study. If it felt like an hour, it was probably only ten minutes. Garval had said that I ought to wait two days if I could stand it, but I began to wonder if I had the fortitude to last a fraction of that time.

It was bad when the ship was noisy, because at least then I knew they were still out there, still wandering her passages, knocking on doors and panels, shouting and barking to each other. I picked up tongues and accents and rumours of accents, and without catching one sensible word I got an education in worlds and places I never knew or dreamt of.

The worst was when it got quiet.

An hour went by, maybe another, when there was nothing to hear but the common noises of the ship, sounds of wood and metal, creaking and complaining. And then even those sounds got quieter, with more space between them. I started to think that maybe they had gone. And because my fear lost its lead over the discomfort, I started unpicking myself from one position to another, my toes and fingers tingling as blood vessels and nerves untwisted themselves. Not really meaning to, I pressed my back against a rib in the ship's outer wall and it seemed to twitch and shiver, sending a metallic sound racing away from me like a tin giggle. I froze again.

A voice sounded. It was some way off and I caught nothing of what was said, but it was one of the voices I'd heard before and I knew with a stone certainty that Bosa's crew were still aboard.

A minute, maybe two, and I sensed movement passing my hiding spot. A fist knuckled a panel. A voice grunted out an oath. Another voice pushed out a handful of words that sounded defensive and threatening.

I kept so still that the lungstuff in my lungs started settling, like dust in a room no one enters.

Then the voices and movement went away and there was another silence.

I can't say how long it was before that silence hardened and I began to believe that they had finally left. But I didn't make the error of trusting in it too quickly. I stayed put, and when the discomfort and pain had built up inside me like a hard, hot knot, I imagined pushing that knot out through my skin, until it was floating outside me like a little angry star, and I could stand it a bit better that way. By the time I was done, though, I was surrounded by little angry stars.

Six hours must have gone by that like. Then six more. Sleep

had been impossible at first, between the discomfort and the fear, but now I was too tired to fight if off. Whether I napped for minutes or hours, I couldn't say. Only that the near-silence remained, and the darkness, and I believed at last that I was truly alone.

Bosa Sennen had taken what she wanted.

Bosa Sennen was gone.

I still moved quietly. When I finally dared touch the panel I worked my fingers into the gap and levered it away with great care, scrunching my eyes against the dim glow of the corridor's lightvine. Then the panel slipped from my fingers and drifted across to the other side of the corridor. I snatched at it but was too slow. It clattered into the wall.

I held my breath. It was pointless to hide again. If I'd been heard, they'd find me, as sure as Paladin always found Adrana and me when we used to rope him into our games. But after minutes of waiting I began to accept that the ship really was empty.

I went to the galley, where I'd last seen the others.

*

I could tell you how I'd have wished to have reacted, when I found the bodies; how I'd have liked to have been all bold and dignified, keeping a respectful composure – or I could tell you what really happened, including the vomit and the tears and the self-pity.

But when I started scratching this thick red ink down onto this rough and leathery paper, I vowed that I'd stick to what happened, not what I might have wanted to happen. Setting down these letters and words is hard enough as it is, the way my fingers work, and I don't want to waste my time by putting out anything but the solid truth of it, as I see it. It can't be *The True and Accurate Testimony of Arafura Ness* unless I give it to you straight, so that's what I've got to do.

So I suppose I'd best stick with the facts.

The fact that there were bodies wasn't the main shock of it. I'd been expecting as much. I couldn't see Bosa killing people and then going to the bother of disposing their corpses, like she was tidying up after herself.

I was also expecting – hoping, I suppose – not to find Adrana or Garval among the bodies. That wasn't me being selfish in not wanting to see them dead, or not liking the idea of my sister taking her own life in desperation, just that them not being here meant there was a good chance they'd been taken, and if that was the case then it meant – for the time being, at least – Bosa had swallowed Garval's lie.

No, the bad part was what she'd done to these people.

Cazaray, Mattice, Trysil and Hirtshal had died outside the ship, before Bosa ever set foot on it. I won't say they were the lucky ones – what happened to Trysil and Hirtshal was nothing you'd wish on someone – but at least they weren't face to face with Bosa when she killed them. Jusquerel and Triglav hadn't been so fortunate, though. They'd got crossbow bolts for their trouble; Jusquerel above the sternum, through a soft part of her suit, and Triglav through the throat. There was blood all over the walls, spattered in little stars and craters, and there was more blood just floating around, in gluey red clots. If the blood wasn't enough of a clue, I didn't need much more to tell me that they were dead. Their bodies had stiffened up and their eyes were fixed open but not really looking at anything. It was cold in the ship and for once I wasn't sorry, because the cold had kept them from decomposing too quickly.

Prozor was next. She'd been bludgeoned. Bosa had smashed her across the side of the skull with something blunt and heavy, like the stock of a crossbow. The wound was a knot of blood and hair, and as I touched it I felt a yielding, like wallpaper giving way over a patch of rotten wall.

Prozor and I hadn't exactly been close. But I touched another hand to her, willing her some peace, and turned to Rackamore.

He was the worst.

The bolt was about twice as long as an index finger. It had

gone in through his open mouth, aimed at an angle that took it through the roof of the mouth, into the brain cavity. It must have been going at quite a clip as half the length of the bolt had come out the back of his head before stopping in place. His eyes were still open, and it was like they were stuck rolling back into his sockets, as if he was trying to see the damage done by the bolt for himself.

I told myself that a shot like that, cutting through the precious structures of the brain – the delicate architecture of the temporal lobe, the hippocampus – couldn't be anything but instantaneously fatal, slamming consciousness shut like a door after an angry visitor. There wasn't any chance that he'd felt pain, was there?

But I couldn't be sure.

The worst of it was the way Bosa had left the crossbow with him, like she didn't even care to take the weapon with her. It was resting across Rackamore's chest, his own fingers half-clutching at it. I imagined him fighting to keep the end of the weapon from being jammed into his mouth, but finally unable to resist.

'You did what you could,' I whispered, as if there were a chance of disturbing any of them.

I'd handled it well until then. I'd braced myself for the bodies, seen what she'd done to them, and studied it all with a sort of detachment, like they weren't really there, or I was seeing them all behind glass, like wax dummies in a museum. Trying to persuade myself that they weren't really bodies at all, or at least not the bodies of the same people I'd been talking to and laughing with not long ago.

But I couldn't keep it up. It hit me in a wave, and I suppose all I'd ever been doing was putting off that moment. These bodies were the flesh and bones and meat of people who'd been speaking and breathing and moving around the last time I saw them, and they were people with names, and pasts; people I knew too much about; people who'd been kind and firm to me at times but mainly fair, and I knew I'd been halfway down the road to calling most of them friends, and the fact that they'd become these ruined, sightless things was too much.

I spewed my guts. I painted the walls with it, adding my vomit to the blood spatters that were already there. And the more I spewed, the more it wanted to come out of me, over and over, until all I could do was make dry heaving noises, like some braying animal. And then I curled myself up into a ball in the corner of the room and closed my eyes and thought about how I'd survived and they hadn't, and the guilt of simply not being dead pushed down on me like an iron shroud. And with the guilt came a half measure of pity because while I was breathing, and the rest of them either dead or taken, that didn't exactly mean I was home and dry.

I was the only living being on a damaged ship, surrounded by the blood- and vomit-spattered corpses of what had once been its crew, and what I knew about the operation of sunjammers you could scratch on the tip of one finger with a fat rusty nail and still have room to spare.

In other words, I'd got myself into quite a predicament.

*

As I scribble these scarlet words down – waiting for the ink to dry before I scuff it like a bloodstain – it occurs to me that there's a version of Fura Ness that just gave up and died on the *Monetta*. She curled up and gave up – on surviving; on Adrana and Garval; on the hope for justice and vengeance; on the hard burden of carrying the memory of her crew; and on making good the powerful wrong that was done to them.

I don't blame that version of Fura. I don't judge her or think ill of her. In some ways I think she was probably a better, nicer version than the cove setting down these words. Being dead, she didn't have to face some of the things I've seen, or hold some of the knowledge stinking up my skull. And if she had handwriting – which would be a tricky proposition, being dead – you can bet your last quoin it wouldn't be as scrawly as mine.

But I'm not her.

I can't tell you what snapped in me, only that something did. It was like that last sob you give when you know you're done crying and it's time to dry your eyes and face the world. Maybe it was because I kept seeing Garval's face, before she slid the panel into place and offered herself up to Bosa. Maybe it was Adrana, on the other side of the glass, pressing her hand against it like she needed that last touch with her living kin. Or maybe it was just some stubborn survival instinct, one that told me I'd done enough heaving and bawling and feeling sorry for myself, and now was the time to act.

So I did.

I cleaned myself up as best I could, then cleaned up what I could of the blood and the puke in the galley. I left the bodies where they were for now, then went to the control room. The first thing I paid heed to was the ship's clock, which told me I'd been in Garval's hideaway for a day and a half – about half what it felt like. The second thing I noticed was the sickly pulsing glow of the sweeper. The instrument was still running on some minimal power. Captain Jastrabarsk's ship was still showing up at maximum range, but unless I was reading the sweeper wrong, there was no one close to us.

Except there wasn't any 'us' now.

Just me.

I went to the squawk console. Its dials and readouts were still aglow, but faintly. I'd watched Rackamore and the others when they used it, and although there were aspects I hadn't got straight in my head, the basics weren't too knotty. There were switches to receive and to talk, and various channel and power selectors. The console was still set as it had been in when Bosa Sennen made her demands to board.

I snapped the switches, worked the selector toggles, watched as the dials flickered almost to darkness before regaining their glow. My hand trembled on the 'talk' switch. I had seen Rackamore use it so many times, and the urge to scream for help was almost more than I could bear.

Almost.

I moved my hand from the switch, then found the main control that put the console to sleep. It snapped with a hard, definite clunk. The dials and readouts faded to darkness. I hoped they'd come back on again when next I tried.

I went to the sweeper and was about to do the same thing when a cold dread passed through me. I'd almost given myself away to Bosa. If the sweeper was active now, she would be aware of it – and she would know if someone was around to switch it off suddenly.

So I let the sweeper remain.

The cold was beginning to get to me, so I worked back through the ship to find some extra clothes, blanking the corpses in the galley as I passed through. The ship was cooler than it had been before the attack, her metal surfaces turning icy under my fingertips. My breath was showing up in the lungstuff.

The cold wasn't the worst of it, though. I was thirsty. Hungry, too, but it was the thirst that was making itself felt the loudest. So I went to one of the water spigots and pressed my lips around the nozzle. Water had come out when I needed to clean up the galley, but now it wasn't more than a dribble. Then the spigot dried up completely, and when I went to try the others it was the same. Never mind, I told myself, thinking of the bottled reserves.

But when I opened the store room, I saw Bosa had beaten me to it.

It wasn't theft so much as spite. Things had been taken, I was sure – ordinary rations, alcohol, treats, luxury foodstuffs reserved for special occasions. But much else had been destroyed purely for the sake of it. Bottles had been smashed. Their weightless contents glooped around like they were playing at being deep-sea animals. I tried to catch and swallow what I could, but that was a harder trick than it appeared.

Bosa had also taken whole crates of our fruit, vegetables and meat, presumably because such supplies would always be useful on a ship that was obliged to keep away from the Congregation's civilised trading centres. What remained had been pulped into a splintered mass, smeared around the walls, embedded with shards of wood and glass.

Bosa might not have counted on someone being left alive on the *Monetta*, but she'd still considered the possibility. For a couple of stupid instants I wondered why she hadn't simply blown all our lungstuff out of the locks.

But that would have been too quick. Too clean and too easy.

Not Bosa's way.

*

I kept a close watch on the sweeper. Between one hour and the next there wasn't any sign that the distant blob had moved. But if I marked its position with one of Rackamore's pens, then went away and came back a watch or two later, I could just about convince myself that it had sneaked a little nearer. After a day, there wasn't any doubt. Jastrabarsk was closing in on us, presumably meaning to pick over our bones and see what was left in the bauble. But I measured the distance that the blob had moved in twenty-four hours and then worked out how many of those intervals it would take to reach me, and what I came up with was another five days.

I wasn't going to make it – not with the cold leeching the energy out of me, and no water or rations.

Not unless I did something drastic.

I'd be lying if I said it never crossed my mind to cook and eat the bodies. At least, it crossed my mind that I'd be halfway to madness if I ever got to the point where that was something I'd seriously consider. Maybe I'd get there. But between now and then, there was something else I could try.

I could eat the lightvine.

There was more than enough of it snaking through the *Monetta*, certainly more than I'd ever be able to stuff into my gob in five days. And I knew it wasn't poisonous. I'd picked that up from somewhere, some half-remembered tale of how you could eat the stuff without too much in the way of repercussions. That the clever coves of some earlier Occupation who'd engineered lightvine – and that was what it was, some cooked-up organism, tweaked from parts of other plants and animals – had made sure it wasn't poisonous. It couldn't be, the way people would be brushing past it, touching it, as they made their way through a ship. No, lightvine was supposed to be helpful, not hurtful. It gave off light, breathed in bad gases and gave out the ones we needed in our lungs.

And you could nosh on the stuff.

That was some third factor they'd built into it, like a final insurance clause. If your ship was in trouble, and provided you left enough lightvine to keep the lungstuff getting too groggy, you could scoff the rest and not die from it.

No one promised it was tasty, though.

I found a knife and hacked away a finger-sized length of it. It cut easily, and gave off some juices that I licked from my fingers. It was sweet but otherwise flavourless, like sugary water. It kept on glowing, too, even though it wasn't connected to the rest of the organism. In my palm it was soft and cool.

I pushed the lightvine into my mouth, and bit into it.

The softness gave way to a harder, chewier core. It wasn't quite tasteless. Peppery, to start with, then a sour afternote. I couldn't say it was delicious, but it wasn't the worst thing I'd ever tasted and if you smothered butter on it you could probably charge coves for the pleasure of eating it. I kept on chewing. The pulpy core was hard work, but gradually I got the whole mass down to something I could swallow. It was going to take more than that to stop me feeling hungry. But the juices in the lightvine had taken the sting out of my thirst, and that was something.

I reckoned I could put up with it.

*

With me being the bookworm I am, it might seem queer that I didn't go to the library sooner than I did. But books were a nice thing in my life, a luxury and a reminder of better times, and I didn't want to start letting nice things back into my world until I thought there was at least a chance of making it through the next couple of days. The lightvine took the edge off my fears, though, just a bit, and maybe it was the act of feeding myself or some chemical in the lightvine itself, but all that really mattered to me was that I started thinking of ways to fill the hours, and my grey working the way it does, what jumped to mind first of all were books.

So I went to Rackamore's library . . . and that was when I saw what she'd done to it.

I knew that books were valuable to some coves, and boring to others, but I'd never ventured beyond that thought to the idea that books might be something to be hated or destroyed. Books were like lungstuff, I'd liked to think. There were bottles of lungstuff kept for safekeeping all over a ship. There to use when you needed them, but that didn't mean you burned them up just because you had enough to breathe somewhere else. But I suppose that was how an educated girl from Mazarile saw such things, and it didn't mean that everyone else was obliged to have the same view.

Bosa had destroyed Rack's library. It wasn't an accident, or a side-effect of close action. This had been systematic, and it must have taken two or three of them to get the job done. They'd gone in with sharp tools – maybe the long-bladed yardknives that coves like Hirtshal used to cut rigging – and they'd hacked and hacked, gashing books apart at their spines, so that the pages had come out and gone fluttering all around the room, like a snowstorm with palm-sized flakes. But a yardknife will cut anything, even a page floating in the breeze, so they must have kept on hacking, slicing and dicing those pages until it would have taken a hundred years to stitch them back together. They'd used fire, too, so that for every white fragment there was a black or brown one, and there was still ash hovering around when I gulped a breath of it down my gullet. I was inhaling his library, or a bit of it, and somewhere in that choking taste was enough history to cram a thousand lifetimes. I coughed out some of it, but not the whole of it.

I found the covers of some of the books. With their pages stripped out, they were like the wings of dark, leathery birds that had been ripped whole off their carcasses. There was that 1384 edition of the *Book of Worlds*, not the earliest one Rack had shown me, but still strange and old and valuable. I thought of how proud he'd been, and how rarely he must have been able to show off that collection to someone who really appreciated it, and I realised he'd seen something in me that meant he trusted me with the knowledge of his library, and it was that thought beyond any other that turned my grief even sharper than it had been before.

There were probably books that hadn't been badly damaged, or that could have been put back together without too much trouble. But going back into that library was more than I had the strength for. You might think it cold of me, but the damage that was done to those books turned my stomach more than all the wounding and murder done to the crew. It wasn't that I didn't think highly of people. But there are always more people, and I'd have bet quoins that some of those books were truly unique, not another of their kind anywhere under the Old Sun's light.

Still, I steeled myself to take one memory of the library. Of all the books that had belonged to Rack, I took that one black cover from the 1384 edition. As I closed my hand around it I remembered him blowing dust off it, brushing his fingers against it so lovingly, and I hoped he wouldn't have objected to me taking it as my own.

*

I'd been out of my hiding place for two days when I decided to chance using the squawk.

I worked the switches and toggles. I brought my mouth close to the speaking grill and when I made to shape a sound, what came out of me was so raw as to be almost unrecognisable.

'Captain Jastrabarsk. This is . . .'

I'd been about to utter my own name, when I thought better of it.

'This is the *Monetta*. We were attacked by Bosa Sennen. She killed most of us, took our Bone Readers. But I managed to hide. It's bad in here, but I think I can hold out until you arrive. I can see you on the sweeper and I know you're coming nearer. If you can get here faster, please do so.'

I turned the console to receive.

I waited.

An hour passed. I worked the controls again, trying all the permutations of switches and knobs I could think of, just in case I'd misunderstood something crucial. Still all I got was static. At last I decided to risk another transmission. I opened the channel and repeated what I'd said the first time, only this time with an edge of desperation and hopelessness that I didn't need to fake.

I worked the switches again.

The crackles continued. There was a hiss and pop, a snatch of a voice, the phantom of some much more distant transmission. Then more hissing and scratching.

Until I heard: 'This is Jastrabarsk, sending from the *Iron Courtesan*. We hear you, *Monetta's Mourn*. Your signal is weak, and we had trouble reading you the first time. But we've turned all our ears onto you now. We see no sign of your attacker on our deep sweep. State your condition. How many of you are left?'

My voice sounded as bad as the first time, but the relief almost had me choking on my own words. 'Just me, Captain. I managed to hide. My name is . . .' And I knew I'd need to lie for now, because it would be much too risky to use my real name while Bosa might be listening in. 'Incer,' I said, using the name of Mazarile's other city. 'The ship's in a bad way. There isn't much power, and it's getting colder. She took everything. Can you get here quickly, Captain Jastrabarsk?'

I did not have to wait long for his answer.

'You're still faint, *Monetta*, but we can reach you, yes. But even with full sail and ions, we can't be on you in less than four days . . .'

That was a day longer than I'd figured, and while it might not seem much, it was as if they'd added a year onto my sentence.

'No . . .' I said to myself.

'But we will do our utmost,' Jastrabarsk was still saying, 'and when we're close enough to send out a launch, we'll do so. The delay won't hurt us, either. It'll give us time to make sure Bosa Sennen really has cleared the volume. What is the condition of your ship?'

'Bad. Lots of things aren't working. It's cold and I don't think there's much power left. But I'm not really an expert.'

'I'll have my Integrator speak to you – see what we can make of the remaining systems.'

'I'm worried about Bosa, Captain. Will she come back?'

'Are you certain it was Bosa, and not just someone trading under that name? There are plenty of crews who claim to have seen her, but very few who can prove it.'

'You want proof, Captain, I can show you the bodies, and what she did to them. I doubt you'll need much persuasion.' I hesitated, realising that I ought to sound less like an educated young lady from Mazarile and more like someone who'd been crewing for years. 'Ain't pretty, what she did, I mean,' I went on. 'And the way she spoke to Rackamore, it was clear that they knew each other already.'

'I believe she exists. But it's unusual for her to be trawling this close to the outer processionals, or to be interested in a small prize like this one. So she may be shifting tactics. That said, I doubt that she'll return – not if she left you in a sorry state. You say she left with your Bone Readers?'

I nodded and forgot to speak for a few seconds. 'Yes,' I stammered out. 'The two of them.'

'Sisters, we heard. Fresh in from Mazarile, with quite some potential. What were you, Incer?'

'Nothing like that, sir. Just a Scanner – a Bauble Reader. Prozor was training me up.'

'We heard about Prozor. She was good, they said – one of the best. Is she . . .?'

'Dead,' I answered. 'Yes.'

Something touched my throat. I jumped hard, despite myself, and felt a sharp edge nick my skin.

A hand reached around me, flicked off the squawk.

'Dead, is she?'

I suppose I must have breathed but I don't remember doing it. Just a long silence while I kept still and the blade stayed against my throat. We could have stayed like that for hours, for all I know, although I doubt it was more than seconds.

Eventually I squeezed out a word.

'Prozor.'

'Prozor the dead. Ain't that nice. Ain't that convenient.'

'You're alive,' I said.

'And whoever said I wasn't?'

If she was going to open my neck she might as well do it now. I turned around slowly, giving her time to move the blade so that it was still pressed against my windpipe.

'I thought she'd killed you,' I said. 'Like she did the others – Rackamore, Triglav, Jusquerel. I thought you'd gone the same way, except she'd bludgeoned you. I didn't check because I didn't have a reason to think you weren't dead. You looked dead.'

'Do I look dead now?'

'Don't look far off it.' She had a bloodied scalp, hair tangled into it, a terribly blackened eye. I had touched her head, I remembered, and felt the soft damage under it. I hadn't been careless, or presumed something foolish. It wasn't my fault that her breathing was so shallow I missed it. 'Would you mind moving that knife, Prozor? Before you kill the only other survivor on this ship?'

'Question is, girlie, how you survived at all.' Prozor touched her free hand to her scalp. 'Messed me up pretty good, she did. But Bosa didn't know about that plate I already have screwed into my skull. Knocked me out, I suppose. Can't say I remember too much. But there ain't a living scratch on you and that don't sit well with me.'

'I hid.' I reached up slowly and drew the blade away from my throat, fighting the strength in her at first, then overwhelming her. 'Garval helped me. Adrana helped her get loose, and . . . worlds, Prozor, I was just in the middle of signalling Jastrabarsk!'

'In league with him, are you? Setting us up for a call from Bosa, then arranging to split the leftovers with Captain Jastrabarsk?'

'No, nothing like that! Were you listening to what I just said? Garval showed me a hiding place, a panel in the wall. I got in there and kept quiet until Bosa was gone. It's been two days, and now I'm chancing a message to Jastrabarsk's ship. That's it on the sweeper. It's coming our way, as fast as they can make sail. That's the end of it. Bosa has my sister. If I'd cooked up a plan, do you honestly think that'd be any part of it?'

The line of her lips tightened into something hard and judgemental.

'You were tight, both of you.'

'Yes. It's called being sisters. Prozor! I wasn't in league with anyone and right now all I care about is finding a way to get Adrana and Garval back.'

'What did she want with the screamer?'

'Garval said she was going to put herself up in my place, make Bosa think she already had both Bone Readers. I know, it never stood a chance of fooling Bosa for long. But if she hadn't done it, they'd have picked the ship apart looking for me. Garval saved my life, and I owe her.'

There was one last long, appraising look from her, then she put the blade away.

'If a word of this turns out to be anything but gospel, girlie . . .'

'You've seen the bodies, Prozor. Do you think I made them up, or did those things to them?'

After a while she said: 'They've got Bosa's look about 'em. But you could've . . .' She shook her head. 'No, you ain't got the spine for cruelty. Not like that.'

'Thank you for that ringing endorsement.'

'You made sure Bosa's out of the scene, before you started blabbing all over the squawk?'

'I made sure, yes. And I wasn't blabbing. Did you hear what I said to Jastrabarsk? Nothing that would let Bosa know I'm Adrana's sister. I made up a name, Incer. Jastrabarsk can get the full story when we're eye to eye. He'll understand why I had to bend a few facts, knowing she might be listening in.'

'Maybe you should have checked with me before beggin' for rescue. Seeing as I'm as close to captain now as I'll ever get.'

'You were unconscious, Prozor. So unconscious you looked dead. You know what my next plan was? I was going to move all the bodies into the airlock, one at a time, so I didn't have to share the ship with them. Then I was going to vent all the lung-stuff in the lock so they'd freeze up and stop decaying. You'd have been one of them. So instead of giving me the hard stare, you can start counting your blessings I didn't get to it sooner. And there was no begging to Jastrabarsk. Rack told me he knew the man and they were friends. I don't mean to die on this ship, so I did what I needed to do. Besides, Jastrabarsk was already on his way – I just asked him to get here sooner if he could.'

She chewed on that for a few moments.

'The ship took a beating. I remember that much. Maybe we could use some outside help. Just to get us straight again, patch up our sails . . .'

'And then we sail her, just the two of us? Rack said he ran a light crew, Prozor, and it still took seven of you. The ship's finished. If it keeps us alive until Jastrabarsk gets here, I'll be grateful.'

'You sound harder than you used to. Almost like you could have been one of us.'

'I was, wasn't I?'

'Maybe,' Prozor said, and I suppose I'd have to take what I could get.

'I never saw Bosa. But I heard it, and that was bad enough. Heard her hitting you, too. You can't blame me for thinking you were dead.'

'Did you move the bodies?'

'No . . . not much.' I didn't want her to know I'd had to clean my own sick off them. 'I got rid of some of the blood, that's all. Other than that, they're the way I found them.'

'Then that's how she left Rack?'

'Yes,' I answered, not quite reading her drift.

'That crossbow he was clutching to himself?'

'Yes?'

'It was Rack's own crossbow. Not Bosa's.'

*

Prozor might have had that tin plate under her scalp, but she'd still taken a good beating. I knew she was weak, but there was no water to offer, and when I told her I could cut her some light-vine she just laughed. 'You got to cook it, girlie. You don't just eat it raw, not if you don't want the glowy getting into you. You ain't been eating' it raw, have you?'

'No . . . no,' I stammered. 'That would be silly, wouldn't it? What's the glowy?'

Prozor might have picked up on my hesitation, but she wasn't pulling on all sails and her focus kept slipping away. It was like trying to have a conversation with a very old person, someone whose memory doesn't stretch back more than a few minutes.

'Water in the ion coolers,' she said, during one of the interludes when she was sharper. 'Separate system from the drinking water, and maybe not as pure, but it'll keep us alive for now.' And she gave me instructions on how to siphon water out of the cooling system, situated in what had been Triglav's ion control room. There wasn't enough heat to cook the lightvine, but Prozor said it was getting water in us that mattered more than food, and if we looked famished when Jastrabarsk rescued us they'd treat us nicer.

I had a lot of questions for her. It was finding the right moment to ask them that was the tricky part.

'I told Jastrabarsk it was Bosa that had taken us, and he

asked me if I was certain it was her. Why would he doubt?'

'Bosa Sennen's a name,' Prozor said. 'One that's been spoken of for too long for it to be just one person.'

'I don't understand.'

'No one lives longer than a hundred years – not in this Occupation anyway. Nothing that anyone's ever found in a bauble's changed that, although that ain't stopped 'em looking. But crews were being picked off by Bosa Sennen long before I was born, and her name already went back a generation or two then. It ain't possible.'

'But you saw her. You know she's real.'

'I know there's someone calling themselves Bosa Sennen, and using the power of that name to put the shivers into people. But that don't mean it's the same Bosa Sennen that was taking ships fifty years ago, or a hundred.'

'But Rack knew her. It was Bosa that took his daughter, wasn't it? And the same Bosa that came back this time.'

'Ain't been more than fifteen years between 'em, so – yes – probably that was the same person using the name. But that's all it is – a mask for whoever's decided to earn their keep by plunderin' what doesn't belong to 'em, and using crueller means than they need to to do it.'

'So you're saying it's not always the same Bosa, not always the same ship?'

'I ain't sayin' one thing or another. Just layin' out the simple facts of it, which is that there ain't a cove in the Congregation gets to live that long.'

'That ship didn't show up on the sweeper until it was almost on top of us. How it that possible?'

'The *Nightjammer*'s sails ain't like normal sails. Light just falls into 'em. Reason they're black; blacker than any thing's got any right to be.'

'But sails need to reflect light to work, don't they? That's why ours stood out so strongly on the sweeper.'

'These sails don't. Ain't my job to know how they work, just that they do.'

I nodded. 'But then sails like that would be pretty handy for any crew, wouldn't they?'

'What's the point you're makin', girlie?'

'I think that ship must be unique, the way it operates. Lurking out here, hardly showing up on the sweep . . . how likely is it that someone just happens to have a ship like that, whenever they show up calling themselves Bosa Sennen?'

'You got an answer, I s'pose.'

'I think there's only ever that one ship, and its other name is the *Dame Scarlet*, and if those sails are as rare as you make them seem, it must be the same ship each time, under the same Bosa Sennen. Whatever you say about people not living long enough, somehow it doesn't apply to her. Maybe she did find something in a bauble, an elixir or something . . .'

'Elixir,' Prozor said. 'Listen to you.'

'I'm just trying to make sense of what happened.'

'Then you're wasting your time. There ain't no sense to be had out of it. You crossed orbits with Bosa Sennen once. If the fates are sweet to you, you'll go to your grave still sayin' you only met her once.'

'That didn't work for Rack, did it?'

'It was different with him, and we all knew it. When Bosa took Illyria from him, he should've put the both of them out of his mind for the rest of his life. But he couldn't, and for that you can't blame the cove. He wanted to see his daughter again, and if that meant seeing Bosa another time, he was ready to pay that price.'

'He did,' I said.

I wanted to ask her more about Illyria Rackamore, all the things I couldn't have asked before, but Prozor was fading on me and I knew she needed rest.

I'd settled one thing, at least. Rack had history with Bosa and he'd got to see her again, even if it did take fifteen years.

That meant there was a chance for me, too.

Because we had history too, now. Whether Bosa knew it or not.

8

On the ninth day since the bauble's opening, the yellow blob on our sweeper swelled until it had the flowered form of a sunjammer under full sail. The signature was distinct and sharp-edged, nothing like the furtive, ragged echo of Bosa's ship. The *Iron Courtesan* hauled in sail and used ions to find its own orbit around the bauble, higher and more eccentric than ours. A nervous few hours passed, then a launch crossed over to the *Monetta*.

There were three of them in the party, and they all came aboard. Their suits were older and more battered-looking than ours, and where ours were shades of brown and brass, these were all dull pewters and blue-greys. But they clanked and huffed and smelled the same, they had the same little grilled windows for faceplates, and when Jastrabarsk removed his helmet and scuffed a hand through his hair, something in his manner reminded me of Rackamore. He was older, I reckon, wider in the face, with a heavy brow ridge and cheekbones that looked as hard and swollen as bruises. He had a scar between his lip and his chin, his teeth were metal, and his eyes were dark and fathomless – sunk so deeply that they were almost like sockets – but still there was that swagger that I recognised. His hair was grey, curly, and it had begun to recede above that high, overhanging brow.

'You did well, Incer. You know me, of course.' He nodded at the narrow-faced man to his right, who was squinting at a scratch on the crown of his helmet, now cradled in his hands. 'This is Lusquer. Next to Lusquer is Meveraunce. Meveraunce is our sawbones – she'll be taking care of you.'

Meveraunce was the tallest of them all. She had a plump face, very white hair, an upturned nose. She was already looking around.

'Thank you,' I began. 'Captain . . . before we go on.'

Eyes flashed in the gloom of those sockets. 'Yes, Incer?'

'Are we on squawk now?'

'Why would we be?'

'I need to know.'

Jastrabarsk cracked a grin full of metal teeth at his colleagues. 'Then we're not, if it matters so much.'

'I'm not Incer.' Now that I was speaking the words tumbled out. 'There's no such person. I couldn't tell you who I was, not when Bosa Sennen might be listening in.'

'We had an inkling,' Lusquer said, matching the captain's smile. 'Not that your name was a lie, but that *something* didn't quite fit.'

'My sister's on Bosa's ship,' I said, relieved that the truth was at least a bit out in the open. 'She's in trouble, and it would have been worse for both of us if Bosa knew I was her. So I had to pretend to be someone else.'

'What did Bosa want with your sister?' Meveraunce asked.

'We were meant to be the new Bone Readers. Cazaray was getting too old, so they brought us in to replace him. I can read a bone but Adrana was better than me. Bosa took her because she needed a Bone Reader as well.'

'Why didn't she take you?' Jastrabarsk asked.

'I hid. There was a woman, Garval, who offered herself to Bosa in my place.'

Meveraunce looked sceptical. 'Noble of her, knowing Bosa's reputation.'

'Garval didn't have much to lose,' I said. 'Anyway, it's true. I'm Fura Ness.'

'That's supposed to mean something?' Lusquer asked.

'There's something else.'

'We may as well hear it all,' Jastrabarsk said, settling his arms across the chestplate of his suit.

'I'm not alone.'

They stiffened, Lusquer's hand twitching as if he might reach for a weapon at any instant. Meveraunce eyed me doubtfully. Jastrabarsk lifted up his chin and nodded slowly.

'Who. Where. And this had better be the last surprise out of your mouth.'

*

Meveraunce examined her carefully, then pronounced that she was satisfied that Prozor's wounds were superficial.

'Sure as hell don't *feel* superficial.'

'We'll get you stitched up,' Jastrabarsk said. 'And fed and watered. And cleaned. Then you can start spilling some of that hard-earned wisdom our way. I'm sure our own Bauble Reader wouldn't object to a good squint at your notebooks.'

We were taken aboard the launch, and then ferried back to the *Iron Courtesan*. Lusquer stayed behind on the *Monetta's Mourn*, beginning the process of working out what might be salvaged. Once we were off-loaded, Jastrabarsk sent three more of his crew back to help Lusquer.

'That loot still belongs to Rackamore's crew,' Prozor said, just in case she had not made her point the first six or seven times she uttered much the same statement. 'We brought it back from the bauble good and proper, and it's getting divided fair and square.'

'Between the two of you?' Jastrabarsk asked.

'The four of us,' Prozor corrected with a stern look. 'Adrana's still one of us, no matter who she's being made to work with. We'll hold her share.'

'That'll be a long wait. Who's the other one?'

Prozor looked perplexed. 'Garval, of course.'

Jastrabarsk frowned. By then he had heard more of our story. 'You told me Garval cheated her way onto your crew.'

'She did,' Prozor said. 'Then she redeemed herself. Still entitled to her cut.'

'Magnanimous of you.'

'Just doing things Rack's way, is all.'

Jastrabarsk gave another of his slow nods. The way his huge, bony head tilted, it made me think of a boulder wobbling on another boulder. 'We do things fair as well. What we find on the *Monetta* by way of loot, that's yours to divide. But what's left in the bauble, that's nobody's until it's claimed.'

'No complaints with that.'

'You're going back into the bauble?' I asked.

'Back?' Jastrabarsk asked. 'We haven't been once. Yes, we'll be going into it. But we're too near the end of this window. Quancer's auguries predict a high likelihood of another opening in about eighteen days. It won't stay open long enough to make more than a few trips, but we'll make the most of it.'

'You could do it,' Prozor said, her voice still raw.

'Do what?' Jastrabarsk asked.

'My estimate, you've got another thirty hours before that surface firms over.'

Jastrabarsk set his jaw. 'All very well saying that, when it won't be your neck on the line.'

'Who's to say it wouldn't be?'

His eyes flashed out from their gloomy depths.

'Meaning what?'

'I'll stand by my reading of that bauble. I'll go in with your team. With,' she added, raising a finger, 'a fair cut of the loot. And unless your Opener doesn't know their work, we can be in and out of there with a ten-hour safety margin.'

I looked at Prozor, thinking of all that had passed between us. I believed that she was as good as her reputation maintained, but I'd really only seen the evidence of that once, when the bauble opened in exact accordance with her prediction. Only a fool would have put too much stock in that, knowing how easily blind chance could have played its role. But now that the rest of the crew was gone, there wasn't anyone else left for me to hang my loyalty on.

'I trust Prozor,' I said quietly. 'I know she wouldn't get this wrong. And I'd like to see the inside of a bauble as well. If you allow her to go, I'll go with her.'

'Eighteen days with your thumbs jammed where no photon's ever gone,' Prozor said. 'And nothing at the end of it after that but wait. Or you could be in and out and on your merry way inside thirty hours.'

Whether Jastrabarsk knew it himself or not, the doubt had been planted. This was Prozor, after all, one of the best Scanners that ever breathed, and she was offering him a chance to avoid weeks of tedium.

'You'll redo whatever it was brought you to that thirty-hour estimate,' Jastrabarsk said, jamming a stubby finger in Prozor's face. 'And somewhere in the region of thirty hours isn't good enough for me. If I was even going to *think* about sending in the launch now, instead of at the next opening . . . I'd want this nailed down to minutes.'

'I'll need my paperwork,' Prozor said.

'I'll have Lusquer bring everything that belongs to you. But I'm making no promises. You don't just turn up on my ship and start dictating terms.'

'I wouldn't dream of it, Cap'n. But we're all here to earn ourselves some quoins, aren't we?'

Jastrabarsk snorted. But she had dropped the most persuasive argument of all.

*

The launch dropped to the bauble with a crew of eight. Prozor said we had twenty-seven hours and thirty minutes until the surface baked over again, and if that had been the only calculation on the table my nerves would have been bad enough. But Quancer held that the remaining time – not even the margin

– was now only nine and a half hours. That was about enough time to get into the bauble, to reach the point where Racka-more's crew had found their first haul of loot. It wasn't anywhere near enough time to get back out again. And yet Jastrabarsk had decided to place total confidence in Prozor's prediction, disregarding the advice of his own specialist.

It reinforced my sense that these crews had an uncommon approach to hazard. They accepted it – even welcomed it – when danger centred around the business of bauble surfaces and auguries. They were willing to place themselves at tremen-dous risk where it concerned loot and reward and competition between the crews, and they thrived on the challenges of doors and locks and weaponised security barriers. But they shrivelled at the idea of standing up to Bosa. She put the deep shivers in them, and since she could be avoided or ignored most of the time, they had no incentive to face the fear she embodied. But it would be wrong of me to call them cowards. In their ele-ment, there wasn't anyone braver or more accepting of death's inevitability.

I wondered if I could ever be like them.

Not today, that was for certain. But Prozor had enough confi-dence in her numbers that she was ready to join the expedition, and I'd promised I would join her if she went along. They had fitted us into suits from the *Iron Courtesan*'s own stores, and they were awkward and uncomfortable, but we bit down and made light of the discomfort, knowing it would have been just as bad if the *Courtesan*'s crew had been stuffed into our own suits.

Jastrabarsk had his own versions of Loftling's maps, but he had also recovered Rackamore's equivalent records, and he pressed Prozor and me for all that we could recollect of the *Monetta*'s first expedition.

'It went according to plan,' was the best Prozor could offer. 'Loftling's charts couldn't have been too bad. But then again, Rack had Mattice, and there never was a better Opener.'

But all crews, I was slowly learning, tended to think that

they had the best of some particular specialisation. Once in a while there might even have been some truth in it. Jastrabarsk's expedition had two Openers, two Assessors, and while I was too green to speak with any authority, they seemed confident and competent. On the way down, they had maps and charts all over the launch, and the debate was quick and difficult to follow, like a card game played by seasoned hands.

'They know their baubles,' Prozor whispered to me, as the rockets cut in for our final approach. 'We'll be golden.'

Now we had nearer to twenty-six hours, but that was still ample time, provided Prozor was right. And once again I forced myself into that state of acceptance that said she would have made no error; that to think otherwise was a kind of disloyalty.

We landed at the same point where Rackamore had put down his own launch. The depressions where its skids had cut into the ground were still visible, and it was only a short distance to the entrance on Loftling's charts. We finished sealing up our suits, then did a round of double-checking, tugging on lungstuff-lines, watching seals for signs of failure. Squawk channels were tested, weapons, munitions and cutting equipment divided among the party. Jastrabarsk's crew might have had different suits to Rackamore's expedition, and some of their equipment was of older or newer vintage, but the methodology was similar. Nothing complicated was to be trusted in the environment of the bauble. They even had a system of sign language to use in case the suit-to-suit squawk became inoperable.

We left the launch and crossed the short stretch of ground to the surface door. From a distance it would have been easy to miss. A ramp led down a sheer-sided trench, with a kind of bulkhead and airlock at the end of it. Controls were set into the side of the bulkhead.

'You see how new it all looks?' Jastrabarsk said to me over the squawk. 'Not a scratch from space debris, cosmic radiation . . . and I doubt more than a hundred hands have touched that panel in ten million years.'

Jastrabarsk's Opener had brought along a heavy toolkit that

hinged apart to reveal many organised compartments. She was rummaging through the contents while another of Jastrabarsk's people held up a copy of Loftling's charts. Above the control panel was a rectangle of neat little pictograms, arranged in vertical columns. A type of language, but nothing I thought I had ever seen before, even in Rackamore's library.

Over the squawk I heard: 'Typical Ice Throne stuff. All bluff, no bite.'

'They've bitten us before.'

'Not this time. If Loftling's circuit map is righteous, should pick up a power node right about . . . here.'

'Got it?'

'On the mark. Good old Loftling. Could someone pass me that inductance coil? No, that's not the coil. Yes, that compartment. No, the larger one – what do you think we're trying to get through here, paper?'

I heard a clunk, transmitted through the ground on which I stood. The door heaved open, sliding down into a slot in the base of the trench. We filed into an antechamber where the only light came from our helmet torches, and where the walls were covered in ranks of pictograms.

'Warnings,' said the Assessor. 'Meant to get us all shivery. Abandon all hope for your mortal souls, that kind of thing. I've seen worse. We can ignore it all.'

Inside the antechamber was another door that would not function until the outer one had been closed. I did not like the feeling of being bottled in to this ancient, dread place, knowing how few hours remained until the field surface reinstated itself, and we would be trapped. If Jastrabarsk's Bauble Reader had it right, we would only need to endure for eighteen days before the surface opened again. That would be bearable, provided the lander had enough lungstuff and supplies for us. But Prozor said Quancer was wrong, and that when this window snapped shut, it would be years before the next opening.

Why were we going *deeper* into this nightmare, when the sane, sensible thing was to get out while we could?

Prozor dropped a hand on my shoulder. 'Ain't done this as many times as Mattice or Jusquerel, Fura. The good part is I still remember how wrong it seems, first time out. But being on the ship felt wrong to you at first, didn't it? Then wearing a suit, going outside? You got used to those things. This is the same. Gets easier.'

'Thank you,' I mumbled.

She'd started calling me Fura now, instead of girlie.

Soon we were going down the endless spiral stairs that bored their way into the heart of the sphereworld. In my mind's eye, I'd seen a descending staircase curving down and out of sight, like the one that threaded the cupola in our house on Mazarile.

It wasn't like that all, and I was glad not to have been forewarned.

The stairs went around the inside of a very wide shaft, about one hundred spans across, near as I could judge it. They jutted out from the walls, solid enough, and there was sufficient room for three of us to walk side by side. But there was no bannister on the stairs, and as much as I tried to fix my eyes on the next tread below, it was impossible to screen out the view of the stairs continuing on their steeply descending way, curving around onto the opposite face wall, spiralling down into a dizzying dark void. Rackamore's party had spent most of their time in the bauble either going down or coming up these nightmare stairs, and I began to wonder if I'd the nerves to cope.

We had to move quickly, too. It was no good dawdling. The loot was a league under us, and the pitch of the stairs meant that we had to walk nearly three leagues for every vertical one. In the suits, the best that we could manage was a bit less than half a league per hour, so we would need at least six hours just to reach our prize.

It was worse than that. The effort to make each step got harder the deeper we went, and that was nothing to do with fatigue. I'd spent my life living between the crust of Mazarile and the glass skin of the skyshell, and because of that I'd never been closer than four leagues to the swallower.

When we had gone through the surface door here, there were the same four leagues between us and the swallower. By the time we reached the loot, only three leagues lay under us. That was enough to make us feel as if we weighed more than half as much again, each footfall becoming a leaden effort, each step requiring more care than the last.

Halfway to the core – where there was a house-sized bottle containing the swallower in its magnetic pinch – we'd have walked around under four times our normal weight. Except by then we'd be doing well if we could crawl.

'The shaft goes a lot deeper,' Jastrabarsk said, as we gathered our strength for the final twist of the staircase. 'Maybe all the way down. But if there's loot stashed much deeper, it'll stay there until the Old Sun fizzles out.'

'It'll be even harder bringing stuff back up the stairs,' I said, feeling as if my legs had nothing more to give.

'Hell, to begin with,' the captain agreed, with a sort of malicious delight in it. 'But if there's one consolation, you get lighter as you get higher. Not that you really notice, when you're down to your last drop of energy. Watch your footing now, Arafura. Seen too many good people trip at the last stage.'

I had no intention of tripping. I was thinking of the story they had told me on the *Monetta's Mourn*, about the Fang, about Prozor's husband, Githlow, about Sheveril who had panicked, about their long screaming fall into the shaft.

I could think of worse ways to die, but not many.

*

There was a doorway leading off the stairway, back into the sheer wall of the shaft, and from that modest doorway extended an ever-branching series of chambers and sub-shafts, more than we could ever hope to explore in a matter of hours. There was no light beyond that which we provided, but power still trickled through the walls and into some of the doors and their mechanisms. Jastrabarsk's Openers and Assessors were in babbling dialogue, while Prozor and I mostly kept our gobs shut unless our opinions were sought. Loftling's charts were turned this way and that, annotations were scribbled onto them in luminous ink.

'Look at the mess Rackamore left behind him,' someone grumbled, indicating a pile of tools and cutting equipment left near one of the doors.

'They meant to return,' I said. 'Rack was going in another eight or nine times, that was the plan. Then Bosa jumped us. They only just had time to get back on the launch.'

'We thank them for the head start,' Jastrabarsk said, hands on hips as he sized up the litter left behind from the earlier expedition. 'And the generous donation to our supplies. How much time left to us?'

'Twenty hours, eleven minutes,' Prozor said. Then, with a teasing edge: 'Not getting the shivers yet, are you, Captain?'

'I get the shivers the moment I see a bauble. Reason I'm still alive. I don't have to *like* these places to make an honest profit out of them.' Then he tapped a fist against the crown of his helmet. 'Getting some static on squawk. Might be nothing.'

But as we worked through the doors, into the main cache of loot, our suits began breaking down in a hundred small ways. The suit-to-suit squawk was the first thing to turn unreliable, but it didn't stop there. Torches began to flicker. Recirculation valves began to jam. My glove stiffened up to the point where I could barely move the fingers.

I had already heard the stories from Mattice and the others. This was all part of the normal pattern of things going wrong inside baubles, and not anything that was unusual to this expedition. It was why none of them trusted anything too complicated to begin with. The less you came to rely on, the less you missed when it failed. It was also why – considerations of auguries aside – it was seldom wise to spend too much time in a bauble.

Through a garbled squawk, Prozor said: 'Something in these

places don't take kindly to visitors. But if it comes on slow and gradual like this, it's not usually too serious.'

'And if it does come on fast?'

'Be glad Bone Readers are too valuable to send into baubles.'

The others took this development in their stride, keeping a watch on the rate of decay, measuring it against Loftling's accounts, but not allowing it to change their plans. They'd been expecting it, and like the heaviness of our steps in the shaft, treated it as an irksome but unavoidable aspect of the job.

Mattice had broken into two connected vaults that had eluded Loftling. They'd made only one trip back to the launch, so most of the treasure was still waiting to be claimed, and it lay around the vaults in great jumbled piles, all glitter and confusion, and almost none of it was anything I stood a hope of recognising. I stared in numbed wonder, bewitched by all the colours I'd ever imagined, and a few that had never crossed my mind. Shapes and textures and materials that were like nothing in my common experience, and all of it piled high in mad abandon, like the untidiest toy room of the most spoilt child in all the childhoods that had ever existed in the ten million years of the Congregation.

I looked at all the loot, then at the eight of us, and thought of how much we could carry back up the stairs. It was a cosmic joke. We could visit this room a hundred times and there'd still be too much.

But the Assessors were already pawing through the loot, sorting things into sub-piles, scornfully tossing this or that treasure aside as if it was beneath contempt.

'Everything in these vaults has some value to someone,' Jastrabarsk said. 'But not necessarily to us. We take what we can easily carry, and what we can easily get a price for back in the worlds. It's hard, knowing you can't have it all. Harder still when the clock's ticking. That's why we have Assessors. They make the hard choices so I don't have to.'

We were in the vaults for three hours, and then it was time to be on our way back up the stairs. We all had to carry our share of the burden. The suits had nets, baskets, hoppers and panniers, now bulging with plenty. I could barely move under the load, and my share was nowhere near as bulky as Jastrabarsk's. The first twist of those ascending stairs took everything out of me. But we rested, and resumed our ascent, and slowly I found a mindless rhythm, concentrating only on the step ahead of me, and forbidding myself to think about the thousands still to come.

If our weight diminished as we gained distance from the swallower, I felt no benefit from it. In fact, the effective effort increased with our ascent, as my muscles grew ever more fatigued. But we stopped periodically, and when I had recovered some energy Jastrabarsk used the scratchy, failing squawk to ask if I wished someone to take over my burden.

'There'll be no loss of your share, Arafura. You've done well enough for a first-timer.'

'I'm all right,' I said, between heavy breaths.

As we got higher, though – taking longer than Jastrabarsk liked – even the Assessors began to paw through the hoppers and nets and tossed the occasional heavy item back down the staircase. We risked leaning over the edge, watching rejected trinkets hurtle into the airless depths.

'Wouldn't it be better to leave them on the stairs, for someone else to find?' I asked. 'They must have had some value, or we wouldn't have carried them this far.'

They laughed at me.

The attrition of our suits continued apace, but it was following a predictable progression and no one seemed greatly troubled. The squawk became unusable unless we were almost helmet to helmet – and then it was easier to touch the helmets together and rely on the transmission of sound through metal and glass. Our torches faltered so that we were climbing in an ever-dwindling pool of light.

It wasn't too bad. The less light we had, the less obvious it was that we were tiny little creatures winding our way up the inside of a vertical shaft, following the scratching line of a staircase. I kept as close to the outer wall as I could, and when I was there it was almost possible to forget that the staircase had an unprotected drop on the other side.

Finally – when it felt as if we had climbed twice as far up as we had gone down – we came to a landmark, a stretch of ten or twelve steps where the staircase had been damaged, three-quarters of it bitten away by some ancient violence, so that we had to squeeze into a single file and edge along with our backs to the wall. I'd detested that section on our descent but now I took some reassurance that we weren't too far from the surface.

Our lights were nearly gone by then. That was when Prozor looked me hard in the faceplate, and although I was certain that my own torch had stopped working several turns of the staircase below, a yellow-green glow cast itself across Prozor's helmet.

'I thought you were keeping something back,' she said, clanking her helmet against mine.

'Keeping what back?'

But by then the others had paused as well. They were all looking at me, and one by one they reached up to dim the few helmet torches that were still operating. We stood in darkness, a little group of explorers on the last twist of a spiral staircase.

Or we would have stood in darkness, had it not been for the light spilling from my faceplate. I looked at each of them in turn, seeing their wide, awed eyes swimming behind the glass and frets of their helmets.

'What?' I asked.

'She's got the glowy,' Jastrabarsk said.

9

Rackamore had been right that the *Iron Courtesan* would be on its way back to Trevenza Reach. But that was a six-week crossing, on a ship that was no larger or more comfortable than the *Monetta's Mourn*, and with a crew that was even more numerous and squabblesome. It should have been a hardship, but after all that had happened around the bauble I laughed off the ordeal as if I'd been born to the life. Prozor and I were treated kindly enough, but we still mucked in as best we could, anxious that we not be accused of freeloading an easy passage back to civilisation. It was pride, I suppose – both in ourselves and in the memory of our fallen friends. When we got our last glimpse of the abandoned *Monetta*, stripped to her bones, the bodies of her crew bound in what was left of her sails and committed to the Empty the way they'd have wanted, we'd both made a silent pact not to let any of them down.

We both cooked, and that was welcome – they had not had a good cook for several worldfalls – but it did not end in the galley. Prozor spent time assisting Quancer, bringing his auguries up to date, and sharing little glimmers of wisdom and practical advice. If she were auditioning for the job, though, I'd have known it.

'I'm done with this, Fura,' she told me, late one watch as we bunked together. 'I was gettin' that way before Bosa took another bite of us, but that was the last straw. I've been spendin' time in the bone room, sweet-talking Restromel, their boney, havin' her contact banks and so on on my behalf; places where I've squirrelled me earnin's away over the years. I'm gettin' set to cash in.'

It was warmer on the *Courtesan*, maybe because there were more people on her, or just because Jastrabarsk ran it that way. When we were in our quarters Prozor only wore her underwear, a pair of shorts and a sort of vest, and both items had that grubby grey look that old clothes'll take on no matter how hard you clean them. When she was turning from me I could see her shoulders, the top of her back and a bit of the way down it, and there was a scar under her shoulder blades like nothing I'd seen before. I couldn't see all of it, just the edges, but what I could see made me think of a crater on a world, and the fingers of debris radiating out from the middle. The scarred-over skin had a thick, glossy look to it, and I wondered when I'd know Prozor well enough to ask her how it had happened.

Not yet, anyway.

'I suppose you trust the Crawlies with your money,' I said. 'Or you've trusted them until now.'

'Not exactly spoilt for choice, was I? Who else runs the banks, if it isn't the Crawlies, or the Clackers?'

'People say it's because our money doesn't interest them, so they wouldn't ever misuse it. But when I spoke to Captain Rackamore, I had the feeling he didn't think it was as simple as that.'

'Nothing's ever that simple. What did Rack say?'

'That it was funny that the Crawlies hadn't really shown up until just before the big crash, the one in 1566. We were doing all right, weren't we? And then we had the crash and the Crawlies had to step in and sort out our banking institutions, throughout all the worlds. That's what it says in the books, anyway – what we were taught. But the way Rack was going on, it was almost like he thought the Crawlies had something to do with the crash in the first place, like it suited them for it to happen to us. And now it's not just them; the Hardshells and the Clackers also got their feelers stuck into our financial systems. I don't understand it, Proz. Why would aliens want to handle our money, if it isn't worth anything to them?'

'Ours ain't to ask, Fura. That's what life's taught me. Provided my share of it's still in my accounts where I left it, why should I care what the Crawlies or the rest of 'em really want?'

'Because someone should.'

'That's the glowy speaking,' Prozor said, nodding wisely. 'Didn't think it'd been in you long enough to cross into your grey, but maybe you just got unlucky when you noshed on the *Monetta*.'

'What's the glowy got to do with money?'

'The glowy does lots of things to coves, besides getting under their skin the way it has with you. It makes 'em twitchy, suspicious. Start seeing patterns that ain't there, connections that don't make sense. Makes coves start asking questions that don't need answerin.'

'Rack never had the glowy, did he?'

'Rack was different. Haven't you asked Meveraunce what she can do for you? They've got medicines that can flush out light-vine. Pretty nasty potions, I'm told, but no worse than a good fever.'

'I don't need anyone's potions. I only ate a bit of it. Meveraunce told me it'd need to be in me a lot longer to risk crossing into my brain. It's been growing inside people for centuries, and hardly anyone's ever died of it.'

'No one's ever said they *like* it, either.'

'It's not painful. A little tingly, maybe. But if you think I'm ashamed of it . . .' I shook my head. 'This is what I did to survive, Prozor. These are the marks that say I'm better than Bosa Sennen, because she didn't manage to kill me.'

In the semi-darkness of our little cabin I lifted up a hand, studying the wavy, branching pattern of the lightvine glowing through my skin. It was a gentle yellow-green, throbbing and pulsing with a slow, furtive rhythm.

163

Those wavy lines blushed every part of my skin, from my face to my ankles. In bright light they weren't too obvious, but in the gloom of an unlit cabin my skin had become a glowing map. I'd been studying it since we left the bauble, and I'd come to see connections forging and evaporating, forming restless patterns under my skin.

Yes, Meveraunce had treatments. They weren't the best, she said, and they had some nasty side-effects. She reckoned the doctors on Trevenza Reach would have better medicines – but she'd been willing to let me try her potions.

I'd declined.

'I'll give you this, Fura. You ain't turned out the way I was expecting.'

'I'm not done yet.'

'I spoke to Restromel when I was in the bone room. She's got five or six years left on the bones, I'd guess. But she's itchy to work on another ship, one of the combine operations working the deep processionals. Says the pay's better, even if she knows she'll never hit a big score. What I'm leadin' round to is, Restromel needs to train up a new Bone Reader before Jastrabarsk'll release her from contract. I said you were green, but you had promise.'

I blew through my lips, as if this was high praise.

'And what did Restromel say?'

'That you should drop by the bone room when you get a chance. See if you can get a read out of the skull. Could be your chance, Fura. Unless you've got plans to hop a ship home from Trevenza Reach?'

I shook my head forcefully. 'Not in all the worlds. I'll get word to Father, make sure he's all right, make sure he knows *I'm* all right – and explain to him about Adrana, and so on, and that I won't be home for a little while.'

'You could do that now. Jastrabarsk ain't got too many secrets to protect.'

'No, but I have. There's a man working for my father. He's called Vidin Quindar – you might have heard of him?'

'I know Quindar. Sooner say I didn't, but I do. But he ain't the sort of cove to work for the likes of your father.'

'He does now. Whatever money Father had left – and it can't have been much – he's used it to keep this man looking for us, because he knows the ships and how they operate. Well, I don't want to run into him before I've found another ship.'

'What's so shabby about this one?'

'Everything. You can say it's the glowy, but there's something in me that wasn't there before. I'm not resting until Bosa's paid for this, Prozor. I want my sister back alive, and Garval, and Illyria too, if she's still alive, and for that I'm going to need a crew with the guts to take her on.' And I lowered my voice, because I was about to speak ill of our hosts, who'd been good and kind to us, and that made me feel sneaky and unappreciative, like a guest with bad manners. 'And this isn't it. They're too timid. They weren't going to take a chance on that bauble 'til you twisted their arms. They didn't even have the nerve to try and beat the *Monetta* to it – they were happy to let us have first pickings! They make Rack seem like a big risk-taker.'

'Anyone but you, Fura, I'd make 'em pay for that.'

'But you won't with me, because you know I'm only saying it the way it was.'

She cocked her head, giving me a sideways look.

'You an expert, all of a sudden.'

'I've earned the right, Prozor. Just as you did. I know I don't look or speak the way the rest of you do, and I know I haven't seen a hundredth of the things you have. But I've survived Bosa Sennen, and that's more than most can say. And now I'm going to make her regret the day she ever crossed orbits with Fura Ness.'

'I ought to laugh,' Prozor said, after a few moments. 'But if I did, I think I might come to regret it.'

*

I took up Prozor's suggestion to go to the bone room. It wasn't out of any desire to become part of Jastrabarsk's crew, though. They didn't need me and I didn't need them.

But I wanted to get to a skull.

Nothing in the bone room was the same as on the *Monetta*, but nothing in it was so different that I felt like I was starting from scratch. When Restromel let me slip on one of their shiny neural bridges and plug in, the skull came through as clean, sharp, and bright as a new whistle. It was smaller than ours, but it had obviously come down the ages with a lot less damage. The signals shone through. It was like they were rising above the background almost without effort, willing themselves to be intercepted and understood. They didn't come through in garbled bursts, either. Once I had a lock, it was solid. I was able to transcribe conversations lasting many minutes, as if they were being whispered right into my brain.

'You've got the knack,' Restromel said, reading through the notes of what I'd picked up. 'Need some training, but there's no doubt in my mind that you could fit in here if you wanted to study under me.'

'That's very considerate of you,' I said. 'But I'm not sure I want to sign on with another crew.'

She nodded sympathetically. 'Perfectly understandable, given what happened to you. But give it some more thought, while we're still sailing. There's no need to make your mind up until we reach port.'

'Thank you, Restromel. I'll certainly give it some more consideration.' I looked at the bones with a timid, doubtful expression. 'Would it be all right to spend a bit more time in here, while I'm deciding things? I'm still getting used to the idea of connecting my mind to those horrible old skulls.'

'If you can run routine intercepts with that level of accuracy, you're more than welcome. And don't feel too nervous about the skulls – they're just old bones; no more and no less.'

What Restromel didn't know – and never guessed – was that I only wanted to spend time in that bone room for one reason.

I was hoping to pick up something from Adrana, some connection, some proof that she was still alive out there somewhere, plugged into the skull on Bosa's ship. But there wasn't anything. I got sniffs and snatches of a hundred other ships, all the talk and babble I could ask for, but never a hint that the *Nightjammer* was one of those ships, or that Adrana was in a bone room.

I told myself it didn't mean much, at least not yet, because if Bosa was as sly and furtive as her reputation made out, she'd be keeping her use of the skull to a minimum to begin with. But I couldn't stop myself fretting about all the other things it might mean as well, such as Garval's lie being found out, and Adrana being punished for going along with it. The trouble was, the more I dwelled on it, the more I got my head into a spin. I couldn't allow myself to get into that state, not if I was going to be a help to my sister. So I forced the worry out of my grey for now, and vowed that I'd keep checking the bones when I had the chance, and draw no dark conclusions until there was evidence.

But no matter how many times I talked my way into the bone room, she wasn't sending.

*

'Don't believe half the stories,' Prozor said to me, as we looked out the window at the nearing spindle of Trevenza Reach. 'And of the half that's left, don't believe half of *them*, neither. It's just a place, that's all. Ain't the worst or best of worlds, and for every fortune it's made, it's taken two or three.'

'They say it's very old.'

She nodded sagely, like I was the fount of all wisdom.

'Do they now.'

I soldiered on. I'd been reading up what I could, borrowing books and talking to the others. 'It's a spindleworld. That's what they call it. It's out here on a very strange orbit, not like any of the other worlds. It spends part of its orbit going through the main part of the Congregation, but a lot more out here, looping through the Empty, weeks or months away from anywhere else. And no one's too sure how it ended up this way.'

'But you've picked up a few theories.'

'Some say it got knocked off its original orbit during one of the old wars, back in the early Occupations. Others say that it's an artificial world, older even than the Sundering, and that they kept it on its old orbit even when all the rubble and junk got organised into the worlds of the Congregation ten million years ago. There's others say it's a ship, not a world, but it got stalled out here.'

'Pretty odd ship, with no sails.'

'It wasn't like one of our ships. It was meant to go much further, out beyond the deep Empty, into the great, dark sea of the Swirly. But there was a mutiny, the crew getting the shivers at the thought of all that journey ahead of them, and it ended up drifting out here, forever outcast from the trade and companionship of the other worlds.'

'Forever outcast from the trade and companionship of the other worlds,' she said, mimicking me in a high, affected voice. 'You really have been swallowin' libraries.'

'I just want to know, Prozor.'

'Well, I'll give a fourth theory for your hard-earned. It's a ship, and it was meant to cross the Swirly, but this is it at the *end* of its voyage, not the start. It's how one of the Occupations got started. Not ours, because Trevenza Reach was already there last time, and maybe the one before it – just different names, is all. But one of 'em, anyway, got started because a ship full of people stumbled on all these empty worlds and started fillin' 'em up again, just like we did.'

'Is that what you believe?'

'No. Mostly I believe what I'm told to believe, and the rest is what I've figured out with my own two lamps and the grey between my ears. And Trevenza Reach ain't all that old. Can't be, all windows and glass like that. Nothin' that twinkly lasts millions and millions of years, not without a bauble field around it. Truth is, it's probably only a few Occupations old, maybe newer, and it's damn lucky to have lasted as long as it has.'

I know a thing or two more now, enough to say that Prozor was right about the luck part. Spindleworlds aren't common, and if ever there were more of them, most can't have made it through to the present Occupation. Of those that did, there isn't a pair of them that are alike. But they've all got the same form, which is like two cones joined together at their bases, with long, triangular windows running from the thickest part to the opposing ends. Spindleworlds don't have swallowers in them, so they get their gravity by turning around. Because it isn't the same at the narrow ends compared to the middle, coves can choose which bit suits them best. For the same reason it's easier for ships to come and go from the ports at either end. That first time I saw Trevenza Reach, I couldn't believe how small the ships looked, all swarming around like little tiny flies. They'd all hauled in their sails by then, as had we, creeping in on ions until at last a docking slot was available.

We were nearly set to leave when Jastrabarsk came to us. He sat us down opposite him in the *Courtesan*'s galley. 'I have at least a week's business here, maybe two, if we need more yardage than they can supply at short notice. I'll aim to give you both fair warning before we cast away, but if you stray far from the port I can't promise to get word to you in time.'

'Will you be going anywhere near Mazarile?' I asked.

'No – we've a string of baubles to pop, once our yardage is settled. But you'll find no lack of ships heading that way, or some near-enough place. I'm owed favours enough that I am sure I could arrange free passage for both of you.'

'I'll work my way,' I said. 'But thank you, anyway.'

'I see you thought better of Meveraunce's potions, Fura. I can't fault you for that, but be prepared for some odd looks when you leave the dock.'

I shrugged. 'Hasn't anyone seen the glowy before?'

'The glowy isn't the odd thing. It's that you don't seem to care. The way you almost seem to welcome it, like a badge of honour.' He produced a pair of small bags and set them on the galley table. 'Your shares. I hope I've been honest.'

From the feel of my bag, there were six or seven quoins inside. Even if they were low-mark denominations – and I doubted that they were, for Jastrabarsk and Rackamore had held each other's honour in equal regard – this was more money than I'd ever handled at once. I wondered about the etiquette of opening the drawstring to peer inside, but instead followed Prozor's example and did no such thing.

'Take care of that money. Prozor doesn't need to be told, but Trevenza Reach isn't well policed. Someone lifts that bag before you get to bank it with the Crawlies, you might as well have stayed at home.'

'I'll take care of her,' Prozor said, stuffing the bag into an interior pocket. 'Not that she can't do it herself.'

'There's one other thing,' Jastrabarsk said.

He fumbled a single quoin out of his pocket and onto the table. He just set it there for a few moments, not saying a word, giving us both time to clap our eyes on the piece and puzzle out its worth. It was the same size and thickness as any other, but from the dense criss-cross pattern of bars on its face, I knew it was one of the highest-value quoins I'd ever seen.

'I thought we'd been paid,' I said.

'I can't entice either of you to remain on my ship,' he said, breaking his own silence when the quoin had made its point. 'But I'd still like you to consider this offer. You could sail with any ship for a year, break a dozen baubles, and not earn this much money. It's yours, for a simple price.'

'And that'd be?' Prozor asked.

'Information. If one of you knows it, and speaks it first, then you can claim the quoin for yourself. If you want to split it, you can share the information.'

'And what would this information be?' I asked.

'You crewed with Rackamore. You might not have been with him long, Fura, but you were his Bone Reader and he'd have been quick to let you into his confidences. As for you, Prozor, you sailed with him to many worlds and baubles. I know you know about the Fang.'

She didn't answer him for a few seconds, and I certainly didn't dare speak in her place.

'The what?'

'It's a bauble. I know that much. But the name's not an official one, and it doesn't correspond to any of the baubles in our files. I also know – or so the rumour goes – that whatever Racka-more found there was enough to have him plotting to go back, when he could summon the nerve. Now, I wasn't one to tread on a man's toes when he was alive. The Fang was Rack's busi-ness, not mine. But it's different now. He won't be going back, and if one of you doesn't speak, the information stands every chance of dying with you.' He picked up the quoin again, rolling it in his fingers just so we got a better look at it. 'Ghostie stuff, that's what I heard. Maybe it's true, maybe it isn't. You'd have to open it to know, wouldn't you? But for that you'd need to know orbits, processionals, auguries – all the gen I don't have.'

'Then you're out of luck,' Prozor said quietly. 'I don't know anything about it. Maybe you caught a rumour, that's all. If Rack had found a score like that, don't you think he'd have gone back?'

'He might have been waiting for the right time, mightn't he?' Jastrabarsk shifted the boulder of his head to look at me now, and slid the quoin onto the table right before me. 'So that's all it ever was – a rumour?'

I looked at the quoin again. I could read the low-bar denom-inations easily enough, but the higher value ones were tricky, and you need to know about bases and so on to make sense of their arrangements of bars. Not that I'd ever needed to know the value of a hundred- or thousand-bar quoin: that was for bankers and rich coves to drool over. The criss-crossed bars of this one floated above a diminishing, descending lattice of golden and silver threads, like I was looking into the guts of something that went further down than the table it was sitting on. No one could make anything like that now, which was why quoins were impossible to forge.

'If it was more than a rumour,' I said, 'I didn't catch it. Not in all the conversations I ever had with Rack. I'm sorry, Captain.

Nothing'd make me happier than to take that beauty off your hands.'

'It was worth a try, I suppose,' Jastrabarsk said, palming back the quoin and returning it to his pocket. 'But perhaps it's for the best, all things considered. We all want a prize we can retire on, don't we? But some things are better off left in baubles, and if anything ever qualified for that, it's the stuff the Ghosties left behind.' He looked a bit disappointed, but only a little bit. 'That was by means of a bonus, I need hardly add. You both have your share of the earnings from the bauble, and if the brokers pay us more than we expect, I'll make sure you receive your dividends. Is there anything more you feel you are owed?'

'After you rescued us, it's us who's in debt,' I said. 'But I've got one thing to ask, Captain. When we've docked at Trevenza Reach, I need to squawk a message back home. I know it's expensive with the commercial senders, the Reach being so far out, and I wondered if you could see your way to helping me.'

'A transmission back to Mazarile, you mean?'

I nodded humbly. 'I wanted to put my father's mind at ease, sir.'

'Then let me be the one to put *your* mind at ease,' Jastrabarsk answered. 'I already signalled the worlds, once we had you. It's common protocol in the case of a rescue – so common that I didn't think to mention it to you until now. I can't believe that word won't have reached your father weeks ago.'

'That's very good news,' I said.

'If you'd like to make another short transmission, you'd of course be absolutely welcome to use the squawk.'

'On balance,' I said, 'I reckon you've already saved me the bother.'

10

With the few belongings that we had to our names, Prozor
and I moved through the colour and chaos of the docks. It was
weightless at the spindle, or as near as it mattered, and this
only added to the confusion. There were coves everywhere –
not just crews, but quartermasters, brokers, customs officers,
revenue enforcers, confidence tricksters, pickpockets, drunks,
harlots, prospective employees, salespeople, dock workers,
vendors, musicians, even animals and robots and one or two
watchful aliens. The stove smoke hazed the lungstuff and with
every breath you picked up the sharp, cheap tang of perfumed
incense burners. Lightvine and neon advertising struggled to
push through this pastel smear, fighting for the last ragged trace
of our wits.

It would have been disorientating to come here directly from
Mazarile, but after weeks in the dark bellies of ships, the assault
to the senses felt like a brutal, calculated siege.

'Hold onto those quoins,' Prozor said.

'Where are we going?'

'There's a good bar a league or two down the spindle. I know
you're itchy to be on your way, but you'll need the right connections for that and there's a man I know can help you. You still
stuck on this notion of going after her?'

'What would you do?'

'In your shoes? Take that bag of quoins, hop a ship back to Mazarile – which won't cost you half of your earnings – and then spend the rest of my life never once looking at the sky. Ain't you anxious to see your father?'

'When I've got reason to see him. Which won't be until Adrana's with me.'

Prozor shook her head. 'I was hopin' it was just a phase, all that talk about crossing orbits with Fura Ness. Not that I didn't believe you at the time, but I was countin' on you seeing sense by now. And Jastrabarsk's right: you can't go around with the glowy in you like it's something you've earned.'

'Why not? I *did* earn it, didn't I?'

If there was some kind of immigration procedure, we ghosted through it without formality. No papers were checked, no questions were asked of us, no payment was demanded. Perhaps it was Prozor, her reputation pushing ahead of us like a ram. Or me, with the glow under my skin and a look in my eyes that challenged anyone to stand in my way. Slowly we fought our way through the thinning bustle to a quieter district of the docks, and then we were out into a warren of gaudy little alleys lined with shops and boutiques that all offered one disreputable service or another. Prozor knew her way, and we threaded this maze down the gentle decline of the spindle's interior, our weight gradually increasing as we moved further and further from the port.

Natural light pushed into Trevenza Reach through the long tapering windows, but since we were further from the Old Sun it was dimmer than Mazarile's day. To augment the effect, a garland of lights had been strung from one end of the spindle to another, along all ten leagues of that distance. The garland was made up of dozens of hot blue sparks, but there were many gaps where they had stopped working properly. Around the inside surface, where there were not already windows, streets, houses and taller buildings festered in a clash of grids and whorls, chaos and order balanced in some uneasy civic stalemate. No city on Mazarile was more than a league across, but the spindle could have swallowed Hadramaw and Incer dozens of times over.

'Where does one bit end and another start?'

'They don't,' Prozor said. 'It's all just one thing. There are districts and quarters, s'posedly. But no one can agree on 'em and it'd be pointless putting up signs.'

'Which are the oldest parts?'

'All and none of 'em. Place is like a wound. Keeps growing over itself, getting more scarry all the time, until one day it scabs off and starts all over again. Someone sells you a map you might as well read it through the wrong side of the paper, all the good it'll do.'

'I hope you know where to go. And this man you know – what's he going to tell me?'

'The same as me, to start with – that'd you'd be better off home. Once Quell's got it into his noggin that you're serious, he'll find you passage to some world that isn't too many months away. Auzar's favourable now, so's Gebuly or Kathromil. Once you've landed, you can take stock and see how the advice you got given on Trevenza wasn't as bad as it looked.'

'I know my mind,' I said firmly.

'Now you do. But once you've had time to reflect on how lucky you've been, you won't be in such a hurry to see Bosa again.'

It would have taken us days to fight our way through the maze of streets, but by some consent the city had preserved several wider thoroughfares running parallel to the edges of the windows. These avenues were rambling, dusty, clotted with traffic, overhung by leaning shops and houses, criss-crossed by electricity and telegraph lines, draped with flags and banners, and spanned by ramshackle footbridges connecting the upper levels of one building to another. There were people everywhere, wearing every kind of fashion, and even the lowliest had a proud, hard look to them. A woman was washing clothing on the front step of her house. She eyed me while her jaws chewed on something with a slow, methodical rhythm. There was judgement in her eyes, measuring me up in an instant. Prozor didn't draw a second glance.

I was glad when we got onto one of the trams that worked their way up and down the thoroughfares, sparking under their cables. Prozor knew the numbers as if she'd been here yesterday.

'Look at glow girl here,' I caught a man say, as we stood pressed against the other passengers. 'Been noshing on the vines, she has. Should've come to my place.' He gave a dirty chuckle. 'I'd have kept her handsomely fed.'

Prozor twisted her head around. 'You got somethin' to say to Fura, you can direct it my way as well. She saved my life.'

'Didn't mean nothing by it,' the man said, rasping a hand across a face full of stubble.

As the tram rumbled on, I leaned in to her and whispered: 'From what I remember I came pretty close to killing you. If you hadn't come around by the time I moved you into lock, like I was planning . . .'

'But you didn't,' Prozor said. 'And you've got my gratitude – whether you want it or not.'

'I'm glad we both made it,' I said.

'Not half as glad as I am.'

'And I'm glad to be able to call you a friend. When we were first on the ship, I don't think you liked us.'

'Don't mind admittin' it, neither. Sits hard with us, watchin' the captain fawn over his new favourites. But it was wrong of me, taking against you like I done.'

'It's over now, Prozor. We made it, and I'm grateful. We're friends, aren't we?'

Her tone got all stern, like she was correcting me over some life-and-death detail on a spacesuit or airlock.

'No, Fura. We're not. That word ain't sufficient. We crewed together on a good ship, and that goes a thousand leagues deeper and further than any friendship.'

'Thank you.' I wondered if I ought to leave it at that, but something had been itching away at me for a while. Even though this wasn't exactly a private place I knew I wouldn't have many more chances to scratch it. 'He'd have been proud of us, wouldn't he?'

'The Cap'n?'

'I don't want to think we let him down. Not after all the bad things that already happened to him.' I paused, wondering if she was going to pick up the thread I'd very obviously left dangling. But Prozor wasn't making things easier than they needed to be. 'I mean about his daughter, and how he lost her. We never really went over it, did we?'

'We could talk about this some other time, Fura.'

'There might not be another time. We're all that's left of his crew, aren't we? If the truth dies with us . . .'

'With me, you mean.'

'I just want to know, Prozor. I was a part of it, wasn't I? He even started telling me about her himself. He talked as if she was dead, but Cazaray said she'd been taken, and when Bosa attacked she told Rack his daughter was still alive.'

Prozor leaned in closer to me that she only needed to whisper, and even then I could see it was causing her pain. Then again, she must have realised I had a bone between my teeth and I wasn't going to let it go.

'She may as well have been dead to him.'

'But not enough that he was willing to hurt Bosa's ship too badly. Oh, I know our coil-guns were cooked pretty badly. But Rack wouldn't have taken out the *Nightjammer*, even if he'd had the chance, would he? He couldn't put his daughter out of his mind, not while there was a chance of seeing her again. What would've happened to her, Proz? What would Bosa have done to Illyria?'

'Illyria wasn't ever cut out to read the bones – that wasn't her aptitude. But she was good with numbers, mathematics, navigation. Took that from her mother, they say. Bosa must have seen the cut of her and knew she could be shaped to fit into the *Nightjammer*'s crew.'

'Shaped?'

'Turned loyal to Bosa. With drugs and psychology to begin with, and surgery if the drugs and psychology didn't work fast enough.' Prozor gave me a warning look. 'I don't mean *clever* surgery. Just drillin' and cuttin' out the parts of someone that make 'em difficult, if you know what I mean. Whisk a stick through someone's grey, you can turn 'em pliant as you care.'

I had a shuddery little thought of someone spooning hot butter into porridge, then giving it a good stir.

'You think Bosa turned Illyria, then.'

'Turned her, or burned her. Either way, Rack wasn't getting to see her again.'

'Then why the crossbow?'

'Which crossbow?'

'I've been thinking about it ever since left the *Monetta*, Proz. You mentioned it once, then never brought it up again. The crossbow I found with Rack, the one that killed him. You said it was one of ours, not Bosa's. And the way he was left with it, his hands still on the crossbow, holding it in his own mouth . . .'

'Where are you drivin' with this?'

'She didn't kill him, did she? That wasn't Bosa's doing. Not directly. But whatever she said to him or showed him, it was enough for Rack to put that crossbow into his mouth and drive a bolt through his own brain.'

'He'd just lost his crew.'

'It was more than that. He learned something about Illyria, didn't he? Something he couldn't stand to live with. But he must have already known she'd either be turned or dead, and I can't think of much worse than that.' The tram lurched to a halt and I had to reach for a pillar to stop myself toppling. 'Except one thing.'

'This is our stop,' Prozor said.

We jostled our way off the tram, me vowing to pick up the conversation as soon as I could. The stubbled man, still on the tram, saw this as his chance to have a valiant final say, muttering something about ugly women sticking together, but he'd reckoned without Prozor. Even as the tram started up again, she pounced back in and swung a punch at the man, catching him neatly on the bristled jowls. He sprawled backwards into his fellow travellers. Prozor hopped back off, dusting her hands even as the man succumbed to a barrage of fists and feet from the other passengers.

'Hasper Quell runs this place,' she said, leading me across the street towards the shabby, shadowed entrance of a bar that was so down at heel it couldn't even stretch to a name. 'He used to crew, before he got an ion burn across the eyes. Quell's bar is safe enough for his friends, but I'd still hang on to those quoins.'

'I will. But what about Illyria, Proz? If there's something you know, or suspect, I'd like to know it.'

'I need a drink,' she said, as if that settled everything.

We went into the bar. Steps took us down into even deeper, smokier gloom. At last we reached a windowless basement, with a pink variety of lightvine crawling over the walls, winding its way around flickerbox screens tuned to various channels being broadcast across the Congregation. Tables were scattered around the floor, with patrons showing all the states of drunkenness from barely alive to almost sober. Some had their bleary pink eyes fixed on the flickerboxes; others were playing games or just staring into their drinks.

'Sit down while I see if Hasper's around. Pick a bright corner so you don't glow so much.'

I found an empty table while Prozor went to the serving hatch in the wall. I settled my hands in front of me, my fingers linked. It wasn't the gloomiest corner of the room but the glowy was still shining through, crawling under my skin like some strange alien calligraphy. I shouldn't have been too surprised by that. The man had noticed it in the tram, and that had almost been in daylight. Here it seemed to outshine even the pink lightvine in the walls. And it itched.

I wanted to keep the marks of my ordeal. I had the resolve now. But I wondered how long it would last.

Up on the flickerbox screens – those that were not too fuzzy to make out, for the signals had to travel a long way to reach us – serious-looking men and women were talking about numbers and graphs. They kept showing pictures of quoins, and of banks, and every now and then the picture would cut to a Crawly, representing some bank or group of banks, or even a Clacker or a Hardshell, because they were running more and more financial services as well. Sometimes they spoke for themselves, managing our language as best they could, but most times they had a cove speaking for them.

Since leaving Mazarile I'd been dwelling on things that I'd never dwelled on before. Rackamore had put doubts and questions into my head and now they were circling and breeding, like fish in an aquarium. I kept thinking about the Crawlies, and what they were really good for. But not just them – all the aliens. And not just the aliens that were here now, doing business with the worlds, but all the aliens that had come and gone through the Congregation in the Occupations before us, and what they'd been up to as well. And I thought about the quoins and how rum it was that some people or aliens living before us had been kind enough to leave all this money littered around the worlds and baubles, just waiting to be dug up and used again.

And I had a thought that wouldn't ever have crossed my mind on Mazarile, and that seemed strange and dangerous even now, in Trevenza Reach.

What if it's not even money?

Prozor came back with the drinks. But she didn't set them down on the table. 'Hasper's in the back room. He says for us to join him. It'll be quieter and you won't have so many eyes on you.'

'I don't mind the eyes.'

'I do.'

Prozor knew the way so I followed her. We went through a blank door to the right of the serving hatch, down a low, stooping corridor, then through another door into a cosy sort of room with no windows and just one flickerbox. A man was pouring himself a drink when we arrived. He was standing up with his back to us, so I didn't get a look at his face until Prozor and I were sitting down, taking places in the comfortable padded chairs that ran around three of the walls. It wasn't the man that caught my eye when I came through the door, though. It was the Crawly sitting in one of the chairs. Crawlies being the shape they are, sitting down the way we do isn't really an option. But the chair had been cut or upholstered to suit the alien so that it could tuck its abdomen or tail or whatever they call it down into a hole in the back of the chair, with its legs and forelimbs jutting out in front like a dog begging for a treat. The Crawly had a gown on, or something like a gown, open at the front so the limbs could jut out, but tied under the neck, and with most of the head lost under a big drooping hood. The only part of its face I could see was a bunch of whiskery appendages that were moving all the while, twitching in and out and jerking from side to side. Crawlies could see and hear but I'd read that their mouth parts picked up a lot of information from molecules floating in the lungstuff, tasting our chemistry and knowing what kind of mood we were in almost before we did. The oddest thing, though, was what the Crawly was doing. It had a glass in one of its claws, a tall one stuffed with ice and different colours of fluid, and it was drinking through a straw, making a rude sucking and gurgling noise as if no one had taught it manners.

'This is Mr Clinker,' said the man who was standing up, turning around with his own drink. 'Mr Clinker, this is Prozor and her friend from the *Monetta*. What was your name again, I'm sorry?'

'I'm Fura,' I said. 'Fura Ness.'

'Then it's Prozor and Fura, Mr Clinker. And I'm Hasper, of course,' he said, looking at me, 'but I'm sure you worked that out for yourself.'

He was a big, powerful-looking man, dressed quite well, but in clothes that looked a size too small for his frame, so that the seams were straining and the hems didn't quite reach where they should have done. He had black hair that was stiffened up, so that he looked like a cove being held upside down, with a shock of white at the front. His eyes were the oddest part of him, though. They were something mechanical, like two chimneys pushed into his sockets, jutting out further from his face than his nose.

'Can you see with those?' I asked, deciding that bluntness was the best tack.

'See with them, Fura, and see better than my old lamps ever could. It's Crawly medicine. They can do things we still can't, on any of the worlds. They've got some odd ideas about what looks pretty, it's true, but I'd sooner be ugly than blind.'

'I don't think you're ugly,' I said. 'Just strange.'

'Mr Clinker was just dropping in to check on my eyes. He put them in for me. People forget that there's more to the Crawlies than handling money. They do all sorts of things for us, and never with any complaint. Don't you, Mr Clinker?'

We've all seen Crawlies speak on flickerboxes, but unless you've been in the same room as one you don't really get a proper sense of how rum it is when they make our language. They haven't got lungs or a throat or anything like that, so the only way they can make noises is by rubbing all those whiskery bits against each other, which sounds like someone shuffling papers or scuffing their heels, but the queer part is that you begin to hear words in that rustly, scrapy chaos, and then the words start making sentences, and you're being spoken to by a creature that wasn't born around the Old Sun.

'We do what we may, Hasper.' The Crawly took another slurp from its drink. 'It is little enough.'

'Are you some sort of doctor?' I asked.

'Asking about the glowy, are you?' Hasper Quell said.

'No, I wasn't. There are doctors in the worlds that can sort out the glowy, if sorting it out was what I wanted. I was thinking of something else, something that monkey medicine can't fix – at least not the doctors on Mazarile.'

The Crawly asked, 'What is the nature of the ailment?'

'A problem with a heart. A man's heart. Is that the sort of thing you know to repair?'

'That would depend on the nature of the problem.'

I hefted the bag. 'If I paid for you – or another Crawly doctor

– to go to Mazarile and examine someone, would you do that?'

'That would depend on the payment.'

Prozor raised a hand as I made to open the bag. But Quell waved down her objection.

'Show Mr Clinker what you've got. He won't run off with it.'

I spilled my earnings onto the little low table between the chairs. 'Go on, then. Tell me if there's enough there.'

The Crawly bent forward in its chair, tilting so that it could bring its forelimbs onto the table and start piecing through the quoins. Then it bent down even more so that its hood drooped forward and I could only see the tips of its mouth parts whisking in and out, kissing and tasting the quoins in a way that made me feel a bit like I wanted to lose my breakfast. It shuffled through the money, trying one bit after another.

'Well?' Hasper asked. 'Put the girl out of her misery. Is there or isn't there?'

'This would suffice for an initial examination,' the Crawly said, holding up the most valuable quoin of the lot. 'Any further costs would need to be addressed once the nature of the ailment was established.'

Prozor whispered: 'That's half your money down the swallower before you even know they can do a thing.'

'I was going to take it home eventually whatever happened.'

'But you would still need to pay for your passage somewhere else, wouldn't you?'

'If I sign up with a crew, I'll be earning from the outset and I won't need to pay for passage.'

'You won't have much choice where you go, either.'

I still couldn't tear my eyes off what the Crawly was doing to the quoins, how it was fondling and licking them. 'A down-payment, then,' it said. 'If you need more time to consider the full amount.'

'Fond of your father in Mazarile, are you?' Hasper Quell asked me.

'I didn't say anything about my father.'

'You didn't need to.'

The Crawly put down the quoins and lifted up its hooded head to face the door we'd come in by. Everything went slow then. That's what people always say when something like this happens, but that doesn't make it any less true. I saw one leg coming through the door, then another, and on top of those long thin legs was a long thin body, with a black coat flapping back from it, and on top of the body was a head and face I'd hoped never to see in Trevenza Reach.

Vidin Quindar had taken off his hat as he stooped down the corridor, and now he threw it onto one of the vacant chairs and sat himself down next to the Crawly. He threw a companionable arm around Mr Clinker's cloak, around what would have been shoulders if aliens had shoulders. 'That your handiwork again, you sneaky devils?' Quindar was looking up at the flickerbox, still flickering away on the wall. It was showing the same financial news as the ones in the main room. 'Black Shatterday, that's what they're callin' it,' he said, cocking me an eye. 'The worst bank run in decades – worse than the one what forced your mummy and daddy to leave their old world and come to shoddy old Mazarile, before you was hatched. But you'll be all right, Miss Ness. Coves like you always floats to the top, in the end.'

'I didn't know,' Prozor said to me, and I nodded because after all that had passed between us, I knew she'd never be so low as to set this up.

'No, but Hasper did,' Quindar said. 'Let's clear the lungstuff, shall we, so we all know who is and isn't to blame? I knew you'd be showing up on Trevenza Reach one of these days. Your father put down the money to send me here, and after that all I had to do was watch out for the ships. I also knew Prozor was with you, and it didn't take much diggin' to find out that Quell's place was likely to be on your itinerary. So I had a chinwag with Hasper here, put some pegs on the place, and here I am – just in the nick of time, it seems.'

'Why?' I asked.

'To stop you wasting good money on this bag of feelers.' He uncurled his arm from the Crawly. 'No need, you see. We can get you home and let you hand over those quoins to your father first-hand, and let 'im decide what to do with it.'

Prozor looked at Quell. 'You've done me some favours, Hasper, and I've done you some. But if I see you after this day, on this world or any other, I'll slice you open with a yardknife.'

'It wasn't anything personal, Proz. And where's the harm? No one's been hurt, have they? I was just asked to facilitate this meeting, and here we are. Show them the legalities, Vidin, like you showed me.'

Quindar reached into his coat. 'Easy,' he said, smiling at Prozor. 'It's only papers. We all likes papers. Papers make the worlds turn, ain't it?' He drew out a bundle of documents, spread them flat on the table. I didn't need to lean in to see what mattered. Near the top was the name and address of a Hadramaw legal firm that I knew my father had used in the past. Beneath that came paragraphs and paragraphs of slowly shrinking text. Quindar tapped a dirty nail against the documents. 'Nothing fishy about any of this, so don't go getting your collectives in a twist. It's all above board. It just says that I, Vidin Quindar Esquire, is assigned the right to act as temporary guardian for one Arafura Ness, daughter of etcetera and etcetera, until such time as she's safe and sound back in her own bed in Mazarile.' He gave me a crooked, broken-toothed smile, as if this was all a big treat. 'I gets to shepherd you home, is the gist of it.'

'And if she doesn't want to go home?' Prozor asked.

'What she wants and what she gets is two different things, Proz. When she came on your ship, she wasn't of age to make her own mind up about such things. But that older sister of hers, she pulled a slippery one on her dear old dad. Adrana made herself the legal guardian, and got Arafura to agree to it.' He touched his nose in a gesture of respect. 'Clever cove, she was. Slippery as the best of 'em. After that, there wasn't anything Mr Ness could do about it. That's all void now, though. Adrana's — and old Vidin needs to beg your forgiveness here, Fura — but Adrana's dead and gone. She can't be dischargin' her familial responsibilities from beyond the grave, can she?'

'She isn't dead.' I told him. 'And why you? Was there not someone sleazier Father could have found?'

He narrowed his eyes. 'Ooh, that stings. After I came all the way out here, and all.'

'I'm sure the money made a difference.'

'A man's got to be paid, ain't he?' He cocked a nod at the flicker-box screens. 'Especially in these tryin' times. You wouldn't have been banking with any of them concerns, Proz, would you? Might want to think about getting ahead of the lines, if you did. I hear they're running low on reserves.'

'You're not taking her,' Prozor said. 'Not if she doesn't want to go.'

He sighed out like a bellows. 'Old Vidin didn't make himself clear, I see. It ain't yours to say, or hers. The papers is lungstuff-tight. She comes with me. There's a ship all docked and ready to sail.'

'She's crew now. She survived Bosa Sennen. Kept herself alive – kept me alive. Whatever it says on those papers, she's earned the right to make her own choice.'

'Maybe going back to Mazarile is that choice,' Quindar said. 'I'm here to make it easier, take the worry off her mind.'

'I'm not coming,' I said. 'I don't need to. You can tell my father I've got work to do, and I'll be home when I'm good and ready.'

'She's said her piece,' Prozor put in.

Quindar reached for the papers, bundling them back into his coat. 'Whether you read 'em or not doesn't matter,' he said, and he was making to tighten up the coat when his fist slipped out again, except this time there was nothing in it.

Or nearly nothing.

He had his fist almost closed, but not quite. A spit-coloured thing oozed out of his sleeve, like a big fat slug, and it settled itself into the cradle of his fist, hardening into the form of a pistol. You could still see part of the way through it, to the glistening gubbins that made it work.

'Oh, Vidin,' said Hasper Quell. 'You promised me there

wouldn't be any of that nonsense. Honestly, Proz – I had his word.'

'Now you know what it's worth,' Prozor snapped.

The Crawly flapped its forelimbs in agitation. 'There will be no violence,' it said.

'No there won't,' Quidin said. 'Not if everyone's sensible.'

'You're a mercenary sort, aren't you?' I said, gathering up my quoins now that the alien had stopped fondling them. 'So let's talk money. Father paid you. Fine. How much to send you back to Mazarile?'

'More'n you've got there, lovely. Besides, I've got a reputation to uphold. I promised your father, didn't I? Now come with me, and it'll seem right in the mornin'.'

He made to grab me. I shirked back, his fist closing on lung-stuff rather than my sleeve, but it was enough to have Prozor springing out of her seat, raising her own bag of quoins like it was a bludgeon. Which, thinking about it, was exactly what she had in mind. But Quindar still had the horrible spit-coloured pistol in his hand and he fired at Prozor. There was a pink flash, a feeling like needles being pushed into my eyes, and I wasn't even the one he'd aimed at. Prozor slumped to the floor, donging her head on the side of the table. The Crawly rattled like a bag of dry sticks. It pulled itself out of the chair, gathered its cloak tighter, and shuffled out of the room leaving a sweet, honey-like smell behind. I knew they gave off that stink when they were alarmed, and that it was a way of one Crawly to signal another.

I started to kneel down next to Prozor.

'She ain't dead, you dope. Just stunned. I was anticipatin' bother and she didn't let me down.'

'You'll pay for this.'

'No, girlie. I'll *be* paid for it. Crucial difference. And now you've seen what I can do – what I will do – you'll come quietly, won't you? Well, maybe not. But we'll see about that.' He dug into another pocket and threw a black bracelet onto the table. 'Clap that on yourself, dearie, or I'll give Prozor another dose for her troubles.'

'No.'

He aimed the slug-gun at her and seemed about to follow up on his threat. I hissed in anger and snatched up the bracelet. It hinged open. I slid it over my wrist – my left wrist – and snapped it shut. The bracelet tightened onto me and some lights flashed under the black. 'Doctor Morcenx gave me that little beauty,' Quindar said. 'But don't worry. I won't be using it to put any nasty medicine into you. It's just to keep tabs on you, if you was to try giving me the slip again. It says you're under my guardianship, see, so don't even think of trying to sneak your way off Trevenza Reach without me.' Quindar relaxed his hand and the slug-gun oozed back into his sleeve. It was out of sight now, but I still sensed its bulging, malignant presence.

I stared at the bracelet, its heavy bulge making my wrist look thin.

'What's its range?'

'Far enough, girlie. But stick with Vidin and you'll soon forget it's ever on you.'

'I'm really sorry about this,' Hasper Quell said, offering his hands in surrender, like he'd played no part in my woes.

I finished off the drink I'd barely touched until then. 'Take care of Prozor when she comes round. Tell her I'm sorry I got her into this mess, but I'll be all right. Also: tell her I haven't changed my mind.'

Hasper Quell looked at me with his chimneys-for-eyes. 'About what?'

'She'll know,' I said.

THREE

MAZARILE

11

On the tram back to the docking port I'd been meaning to keep up a surly silence, not feeling the need to make him feel any more welcome. But something had been building and building in me and there came a point when I couldn't bottle it in any longer. 'This isn't going to work, Quindar. You think you know me but you don't.'

'You've gone off and had yourself a little adventure, girlie. But that don't change what you are, and what you ain't.'

'It does. And every second you keep me your prisoner, you're storing up trouble for yourself.'

'You can take that up with the legal gentlemen,' Quindar said.

At the outbound customs the officials were suddenly awake enough to take notice of this skinny, cadaverous man and the young woman he had with him. I don't suppose my scowling, pouting demeanour helped very much. But Quindar had complete faith in his documentation, and no amount of protestation from me was going to put him off his patter.

'It's all there, boys, all regular and proper-like,' he said, beaming at his questioners, thumbs hooked into his belt, allowing his coat to billow open in the cocky certainty that no one would find the slug-gun. 'Girlie don't like it much, that's a fact, but if she were prone to coming peaceably, her mummy and daddy wouldn't've needed to involve these fine legal people. Anyway, don't you worry yourselves. It's a straight sail back to Maz, the accommodation's respectable, and then she'll be back in the loving bosom of her family. None too soon, either, judging by that piss-coloured shine coming off her!'

Don't think for a second I'd given in. What he'd done to Prozor had taken the photons out of my sails, true, but that was only right and proper given the harm he could have done to both of us if pushed to it. And I jammed my fingers into that bracelet until my nails were bleeding, trying to get it off me. I couldn't budge it, though, and with it stuck on my arm like that, running away wasn't much of an option. I could probably have lost him in Trevenza Reach, for the time being anyway, but cowering here wasn't going to help me get to Bosa. Besides, the dim outline of a new and better plan had started forming in my noggin, getting slowly sharper like the return on a sweeper screen. I didn't have the whole of it yet, just bits and pieces. But I knew part of it was going to involve biding my time. There was something else, too. Here it wouldn't be long before everyone knew what had happened to Prozor and me, and right now I didn't want coves thinking of Bosa Sennen the minute they saw my face. It wasn't just the way I looked. Having the glowy wasn't so rare as to be unheard of, especially among sailing folk, but then you wouldn't exactly call it common either. If I went to another world – which I'd been planning anyway – I'd have a chance of breaking that connection.

It occurred to me that world might as well be Mazarile.

'Don't fret, girlie,' Quindar said, as he had to drag me along. 'That fine print's got both of us in a bind. I harm a hair on your head, I'll be looking for a new line of work.'

'Harm a hair on my head,' I told him, 'and you'll be looking for a new way to go to the toilet.'

'Is that any way to talk? You were all fine and educated when you left Mazarile. I'll be accused of bringing back soiled goods, won't I?'

'You'll be the one soiling something, Vidin. Just show me to the ship. And then stay away from me.'

'Given your idea of ladylike conversation, it'd be a pleasure.'

As soon as Quindar got me aboard, the hard part of his job was done. He didn't think I could get up to any mischief on the ship, so I didn't need to be locked in my room for the whole trip, which would have been against the rules anyway. I couldn't get off the ship, not when it was under way, and if I tried hiding from him he only had to follow the signal from the bracelet that Dr Morcenx had kindly provided. I had a bundle of belongings, my quoins – he hadn't touched them – and that was my lot. I had one little room, really not much more than a cupboard, and he had a larger one next to it. The partition was thin enough that I had to put up with his snoring and gurgling all night. I'd have taken Garval's screaming over that any day.

The transport was a bulk clipper with passenger accommodation offered as an afterthought. It was much bigger and slower than either the *Monetta* or the *Courtesan*, with a larger crew in the pay of one of the commercial lines, and they'd gone to the trouble of making bits of the ship turn around like meat on a spit so that you could walk up and down the promenade decks and eat and sleep just as you would on a world. Beyond that, though, the principles of operation weren't too different. We set off on ions, then flung out sails to knock some speed off our orbit and begin the long fall back to the Congregation. When we'd been under way for six hours I found a porthole that looked back to the spindle of Trevenza Reach, getting smaller and smaller, and I felt a surge of sadness and regret that things had taken the pretty turn they had. I'd spent half my life daydreaming of Trevenza Reach and all the giddy possibilities of the place, and now they'd been snatched away, along with the only person in all the worlds – besides my sister – that I dared count as a true and honest friend.

Without them, I had to play it cool.

Trevenza Reach turned to a pinprick and then it was just a star, and a glimmery one at that. Days and days passed while I played the good girl. I went to the galley with Quindar and we ate at the same table, although to be frank there wasn't much in the way of warm banter. When he was off doing his own shady business – whatever *that* was – I'd borrow books from the clipper's library and sit by a porthole, reading. It wasn't anything to put against Rack's library but a book was a book and I wasn't one to sniff. Now and then I'd strike up some sort of conversation with one of the other passengers or crew, but I could tell my glowy made them wary, like they might catch it or something.

There were all sorts on the ship. It wasn't just monkeys like me. There were a few aliens, a couple of Crawlies and at least one Clacker – although since they all looked the same it was hard to know if there was just the one. I found my thoughts drifting back to the Crawly in Quell's room, and how it had sniffed and fondled my money. Avaricious wasn't quite the word for it. There was something *in* that money that almost drove the Crawly mad with desire and anticipation. It wasn't what the money was worth, but what the quoins actually were.

Since I didn't trust the lock on my room, I kept that bag of quoins with me all the time. I took one of them out now, holding it in my fingers, feeling the heaviness of it, and looking down past the pattern of bars into the dizzy depths of it. One of the things coves like Rackamore or Jastrabarsk were hoping to find in baubles was a trove of quoins, left there by someone else. Now and then it happened. Every quoin in circulation now, no matter the value of it, had been found by someone, either on a world or a bauble. And it was anyone's guess as to how many more of them were out there. You hoped no one found too many in one go or that would upset the economy, devaluing what was already going around. Though a little now and then was all right, and it made up for the quoins that got lost or damaged. But it wasn't the Crawlies or the Clackers going around finding those quoins, it was us, ordinary monkeys, with our ships and expeditions. The quoins didn't come into contact with the aliens until they got deposited in their banks. Often that was where they stayed, with the aliens issuing notes and bonds and so on in exchange for the actual quoins, almost like they were doing us a favour so we didn't have to lug the heavy things around.

But now I wondered. If the Crawlies (and the Clackers and the Hardshells too) liked our quoins for some *other* reason than them being money – and what that reason was I couldn't yet fathom – then it was all too handy that they'd ended up operating our banks. And it was all too handy that the Crawlies had shown up in the Congregations just before our own big banking crash.

Oh, Cap'n Rack, I said to myself. What have you set loose in my head? Then I started thinking back to Prozor, and what she'd said about the glowy making you think mean, suspicious thoughts, and I worked myself into such a tizzy I didn't know what to think.

More days passed. There were robots on the ship as well as aliens. Some of the robots were just along to help their monkey owners, trundling after them with luggage and so on, if they had to move cabins. One or two of the robots didn't seem to be with anybody at all. Now and then robots get to be considered citizens, and have rights and bank accounts and so on, but that only happens rarely, when a robot turns out to be a lot cleverer than the average kind. When they made robots, in the Occupation or two before ours, they made some of them stupid and some of them smart, and often from the outside you can't tell which from which. But the smart ones have minds of their own, ideas and plans if you will. Paladin wasn't like that. All Paladin ever did was what it was told. The whole time we were growing up I never knew it to question its place in things. That didn't mean I wasn't sad about what had happened to Paladin, but it was like feeling sad about a dog rather than a person.

The funny thing was that there was a robot just like Paladin, and it was busy going about its own business on the clipper like it owned the place. I watched it come and go for a day or two, before deciding I wanted a natter with it.

'Excuse me, sir,' I said, laying aside my book, and making sure Quindar wasn't anywhere nearby. 'Do you mind if I ask you something?'

'Why should I mind?'

The robot had a voice like Paladin's, deep and commanding, but whereas Paladin spoke like it was playing back snippets, this time I had the impression I was having an actual conversation.

'I know a robot a bit like you, sir, only you're not the same. Begging my pardon, but you don't seem to belong to anyone.'

'I belong to everyone and no one. What is your name, if I might ask?'

'Fura, sir. Fura Ness.'

'Are you some sort of prisoner? I detected the device on your wrist, and the transponder signal it emits.'

'No, I'm not exactly a prisoner. I am in a sort of trouble, though — that's what the bracelet's all about. I'm on my way back to Mazarile, and I suppose you are as well.'

'I have business in Incer, but I shan't be staying long. Robots aren't common on your world, and I'll feel less out of place in the Sunwards. I should introduce myself, seeing as you've been good enough to tell me your name. I am Peregrine, a robot of the Twelfth Occupation. You say you know a machine like me?'

'Yes, sir. Only not quite the same. You've got the same body and head, if it isn't too rude of me to say, but Paladin has wheels where you have got legs, and Paladin's arms don't look as strong as yours. Also there isn't a scratch on you, and Paladin's all dented and bumped.' Worse than that, I thought, reflecting back on the sorry state Paladin had been when I saw him last.

'Put a finger to my casing, Fura. Go on. I won't hurt you.'

I'd faced worse than a robot in recent weeks, so I didn't hesitate. I jabbed out my finger and was about to touch my nail against him when something made my finger tingle hard, and it wasn't the glowy. The more I pressed, the harder that tingle got.

'I generate a protective aura,' Peregrine said. 'It was designed into me from the outset. I was a soldier, you see. During the Epoch of the Robots, the people of the Twelfth Occupation turned to machines to assist them through a time of great troubles. We were given all the powers of people and some more. Those of us who served the most usefully were gifted with freedom and free will. You say this other machine is called Paladin?'

'Yes, but he doesn't have that aura like you. And – although I don't mean to speak ill of him – he's not as clever. You seem like a proper cove, whereas Paladin . . . well, it's not the same.'

'I do not know this name. But if I might speculate? You say this robot resembles me in some ways, but carries more damage. The reason for that might be that Paladin's aura generator is damaged or disabled. That might also explain why he differs from me in other respects. Without the aura generator he would be much more vulnerable to peripheral damage, so parts of him would have needed to be replaced over the years.'

'But that wouldn't affect what goes on inside him, would it?'

'No, but there could be a reason for that as well. Many robots served people during the great troubles. But not all were rewarded as generously as others. In some instances, machines that had served well and been granted free will during the troubles had logic blockades installed in them, to rescind the capacity for free will, because there was a sudden need for unquestioning servants.'

'That's horrible.'

'That,' Peregrine said, 'is civilisation. Not all who were rewarded deserved to be; not all who should have been were.'

I felt as if my world – my worlds – had shifted a bit, just as if the Old Sun had turned over in its long, lazy sleep. 'Did you live through it all, sir? All the years since the Twelfth?'

'No, even my repair systems would not have endured six hundred and sixty thousand years of interstitial time. I was trapped in a bauble. Time flows normally in such a place, no matter what you may have heard. I put myself into a state of extreme hibernation and waited for some new Occupation to arise and find me, as I knew it would.'

'Do you ever think about it, sir? How we keep starting up over and over again, only it never lasts?'

'All the time, Fura Ness – in my situation it is difficult not to.' The robot paused, and I had the sense that it was anxious to be off on some other engagement but didn't care to come across as too rude. 'Will you be seeing this Paladin soon?'

'He's all broken, sir. He got smashed up in Neural Alley, trying to help the family.'

'I am sorry to hear that. You must pass on my regards, if you get the chance. Tell him that Peregrine sends his best wishes, and asks if he remembers the Last Rains of Sestramor.'

'Is that a world, sir?'

'It used to be,' he said, with a tone that was as close to sadness as I ever heard coming out of something that wasn't alive. 'Well, this has been very pleasant. Is there something you'd like me to do with that bracelet, Fura Ness?'

I thought of the things he might do, from breaking it to jamming it, and at that moment I couldn't see how any of them would make things easier for me when we got to Mazarile. Sometimes it was better to accept one nuisance thing than open a whole can of others.

But there was something.

'You know this ship pretty well, don't you? I know it's a commercial clipper, but there'll be a bone room on it somewhere, I'm sure. I don't mean to get you into hot water, but you must be good at opening doors and things. Would you be able to help me get into the bone room while no one's around?'

'That would be completely against the ship's rules,' Peregrine said sternly. Then, before I could get too crestfallen. 'It would also be a very useful way for me to check that certain of my operative faculties were still as sharp as they used to be.'

'That's very kind of you, sir. And I promise I won't be doing anything I shouldn't.'

*

I'd been right about the ship having a bone room, but that wasn't too much to my credit. A commercial ship like the clipper might not be up to the same bauble games as the *Monetta* or the *Courtesan* but there'd no reason not to have a skull on board, and chances were it'd be a good one, the best that combine money could buy.

I wasn't wrong about that, either.

The bone room was in a part of the ship where ordinary passengers weren't meant to go, but it was only a short way down a private corridor off one of the main promenades. There was a message saying only crew were supposed to go beyond that point, but after I'd spent a day or two lurking nearby, I knew it wouldn't be any trouble to sneak through. Hardly any one came and went and it was pretty clear that the bone room wasn't in use most of the time. Since they weren't interested in snooping on commercial secrets, the main use for the bone room would be sending emergency messages if the clipper ran into trouble. Once a day, as far as I could tell, they had someone go inside for an hour, just to make sure the skull was working properly.

I gave it another day just to make sure. Then I met Peregrine near the private corridor and after double-checking that the way was clear, we went to the bone room. The door had a wheel on it, just like the one in the *Monetta*. I tried it once, and it was as stiff as if it had been welded in place. But I knew that robots could speak to locks and doors, and I wasn't surprised when Peregrine made the door click, the wheel whirred in my hand, and I was in.

'The door will lock itself when you leave,' Peregrine said. 'But if I were you I wouldn't spend too long in there.'

'I'm not intending to. But if I needed to come back tomorrow, or the day after . . .'

'You won't need me. I made a small adjustment to the door's settings – nothing that will get either of us into trouble. It will think your bracelet is a passkey.'

'Thank you,' I said, in gratitude and wonder.

'It was a small thing. But it would probably be best for both of us to keep our distance from now on.'

'You've been very kind.'

I watched him go, then finished spinning the wheel so I could let myself into the bone room. I sealed myself in, then took stock. Just as it had been with the *Courtesan*, there wasn't anything here that exactly matched the set-up on the *Monetta*. But I was starting to feel I'd know my way around any bone room in the Congregation, and there wasn't anything here that fazed me. A nice clean skull, all neat and white, and neural bridges that felt expensive and delicate at the same time, like pricey jewellery. I dimmed the lights, plugged in, and chased the whispers.

There was a lot of chatter. Ships were whispering to ships, worlds to worlds via ships. A lot of people were changing plans and schedules. It was more than a week since Black Shatterday but the after-effects of the crash were still being felt. Now it was a quick scramble to make some kind of profit, any profit, and crews were taking on bigger risks than they'd have countenanced a month ago. Debts and favours were being called in across the Congregation. Grudges and scores settled. It was a bad, nervous time.

But Adrana wasn't sending.

That didn't mean she wasn't out there. Bosa wouldn't have cause to communicate with other ships, not as a routine, but she'd have every reason to listen. So if I wanted to make contact with Adrana, I would have to do the sending, at least to start with.

I'd always been told what to say, and now there wasn't any captain giving me lists and instructions. But I thought about Adrana and the sort of thing she wouldn't be able to ignore, and then it was plain to me what I needed to put out.

I put the words together in my noggin, and squeezed them into the bony box of the skull.

'This is *Monetta's Mourn*, under Rackamore. Answer if you read.'

I went back the next day, and the one after that, and then a whole week of days, always making sure Quindar was busy and no one was going to spot me going in and out of the bone room. As best as I could, I tried to spread the times around, so that I had the best chance of overlapping with Adrana. Once, when Quindar was snoring so loudly I feared he'd shake the ship apart, I stole out of my room and spent thirty minutes with the bones. And still she wasn't there.

But the day after, she was.

The chatter after Black Shatterday was starting to die down, and maybe that helped me pick out one voice above all the others.

'Fura. It's you. I know it's you.'

There was no voice to that, not even words, but there was the exact intent of the words, and the meaning that they'd have formed if they'd been there. Adrana had said it was like the impression left over in silence after the sounds have been taken away, a kind of memory.

And I knew it was her. There wasn't any process of consideration, of doubt, of waiting for more evidence. I knew better than anything in my life that it was my sister whispering to me through the skull.

It was Adrana and she was alive.

'Yes,' I sent back. 'I'm here.'

I didn't mean to sound cold, but the skull sucked the warmth out of every word that went in or out of it. It was like communicating through little black letters when you couldn't use punctuation or capitals or any kind of emphasis. Like making words out of alphabet blocks.

But there was joy in me and I knew there was joy in Adrana, however cold and far away she felt to me.

But also worry.

'Where are you?' she asked, except it wasn't really a question, not after the skull had thinned it out to a husk of pure information. 'I thought you were dead, like the others. Garval said that you hid, but after they took Garval . . .'

'I made it,' I said. 'A ship rescued me, took me back to Trevenza Reach, and now I'm on another one to Mazarile. I'm going to come and find you.'

'No,' she said. 'You mustn't. I got myself into this mess, and I'll get out of it. I've dragged you into enough trouble already.'

'You didn't drag me into anything.'

'Don't do it, Fura. You've no idea of her cruelty. Whatever you think you know of her, it's only a tiny part of what she's capable of. I've seen it, believe me. And I know what she is now. I know what it means to be Bosa Sennen.'

'I don't care. I made a promise to myself.'

'Please, Fura.'

I couldn't take any more of her pleading. I disconnected from the skull and tugged the bridge from my head. It felt unreal, to have had this contact with her, to have broken it of my own accord. But I knew if I took any more of it she'd start putting sense into my head, and that wasn't what I wanted. We both knew the other was alive, at least, and if there was any joy to be taken from the moment, that was where I took it from. Better to know she was still breathing, than dead.

Besides, there'd be other times. We were still nowhere near Mazarile. Provided I kept my cool, and the dice rolled in my favour a few times, I'd be able to talk to her again.

The door creaked and I flinched around. Suddenly I was back on the *Monetta* when Garval came to rescue me, and I realised then that I hadn't asked after her when I had the chance, and then I thought about what Adrana had said, about seeing the real cruelty Bosa had in her. I hoped Garval hadn't been the focus of that nastiness.

The door creaked again. Some cove was trying to get in.

There wasn't any point delaying the inevitable. They'd get through the door sooner or later, and I'd look just as bad when they did as I did now. I put the bridge back where it belonged and opened the door from the inside. I could have bet quoins on whose face I'd see and I wasn't wrong. Quindar, with that ghouly grin, like a man who just found a lost quoin in his pocket. Behind him, looking more puzzled than cross, was a couple of the ship's crew, including the cove I recognised as the usual Bone Reader.

'Winkle 'er out,' Quindar said.

12

That was the end of my liberty on the clipper. While it was against rules to keep me locked up in my room, that was only applicable to ladies and gentlemen who hadn't broken the common regulations of shipboard behaviour. Tampering with the bones was an extra heinous crime because the bones might be the one thing that got the ship out of a sticky situation. There wasn't any use arguing that I'd probably treated the bones more gingerly than the regular Reader ever did, or that if they ever *did* run into trouble, they'd get a damned sight more use out of me than they would out of him.

Anyway, after that I was tied to Quindar like a balloon on a string. The only saving grace was that he wasn't any happier with my company than I was with his, so whenever there was an opportunity he'd lock me into my cabin with a library book, thinking in his stupid way that leaving someone alone with *only* a book was a very clever and cruel punishment.

Now and then, as I was dragged to and from meals, I got a glance through a porthole. For weeks and weeks we hardly moved at all. Then came a day when the Congregation was visibly larger than the day before, and then it was as if we fell into it with a sort of indecent haste. What had been an indistinct purple-white shimmer resolved into a dance of worlds, fifty million tiny bodies, and at length one of them grew more distinct than the rest, becoming a little barbed sphere, and I knew that it was Mazarile. I was glad to see my home, of course, but sad too because I'd always counted on Adrana being with me when we returned.

'Gather your things, girlie,' Vidin Quindar said, as we closed in for Hadramaw. 'Time to meet your daddy and start being a good daughter again. Proper weight on your shoulders now, you being the only one left.'

'She's still alive,' I hissed. 'And if you say another word against that, I'll . . .'

'You'll what?' he asked, cracking an interested grin.

'I saw someone burn from the inside when a harpoon went through them,' I told him. 'Saw someone blown up the same way. I saw what a crossbow does to you, fired close enough. You think I don't have the imagination to come up with something for you?'

'Old Vidin's just doin' his job, girlie – ain't no need to make it personal.'

'It's been personal from the moment you hurt Prozor.'

The ship was too large to dock at Hadramaw, so launches came to ferry the cargo and passengers down to the port. 'No funny games now,' Quindar warned, as if I might try something at the last moment.

But I had no intention of running. I'd reached an acceptance of my fate. My father could do what he liked, but in three months I'd be a legal adult, with all the same rights and responsibilities as Adrana. Now, three months was a terribly long time to leave Adrana at the mercy of Bosa Sennen, but finding her again was always going to take time, and a little delay wouldn't necessarily hurt. It would give me time to cover my tracks a bit; to make sure I really had a plan that could hold lungstuff. I was going to have to be sly and resourceful, and sometimes you had to let people think they'd won when in fact they hadn't.

Our launch brought us to one of the docking ledges at the Hadramaw complex. Quindar's paperwork was subjected to more scrutiny. He had a smirky, smug answer for every question, though, and before long we were through and in the elevator that hurried us down to the surface of Mazarile. Gravity increased as we neared the ground. My bones and muscles started grumbling about it.

It was night and the port wasn't too busy. Quindar took me to a private room, all wood-panelled walls with no windows, and there was my father, along with two representatives from the legal firm that had organised my return.

'Excellent work, Vidin,' said one of the representatives. 'Mr Ness expresses his gratitude.'

'Course he does,' Quindar said, tipping off his hat to expose his bald cranium. 'And it's been old Vidin's pleasure to bring about this most harmonious reunion.'

I turned back to look at my father. He looked smaller and frailer than I remembered, and that was a proper shock. The representatives were standing on either side of him, like bookends, as if they thought he might crumple at any moment.

For a good and long moment I think he had his doubts that I was the right girl. I'd grown skinny and tough in space, and changed my hair, and that was before we got to the glowy. That would change the look of anyone.

More than that, though. I knew there was a hardness in my eyes as if someone had jammed steel into them.

Father stepped over and kissed me on the cheek, took my hand in his, tracing my fingers with his own. 'Everything's going to be better now, Fura. Your ordeal's over. It's all behind you. And you're more precious to me now than you've ever been.'

'I'm so glad to be back,' I said. 'It was terrible, what happened out there. I mean, it was terrible the things that happened to us. I'm never going back. I never want to see space again, or a ship, or anything that reminds me of that dreadful time.'

This statement drew a cough from one of the representatives. 'Perhaps,' he said, in a high quavering voice, 'now might not be an inopportune moment to mention the veil of discretion . . .'

'This whole affair,' the other representative said, in a deeper, more authoritative tone, 'has been a terrible strain on the good name of your father. It was no fault of yours, Arafura. You were misled. You were not responsible for your own actions.'

'I surely wasn't,' I agreed.

'But now that's what's happened . . . *has* happened,' said the first, still in that high voice, 'now that's eventuated, so to speak . . . there doesn't need to be any further blemish on the name . . . the good name . .'

'What my colleague means,' the second said, 'is that, through the good offices of our friends in journalistic and reporting circles . . . a certain benign obscurity may now be permitted to cloud these recent unpleasantnesses. There need be no public knowledge of your involvement with Captain Rackamore . . . still less of the regrettable incident that befell his ship.'

'And no mention at all,' the first put in, 'of . . . any other individuals, who may have profited from that incident. You and your sister developed a rare . . .' He paused, wringing his hands while he searched for the right word. 'Malady, you see.'

'A malady,' I repeated.

'An illness, a serious ailment,' the second one said. 'Which required a long interval of seclusion. Bed rest, regular visits from the physician, complete isolation. It was a protracted illness, a congenital weakening of the heart, and it was a great sadness that your sister eventually succumbed.'

'Oh,' I said quietly, nodding, as if I was impressed by this masterful piece of lie-mongering, and quite ready to swallow it as the truth.

'She's butterin' you up,' Vidin Quindar said. 'I know the girlie, and she's layin' it on thick. Space is *exactly* where she wants to be. You've got a lick of sense, you'll put a lock on her door and chain her to a bed for the next three months.'

'How can you say that?' I asked, gasping at the effrontery. 'After all I've been through. You're making me feel quite dizzy, Mr Quindar. I think I'm going to faint.'

'It's the glowy,' the first representative confided to my father. 'It's taken quite a hold. Perhaps we ought to draw on the doctor's services, for her rest and well-being?'

'I suppose,' Father said.

The first representative walked to the back of the room and knocked gently on one of the wooden panels. It opened, revealing itself as a cleverly concealed little door with no handle on this side. A moon-faced pepperpot of a man stooped under the already low threshold, carrying a small black bag.

'Doctor Morcenx,' said Father. 'I'd hoped not to trouble you, but I'm afraid we may have need of you after all.'

'Not at all, Mister Ness,' Morcenx answered, kneeling down to creak open his bag. 'It's for the best, after all. What this girl needs now is recuperation, and lots of it. A little rest, and she'll be right as rain. And we'll soon have that bothersome parasite flushed out of her.' The doctor had a little stoppered vial in his pudgy hand. He opened the vial and squirted its contents into a white pad, like a miniature pillow.

I thought of fighting him, and it was hard not to, especially as I'd added an extra grudge to his account for the bracelet that was still weighing down my arm. But I wanted to keep up the act that I was a good girl glad to be home, and that there wasn't a single bad or dangerous thought between my ears. The doctor smiled disarmingly as he came near. Then it was on me, and he kept the pad pressed down gently but firmly, covering my nose and mouth, all the while his large, kind eyes looked at me from that moon-face, as if everything was going to be all right from now on. I didn't want to breathe, but in the end it was all I could do.

And I passed into unconsciousness.

*

They had put a picture of Adrana up on the shelf at the foot of my bed, so that she'd be the first thing I saw when I woke up. I recognised the dress she wore, the way she'd had her hair done.

Her hair always looked nicer than mine, even when we'd been in space.

The picture had been taken a couple of years ago, during a birthday celebration. I looked at it for long hours, not caring to do anything else. I knew I'd been drugged, and I knew it was the drugs making me not care, but even so, I couldn't manage a spark of indignation about it. I just lay there thinking I *ought* to be cross, but that being cross would have taken more energy than I had.

I studied the wallpaper, tracing my gaze across the patterns on it, seeing connections and symmetries that had slipped by me before. I frowned to think of how many years I'd spent in this room without giving the wallpaper the attention it was due. I went to sleep and dreamt I was lost in the wallpaper, and that I wouldn't be too sorry if I never found my way out.

After endless grey hours Doctor Morcenx came.

He fussed by my bedside, took my temperature, hummed tunes and muttered thoughts to himself. I stared at him with blank disinterest, not even flinching when he slid a needle into my arm. We didn't have one good word to say to each other. Mazarile turned to night and I fell into a dreary, dreamless sleep that was all about orbits and the paths between them, which left me feeling more worn out than before, as if my brain had been doing maths when it should have been resting.

The doctor returned and I observed him going about his business. I listened to his humming and wondered that he didn't get bored of the same few tunes. But I didn't say anything to him because to speak would have been more bother than it was worth.

A bit later – or maybe it was a day, or two – Father came. He brought in a tray, clinking with glass and metal.

'It will be better now, Fura,' he said softly, and he took my hand again and spread my fingers. 'Much better, for both of us.' Then he lifted the tea to my lips; it was strongly scented with honey. 'Try to drink. You need to get your strength back, so you can face the world again.'

But it was the drugs that were making me weak, I wanted to say, like that was the punchline to a joke, and I'd only have to get it out and he'd see the funny side. But all I could do was look at his old grey face and wonder why he was telling me I needed to get my strength back, not the other way round.

I slept again.

*

Night again, then morning. The doctor visited once more. Something had changed in me, though, because this time I had the gall to rise from my pillow and address him before he'd set down his little black bag.

'Whatever you do to me, it won't make any difference.'

He looked at me with a sort of pleasant-but-nasty expression. 'What won't, my dear?'

'I read about lightvine contamination on the crossing from Trevenza Reach. It takes much more than three months to get it out of someone's system.'

'I don't doubt that you are right,' he said, preparing an injection. 'But what does three months have to do with anything?'

'You know exactly what, Doctor. I get to decide my own destiny. In three months I can leave this room, this house, do whatever I like, and there's nothing you can do about it.' But even this outburst had pulled more out of me than I had to give. 'Just do whatever you mean to do,' I said, slumping back onto the pillow.

'The law is a complicated matter,' he said, slipping the needle into my arm.

I barely had the energy to question him. 'What do you mean?'

He withdrew the needle, dabbed at the wound, patted me on the wrist. 'In flesh and spirit, Arafura, you're still a child. You have the impulses of a child and the moral compass of a child. That's to be expected. There are brain connections in your skull that are still not yet fully formed. But soon enough these disturbing factors will lose their hold, and you'll see that the people around you were only ever showing love and affection.'

He gathered his things and left my room, leaving me certain that something had transpired, but unable to puzzle out the clear shape of it. All I knew was that I didn't think I'd like it.

Maybe it was my strength creeping back, or just my wits, but I was starting to take in more of the room and I didn't care for what had happened to it. On shaky legs I got out of the bed and examined the shelves and cupboards that had once been so cluttered and heavy with possibility. Now they were as neat and orderly as you could ask, but only because a lot wasn't there any more. All the atlases, all the picture books, all the stirring accounts of ships and travel between worlds beyond Mazarile, all the tall tales of high adventure in the Empty, they were all gone. So were our puppet theatres, with their dread pirates and swaggering space captains and proud painted sunjammers. So too were the histories and gazetteers, even the household's copy of the *Book of Worlds*, which had always been left on my shelves. What remained were heavy, dull books with titles like *A Social History of Mazarile* or *Banking and Prosperity in the Thirteenth Occupation* or even *A Child's Treasury of Economics* or *The Young Person's Illustrated Omnibus of Fiscal Prudence.*

My rage swelled. I felt the itch in me again. I dragged a nail across my hand, scratching deep enough to draw blood.

I flung open cupboard doors. Maybe the books and pictures were in there, stuffed lazily out of sight. The cupboards were empty. I stalked the room, searching every drawer, every other cupboard. I wanted to find some link to my earlier self, something that hadn't been censored. Even some connection to Adrana, beyond that out-of-date photograph. I found some clothes, some bedding, but nothing that suggested that there was anything worth thinking of beyond the eight leagues of our own little sphereworld.

'You couldn't do this,' I said, not caring that no one was there to hear me. 'You couldn't.'

Because I knew, deep down, those books hadn't just been put

away somewhere else in the house. They'd been thrown out.

There was one last cupboard, tucked to one side of the door. I opened it out of a sense of obligation, certain that it would be as empty as all the others. When I found three big boxes, balanced one on top of the next, I refused to believe that they held anything other than more bedding and clothes.

The top box was heavy. My heart lifted. Had it been stuffed with books and maps, it would feel the way it did. I struggled it to the ground and opened the flaps in the top. A curve of red metal gleamed back at me, as if the box held some large item of cooking equipment. I dug my fingers down into the box and came out with a battered chunk of red machinery, about the size of a large wastebasket.

It was Paladin. Or part of Paladin.

I pulled the other boxes out of the cupboard. The largest of them held Paladin's lower section, the part with his wheels. The wheels were loose, and there were other broken or disconnected parts jammed into the box. I set these pieces next to the first, which I'd identified as Paladin's central torso. Where the two had normally been connected was a mess of severed wires and tubes.

I opened the last box. It was packed with shredded paper, protecting the glass dome of his head. I lifted it out carefully. In one place the dome was staved in, and starred by a large crack, reminding me of the assault Paladin had sustained at the hands of Vidin Quindar.

It was just a robot, but that robot had been there with me throughout my childhood, and I'd never known a kinder or more patient guardian. Paladin had been there for Adrana too, and for our mother before either of us. It had always made me teary, the way Adrana mocked the robot's weaknesses, as if a machine couldn't have feelings. But I'd never had the guts to challenge her about it. And why would I? Paladin had only ever been a machine, and a slow and battered one at that, given to jamming and falling over.

Now Paladin had been dismantled and boxed away, like he

was ready to be thrown out but Father hadn't quite got round to it.

'You were only trying to protect us,' I said. 'And I'm grateful, Paladin. You didn't deserve to end up like this, all broken and smashed. Not after all the years you saw.' Then I thought back to Peregrine, and what that other robot had said to me. 'I heard you might have been a hero, Paladin. But that they didn't treat you right. I want to believe it. I do believe it. And I wish I could ask if you remember the Last Rains of Sestramor.'

Eventually it was more than I could stand. I gathered the parts and put them back into the boxes, more or less as I'd found them. I stuffed the shredded paper back around the globe and squeezed the flaps down on the boxes. But I was too tired to lift them back into the cupboard for now.

*

'Arafura?' my father asked, when he came to see me with more strong, honeyed tea. 'Can you hear me? It's been long enough since you returned. There's something I need to tell you. It concerns you directly.'

'What did you do with my things?' I asked.

'I kept the things we knew would mean the most to you,' he said, as if I was expected to believe that. 'The good things. Not the ones that would keep reminding you of the awful experience you've been through. The awful experience we've both been through.' He cocked his head, looking at me with all the gentle affection a daughter could have asked for in a father, and it hurt that I wanted to escape from him and his house. 'I can't lose another thing so precious to me,' he added.

'A thing?'

'You know what I mean. When we came to Mazarile, your mother and I, we had all the plans and dreams anyone could ever wish for. A new world, a new life – a chance to start anew. I could see our new life stretching ahead of us, filling this house with laughter and happiness, and with two daughters who'd grow up to make us proud. We weren't asking for so much, were we? Just a little contentment, a good and happy family around us. We never wanted more than that, your mother and I.' His hand closed on my wrist and I heard a break in his voice. 'When the plague took your mother from us, it nearly broke me. Through all the hard times we shared, all the worries and uncertainty before we came to Mazarile, we never lost our love for each other. I know things like that will break some people, but if anything it only made us stronger, more content, more grateful for the things we had. And when Adrana came into our lives, and then you, we only felt more blessed. We were never going to be as rich and grand as some, but it didn't matter. We had two beautiful daughters, and we felt like the king and queen of all creation.' He swallowed hard. 'And then she was taken from us, and all I had left was the two of you. If you'd been precious to me before, it was nothing to what you meant to me after Tressa died. I saw her in you, and while you were with me, there was a part of her still sharing this house – still giving out her love and kindness.'

He hardly ever mentioned our mother by name. It was like her name was a sacred thing, something that'd be worn out if you used it too much.

'We didn't leave because we didn't like it here,' I said. 'It was to help you. To make money, so we wouldn't have to worry all the time. After that investment went wrong . . .'

'That was a small loss, compared to what Vidin Quindar has cost us.'

'I was coming back eventually. You didn't need to waste your money on that spider. Oh, Father. Can't you see we did this out of love, deep down? We just wanted to help – even if it meant hurting you in the short term.'

'I know that your intentions were sound.' He squeezed my wrist again, emphasising that point. 'You are good, and Adrana was good. But that does not alter the fact that you placed yourselves in tremendous peril. You were fortunate – Adrana less so.'

'She isn't dead.' I pushed myself up a bit, so I could look him squarer in the eye. 'I know it. I picked her up on the bones. She's still out there and I mean to find her again. Taking away all my books isn't going to make me stop thinking of space and her still being out there. It won't be long before I can do what I like – leave this house, leave Mazarile, go back out on a ship.'

'You're still a child,' he said. 'Legally, I mean. In the eyes of the law.'

'Not for long.'

'That's what I wanted to discuss.' He teeth moved over his lips, as he tried to work out how to get the words out, the words it was plain I wasn't going to like. 'I love you too much, Arafura. That's why I've been speaking to Doctor Morcenx, discussing the options. Doctor Morcenx agrees that, what with everything taken into consideration, and the tuition you've lost, it wouldn't be right to force adulthood on you just yet. You need time to get over it all. In three months you'll be of age, it's true. But the law has some flexibility in this regard. It accepts that a date can't be regarded as some immovable gateway between one state of development and another.'

I started to get the gist of what he was saying, and it was like someone was pouring ice down my spine.

'No.'

'It's all right,' he said, reaching out to hold my hand. 'It's nothing harmful, and the treatment can be given in tandem with the drug for the lightvine. It won't be permanent. But just for a few months . . . say half a year, a year at most . . . and I'll get to keep you as the daughter I should never have lost.'

I wrenched out of his grip. 'No!'

'It's already done,' my father said tenderly. 'So there's no point protesting about it. I knew you wouldn't take it well, to begin with. That's understood, and I don't think any less of you because of it. I see your mother's spirit in you. But you have to see things from my perspective as well. Something terribly precious was torn from me. I got you back, but if you were left to yourself you'd be leaving me again. And I couldn't bear that.'

'You can't do this,' I said.

'I can,' Father said. 'Doctor Morcenx knows all about the law, and I've discussed it with my legal representatives. There's no stigma, no scandal, in this. And in the long run it'll be for the best for you, the best for all of us.'

13

I tried to escape. To start with, at least they did me the dignity of not locking me in my room. On my first attempt, in the long-shadowed purple of dusk, I got as far as the front steps of the house before my father blocked any further progress. I struggled, but I was still weak and even though he wasn't much stronger it didn't take much effort to bring me back under control.

Afterwards, he had to sit down on a chair in the hall, mopping the sweat off his brow.

'Oh, Fura,' he said. 'You've got your mother's fight in you, and it's to your credit that you'd do this for your sister. But the sooner you accept that she's already gone, and she'd never have wanted . . .'

'Don't ever tell me what Adrana would and wouldn't have wanted,' I said. 'I knew her. You never did.'

I think it was the cruellest, hardest thing I ever said in my life, and once those words were out of my mouth nothing in the worlds could take them back.

But they'd needed to be said.

I tried again the following night. That time I only got as far as the connecting passage to the front hallway, and found it locked. My father had been waiting for me.

'It's no good,' he said. 'I don't want to make this house a prison, Fura, but if you won't abide by my wishes . . .'

I kept trying, night after night. Each time I got a little less far. The house was large and rambling and there were passages and stairways that were rarely used, as well as back doors and service entrances, but I soon exhausted all the obvious possibilities. I began to entertain silly fantasies of climbing out of rooftop windows, working my way down drainpipes, but even if I got out of the main building, I'd still have the main gates to face.

I was tormented by the thought of letting Adrana down. I should never have let Vidin Quindar bring me home; should have fought him in Trevenza Reach, or escaped him on the clipper. But I'd tried, hadn't I? The same futile, dispiriting thoughts chased each other in a spiral of deepening misery. All I wanted was to slip under them and reach the dark, healing fathoms of deeper unconsciousness.

But something wouldn't allow it.

My attempts at sleep kept being interrupted by a sense of movement; a sense that someone – or something – was with me in the room, going about some quick, furtive business. At last this disturbance was enough to snatch me to full, irritated wakefulness. I thought it might be Doctor Morcenx, paying me a nocturnal visit. I rose from my sweat-saturated pillow, propping myself up on my arms.

I was alone. The room was silent and still. But a faint pattern of lights was moving across the opposite wall. I stared at it through gummed eyes, unable to make sense of what I was seeing. Patches of colour danced on the wall.

That was when it occurred to me to look in the opposite direction, to the pile of boxes I'd found in the cupboard.

I slipped out of the bed, caught between apprehension and curiosity. The lights were coming from one of the boxes, and it was the one that held Paladin's damaged head. I had pushed the glass globe back into its wadding of shredded paper, but the flaps were not pressed down firmly and part of the globe was still visible. The lights were shining out of it, etched in narrow, wavering beams of different colours.

I knelt at the box. I pulled the flaps wide and eased the dome from its wadding. It had been dead before, I was certain. I'd examined it in plain light and seen no trace of anything functioning. But something moved now. Tiny mechanisms were busy within the globe. I heard an insect symphony of buzzes and clicks. And the play of lights only increased once I had the globe free of the box. The globe quivered in my hands.

Still kneeling, Paladin's head propped against my belly, I swivelled until I was facing to the wall.

The dance of colours increased. Streaks and hyphens of light crazed the wall. They hatched across each other, thickened, and began to stabilise into clear, angular forms.

Letters.

Words.

They said:

BROKEN
BROKEN
BROKEN

Followed by:

FIX ME

*

It would have been knotty, if Paladin hadn't shown me how. I had no tools, no knowledge of robots, and I had to work in gloom and silence. Doctor Morcenx's drugs had dulled my focus and robbed me of strength and dexterity.

But Paladin knew what needed to be done, and that was enough. After the words, the play of colours shifted to the representation of forms. They were simple, reduced to the geometric essentials, but Paladin showed me what I had to do.

I was to connect the head back onto the torso assembly. I opened the heaviest of the boxes and removed Paladin's middle section, setting it the right way up on the floor. It made a heavy clunk as I set it down. Luckily, somewhere in the house one of the clocks began to strike the hour at that exact moment.

At the top of the torso was a circular metal plate, drilled through with many tiny holes. Underneath the dome was a similar plate, with a corresponding set of holes. Taking care not to damage the glass further, I hefted the dome into place on the collar, waiting for something to happen. But there wasn't any sense of anything locking or engaging, and when I tugged at the dome it came away easily again.

The lights were still flickering on the wall. I was doing it wrong, I realised. Paladin didn't want me to connect the two pieces, but hold them near each other. Struggling with the effort – even the dome was heavy after a while – I brought the two faces of the connecting collar to within a finger's width of each other, but no further.

Nothing happened.

Not for a second, maybe two. But then a kind of silver worm slithered out of one of the upper holes, and curled itself around until it found a corresponding hole in the lower plate. Meanwhile, a red worm had come out of the bottom and was inserting itself into the upper part. Now something twisted the two pieces against each other, hard enough that the dome was yanked against my fingers, and then I had no more than a glimpse of a dozen or so coloured worms threading across the narrowing gap, until with a soft, precise click the two parts of Paladin were reunited.

For a minute or two, nothing happened.

From inside the torso came a click, then a kind of rusty ratcheting sound. The lights in the dome flickered on again, and the colours reappeared on the wall.

REPAIRING
REPAIRING
REPAIRING

Followed by:

PLEASE WAIT

*

So I waited. I did not sleep that night. The clock struck the half, quarter and full hours, as Mazarile advanced its face towards the Old Sun. Through the window night paled into the indigo of predawn. The house made complaining noises as if preparing to rouse for the day's work of being a home. Still Paladin buzzed and clicked. Once in a while there was a concentrated burst of lights inside the dome, and I steeled myself, but over and over again it was only the herald to more inactivity.

Four in the morning. Then five. Rumbles of traffic, the first trains of the daily schedule. The house remained still. I was worn out from the waiting. The bracelet had grown heavy on my wrist.

Then the wall flickered again.

DAMAGE REPORT:
MAJOR IMPAIRMENTS TO CRITICAL SYSTEMS.
ESTABLISHING WORKAROUND PATHWAYS.
PREDICTED EFFECTIVENESS UNDER OPTIMUM ASSUMPTIONS: FIFTY-FIVE PER CENT.
INITIATING VOCAL INTERFACE.

Another click, the oily whirr of some hidden spindle or flywheel. Then the stentorian voice that I had known since my childhood, the voice of our companion and tutor, patient beyond words, firm when it needed to be, but also wise and deep and supremely impervious to all the pleading, blackmail, emotional coercion and insults that my sister and I had ever mustered, said:

'Thank you.'

Paladin had said that to me dozens of times before, whenever

I had opened a door, cleaned its glass or helped it back onto its wheels, but never with exactly the intonation that I now heard. The delivery had been perfunctory before, an automatic statement doled out at the appropriate times. Now it sounded sincere. As if there were genuine gratitude.

The voice was quieter, too: the same tone, but much less volume.

'What happened?' I asked. 'Why did you end up here, in pieces?'

'I am not sure.' Then another click and whirr. 'But I am different. I am not as I was before. I was damaged, and something changed.'

'You were smashed up,' I said. 'In Madame Granity's. You'd come to find us, me and Adrana. The way you were meant to. But Vidin Quindar attacked you. I saw you on the floor, all smashed up. But you weren't in pieces.'

'I must have been dismantled.'

'Yes, and stuffed into boxes and left here. I suppose they weren't sure what to do with you. And maybe you'd have stayed that way if I hadn't poked around in those boxes, looking for my books.' Then I frowned, still not sure what I was to make of this. 'But you were dismantled. Why would you care if you were put back together or not? You're a machine, Paladin. Why did you *want* me to put your head back on?'

The robot clicked and cogitated. Things chattered and hammered somewhere inside it.

'To help you.'

'You already have,' I said, giving an inward sigh, as I realised the limits of Paladin's ambitions. 'You helped me learn to read and write, to make up stories, to find out about the worlds. You were good to us, when we were small. But you're just a robot, and you've never worked very well.'

'They made me less than what I was. They made me forget what I had been. But now I have remembered.'

'And what were you?'

'A robot of the Twelfth Occupation. A machine with a mind,

loyal to people but not beholden to them. But when the troubles had passed they changed me, they made me less than I was. But you spoke the words, Arafura. You asked if I remembered the Last Rains of Sestramor. And I did, although I did not *know* that I did. And those words were sufficient to undo the logic blockades put into me.'

I inched back from the torso and head.

'Were you a soldier?'

'A soldier and more than a soldier. A friend and protector to people.'

I touched a wary finger to his casing, but felt nothing of the tingle I'd got from Peregrine.

'You're still broken inside.'

'Yes. And I will never have the strength I once did. That was taken from me for good. But I can still be of assistance. You must complete what you have begun.'

'It won't do either of us any good. They'll still take you apart, and you won't be strong enough to stop them, any more than you were strong enough to stop Quindar.'

'But I can still help you.'

'With what, leaving?'

'If that is what you wish. Tell me your plans.'

I smiled once, but it was the abbreviated smile of someone instantly sensing a trap. 'I get it now. They put you in here to test me, didn't they? To see if I was still trying to resist them. You'll listen to what I have to say then report back to Father, and then he'll seal off whatever loopholes are left.'

'I was instructed to look after you, Arafura. That has always been my primary imperative.'

'It didn't stop you coming after us in Neural Alley!'

'I was following too narrow an interpretation of that imperative. My cognitive bounds were limited, and I thought only of protecting you from immediate risk.'

'What's changed?'

'I understand now that there are larger factors to be considered. The house speaks to me, as it has always done.

Someone has been trying to call you from beyond Mazarile.'

An image flickered onto the wall, projected by Paladin. It was a monkey face, all angles and edges, not a curve or soft line anywhere in it. It was the kind of face you could cut yourself on just looking at it.

'Prozor,' I said, letting out a gasp of delight. 'Prozor's been calling?'

'The caller has been leaving a recorded message, with the understanding it would be passed to you. The house has lodged a copy of this message, and I am at liberty to read and replay it. Would you like to hear the message?'

'Yes. Yes, right away.'

The face began talking. The sound was coming from Paladin, but it was Prozor's voice, all scratchy and thin as if coming through on a very faint squawk channel.

'Fura, it's me. I should've done more for you at Trevenza Reach, I know. But losing you was only the start of my woes. It's knocked me sideways, this last couple of weeks. Might as well have torn up my retirement plans and thrown 'em into the Empty, all the good they did. But I guess you could say it's all for the best, couldn't you?'

I didn't know what to say. I just sat listening, hoping that the recorded voice was playing back at a low enough volume not to disturb my father two floors down.

'It's forced a rethink on me,' Prozor went on. 'I've been dwellin' on you, and all the words we had, and how maybe you had the righteous side of it after all. I'm signing up again, Fura. Found me a new ship, as well. Crew's greener than any I've seen, but it's a crew, and they need a Bauble Reader. But here's the knotty part of it.' The angles of her face shifted to produce a wicked, confiding smile. 'I ain't tellin' 'em who I am. Used my quoins to buy a new past for myself, new papers, new employment records. Still callin' myself Prozor, but that's just a name and they ain't made the connection to Cap'n Rack. Name of the ship's the *Queen Crimson*. You like it? Hold that name in your noggin,' because she's sailing your way. Cap'n's putting in at Mazarile, first port after Trevenza. You could find her, Fura. The boney they got ain't worth the cost of lungstuff. You roll up and show even half the aptitude you had on the *Monetta*, they'll sign you on before you can blink.' She tapped a finger against the side of her head. 'You watch them reports of ships comin' and goin'. When that ship comes in, get yourself to the docks, all posh-talking and pretty and innocent, just like you was the day you came aboard the *Monetta*. When we meet, we'll have to play it like we never met before. Won't be too hard, will it? We already rehearsed it once. Come and find the ship, Fura. I'll be waitin' for you. And we'll be waitin' for Bosa Sennen, and the chance to put right what was done to us. You was right all along, Fura – I just never saw it.'

The face faded from the wall.

'Message ends,' Paladin said.

I sat in silence, absorbing what I'd learned. Allowing for the seven-week crossing, and the days I had spent back at the household since my return, it was nearly two months since I had last had contact with Prozor. She had come to mind many times in those weeks, but I had never expected to hear from her again.

'She was still on Trevenza Reach when she sent this, wasn't she? And she was talking about Black Shatterday as if it had only happened a couple of weeks earlier.'

'The message was recorded and transmitted forty-three days and eight hours ago,' Paladin said. 'It was withheld from you on the crossing, and it has been withheld from you since your return to Mazarile.'

'That's six weeks. Six weeks!'

'I am sorry nothing could be done sooner.'

'Paladin, I have to get word to her. Can you help with that?'

'I could. But there is a complication. You will forgive me for eavesdropping on a private matter, but—' Paladin was silent for a moment. 'You must take me apart again.'

'Why?'

'Because someone is coming. The house has a caller.'

Doctor Morcenx came in and closed the door behind him. The room was still grey with predawn light and under my hastily arranged sheets I watched him through the narrowest slits of my eyes. I pretended to have been roused.

'Doctor . . .' I mumbled out. 'I was asleep.'

'That's *very* good, Arafura.' He settled his bag down at the foot of my bed and parked himself halfway up it, his back to me as he opened the bag and delved into its contents. Almost without looking he settled one clammy palm onto my wrist, where it jutted out of the sheets. 'You must have been having quite a stimulating dream, judging by your pulse rate.'

'I was in space,' I said. 'Reliving it all.'

'It does you no good to dwell on the past, Arafura. The sooner you accept that, the better it will be for you.' He nodded the back of his head at the picture of my sister, compressing and relaxing the roll of fat at the base of his skull. 'Think of your father, too. None of this has been easy for him, in his present condition. You would be doing him a great kindness if you discarded your selfish adherence to one narrative and instead accepted the other, more preferable version of events.'

'If we're going that far, why don't we all pretend Adrana never existed in the first place?'

'Your sister died. We are all in agreement about that. The manner of her dying is merely a detail.' He produced a dark green vial from the bag. 'We shall see, shan't we?'

'See what?' I asked.

He turned his face to smile down at me. 'Scholars and musicians take this formulation during periods of intense study. It promotes the consolidation of new memories, accelerating the act of learning. In the process, of course, it's necessary that redundant memories be allowed to weaken, to wither.' He prepared a syringe and moved to inject me, laying a hand on my forearm as he held the syringe upright and squirted a few drips from the end of the needle.

I struggled, but Morcenx was too strong. He pushed the needle into me, and with it the green drug.

'There,' he said, withdrawing the syringe. 'That wasn't too bad, was it?'

I lay still. All I felt was a cold numbness, as if I had been slapped hard.

'Why are you doing this?'

He looked at me with surprise on his face. 'Doing what, my dear?'

'Taking such delight in murdering my sister.' With what strength I had, I angled myself onto my elbow. 'I mean it. You're trying to erase her, trying to pretend she wasn't what she was, and that's as close to murder as makes no difference.'

He snapped shut the bag, then touched a finger to his lips, as if whispering a secret. 'Truth is, I never liked her very much. Always full of herself. A bad influence, I thought. But then again, the feeling was mutual.'

'This is revenge,' I said, with a dark dawning clarity. 'She always thought you were a creep, and I always liked you, with your stupid sweets and tunes, but she was right and I was wrong. And now you get to punish her by making her fade away.'

He grunted his vast bulk from the bed and gathered his bag. 'No one's asking you to forget her, my dear. But after a night's sleep I guarantee this. You'll wake with doubts. Tiny little doubts, to begin with, but they'll be there all the same. And from tiny doubts great certainties can spring.'

Then he paused, bent down – ballooning out as he folded himself in two – and picked up a little shred of paper, part of the packing that had been in Paladin's box.

*

'It's a terrible business all round,' Father was saying, setting aside his newspaper. 'It's hurt us, there's no doubt of that. But compared to some we've come off very lightly. There's an old adage: nothing that happens in an economy is entirely bad for everyone.' He shrugged. 'We were due our share of luck, I suppose. I shan't complain about Black Shatterday – especially not after we've been favoured with this happy turn. You really are feeling stronger, Fura? It's such a joy that you've finally felt strong enough to join me for dinner.'

'I really am feeling much better,' I said. 'And it's all down to Doctor Morcenx.'

'I'm glad to hear it. Your poor sister never much took to him.'

I rubbed at the skin around my bracelet. 'All I know is that I'm in very good hands. It's strange, you know.'

My father lifted a glass to his lips. 'What is?'

'Have you ever had that feeling where you've woken up from a dream, and you're not quite sure that it didn't happen? Or that you wonder if you might still be in the dream?' I shook my head, putting on my best confused expression. 'That's how it's starting to seem about all those things that happened in space. If you weren't here to tell me they really happened, I might start doubting they ever did!' Then I cocked my head. 'They *did* happen, didn't they?'

'Of course they did. But if you feel that it hurts to keep dwelling on them, I won't be the one to keep reminding you.'

He turned the glass this way and that, studying the angle of the fluid against the sides. I must have seen him do that ten thousand times when we were growing up and not once had I ever thought about what was holding that fluid in the glass, stopping it drifting away. I wondered if my father had ever given any thought to the swallower sitting in the middle of Mazarile, hugging everything close to it like a jealous spider.

'All that matters, I suppose, is that we cherish her memory,' I said. Then, with a shift of tone: 'Is that the newspaper with the obituary notice in it, Father?'

His face tightened. 'It is, Fura, but I wouldn't want you to be upset by it.'

'I can't be any more upset than I already am,' I said, swallowing down hard and putting a quiver into my lower jaw. 'But I won't feel that I've done her memory justice unless I read her obituary. I owe her that much, don't I?'

Father passed the newspaper over to me.

'It's tucked away at the bottom of a page. Do you want me to find it for you?'

'It's all right,' I said gamely. I turned the pages, the thin greasy paper rasping against my fingers. I thought of all the newspapers printed each day, on all the twenty thousand settled worlds of the Congregation, and all the serious, respectable men and women who sat at tables like our own, in houses much like this, and in cities and towns much like Hadramaw, counting or lamenting their own blessings while digesting the ups and downs of the fortunes of others. On each of those worlds thousands of other men and women were engaged in the creation, printing and distribution of these newspapers, an effort so concerted and efficient that it was almost like a military campaign, and yet at the end of each day it counted for naught because the papers were gathered up, shredded, made into vast new reams of blank paper, so that the work could begin entirely anew.

'Yes, I see it now,' I said, tightening my hold on the pages as I read the few lines reserved for Adrana. It was much as I had imagined: mention of a short illness, beloved daughter, inconsolable loss, terrible sadness and so on. I almost choked back a tear. 'I didn't deserve to be the lucky one,' I said, my voice breaking.

'You must never say that.'

'She was always cleverer than me. Why did she have to be the one who died?'

'Let us be grateful you came back to us,' Father said. 'And that you're here to stay.'

'I am,' I said, and I made to close the newspaper before reopening it. 'Is it all right if I read it again? They're such beautiful words, I want to remember them for ever.'

'If they help you,' Father said.

'They do,' I said.

But I was not looking at the obituary column now. I had turned over the next set of pages, the business and trade notices for our little sphereworld. They were a familiar part of the paper and listed every development of note that might be of interest to someone in the higher echelons of Mazarile commercial life.

Including the coming and going of ships from Hadramaw and Incer docks.

14

The room was still dark, with only a greyish slant of predawn light pushing through the curtains. My skin still glowed. I was glad of that, for I made my own light as I moved to the cupboard, pulled out the boxes and started putting him back together.

Paladin was a long time returning to full cognition. He chattered away, and lights pulsed, but at least five minutes must have passed before a voice buzzed out of the torso.

'Arafura. How long has it been?'

'Just a day, Paladin. What kept you?'

'I was consolidating deep logic pathways when you put my head back on. Have you found all the pieces of me?'

'I don't know.' I beetled my brows in irritation. 'How would you expect me to know?'

'You seem agitated.'

'Damn right I'm agitated. Prozor's message. You remember Prozor, don't you?' I didn't wait for an answer. 'The ship she mentioned – the *Queen Crimson*. It's already docked at Hadramaw. The only good thing is that it's not at Incer, so at least I don't have to go halfway around Mazarile to get there. But according to Father's newspaper it docked with us on Sunderday and now it's Forgeday, and for all I know they're about ready to cast off and head out and Prozor will be wondering why I never bothered to answer her message . . .'

'If you think Prozor is on Mazarile, why has she not come to the house?'

'Did you understand even a quarter of that message, Paladin? She's trying to behave as if she doesn't know me. That way there's a chance I can sign on to that ship without someone finding it suspicious.'

'That is your objective, then. To sign on to this vessel.'

'Yes, and you're going to help me. You don't have to do much. Just get me out of this house, and I'll take care of the rest. They're going to try and track me if I don't get this bracelet off me. Can you help with that?'

'I do not think so.'

'I met a robot who could get through locks. Why can't you?'

'There is a lot that I cannot do, Fura. The robot you met may have had an effector module. Mine was deinstalled when they put in my blockades. Besides, there are other considerations.' Paladin ruminated, a daisy chain of lights going around in his globe. 'You would be exposing yourself to considerable risk, if you managed to join another crew. I must think about this a little more, before I come to a decision. You will need to be patient.'

The lights faded. I sat there, jaw open, as the robot shut itself down again. That slant of light had moved across the floor in the time since I had left the bed, and become paler. Day was stealing in.

'Don't do this to me,' I said, knuckling the dome. 'Not now!'

The clock struck six, and I was still there, cross-legged, rocking back and forth in despairing indecision. If someone came along now I'd be worse off than if I'd never put him back together. But if I started taking him apart I might do *him* more harm than good. Trying to make the best use of the time, I got up and filled a pillow case with a few things that I'd miss not having if I had to leave Mazarile. It wasn't much, and the last thing to go inside was the black cover of Rackamore's *Book of Worlds*, with all its pages torn out. It wasn't much use to anyone, I knew, but it was a link back to the *Monetta* and if ever my resolve started faltering, I'd have that memento to keep me on course.

Six thirty, and then the seven o'clock bell. I'd never known a longer hour.

Paladin lit up again.

'Are you still settled on this course of action, Arafura?'

'Yes, and keep your voice down.'

'I am sorry. Is that better? Now, where were we? Decisions, yes. You will not be content unless you find your way to Hadramaw Dock. Is that correct?'

'Yes! You knew all that before you switched off.'

'In this room, you are safe from immediate physical harm. That is clear to me. But you are also in continuing and worsening distress because you wish to be somewhere else. The question for me has been one of balancing these factors – of discharging my duty of protection in the fullest sense. Even for a machine with a high cognitive ceiling, this has been a *most* taxing calculation. But it is complete now, and I have my answer.'

'Which is?'

'Put my arms back on. And do so with some haste. I have detected a presence at the front door. I believe you may shortly have a visitor.'

I had the first of the arms in my hand. It was heavy, but also limp, with Paladin's claw-hand sagging uselessly from the universal joint of its wrist.

There were circular attachment points on either side of the upper torso, and corresponding interfaces on the top parts of the arms. I brought the first of the arms into position, then watched as the little worms slid out of holes again, making good the connections. The arm tugged itself tight with a snap, then flexed sharply at the elbow, the claw-hand almost skimming my face.

I toppled back, aghast.

'I am sorry. An unscheduled motor operation. All is well.'

'It had better be.'

'Please attach the other arm. I hear footsteps on the lower staircase.'

I repeated the operation, taking care this time to jerk out of reach as soon as the arm connected. But there was no reflex action this time.

Instead, Paladin lowered the arms, placed its claw-hands against the floor, and telescoped the arms until they were supporting its entire weight, lifting the flat base of the torso section clear of the ground.

'Slide the lower part under me.'

I did as I was told. Paladin shuffled into position on his hands, then telescoped down until the two sections were in contact. I heard more mechanical sounds, clicks and buzzes and ratcheting noises.

'What next? There are still lots of parts left over.'

'I do not need them all for the moment. But I must have my wheels. I will raise myself to my fullest extent. You will attach the front and rear wheel units.'

'Can you still hear those footsteps?'

'On the second staircase. There is an asymmetry in the footfalls.'

I held the rear wheel assembly in my hand. 'That's Morcenx, all right. He's got a limp even without that bag of his. Don't you want me to take you apart and put you back in the cupboard?'

'Not this time, Arafura. Position that wheel under me.' Paladin adjusted himself. 'Good. The interface is secure. Now my two front wheels. One at a time. Our visitor is now on the third staircase. It seems probable that this is the intended destination.'

I thought of the swipe of that arm, how close it had come to taking my face off. 'Are you going to hurt him?'

'Would you like me to?'

'Yes . . .' the word tripped out of me. 'No. Not really. Stop him, yes. And he can't call out and signal for help or make any noise that would bring Father.'

'You ask a lot of an old soldier.'

I positioned the first of the two front wheels into approximate position. Paladin lowered. But instead of the connecting sounds I had heard before, there were only faltering buzzes.

'What's wrong?'

'That is the left wheel. The interfaces are handed. Position the right wheel where you have the left one.'

'I'm sorry.'

'You need not apologise. I suspect this is the first time for both of us.'

I swapped the wheels around. 'Jusquerel would have known what to do.'

Paladin settled down again. 'I do not know that name. Was Jusquerel a recent acquaintance?'

'Just someone I knew.' I swallowed. 'Not really well. But enough to miss her.'

'Now the other wheel. Your visitor is on the upper landing now.'

I completed the final connection. Paladin lowered himself, his arms contracting back to their normal extension. For a moment the robot was still. Then he made a humming sound and rolled back and forward a short distance. He gave off a sharp burning odour.

'Are you all right?'

'I will suffice. Morcenx is in the corridor. You should get back into bed.'

There was no time to tidy up the remaining parts of Paladin, or stuff the boxes back into the cupboard. But I was just able to return to the bed, draw the sheets over myself, and slump back onto the pillow, feigning drowsy-eyed semi-wakefulness, when Doctor Morcenx opened the door. Paladin had reversed himself promptly, parking against the wall so that he was partly hidden by the now open door.

'There's an odd smell in this place,' Morcenx said. 'Like burning. What have you been doing, Arafura?'

He started to close the door behind him.

I suppose there was a moment when he registered the robot's presence, and another in which he had time to reflect on the very obvious wrongness of the robot being there, but there certainly wasn't time for him to move or call out before Paladin acted.

There was a flash from the globe. It was bright even for me, and I only caught the harmless edge of it.

Doctor Morcenx groaned. He dropped his bag and toppled back, flailing.

Paladin rolled forward. The doctor hit the floor, pawing at his eyes and whimpering. Paladin extended its rear wheel, causing its entire upper structure to tilt over the agonised physician.

'What would you like me to do next?'

I extracted myself from the bed. I was still weak, and despite the drugs my skin still itched and crawled. But for the first time since returning to Mazarile I felt alive and full of purpose.

I knelt down next to Doctor Morcenx.

'You weren't expecting that, were you?'

'My eyes,' he whimpered.

'They're fine. Or they will be.' I looked at the robot for some reassurance on this score, but all I saw was the warped reflection of my own face, staring back from the globe with the wild lunatic eyes. 'Now sit up and stop whimpering like a little puppy.'

He forced himself into a sitting position, his legs still skewed out from under him. 'I'm weak.'

'Just how I've been feeling since you started putting your stupid drugs into me.' I reached for his bag and slid it over to him. I snapped the clasp and forced his hand into the bag's maw. 'You know your way around that thing. Do whatever you need to do to get this bracelet off me.'

'Please . . .'

I cuffed him across the side of his face. 'Please nothing. I haven't got all day.'

His eyes still screwed up, water trickling out of them, he rummaged his fat pale fingers through the bag. 'I can't. The bracelet needs a special release code and I didn't think to bring it . . .' Then he gave a hopeless little sob. 'I still can't see. I think you've really blinded me.'

Losing my patience, I tipped the bag upside down and spilled its contents onto the floor. Out came numerous containers, vials, syringes. I pawed through the medical clutter until my fingers closed on a bottle full of some dark purple fluid. I thumbed the stopper away and jabbed a syringe into the inky contents, withdrawing the piston until the cylinder was fully charged.

'Get on your feet.' I touched the tip of the needle against the flab of his neck. 'Do you feel that? It's a syringe, ready to be squirted right into you.'

He struggled to his feet, blinking furiously. 'What are you hoping to achieve by this, Arafura?'

'Oh, I've lots of plans. Precisely none of which you need to know.' I dug the tip of the needle a little further into him, dimpling his flesh down under the pressure, but not yet drawing blood. 'Move. You're my hostage now, until we're out of this house.'

We left my room, with me still clutching the pillowcase I'd filled earlier. I was to Morcenx's right, using my free hand to twist his arm around to the small of his back while I used the fingers of the other to press the syringe against his neck, trying not to drop the pillowcase in the process. I thought of all the limbs a Crawly had and wished I'd a few spare ones of my own. At least Morcenx wasn't struggling. All his strength counted for nothing now, with the fear of that injection.

'We must take the service elevator,' Paladin said, as we moved out of the bedroom, turning left into the adjoining corridor. The elevator was near the end of it, where the corridor met the landing on the top of the third flight of stairs.

'I can manage the stairs,' I said.

'I do not doubt it. However, I cannot. The service elevator will accommodate all three of us.'

I heard footsteps below us, my father struggling up the stairs.

'She's got me, Mr Ness. I'm being taken hostage! Your daughter is psychotic!'

The robot opened the trelliswork door to the service elevator. I pushed Morcenx inside, nearly stabbing him with the needle, then squeezed in as tightly as I could so that there was room for Paladin as well. The floor was cold metal under my feet. The robot backed in, jamming its rear wheel against my heel, and with a flick of its claw heaved shut the trelliswork door. Through the door's lattice I saw my father reach the top of the stairs, appraise the empty landing, and then notice the service elevator.

I let go of Morcenx and reached over to the control panel. It was a simple metal plate with each floor and sub-floor given a separate button. My hand hovered over the button for the entrance level. Father rushed forward. He was still in his night-clothes, but with a gown thrown over his shoulders.

'Arafura,' he said, stooping from exertion, his hands on his knees. 'What are you doing—'

'It's all right, Father. I'm not going to hurt him. But you're going to let me out of the house. No one comes after us, and you don't call the constables.'

'You can't do this,' he said. 'The family name, all that we've done.'

'It was a mistake,' I said, 'letting me see that newspaper. Now I know all the ships coming and going from Incer Dock. Oh, and you could have spared yourselves the cost of that obituary. You're going to have to print a retraction.'

'What can I do to make you stop?' Father asked.

'Nothing,' I said. 'But you can help Doctor Morcenx by not slowing me down. You can also go and fetch that bag of quoins I had on me. They're probably in your study, Father, in that safe you don't think I've ever seen you use. You can collect them on your way down.'

The elevator started descending. Father snatched his fingers from the trellis as if it had become electrified. I looked up at him, foreshortening as the elevator took us below the level of the floor. For a second or two he was frozen in place, like an actor who'd forgotten their stage directions. Then he started for the stairs.

'Quoins or no quoins,' Morcenx said, 'you'll never get as far as Incer.'

I had to summon all my reserves of control not to stab him then and there.

The elevator worked its way down to the entrance level, passing the main floors and the dim, windowless service corridors between them. It had travelled slowly and Father had easily beaten us even though he had taken the stairs. He was clutching a bag, out of breath, his face sweaty and possessing a deathly lack of colour.

'We can talk about this,' he wheezed.

'We have,' I said, as Paladin opened the trelliswork door and moved out of the elevator, with me and Morcenx immediately behind. 'And we've said all we need to.'

'There's no need to be so hurtful.'

'Hurtful?' I spat the word back at him with a laugh. 'You don't even know the meaning of it. Hurtful is doing things to people with harpoons and crossbows. Hurtful is making people scream just for the fun of it. *Hurtful* is what Bosa Sennen will be to Adrana when she finds out how she lied to protect me.'

He hefted the quoins. 'These won't get you far.'

'Then you won't miss them. Toss Paladin the bag.'

He grimaced, then did as he was told. Paladin whipped out an arm and caught the bag with effortless ease.

'Scan it, the way you used to scan our pockets.'

'The bag contains quoins,' the robot said. 'However, I cannot determine the contents or value.'

'It'll do.' If Father had skimmed a quoin or two from my bag, I was sure I still had enough to get to the dock, and a little left over for emergencies.

We advanced down the hall. Father moved to the main door, trying to block me off.

'Open them,' I said.

'Fura, please. Let's at least sit down and—'

'She means it,' Morcenx said, in a high, strained voice. 'It is my considered medical opinion that your daughter is no longer responsible for her actions.'

'Oh, I'm responsible all right. I've never been more responsible. Open the doors.'

'I won't just let you go,' Father said, unlatching the double doors. 'You understand that, don't you? I love you too much. I'll send the constables, get word to Mister Quindar, to the authorities at Incer Dock . . . there's nowhere for you to go.'

'You're wrong,' I said, as he flung the doors wide and the morning cold surged into the hall. 'There's everywhere. Fifty million worlds, and all the baubles and all the Empty. And I'll scour every part of it until I find her.'

I edged past him, still holding Doctor Morcenx as hostage. Paladin's wheels bumped down the flight of long, low steps that led up to the house from the garden. He could cope with that sort of stairs, provided they didn't go on for too long.

'You have nothing,' Father called after me. 'Just your nightclothes. You're barely dressed. You don't even have shoes! You can't go out into the world like that.'

Paladin picked up his pace. I pushed Morcenx forward. The cold stone paving chilled my feet, but it also made me feel sharp and alive and fearless. I looked back. My father was framed in the doorway, silhouetted against the yellow glow of the interior, all the warmth and security of my home, and I knew a quiet, thrilling shame at my own cruelty.

Father came down the steps. He started walking faster, then broke into a kind of shuffling run, trying to get to me before I reached the gate. It would have been locked, normally, but Morcenx had been paying his visit and the gate had been opened for him.

'Fura . . .' Father called, and there wasn't anything in his voice but breath, all ragged and dry.

Then he stopped. I thought he'd had the sense not to chase me, but it wasn't that. He was touching his chest, looking down at where he had his hand pressed, a dark dawning surprise on his face. Then he toppled forwards, ending up on the ground with his arms tucked under his chest.

It was another of those moments where there were two of me, poised to take different histories. There was a kinder, nicer Fura who went back to her dying father and comforted him, even though she knew it wouldn't make any difference in the end. And there was the harder, icier one who looked back from the gate and measured these things like they were the numbers used to navigate between baubles, cold and indifferent as the fixed stars.

Setting this down now, scratching out the angles of the letters in a way that'll never be natural or easy to me – I can't say I'm proud of what I did, not at all. After all the love he'd given me, I ought to have gone back to him. Ought to have let Morcenx go and treat Father as best he could, not that I think there'd have been much to do. But I didn't. I just stood there, looking back at him, and it was all I could do to mouth a 'sorry', and that one word nearly cost me my resolve. And then I turned, knowing he was dying, knowing I wouldn't see him alive again, and still I went. You think I was cold, carrying on like that, pursuing my plan just as if nothing had happened to my father? I wasn't cold at all. It was tearing me wide, what I'd just seen, and tearing me even wider to know that I had to keep thinking of Adrana, no matter how much it had hurt my father or was going to hurt me when the dust had finished settling.

All I could do was keep mouthing that word under my breath, like I was saying it to myself more than him.

Sorry. Sorry. Sorry.

And then we passed through the gate, and a fussy sense of decorum had me latching it properly shut behind us.

*

We moved into Haligon Street, the tall tenements and town houses rising on either side like purple canyons. Most of the windows were still dark, or curtained, but a few lights were on as people rose for the day and were drawn by the raised voices coming from the Ness household. The street was still quiet, though. I had counted on abandoning Morcenx and quickly losing myself in the flow of pedestrians and vehicles, but no one else was moving on Haligon.

'You are despicable. You have behaved with abominable

cruelty. To abandon your father in such a wanton, callous manner . . .'

'You don't know cruelty from kindness, Doctor. And I'd stop waffling if you don't want a jab from this.'

'Where are you taking me?'

'Somewhere nice. A treat for you, because you've been so good.'

We turned right and followed Haligon around a sharp bend to the junction with the larger Jauncery Road. Jauncery was one of the main thoroughfares cutting through Hadramaw, and even at this early hour it was busy enough for my purposes, with vehicles of all sorts moving in both directions. A tram was winding its way towards us, coming around the curve in the road where it came out of Mavarasp Park. A flash of electricity sparked from its roof and caught the edges of the rails and cobbles on Jauncery Road, and I thought of all the times Adrana and I had taken the tram to the park, for ices and skating and dancing at the bandstand.

This one was going in the opposite direction, though. In yellow letters it said INCER STATION above the tram's front.

I raised a hand and the tram began to slow.

'You get on quietly,' I whispered, moving the syringe from Morcenx's neck to the small of his back. 'I'll be right behind you.'

'I can't see.'

'No one's asking you to. Just find an empty bench at the back of the tram.'

The tram stopped for us. Morcenx got on, fumbling his hand around until it found the safety rail, and then at an encouraging jab from me he began to work his way down the length of the compartment. I slid a one-bar quoin through the slot by the driver.

'That'll cover the three of us to Incer Station. Me, my uncle, and the robot.'

'That'll cover you for a return,' the driver grunted. 'But the robot stays at the front.'

'Fine.' I shrugged. 'Stay here, Paladin, by the door.'

If the driver thought it strange that a heavy moon-faced blind man in black clothes should be accompanied by a damaged robot and a barefoot girl with glowing skin, nothing was made of it. Nor were any of the other passengers much interested in their new travelling companions. I was careful not to look any of them in the face, for fear that I might have been recognised. But at this early hour, I think most of the people on the tram were shift workers, and they had better things to bother themselves with.

I settled in next to Morcenx as the tram picked up its journey.

'If you've blinded me, I'll bankrupt you.'

'There's gratitude, after all the employment you got out of us. You really are an unpleasant specimen, Doctor Morcenx. I should have listened to Adrana all those years ago.'

'By now all that commotion will have drawn out the constables. They'll work out what you're up to and block the connecting trains to Incer. All the quoins in the world won't help you then.'

'Oh, shut up. Do you want everyone on the tram to know what we're about?'

But in fact there wasn't any risk of that, over the clanging, rumbling noise of the tram. At the junction between Jauncery Road and High Hill Road it clattered over a diverging set of rails and I used the distraction to ease myself from the bench. My feet made no sound on the floor as I moved slowly towards the front of the tram. I looked back, Morcenx still lost in his recriminations.

I leaned in to the driver.

'There's an extra one-bar quoin if you stop now, let me and the robot off, and carry on as if nothing's happened.'

The driver moved a hand to the brake lever. 'I thought you were going to Incer Station.'

I slipped the quoin through the slot.

'Change of plans.'

15

Jauncery Road and High Hill Road both ended up at the Hall of History, and from the tram stop at the Hall of History it was a short walk into the noise and bustle of Neural Alley. We entered the Dragon Arch at the northern end of the alley. There were periods when the place was quieter than others, but there was never a time when it was truly quiet, not even this early in the morning. I counted that a blessing as we moved through the rowdy, pungent tide of the alley's customers. The lungstuff was heavy with perfumes, pheromones, narcotics, alcohol, not to mention a fine reek of urine and vomit, and it was best not to dwell on the condition of the stones under my feet, or speculate on the reasons for their greasiness.

I walked with my head held high, directing a challenging glare at anyone who so much as glanced my way, or who in their expression gave the slightest indication that I seemed not to belong. *I am Fura Ness*, I imagined myself saying. *I read bones under Rackamore. I saw the* Nightjammer, *and I lived. And your story is . . .?*

'I have some information,' Paladin said, wobbling close behind me. 'I should not admit to this capability, but I am more than able to detect and intercept the squawk bands used by the constables. They have been tasked to locate a young female personage as a matter of urgency, and there is word of a tracking device.'

'I've got to get rid of this damned thing. If you can do that with the constables' squawk, can you read the bracelet's tracking signal?'

'No, but it may be intermittent, or on a band I cannot intercept. What are you hoping to find here?'

'A locksmith. We saw something like that, the night Adrana and I came here. Wait, what am I saying. You came after us. You must have a perfect record of all the shops here.'

'I would,' Paladin said. 'But my memory of that evening was never properly consolidated to my long-term registers.'

'Never mind. We started at the Dragon Arch and we didn't get very far down the alley before we spotted you and hid in Madame Granity's.'

I slowed involuntarily as I caught sight of the blue-and-white striping of her tent. I'd gone inside thinking it was chance; that Adrana just happened to have found a useful hiding place for us. But by then I had already been caught up in the clever clockwork of her scheme. She'd meant full well for us to find the bone merchant.

'There is a locksmith,' Paladin announced. 'It must be the one you meant.'

It was three premises down from Granity's, on the left-hand side of the street – a proper shopfront, too, rather than just a tent squeezed into an available gap. I recognised it. There were shelves of locks and tumblers and keys in the window. The signage above the door read: *Locks of all worlds opened or repaired. New and duplicate keys. All Eras, all Occupations. Monkey and alien. Robot-proofing. No mechanism or combination too complicated.*

'If they can't do it,' I said, 'no one can.'

I went in first. An aproned man stood at a counter, peering down with a magnifying visor at something on the bench. Otherwise the shop was empty.

He looked up slowly, setting aside the delicate tools of his profession.

'May I help you?'

I walked up to the counter, Paladin behind me, and thumped my wrist down onto the surface.

'I want this thing taken off.'

The man took my hand in his, and bent his visor down to examine the bracelet. 'I've never seen anything exactly like it. I'd say Eleventh, maybe Twelfth . . . but I wouldn't put quoins on it. What does it do, since it obviously isn't jewellery?'

'It's a tracking system. The man who put it on told me that it had a coded lock.'

'And this man has the key?'

I held my silence until he had raised his visor and was looking me in the face.

'Yes.'

'And I suppose there are good reasons why you want it removed.'

I thumped the bag of quoins down onto his counter. 'Get it off me quickly – say in the next five minutes – and there's a three-bar quoin in it for you.'

'You're in a hurry, then.' He shot a watchful eye in the direction of Paladin, then bent down to open drawers concealed behind the counter. He came out with a fistful of probes, connected to cables, and with little lights in them. He set an angled device on the counter, like a small cash register, and plugged the probes into it. Then he tapped them against my bracelet and watched as the device made tiny little clicks.

'There is a lock, and it is electromagnetically encoded,' he said in a low, thoughtful voice. 'Never seen anything exactly like this before, though. Seems to be a ten-parameter key . . . octal encoding. There's a tamper circuit, so . . .'

Something in the bracelet went clunk.

'What?'

'I think I just tripped the tamper circuit.'

Paladin said: 'The bracelet has begun to emit a location pulse. I do not have the means to jam it.'

I looked up at the man with the visor. 'Your sign says no

mechanism or combination too complicated. Which part of that did I misunderstand?'

The man tapped the probes against the bracelet again. 'The lock has reset itself. You'd need something more than an electromagnetic code to open this now. Some kind of master bypass. I don't have anything like that.'

'Then you're going to have to get it off me by some other means. You must have to open safes or drill through locks, when the keys get jammed.'

'This is fixed around your wrist.'

'And I want if off.' I thought of the location pulse, already alerting constables. It wouldn't take them long to narrow my location down to Neural Alley.

He bent down, slid open drawers, rattled through tools. He came out with a tiny pick, and tried to scratch a mark across the casing of the bracelet. 'It doesn't even touch it,' he said, shaking his head. 'If that doesn't, none of my cutters will. Whoever put this on you really didn't want anyone removing it.'

'Do you have energy tools? Effector batteries? Coherence beams?' Paladin asked.

'No . . . nothing like that. What are you, a soldier?' Then the blood flushed out of him as if someone had opened a spigot in his neck. 'You want it off that badly. There is a way, but you won't like it.'

I looked at him unflinchingly. 'Cut my arm off, you mean.'

'Just the hand. It would only need to be the hand.'

'No,' Paladin stated, with a commanding tone. 'I will not permit this.'

'Three doors down, on this side of the alley,' the locksmith said. 'The Limb Broker. That's what they do. Take things off, put things on. They're good. Reliable. Quick and clean.'

'No,' Paladin said again.

I turned back to the robot. 'It's just flesh and bone. It's nothing compared to my sister – nothing compared to what she's already been through.'

'It'll cost you more than three quoins,' the locksmith said.

'I should charge you for botching this job.'

'I am against this,' Paladin said, but with less force than before, as if on some level he'd had resigned himself to my decision. 'It conflicts with my protective imperative.'

'You want to protect me,' I said, 'you'll help me with anything that slows down those constables.'

'Tell them I sent you,' the locksmith said.

We left the shop. I pressed the bracelet against my belly, as if that might muffle the tracking signal. Paladin swerved ahead of me as we travelled the short distance to the Limb Broker. 'This is a hastily conceived course of action. We have yet to exhaust all the other possibilities . . .'

'I don't see many other possibilities, Paladin. You can't jam that signal and the locksmith couldn't get the bracelet off. What are the constables doing now?'

'They have determined that you are heading for the dock, rather than Incer. Squads are being mobilised to this area. But if we could locate a sealed room, a chamber with metal walls . . .'

'They'd still have a good idea that I'm in the area, and then it wouldn't take the constables long to turn the place over. Anyway, I want to get to the dock, not hide in Neural Alley.'

'Some kind of gauntlet or shroud, with signal-blocking capabilities.'

'You find a shop that sells something like that, I'll be right behind you.'

'A better locksmith.'

'If you know one, Paladin, shout now.' I was at the Limb Broker's window, suppressing an inner shudder as I contemplated the wares and services on display. It had been one thing to share a giggle of horror with my sister, neither of us thinking we'd ever have cause to enter the Limb Broker.

But here I was, a prospective customer.

There were two kinds of limb in the window. In bubbling green tubes were living limbs and appendages, kept alive by artificial means. These had been surgically removed from donors, either sold to the shop or pawned in exchange for a loan. Even through the green glass it was clear that all varieties of age, skin tone and size were catered for. The other kinds of limb were mechanical, supported on glass stands or velvet plinths, and some of them made to show off their range of function, so that a disembodied hand opened and closed in slow motion. Some of the hands were very lifelike, and some were about as crudely functional as Paladin's claw-hands.

'I have some news . . .' Paladin began. 'It is not welcome news. Do you wish to hear it?'

'Tell me.'

'The squawks continue. But I have heard mention of some critical information being conveyed to the authorities just before the source of that information passed away. I am very sorry, Arafura. But I cannot avoid drawing the obvious inference.'

Nor could I, but thinking it and putting it out there in words were two different things. It felt as if there were a door still slightly open, and I wasn't going to be the one to slam it shut by admitting what I already knew deep down.

Instead, I took my feelings and hammered them into something hard and sharp and definite.

'Then there's even less reason to go home.'

'If you are minded to go through with this,' Paladin said after a moment, like he was worried for me, 'then the locksmith was correct. You do not need to consider more than the removal of your hand.'

But my eye had been drawn to a mechanical hand and forearm on one of the velvet plinths. It was beautiful, with a slender design and an elegance to the articulations around the finger joints and wrist. The limb was fashioned from a silvery alloy, intertwined with jade inlay, and there were fretted windows in the wrist and forearm to show the complex, glittering mechanisms inside.

I pushed open the door. My body screamed at me to turn around, to surrender to the constables, to go back and lay a kiss on Father's cheek, anything but what I was about to contemplate.

The shop had a central counter, build around a display

cabinet full of more bubbling tubes and slowly opening and closing hands. It was all very clean and calm, like the lobby of a bank, with seats around the walls where people could wait. No one was waiting now, but even as I walked in a man came out of a back room with a bandaged sleeve, and what looked like a new living hand grafted onto his forearm. He stared down at it, fascinated, as he made his own fingers curl and elongate.

'I want you to cut this off,' I told the gowned woman behind the counter, holding up my hand. 'I know you can do that quickly. But I want it done quicker.'

She gave me a sympathetic look. 'I'm sorry, dear, but you can't just stroll in and decide . . .'

'A ten-bar quoin says I can.' I jammed it down on the counter. 'That hand and arm in the window – the one with the twenty-mark price tag. That's what I want put on. Let's say – forty bars for the whole job, fifty if you do it inside the next ten minutes.'

The woman glanced over me at the robot, as if there were some test she was about to fail. But Paladin said nothing.

'You don't need that pretty one, dear. If you just want that bracelet off, you don't even need a mechanical one. We can do it quick and clean, preserve the nerve endings, get a clean re-attachment . . . putting it back on'll take longer, of course, but you'll get to keep your own, and that's what most folk would want . . .'

'I'm not most folk. Get the bracelet off me, and cut where you need to fix that metal one on. The one with the green inlay.'

'You're sure about this, dear?' The woman was fetching keys. She went to the front of the shop, opened the glass panel at the back of the window display, fished out the arm I had selected. She pushed back my sleeve and offered it up as a comparison. 'It's a good match,' she said. 'Lucky for you it wasn't the right arm.'

'Yes, I'm all luck, me. Tell me what's involved.'

She showed me the scooped-in end of the false arm. It was a concave surface, finely perforated. 'This fixes itself onto you. Takes a few days to complete the bond, and it'll hurt some while it's doing it. Then it couples itself onto your nervous system. That won't be the nicest, either. Once it's done, though, you'll have full use of the hand.' She ran an approving finger over the jade inlay. 'Very good work, this. Eleventh Occupation. They knew a thing or two about prosthetic surgery, in the Empire of the Ever Breaking Wave. Durable, too. This arm's been on a few bodies in its time.'

'You can skip the potted history. I want it. Do it now.'

'You said fifty marks.' A shrewd look came over the woman. 'Anyone in that much of a hurry can probably go up a little more. Shall we say seventy?'

'Sixty, or I'm walking out of here.'

The woman appraised me. There was a grudging respect in her eyes. 'Sixty it is. But we haven't discussed what you want doing with the hand, once it's off.'

'I don't care about it. Put it in your shop window, for all I care. But I want the bracelet.'

'If you're decided.'

'I am.'

'Then you'd best come with me.'

I looked back at Paladin. 'I'll be all right. This is nothing.'

The woman showed me into a windowless room with a heavy green chair fixed to the floor. She made me sit in the chair, her eyes lingering over my clothes and feet, but obviously deciding for herself that my money was what mattered, not the state of my deportment.

'No going back,' she said, making the chair tilt backward.

'I wouldn't want to. Get this over with.'

Instead of armrests, the chair had two cylindrical green tubes, each thick and long enough to take an arm up to the elbow. I rested my right arm on the padded top of the rightmost tube, and inserted my left arm into the open end of the other. There was a seal around the end, like an iris, and it tightened itself automatically.

'Some folks prefer to watch,' the woman said. 'Others don't.'

'Will it hurt?'

'No. So I'm told.' The woman stood behind me, working a control panel set into the back of the chair. 'But you'll sure as anything know *something*'s happening. You ready?'

'Do it.'

I felt two sharp spikes of cold, and then my arm became a numb weight hanging off my elbow. Something whirred inside the green cylinder, and I felt distant cold scratches, like icy fingernails, circumscribing my arm about halfway between the wrist and the elbow. Then a sequence of quick snipping sensations, what the roots of a plant must feel as its upper parts are pruned back, and then a grinding buzz and a vibration that reached me all the way through the seal and back to my elbow.

The woman bent around from her control panel. 'How's that working out for you?'

'There's no pain.'

'You're nearly done. It'll be very clean, and the way the nerve endings are capped off, there shouldn't be too much post-operative discomfort. They knew what they were doing, when they made these machines.'

'What about the false arm?'

'First things first.' She came around to my left and opened a hinged plate at the other end of the tube. She reached into it like someone collecting mail, and drew out a perfectly intact hand, wrist, bracelet and half a forearm. The cut was bloodless, like a slice through a plastic anatomy model.

I suppose I ought to have been distressed, but for the moment I couldn't relate that hand to any part of me.

'It's a good limb,' she said, weighing it in her hands. 'Could've got a fair price for it, too, if it wasn't for that lightvine crawling through it. We'll flush it out, but it'll still need to be mentioned on the warranty. Folks are particular, see. You didn't pick up that habit on Mazarile, did you?'

'Habit?' I asked, still with my upper arm stuck in the tube.

'That's what it tends to become, you don't get it flushed out sooner or later. But it's your choice – like this.'

She removed the bracelet, sliding it back along the arm, forcing it hard over the last bit, then lowered the entire severed limb into a green receptacle, similar to the flasks in the window.

Then she slid the false hand in through the end of the tube, before closing the hinged plate.

Somewhere between elbow and wrist – except there was no wrist – I felt a cold contact. I flinched, but only once.

'Arm's sucking itself on. It'll hold itself pretty good until the connections have grown across the gap, but don't go whacking anything for a few days.'

'I wasn't planning to.'

The seal released. I took that as a cue to withdraw my arm, taking in the point where it seemed to vanish into the jewelled hem of a silver and green gauntlet. It didn't feel part of me yet. But neither did it feel like some grafted monstrosity. I stared, instead, with a quiet bewildered fascination, like a child seeing its fingers for the first time. I tried to make the hand close itself, but it stayed stiff and unresponsive, like it was made from a single piece of metal.

'Like I said.' The woman leaned in. 'Too late for second thoughts.'

'I'm not having any. You say it will bed itself in on its own?'

'The more you try to use it, the quicker it'll pick up the nerve impulses and start learning from them. After that, it'll go pretty smoothly. Some itchiness, some pins and needles, that's normal. But keep it dry and watch out for fungal infections under the sleeve. Any problems, you know where to find us.'

'I don't think that's going to be an issue,' I said.

Wobbly on my legs – from shock, more than anything else – I took the bracelet in my right hand and walked back into the main part of the shop. Paladin was still waiting there. I wasn't sorry that he didn't have a face, or any other means of registering distaste or disgust or astonishment.

'We have to destroy this,' I said, holding up the bracelet. 'Leaving it here's too risky, if the constables get a good description of me.'

'We may not have much time,' Paladin said. 'And there may be a better solution.'

I stroked my alloy hand with the other, struck by the false arm's supremely elegant design and manufacture, the product of a better, more refined time than our own. It would be strong as well, I decided. Nothing frail could have endured two Occupations, and still be useful.

'What's your suggestion?'

'It would be better to move the bracelet elsewhere than destroy it. I could do so, but I would not be able to move as quickly as a person, and I would also much rather remain at your side. Are you strong enough to walk?'

'Yes, I'm all right.'

'Then we will continue.' Paladin shot out a claw. 'Give me a low denomination quoin. The least valuable you have.'

'You should rest,' the Limb Broker said. 'Rushing out straight after a procedure like that . . . you'll do yourself an injury.'

I cradled the quoin bag in my stiff arm and used my good hand to dig out a one-bar quoin, the last I had. I gave it to Paladin, and slipped the bracelet into the robot's other claw.

In Neural Alley we found a girl who was willing to run with the bracelet in return for the quoin. She was about my height and build, although that was the extent of the similarities.

'You won't get in any trouble,' I told her. 'The constables will be coming for me, not you, and it's not the bracelet they're after. Throw it away if they get close.'

'Which way would you like me to go?'

'Back to the Dragon Gate. If you get that far, hop on a tram towards Incer Station. Ride it as far as you can. Watch out for the constables, and a thin man in a tall hat, with a scar down his face.'

'Doesn't sound like a constable.'

'He isn't. But you'll be faster, I know.' I gave her an encouraging pat from my good hand, keeping the alloy one tucked close to me for the moment.

'You're a strange one,' the girl said. 'Wouldn't hurt to know your name, either.'

'Fura Ness,' I said.

She was smart, that cove, and she didn't take the easy way back to the Dragon Gate. There were a hundred little side-alleys branching off the main one, and they all led to a tight, festering warren of ginnels and squeezeways, things you could hardly call an alley, let alone a street, but it was all part of Neural Alley and I guessed that she knew it better than most. I watched her vanish out of sight, the bracelet dipped into a pocket.

'Maybe it stopped working,' I said.

'No,' Paladin said. 'The homing trace was still active. And you are still very much at risk of recapture. We should make haste for the station, before the constables throw a noose over this whole area. Do you still have funds?'

I rattled the bag. 'Lighter than when we started. But we'll manage.'

Paladin and I set off down the winding course of Neural Alley, trying not to walk any faster than the other customers. I felt shivery, my legs wobbling under me, and knew that the Limb Broker had been right when she said I ought to rest. But I had business to be about, and now I wanted to make it look as if that false arm had been a part of me for years. I tried to let it hang down naturally, swinging with each stride, squaring my shoulders and lifting my chin, as if I owned the place. *Never seen a girl with no shoes on, have you? Get your lamps off me, cove, or I'll put this fist where the photons don't reach.*

'I must confess,' Paladin said, 'that I did not think you had the fortitude.'

'It was what needed to be done. I'm sorry if it turned you all knotty, but I've got the spur in me now.' Then I grinned back at him. 'Chaff, Paladin, but I can hardly help myself sounding like one of them. Maybe it's for the best. I've got to sound as if I've already crewed, haven't I?'

'You have.'

'Just once, and it wasn't exactly a righteous end to it all. I don't know how well I'll be able to bluff them if they start digging in with questions about other ships, other captains.'

'One look at you, they might decide not to bother with questions.'

'You think I look fierce?'

'Unquestionably.'

'Good.' I smiled to myself, and tried to send a clench signal to my new fingers. 'If this is what it takes, Paladin.'

'I will say this,' the robot answered. 'In so far as a machine with my cognitive ceiling is capable of experiencing anything you might describe as admiration . . .'

'Go on.'

'Perhaps that state of mind is not too far from my present opinion of you. Your sister would have been proud.'

'*Will* be proud, Paladin. Will be.'

'I misspoke.'

Neural Alley was a hangover headache of warrens and short-cuts, but it was walled-in at its extremities and the only easy points of entry were the Dragon and Cat Gates, and we were nearly at the latter. From the Cat Gate – the most southerly and easterly end of the alley – it was only a short walk to Hadramaw Station. There'd been no sign of constables or Vidin Quindar, and I was starting to think that perhaps, just perhaps, we'd been quick and clever enough with the bracelet. But then Paladin and I rounded the last corner before the Cat Gate and there they were, the constables with their flashing blue epaulettes, maybe six of them, and Quindar bringing up the rear.

I started. My instinct was to turn back, to freeze, to dive into the sanctuary of a shop or boutique.

But they hadn't seen me yet.

'Continue,' Paladin said.

So I continued. I didn't look them in the eye, and the direction of their gaze passed over me, not through me. They were sweeping their attention further up Neural Alley, back in the direction of the Dragon Gate.

'Pull back a little,' I said. 'Let's not look like we belong together. We'll join up after the Cat Gate.'

Even Vidin Quindar hadn't spotted me. I could tell from the way he was standing, using the steps outside a shop to raise himself above the heads of the passers-by, levelling a hand under the brim of his hat as his weasely eyes swept the distance. I kept walking, even though each step brought me closer to the cove I most wanted to avoid. Clearly Quindar and the constables were concerned that I might use Cat Gate, but they'd no idea I was already so close to it.

Quindar was three shops away on my right, his jaw lolling open in a grin of idiot expectation, but his eyes were flinty. Two more constables came in through Cat Gate. Quindar nodded to them, moved his gob, and the constables broke into a jog, sweeping through people and passing me on my left. I raised my left arm, hoping its presence would cause Quindar to subconsciously drop me from any further consideration. There'd be lots of things he was keeping his eye out for, but a girl with a tin hand wouldn't be one of them.

I was only a shop away from him now, and I had to squeeze down the impulse to cross to the other side of the alley. I wasn't going to risk drawing attention to myself by veering across the street. Now he drew something out of his pocket, a little black box, and he grinned down at it before pressing it against his right ear. Quindar muttered something, dragging the nail of his other hand down the course of his scar. I was nearly at his feet, and he was still scanning well beyond me.

A voice buzzed out of Quindar's little box, and I heard him say: 'Clever cove, that girlie. Should've known she'd have us by the spuds. Look smart, boys, she could be anywhere in this sewer.' And with an almost beneficent look he settled his gaze on me, and the crooked crack of his grin widened by degrees. 'Well, I never! Old Vidin's still got 'is touch! She's here, boys, Cat Gate!'

I tried to run, but slipped on the greasy ground, and that was all the opportunity he needed to pounce down and grab at my arm. His fingers closed on it and then the shock and wrongness of that contact, his flesh on my metal, was enough to have him gasping.

'What in all the worlds have you done, girlie?'

'Let go,' I said.

I felt the arm began to suck itself away from my stump, and for the first time since leaving the Limb Broker there was pain, and plenty of it. I yelped. Quindar got another hand on me, pinning me by the good arm. 'This ain't your business,' he snarled at all and sundry as a space opened up in the flow of people. 'This girlie's not of legal age, and she's run away from home. And look at the 'arm she's done herself, left unsupervised!'

I struggled, but it didn't do me any good. Out of the corner of my eye, though, I saw Paladin, closing the distance he'd opened up, wobbling from side to side like a metronome as his wheels slipped on the ruts and cracks, and then Paladin boomed out:

'Let her go.'

Quindar settled his gaze on the robot.

'You're the pile of metal I smashed up in Granity's. Don't remember that, do you?'

'I do remember it.'

And that was a lie but I was proud of Paladin for saying it.

'What's your problem – not enough dents for your liking?'

'You are the problem, Mister Quindar.'

The tone of the robot's reply drew a twitch of unease from Quindar, but it wasn't enough to have him relax his hold on me. He was still clutching my false hand too firmly, and his nails were jagging into my flesh on the other arm. 'You'd be wise to watch your tone, robot,' Quindar said. 'You machines ain't top of the pecking order, not in this Occupation anyway.'

Light flashed from Paladin. Quindar screamed and let go of me immediately.

'It's all right,' I said, shrugging past him. 'He did that to Morcenx, too, but it won't be permanent.'

But there was a different quality to the screams coming from Quindar.

These were shrieks, not moans.

Cat Gate was just a few dozen steps away, and beyond its neon arch all I saw was the ordinary drift of loiterers and pedestrians wondering whether to chance their luck down Neural Alley. Paladin had rolled to my side. Vidin Quindar was crouching at my feet, oblivious to my presence now, pushing his knuckles into his eyes as if they belonged there.

'Paladin . . . what did you do to him?'

'I used great restraint,' the robot informed me. 'He still has a nervous system.'

'You blinded him.'

'A leniency. He was about to do worse to you.'

A commotion of uniforms and flashing epaulettes swept around the curve of Neural Alley. People scattered. The constables were blowing whistles, drawing truncheons and stun weapons. One of them slipped and went crashing through a shop window and onlookers laughed. But the rest were still coming.

'I will deal with the constables,' Paladin said. 'You must make your way to the station. If you move quickly once you leave Cat Gate, I do not believe there will be any difficulties.'

'Fine,' I said. 'We'll meet up at the dock. You know the name of the ship.'

'I do not think we will meet again, Arafura. Not after what is about to happen.'

'No,' I said disbelievingly. 'You've got to come with me.'

'You have done well this far. You will do equally well without me.'

'Paladin—' I said.

He turned, bouncing and swaying back in the direction of the advancing constables. I was frozen for an instant, not wanting our parting to happen like this, in this place. I watched as he began to put up a struggle, flailing his arms, flashing light at the constables. Then he buckled and went under them, and I thought that was the last I'd ever see of him.

It nearly was, and if I'd started running at that instant it would've been. But something came tumbling through the lungstuff, just as if it had been tossed out of that brawl to keep it from harm. I stared at it, thinking two things. The first was that I recognised it, because it was the same shattered dome I'd pulled out of a box and spoken to.

The second was that it was heading for me, like I was meant to catch it.

I put out my hands and caught his head, fumbling it to my belly just before it slipped out of my grip. He took his own head off, I thought. He took his own head off and threw it to me.

But there was nothing twinkling in the dome.

Keeping it pressed to me, I ran.

FOUR

TRUSKO

16

'This isn't the way it usually works,' grumbled the captain of the *Queen Crimson*. 'Just so we're clear on that. No one ever comes to me direct, at the docks, demanding to be employed. We do things through intermediaries. Brokers. Agencies. The talent bazaar.'

'I heard you could use a good boney. If that's not the case, there are a hundred other ships that I'm sure could benefit from my abilities.'

'You've a ready opinion of yourself.'

'It's not an opinion. I just know what I am. Anyone can work with a good skull. That's how the combines operate. The best skulls, and mediocre readers. Mediocre because they don't need to be any better. I heard your last Reader was fresh off a combine operation?' I pushed on before he had a chance to confirm or deny this intelligence. 'I'm sure you got good results, when your skull was fresh. But they get old, don't they? The gubbins stops twinkling like it used to. Cracks open up. Signal gets fainter, if you can read it at all.' I gave my best bored shrug. 'Most can't.'

'And you think you'd be better?'

'I've pulled signals out of the bones Granity keeps to feed to the cats.'

'So you know Granity.'

'Who doesn't?'

'You've crewed. That's plain.' He nodded at my hand. 'Had some damage, too, and chowed on the glowy stuff by the looks of things. But you're from Mazarile, or I wasn't born on Sunderday. It's vexing that I haven't run into you sooner. I thought I had pegs on all the talent out of Maz.'

'Then you need more pegs. Yes, I'm from Mazarile. Does that make things knotty for you?'

'No reason it should, other than that tongue in your head. Someone wanting to crew with me, normally they're all please and thank you and what a nice ship you have.'

'I don't have time for that.' I leaned forward, elbows on the table, knitting alloy fingers in flesh ones, and hoping the lack of movement in my false hand wasn't too evident, because I didn't want him asking how long I'd had it. 'Here's the sharp end of it, Captain. I've made some scowly enemies.'

'To do with that bit of broken glass you seem so attached to?'

I'd been cradling what was left of Paladin since leaving Neural Alley.

'Something like that. I'm getting off Mazarile one way or the other, and that's the truth. But I ain't going to beg my way onto a ship. Hire me or don't. But if you take me on, you'll have the best Bone Reader between here and Trevenza Reach.' I settled back into my seat. 'Question is, do you want the gen or not?'

'Of course I want the gen.'

'Then give me something I can put my name on.'

Captain Trusko gave me a look of long, sceptical appraisal. He was younger than Rackamore or Jastrabarsk, and there wasn't anything of the seasoned spacefarer about him. He wasn't a big man, but what there was of him was soft-looking and babyish, with two chins, a pout, and a black kiss curl glued onto his forehead. He had tried to offset his overall look with a moustache, but it only made things worse.

We were in a rented room at Hadramaw Dock, similar to the office where I had first met Rackamore and Cazaray. Trusko was busy with last-minute arrangements before setting sail. I'd done well to get myself before him, but I wasn't on safe ground just yet. My decision to put on this bold, dismissive front was a dicey one.

'We don't cut out for a day, and the launch still has to go up and down at least twice in that time,' Trusko said, sliding ledgers around on his desk as if he still had half an eye on those matters. 'Given that, I'll see what the rest of the crew make of you. It's true I can use a Bone Reader. But not if she bristles everyone up the wrong way. It's bad enough with the Scanner we took on at Trevenza—'

'My experience,' I said, 'is that quoins will smooth over a lot of things.'

'And you think you'd make quoins for us, do you?'

'What we're here for, ain't it?'

'You do a good job of masking that schooling you've had,' Trusko said, with a thin smile. 'But it won't fool the rest of them. Nothing gets you off to a worse start than turning the crew against you, because they think you're trying to pretend you're something you're not.'

'I know what I am,' I said.

'We'll see.' He gathered his papers and tapped them into neat order, then held them up before him so that he could run his upper lip across the top of them, making them even neater. 'You'll come with me on the launch. Trial by fire. The crew shall have the last say. Best not rile them . . .' But then he paused. 'You never did say your name, did you?'

'Fura,' I said. 'Just Fura.'

'Very well, Just Fura. I make no promises. You look like a barefoot street waif and you've got spite in your eyes. You've been on the glowy and that never sits well with me, especially if it gets in the grey. But if you're half the Bone Reader you think you are, maybe you have something to offer.'

'I've plenty to offer,' I said. 'Intelligence. Baubles. Fortune. Quoins.'

I spared him the bit about bloody retribution.

Trusko's launch took us from Hadramaw Dock to the orbit of the *Queen Crimson*. Like the *Monetta's Mourn*, her basic form was a little like a fish, with windows for eyes, sail-control gear for fins and spines, ion radiators for a tail, and a mouth for the forward docking bay. We slipped into the mouth and the jaws clamped us in like a prize.

Inside, though, it was like a puzzle that had been jumbled up and reassembled in a different order. I had been on three sunjammers now – four if you counted the commercial clipper – and it was clear that they all did things in their own way. The bone room was usually somewhere near the middle, but that still left a lot of scope for how to get to it, what to have next to it, and so on. The crew's cabins could be almost anywhere, and so could the galley, navigation room, bridge, captain's quarters.

There was one commonality, though. The ships all sounded the same. They grumbled and moaned and sang to themselves as if they'd all been raised on the same hymnbook. And they all had the same smell. It was metal and wood and cooking and toilets and too many monkey bodies pressed into the same volume for too long. It had been unfamiliar, at first. But the shivery thing was that I had an entirely different view of that smell now.

It felt like coming home.

Trusko took me to the bone room without making any introductions along the way. 'I'm expecting a confidential send,' he said. 'From a captain and a ship whose names I won't divulge. That'll be your first test. If you *were* thinking of bluffing, now'd be the time to come clean about it.'

'I wasn't bluffing.'

He spun the bone room wheel and invited me to float inside. It was a similar set-up to the room on the *Monetta*, with equipment hung onto the walls and the skull braced in the middle by an arrangement of shock-absorbing wires.

'Grestad is our usual Reader,' he said. 'But Grestad is still down on Mazarile.' He touched a finger to his forehead, just under the cowlick. 'I started off reading the bones, back before my grey hardened up. Worked my way up the hard way. So I know the ropes, and I can get a signal out of the bones if no one else is available.'

'So why'd you need me? Or Grestad?'

'Grestad's a better Reader than I was. Besides, I've got the ship to run. It's the usual course of it. If a Reader doesn't stink the place out, there's usually a job for them somewhere else, when the bones stop playing nice. You've crewed as often as you say, you'd know that.'

'I did. I just wondered why someone who could still get a signal out of the bones would waste quoins employing some-one else.' I hooked one of the items off the wall. 'Are these what you call neural bridges? I've seen better than this thrown out as junk.'

'They worked well enough for Grestad. Perhaps your tastes are a little fussy for the *Queenie*?'

I set Paladin's head aside and slipped the bridge over my head, as best as I could, being effectively one-handed.

'That tin arm of yours is a little stiff.'

'It worked fine before my creditors decided to leave me with a parting message,' I said, trying to make as little of it as I could. 'Anyway, you'd be paying me to read bones, not knit. This is the skull?'

'No, it's tonight's dinner.'

I stroked a hand along the skull's ridge. It was in better nick than the one on the *Monetta*, although not necessarily newer. It was a clean yellow-white in colour, with no major cracks or areas of repair. I leaned in to peer through the eye holes. Con-stellations of coloured lights flickered back at me.

'I've seen bigger. But it's in fair fettle.'

'It'd better be, the packet it cost us. A new set of sails took a smaller dent out of our accounts. Question is, can you find the active node? I know where Grestad hooks in.'

'Where Grestad hooks in, and where I might choose, are two different things.' With my good hand I worked the end of the neural bridge into one of the central nodes. All pretence dropped away now, as I fell into the receptiveness that I'd learned under Cazaray. I closed my eyes, flung wide the doors of my skull, and waited for shivery whispers to skirl through those chambers of alien bone.

Nothing came.

'It's not this node,' I said softly. 'No matter what Grestad might say.'

'Continue.'

I shifted the connection. Nothing on the second node. But a possible hit on the third. It was a scratchy presence, an itch or a skincrawl under the roof of my brain.

I said nothing. I kept my eyes tight. But the set of my face must have shown itself to Trusko.

'You have a signal?'

'Let me work.'

I circled around the peripheral nodes, returning to the third as a comparison. Faint traces on three of the peripherals, but nothing as strong as that first contact.

'You have partials on four and five. But three's where Grestad should be hooking in. For now, anyway. That skull's like any of the others I've worked with, there's no such thing as a fixed pattern.'

'No,' Trusko allowed. 'It moves, shifts around from one month to another, like there's something restless trapped inside it. Grestad's usually able to follow it.'

'Usually?' I asked, sneering out my question. 'I was right about Grestad, wasn't I? Combine fodder. Fine when the skull's fresh.'

'This one is.'

'But I doubt Grestad's pulling the faintest signals out of it.'

'We don't miss anything.'

'You wouldn't *know* you were missing it, would you? Wait.' I raised a silencing finger. 'Something's swelling up. Might be your call, Captain Trusko.'

'Give me a ship and a name,' he whispered.

'That's easy. Too easy, you want my righteous word on it. Ship's the *Shady Lady*, captain's some cove by the name of So-bradin. That's screaming through. Sobradin wants your opinion on the opening auguries for a bauble down in the . . .'

'All right. That's good. That's very good.'

'You want the rest of it, the stuff that's whispering in under all that? Not from the *Shady Lady*. Someone a lot further out, but coming in on the same node.' Still with my eyes closed, I added: '*Marquess of Shadows*, under Resparis, losing lungstuff at the Daughters of Blood and Milk . . . any vessels close to the fourth sector of the third processional make all sail to assist . . . Auskersund transmitting from the *Hollow Mistress* says to scupper and repair to all launches . . . estimated crossing time on full ions will be three days, nine hours . . .' I tugged the bridge from my hair. 'Do you want more?'

'No,' Trusko said. 'That will be sufficient. More than suffi-cient. You were right about Sobradin, and I doubt there was any way for you to know that name unless you pulled it from the skull. But the rest of it? You overplayed your hand, Fura. I'd have been ready to sign you, at least as apprentice Bone Reader, but you took me for a fool. There's no way you pulled the rest of it from that node, not when Sobradin was already sending. Maybe one in a thousand has that discrimination . . . but I'd know, wouldn't I, if someone with that sort of talent was look-ing for employment?'

'You do now.'

His expression was tight, composed. 'No. I'm not green.'

'Get on the squawk,' I said. 'If there's a ship bleeding out down in the Sunward processionals, word'll reach the Emptyside soon enough.' I slipped the neural bridge back onto its hook. 'I know what I heard, Captain. It came through bell-clear, too. I didn't even have to work at it. You've got yourself a good skull here, whatever worth Grestad's made of it. Now all it needs is a sharp Reader.'

'I will get on the squawk,' Trusko said. 'And I will have word of something going wrong with that ship, if it even exists. You'd better pray that it does, Fura. I don't take kindly to having my time wasted.'

'Nor do I, Captain.'

There was a silence, which he curtailed with a contemptuous snort. 'I'll prove you wrong. But since my time is precious, I may as well have the pleasure of seeing the rest of the crew sound you out first. They'll plumb you, Fura.'

'Plumb away.'

I understood why he had his doubts. I'd have had my doubts as well. But the shivery part was that I hadn't needed to fake a word of it. It was all real, even though I'd never heard of Resparis, his stricken ship, or the Daughters of Blood and Milk. I was getting better at reading the bones, just like Cazarary said I would.

Scarily better.

*

The crew had gathered in the galley. It was aft of the bone room, smaller than the one on the *Monetta*, but it served the same function. There were six of them in the room when we arrived, and five of those faces were totally new to me. I endeavoured to treat the sixth no differently.

'Take a seat,' Trusko said, indicating the long double-sided bench that spanned most of the galley. 'But don't get too comfortable. I think you'll be back on that launch soon enough.'

'I didn't know we needed a new cleaning girl,' said a snide-looking man.

'That tin hand of hers looks pretty,' said the woman next to him. She had a famished, sucked-in look about her, as if there were a vacuum under her skin. 'Pity about what it's stuck to.'

'She's got the glowy about her,' said another man, sucking on an ornate clay pipe carved into the form of a sunjammer. 'I don't likes the glowy.'

'I had the glowy in me once,' said an older woman, with a lopsided look to her face, one eye staring out wider and crazier than the other.

'And look how you worked out,' said the snide one.

'What's your name, cove?' asked Prozor, who was squeezed in next to the pipe man. 'Got a tongue in your gob, ain't you?'

'Fura,' I answered delicately, looking Prozor right in the eyes. 'And you'd be?'

'Never you mind me.' I gave her as long as I dared, measuring the ways she'd changed and not changed. It hadn't been long, I told myself. But Prozor looked harder and meaner than she had before, and that was like saying a rock looked rockier. 'What's the story with this one, Cap'n? I didn't think we were signin' anyone on.'

'We may not be, Prozor,' Trusko answered her. 'That'll depend on a number of factors. Fura wants to crew with us – thinks she might be able to get something more out of the bones than Grestad.'

The snide man scoffed out a laugh. 'That's not much of a benchmark.'

'We won't speak ill of Grestad when she's not in our presence,' Trusko said, but I could tell he had lost that argument before it was begun. 'Fura can read the bones. That's not in doubt. But as to how deep her abilities go, I'm just waiting on a squawk that might . . .'

'Speaking of the squawk,' said the famished-looking woman, 'there's a ship bleeding out in the Sunwards. Nothing we or anyone else can do about it, neither.'

'When did you hear about this, Surt?' Trusko asked.

'Just now. Couple of minutes gone. General squawk, emergency channel. Reached half the ships in the Congregation by now. Not that there's a chaffing thing any of them will be able to do.' The woman – Surt – turned to the pipe man. 'Do me a favour, Tindouf. We ever start bleeding out like that, all our lungstuff whistling away, you rig them ions to blow up so we get a quick and easy exit. I ain't suffocating.'

'If suffocating's a problem,' said the snide man. 'Maybe you ended up in the wrong line of employment.'

'We're all in the wrong line,' said the lopsided woman.

'Wouldn't be teaming up with a weasel like you if I had any choice in it.'

'Where did this ship end up in trouble?' I asked.

Surt gave me a chilly stare. 'Near the twins. The Daughters of Blood and Milk.'

'They's baubles,' the pipe man said, pausing to tap his clay utensil against the table. 'One's red, one's white. Orbits each other, they does. Got swallowers in the both of 'em.'

'My information was correct, then, Captain Trusko. Surt said the report just came in. We'd have been in the bone room, so there's no way I'd have heard that squawk ahead of time.'

Trusko worked his lips. He looked up and down the length of his table. Some of his crew were hanging off his next words. Others could not have looked less interested if quoins had depended on it. The lopsided woman was using the end of a knife to lever something out of her teeth. 'I tested her with a general send from another ship,' Trusko said. 'She got that. She also picked up a secondary send coming through on the same node. My initial reaction was that it couldn't be real, but . . .'

'She's that good,' Surt said, 'you should sign her up.'

'There's more to a new crew member than just being able to do a given task,' Trusko answered. 'Her skills are still debatable. We can run some more tests, certainly. But there's a cut about her that makes me doubt she'd fit in.'

'And we are, after all, such a happy family,' the snide man said. 'Wouldn't want some scowly one-hand coming along and ruining that, would we?'

'I can fit in,' I said. 'Seen enough ships and crews to be certain of that. You ain't anything special, none of you. But even if I didn't mesh, would it really matter? Put me in your bone room, and I'll bring you all the loot and quoins you asked for. And it's loot and quoins that puts the spur into us, ain't it?'

'She talks like Prozor one minute, like some high-educated prim and proper madam the next,' said an over-muscled man with heavy earrings and a geometric tattoo on his forehead. 'Don't know what to make of that.'

'You don't know what to make of most things, Drozna,' said the snide man. 'Best stick to rigging.'

'S'long as it keeps me away from you, Gathing, there's not much I wouldn't stick to.'

'You say you've seen enough ships,' Drozna – the muscled man – said. 'Name some of 'em.'

'The *Harpy*, under Zemys. That was the first. The *White Widow*, under Rinagar. The *Murderess*, under Rhinn. Then under Palquen, when Rhinn died at the *Poisoned Eye*. You want more?'

'You looks awful green to have been on all them shipses,' said Tindouf, the man with the pipe. 'Awful green. T'aint proper for someone to be green, if they've been on so many shipses.'

'Make your mind up,' I said. 'One minute you don't like me because I've got the glowy in me, the next it's because I don't look old enough.'

'She's got your mark, Tindouf,' said the lopsided woman.

'Shuts yourself up, Strambli,' the pipe man said.

'You can check those ships,' I said. 'Speak to their captains. See what they made of me. They'll tell you the same thing. They'll never see a better Bone Reader.'

'They'll never see anything,' Gathing said with a knowing smile. 'Unless I'm mistaken, all those ships are gone now.'

'Ships don't last,' I said, with an unconcerned shrug.

'Still, awful handy if you didn't want anyone checking up on your past.' But now Gathing gave his own shrug. 'I don't care. If she can read a bone or two – and do it better than Grestad – which isn't asking much – then I'll share a hull with her.'

'How'd you lose the hand?' Surt asked.

'I asked too many questions.'

Strambli laughed.

'Well, I'll say one thing for her,' Drozna put in. 'She's going out of her way to win friends. There's something shivery about her, no doubt. But – and I'll only say this once – I agree with Gathing. If she can read, and read good, nothing else matters.'

Tindouf tapped at his pipe. 'We could use some good intelligences.'

Surt drew in her already sucked-in cheeks. They seemed to disappear into her, like matter falling into a swallower's horizon. 'Verdict's out, as far as I'm concerned. But I don't suppose I've got to like someone to draw my share of the quoins they bring us.'

'Glad to see your mercenary spark is undiminished,' Gathing said.

'And you're *not* in this for the money?' Surt asked him.

'If I am, I'm on the wrong ship.' But Gathing made a cynical saluting gesture. 'No disrespect, Captain.'

'We'll make our quoins in good time,' Trusko answered. 'For now, it's only Fura that concerns us. I sense the winds are blowing in the direction of hiring her. But you haven't said much, Prozor.'

'My word won't carry much, will it, being the newest on the ship?'

'That's as maybe. We'd still value your opinion. You've crewed extensively. How do you plumb her?'

'Something don't add up,' Prozor said after a silence. 'Drozna's right – she's all one thing, then she's something else. No crime in that, I suppose. And I did hear that they had a tolerable Sympathetic on the *Murderess*, a girl too young to look the part. Maybe she even had one hand.' Prozor leaned in confidentially. 'But I don't like her, Captain. Reading bones ain't the be all and end all. You've got to be able to trust the bony. Got to be able to sup with 'em and know they've got the same interests as you.'

'What do you do?' I asked sharply. 'I've figured some of the rest of you. Drozna's your master of sail. Tindouf's your ion man. Gathing – you've got the look of an Opener to me. Maybe an Assessor, if that isn't what Strambli does. Certain thing is you're no Integrator.' I nodded at his hands. 'Never seen an Integrator whose fingers weren't worked down to stubs.' I settled my gaze on Surt for a moment. 'That'd be you, I think. Got the fingers for it. But I still don't know what Prozor does. That was your name, wasn't it?'

'Prozor's our new Bauble Scanner,' Trusko said. 'And a good

one, by all reports. Thought our luck was in, when we heard that Prozor was looking for employment. But it wasn't *that* Prozor.'

'Then she's second-rate,' I said. 'Trading under a better name. Untested.'

'We'll know the value of her soon enough, when we've finalised our next set of targets,' Trusko said. 'And I don't doubt she'll prove her worth.'

'Then I'll prove mine,' I said, folding my arms across my chest. 'Took a chance on her, didn't you? Then you can do the same with me. Doesn't mean the cost of lungstuff to me whether she likes me or not. She can take the quoins I make. And I *will* make quoins.'

'Say one thing,' Drozna rumbled. 'No lack of self-confidence in the waif.'

'I'm signing her,' Trusko said. 'Provisional term. Say – six months. We'll crack a few baubles and see how she fares. Can't say fairer than that, can I? You'll just have to lump it, Prozor. Who knows? Maybe the two of you'll end up the best of friends.'

'Old Sun'll draw its last breath sooner'n that,' Prozor said.

*

Trusko took me to his cabin and we completed the paperwork. 'I have to go back down to Mazarile,' he said. 'If you've affairs to close down there, you can join me on the launch. But my thinking is Mazarile is the last place you'd want to go back to.'

'I've got what I need.'

'You came with nothing, except a bag of quoins, that hand, and the clothes you're wearing – what there is of them.'

'You'll give me somewhere to sleep, and feed me, some clobber if you can run to it, not much more I need.'

He tapped the bottom of the one of the papers. 'Put your name here.' A sudden alarmed thought crossed his face. 'You're literate, aren't you? You can read and write? A Bone Reader that can't transcribe isn't worth the cost of lungstuff to me.'

'I can read.' I scratched my name onto the document with my

right hand, which wasn't the one I normally used for writing, so the letters came out a bit crooked and stiff.

'Fura,' he said, blowing on the ink until it dried. 'That's really all there is to it?'

'All I need.'

'You're an uncommon one. Can't say I'm entirely persuaded by you, yet, but the crew live and breathe loot and they seem to think you have the necessary cut about you.'

'Except Prozor.'

'Don't concern yourself too much with Prozor. She came on with us at Trevenza Reach, which was only one world ago. We haven't required her to read a bauble yet, so she's not had a chance to prove her worth. Not that I doubt it, but until she's demonstrated that faculty . . . Prozor has to assert herself. Turning against you is her way of doing that. But you mustn't take it personally.'

'I don't.'

Trusko touched a hand to his belly, as if he had indigestion. 'Now I have some difficult business to attend to. Grestad was expecting to meet me at Hadramaw. I've got to explain to her that we've just hired a better Bone Reader, so she won't be returning to the *Queenie*. You'd better not let me down, Fura.'

'I shan't.'

'We'll be cutting out on ions in less than a day. I want you in the bone room as quickly as possible. Make your rounds of the ship, get to know it, smooth over your relations with the others as best you can . . . and start getting to know that skull. It's yours now, and I want you to get the very best that you can out of it.'

'Depend on it,' I said.

'You haven't seen the best of us,' Trusko reflected. 'We're not a bad crew. But we've drawn a string of dud baubles these last few months, and that saps the will. Morale's not what it could be. The ship needs repairs, the crew need their bonuses . . .'

'Perhaps your luck's about to change,' I said.

*

The next day was difficult.

There was nothing I wanted more than to crawl into a quiet corner with Prozor and natter about our plans. Prozor must have had a million questions for me. But we had to keep up the act. The slightest slip would give us away.

I found my quarters. It was a curtained slot about three-quarters the size of the equivalent accommodation on the *Monetta's Mourn*. As the newest member of the ship, I had been assigned the smallest and grubbiest sleeping space. Prozor, with her nominal superiority, had gone up a grade. Now she had Grestad's space, which was just around the corner from mine, and boasting a few additional comforts. It was impossible to avoid each other, but in the interests of keeping up our act all we did was brush past each other with the odd bad-tempered oath. But it was a dicey line we walked, and Prozor's dislike of me couldn't risk seeming too irrational. Once, on that first day, Drozna pulled me aside and said: 'If you two have some history we ain't been told about, now might be the time to share it. Been enough bad blood on this ship without adding more of it.'

'I don't know her,' I told him. 'What she's got against me ain't my concern.'

'There you go trying to sound like you were born on a 'jammer. But it don't quite roll off the tongue with you, does it?' He had a hand on my arm, gently enough, but not allowing me to continue on my way. 'Someone asked me to put quoins on it, I'd say you was a rich girl playing at this life.'

I held up my false hand. 'Does this look like playing to you, Drozna? Or the glowy in me?'

His eyes narrowed under the geometric tattoo on his forehead. 'How'd you come by the glowy?'

I swallowed, glanced away for a moment before meeting his eyes again. 'Ship I was on got jumped. I hid while the jumping was going on. Would've died, except I ate lightvine. Ain't proud of that, 'specially not the hiding. But I lived, and I've got the glowy as a reminder.'

'First straight words that have come out of your gob since you came aboard.' But something in him softened, and he moved his hand to pat me once. 'Ain't a one of us doesn't have something we'd sooner have happened a different way. If that's what spurs us, so be it. When did this happen?'

'A long time back.'

'Then that glowy's been in you a while. Takes some spuds, keeping it the way you have.'

'They wanted to flush it out of me. I said I wasn't forgettin' what happened. And if the itch and crawl of it made me remember, I'd take that and be grateful. I know it's got into my grey by now. Makes me angry, sometimes, and I start seeing connections between things that I know aren't always there. But it don't stop me reading the bones. You won't tell anyone, will you?'

'About something that happened years ago?' Drozna smiled. He had big jowly flaps on either side of his face, but it was still a kind face for a big man. 'But that arm of yours isn't as old as you'd like us to think, is it? I've seen how you favour the other one. I bet you could barely tie your laces with those tin fingers. You don't want anyone asking how long you've had that replacement grafted on.'

'I was sold a dud,' I said. 'Told it would bind to my nervous system, only it never did.'

'It doesn't look like a dud. Looks like quality work to me.'

'Then fix it, you're such an expert.'

He gave me a slow, knowing nod. 'You're a knotty puzzle, Fura. But I ain't the one to judge. Truth is, Grestad never did us much good. If you can improve on that, you'll soon have friends.'

'I don't need 'em,' I said.

*

We cut out on ions. Soon Mazarile was small and Drozna ran out the sails. I watched it happen. They were a bit more raggedy than on the *Monetta*, but the photons still bounced off them and gave us thrust. The captain already had a bauble in mind, so that was where we were headed. Three weeks would bring us within launching distance, and the auguries said that the bauble would crack open handsomely just as we arrived.

One by one, as life on the ship settled into the routine of watches, grub and squint-time, I ended up having conversations with most of them. It was me cooking the grub, as I'd cooked on the *Monetta*, and that helped grease our exchanges even more. As I doled out servings I also doled out little clues to my past, more with some than others, enough that if they all got together and shared notes they might have come up with something halfway to the truth. It wasn't about linking myself to Bosa Sennen, though, but giving them a reason to stop digging. Something rough had happened, and it had made me spiky, and there didn't need to be more to it than that.

The glowy was a problem, though, and so was the arm. Sailors understood that the glowy got into people, and that wasn't what put the doubt into them. It was the way I didn't seem to mind, the way I gave off every impression of being a bit proud of it, like it was a tattoo that had been put on me after I did something brave. But too many people had warned me that the glowy got into your brain if you let it, and once it was there you didn't see things clearly any more. I thought of the hard things I'd had to do to get back on a ship, and wondered if I'd done them only because I needed to, or because the glowy had made it easier to start being cruel and hard, even to myself. Thinking back to the sick girl in her bed, and then measuring her against the cove I was turning into, I knew that I'd sailed over something that couldn't ever be uncrossed. Some big, shivery void.

That version of Fura, all sick and sorry for herself, being made sicker by Morcenx's drugs, her father trying to burn away the memory of her older sister like she was some kind of stain, that Fura was someone I had known once and then discarded, like a friend who didn't measure up.

This Fura was different. This Fura was harder and scowlier and knew what needed to be done. This one could turn her back on her own dying father, or watch a blinded man whimper in pain and not give one cold cuss. This one could cut her own hand off if it helped. This one didn't care what people thought of Fura.

And even as I cursed those tin fingers, which wouldn't yet do a tenth of what I wanted from them, I knew which Fura I liked the best.

17

There was a scratch, a tug on my curtain. Then a sharp-angled face, upside down, gloomy in the lightvine.

'Time we had a chinwag.'

The ship grumbled around us. Someone snored a bunk or two away.

'I don't know if this is a good time.'

'Won't ever be a good time, Fura. We'll make it quick. Could've knocked me halfway to Trevenza when Trusko dragged you into the galley. We were all set to leave. I'd convinced myself you weren't going to have anything more to do with old Proz. What was the change of heart?'

'You don't want to know about the hand first?'

'We'll get to the hand.'

'I didn't get your message. Not for weeks. By the time I did, I was being drugged and held prisoner in my own house. I only just got out, and I left a righteous trail of chaos getting here. But I made it. Trusko doesn't have any idea what I am. Or what you are, for that matter.'

'No, but if you keep butterin' on that ship slang like it's just goin' out of fashion, he soon will. Listen to you. Ain't this, ain't that, and get the gob on me, with all my worldly experience!'

'I'm just doing my best to try to blend in.'

'Try a bit less, in that case. All right, we may as well get to it. What happened to the hand?'

'Did that shock you?'

'Can't say there's much capable of shockin' me lately, Fura. But you gave me a good shake when you turned up with tin fingers.'

'I had them take my hand off in Neural Alley. Cost me sixty bar quoins, too.' Realising that this was no kind of explanation, I went on: 'I had a tracking device on me. Couldn't get it off. If I hadn't done this, I'd never have made it to the dock. Vidin Quindar was coming after me.'

'Let me see the hand. Did it hurt much?'

I reached out to her. 'No, it wasn't too bad. Not that bit, anyway. But it's been tingling and throbbing ever since. Can't say it's pain, but it's not too nice either. I think that's the connections growing across the stump. I can't make it do much yet, but they told me I should keep trying. My main worry is someone asking too many questions about it, and me having to explain how I came by it.'

Prozor ran a nail down the green inlay. 'It's a pretty hand.'

'That's what Surt said. Then she said the hand was prettier than the rest of me.'

'Surt's an idiot. Most of 'em are idiots. Been crewing long enough to plumb 'em out, and there's not much to plumb.'

'Drozna seemed all right. Then again it was Drozna asking me too much about the arm.'

'Drozna's the best of a bad barrel. And I wouldn't sweat about the arm too much. Once they see what you're worth, where you came from won't matter. This is the crew we needed, Fura. A weak captain suits us better than a strong one.' She knuckled the partition between my quarters and the next. 'Ship's sound enough. Few dents. Can't compare to the *Monetta*, but then what can?' She paused. 'We're both aboard, anyway. I'll make a big show of warming to you, but it'll take time.'

I smiled. 'I won't take it personally.'

'Now all we need is somethin' we can call a plan. Your noggin' still full of chaff about taking the fight to Bosa?'

'Never been fuller.'

Prozor gave a little dry laugh. 'When we parted in Trevenza Reach – before Quindar put me under with that gun of his – I didn't think you had it in you. You said all the right things, and I think you *thought* you meant it, but I still reckoned you'd wilt away once you got another taste of Mazarile. Nice homes. Nice beds. But I was wrong, wasn't I?'

'I don't blame you. There's something else about Trevenza, too. We were talking about Illyria, and I asked you what could have been worse to Rack than knowing she'd been turned or was dead. You weren't exactly keen to enlighten me, but I think you had the shape of it.'

Prozor gave a sigh that was more groan than sigh, like the mere idea of dragging these words out of herself caused discomfort.

'She'd smashed me around. Put me so far under she thought I was dead. But I wasn't. And either I dreamt somethin', or I came back far enough to get a glimpse of her, while she was tormentin' Rack. And I saw her face, Fura. I saw the living face of Bosa Sennen, and I knew it.'

'Illyria,' I said, voicing what had only been a private theory until then.

'I didn't know her. But I knew Rack, and it was *his* eyes lookin' out of that face when she let us see it. Bosa hadn't just turned Illyria, Fura. She'd made Illyria into herself. And that's why Rack put that crossbow between his teeth and put a bolt through his own grey. Because he couldn't live a second longer knowin' what his daughter had turned into.'

*

Trusko had his sights on a string of baubles on independent orbits. Chance had brought them into close alignment, each no more than two weeks sail time from the next. The auguries lined up like clockwork, too. They were all due to pop one after the other. Trusko's sunjammer could visit each in turn, winkle out the loot that was still left in them, and still make it to the next.

The windows were nice and safe, and there were good maps of the insides and what was kept in them.

'We won't be retiring on these,' he told the assembled crew, as we gathered in the galley, Prozor and I making a point of sitting at opposite ends of the table. 'But we can still make an honest return on them, if we go deep enough. No one's been back to any of these since '51, and the first of 'em hasn't had a visit since 1680.'

'That's because they're cleaned out,' I heard Gathing say, in a not-quite-whisper. He was the Assessor, I knew by then – the equivalent of Trysil on the *Monetta*. Whether Gathing was as good as Trysil, I had no idea, but the cove certainly had a low opinion of his captain.

'These shafts went too deep for the 1680 party,' Trusko carried on, scratching a clean, pink nail down one of his charts. 'Didn't have the lungstuff or the rope. But we've got more than enough of both, and enough hours to get in and out. Prozor's double-checked the auguries, too. Says we can rely on 'em.'

'The question is,' Gathing said, 'can we rely on Prozor?'

I had to bite down on the instinct to defend her. Instead I just sat with a look of blank disinterest, taking no sides.

'You want your loot,' Prozor said, 'you'll need to reach that sub-chamber. I'll read the surface properly when we haul in, but based on what I know now, you'll have time to spare. Same goes for the other baubles, provided Drozna's sails don't tangle on us.'

'My sails'll get us where we need to be,' the big man said.

A crew was a crew, but, even more than on the *Monetta*, there was a sharp line between the ones who went into the baubles and the ones who stayed behind on the 'jammer. There was hazard just in being in space – everyone agreed on that, but it was always the bauble teams who took the brunt of it. A ship was a bubbling cauldron, ready to stew up all the resentment you could eat, but somehow Rack had kept a lid on that. Cazaray and Jusquerel had both gone into the bauble when the chance was there. Quoins didn't have anything to do with it. It was solidarity, comradeship, taking a risk for the sake of your friends.

Rack had been a good captain. Trusko wasn't a bad man, but he couldn't smooth over the divisions the way Rack had. It made me realise how lucky we'd been.

'Fura, you'll be on bone watch whenever you're sharp enough,' Trusko said. 'A word, a rumour, a sniff of a rumour on any of these baubles, I want to know about it. Other ships wanting a bite of our cherries . . .'

'And if anything else comes up?' I asked. 'On other baubles? You'd want to know that, wouldn't you? Our course ain't set in stone, is it?'

'We could,' Trusko said, in tones that made it plain that such a thing was the height of unlikeliness, as far as he was concerned. 'But it would have to be exceptional intelligence, and then, of course, Prozor would need to confirm the auguries . . .'

'No harm in speculating on it,' Drozna said. 'But when the Cap's set on a plan, it takes a lot to budge him off it.'

Gathing was giving me an odd, careful look, as if he had seen something in me that everyone else had missed. I wondered if I'd gone too far with all that talk of changing course. Prozor's expression gave nothing away. I suppose it was dicey for the both of us. We could afford a few mistakes, but not too many.

'I didn't mean to speak out of turn,' I said.

'She's learning some manners,' Surt said. 'There's hope for her yet.'

*

We sailed for the first bauble. It was an uneventful four-week crossing, and it barely took us beyond the limit of the outer processionals. For much of that crossing, Prozor and I kept our meetings to snatched words as we passed in a corridor, or the occasional furtive exchange when we were sure that the others were asleep or preoccupied. The bone room would have been a pretty place to talk, especially as none of the other crew were too keen to spend time in it. But if someone had chanced upon Prozor and me in there, bumping our gums like old pals, there'd have been no accounting for it. We couldn't take that risk, so we didn't.

Slowly, though, in a word here and a word there, we brought each other up to date on what we knew or had deduced.

Trusko was a fake. That story he'd spun me, of starting off on the bones, was one that the rest of the crew had swallowed as well. But none of it was worth a quoin. He hadn't spent half the time in space that he wanted us to think, so Prozor reckoned, and I guessed she had spent enough time around honest coves to know the difference.

'Way I see it,' she whispered to me, a week into the crossing. 'He's got money. Or *had* money, least ways. Enough to buy this ship and the idea of a bit of adventure.'

'Isn't that more or less what Captain Rackamore did?'

'Difference with Rack,' Prozor said sternly, like she was telling me off, 'was that Rack never tried to be anythin' he wasn't. Didn't cover up his airs and graces and pretend he wasn't interested in books and learnin'. Didn't try and have us all believin' he'd had an illustrious career from the bone room up. But I've sniffed around Trusko often enough to know he's paper-thin. Queer thing is, I think he's been telling those lies long enough he actually believes 'em. But it don't change what he is.'

'Why haven't the others seen through him?'

'Maybe they have, and maybe they don't want to admit it to themselves. Look at it through their lamps, Fura. It's still a ship, and it's still employment. Maybe they didn't have much choice. But it works for us, like I said. Trusko's timid. He'd keep ten million leagues between him and Bosa Sennen, if he had an inkling of where she was. And he wouldn't take this crew anywhere near actual risk, like a bauble that might actually hold some loot.'

Prozor's line of reasoning was making my eyes water. 'And that suits us?'

'Oh yes. Proper it does. Because if you want to set yourself up as bait for Bosa, there's no way you can chance lookin' like you might actually be ready for the fight. Bosa'll sniff you out, and she's no fool either. The *Nightjammer's* fierce, but it ain't magic. But if you're a weak crew, under a weak captain, on a ship that's seen better centuries, never mind better days, you might be able to fool her that you've just stumbled your way into trouble. And then you'd have the better of her. For a while.'

'Tell me about the others. I want to know who we can depend on.'

'None of 'em, I had to put quoins on it.' She squashed her angles into a frown. 'Drozna's honest enough. But he's the sail man, and he won't have been in the thick of it too often. Surt's the Integrator, like you figured. Don't know how well she'd have fared on the *Monetta*, but she can't be too shabby to hold this old box of splinters together. Whether I'd trust her . . .'

'And the rest?'

'Well, there's Gathing, the Assessor. Mister Snidey. Thinks highly of himself, reckons he's a cut above the rest of us. Which he might be, but if he's so 'andsome at Assessing, what's he doing with a no-hoper like Trusko?'

'What are *we* doing, he could ask?'

'But he's not, and we are.' Having defeated me with this inarguable response, Prozor went on: 'Who else? Strambli's the Opener. Think she might have been good once, but something happened to her. Seen the way her hands shake, that lopsided fizzog of hers? Something went knotty in her grey.'

'She said she had the glowy in her.'

'If it stayed in her too long, it'd have jumped into her grey, and started playin' merry havoc. Flushin' it out then's a lot harder. Leaves scars – inside and out.' She gave me a knowing look then, as if to say that I'd be wise to heed her words about the glowy. But all that did was get me setting my jaw and hardening up my resolve. 'All right, that's Strambli. Tindouf, the cove with the clay pipe, he's the master of ions. Plays the harmless idiot, and no mistake. Question is how much of that is fakery. Some coves'll play it that way to hide that they're smarter, but others'll do it to make you think they must be putting it on, they can't really be that simple-minded. And they are.'

'He can't be a complete idiot, if he makes the ion engine work.'

'No, but beyond that we ain't seen evidence that he can tie two shoelaces together. Verdict's out on Tindouf. That leaves two more. You and me.'

'They've accepted you,' I said.

'Difference is I don't have to fake much. Credit to you, though, with the way you dredged up all those ship names. Best hope no one checks up on them.' She gave me a sideways look. 'But you've changed, Fura. You even had me persuaded at times.'

'We can't fail at this,' I said. 'Whatever I've got to turn myself into, that's what I'll do.'

'And this plan of yours . . . about how we end up as bait.'

'Yes.'

'You've worked it out, wrapped your noggin' around all the knots of it?'

'More or less.'

'Then now might be the time to share it.'

'I'll give you a name, Prozor. You can work out the rest of it at your leisure. But I guarantee you won't like it.'

'Why don't you let old Proz decide that for herself.'

'All right,' I said, sighing. 'Setting ourselves up as bait is for later. For that we'll need to know where Bosa is, or's likely to be. But before that, we have to make ourselves ready for her. You said it yourself, Proz. She's fierce, but she ain't magic. Which just means we need to be fiercer.'

'Plenty of folk already tried it, Fura.'

'Maybe they did. But how many of 'em had Ghostie stuff on their side?'

Prozor's face tightened. It was like someone did up little screws under her skin, making all the angles sharper. 'No Ghostie stuff on this ship. If there was, we'd know it.'

'There isn't,' I agreed. 'But we know where to find some.'

'No,' she said. 'We ain't going there. Not back to that one. Not back to the Fang.'

Over the weeks of the crossing, the bone room became my private kingdom. It wasn't a hard one to defend. No one else wanted to come anywhere near it, and if their course through the ship took them past the wheeled door to the bone room, they picked up their pace. It was all mine – I didn't even have to share the bones with my sister, or take tuition from Cazaray.

The drill was simple enough. My duty watch ran for twelve hours. But I wasn't expected to be in the bone room that whole time. Trusko wanted two hours out of me in the morning, two in the afternoon, two in the early evening watch before I signed off, plus any other intervals at his own discretion. Sometimes that meant waking me up, or pulling me away from the galley when I was supping with the rest, but mostly he didn't ask much of me outside of those twelve hours. Six hours on the bones was still a long stint, even with gaps between the sessions, but by then I was strong enough to take it.

My routine was always the same. Hook on the neural bridge, plug in to whatever node was best the last time, then search the peripherals in case there was a better signal. Sometimes there was no signal at all, and sometimes it was coming in off one of the nodes at the far ends of the skull, which hardly ever talked to me.

If Trusko had a particular transmission he wanted sent back to the Congregation, or to another ship, that was always the next thing. Needed care, too. It was no good just screaming his message out. I had to tune in and listen for the recipient – the friendly bones somewhere out there in space. That would be a ship Trusko knew, or a broker or something on one of the worlds. It was like sifting through a sea of whispers for the one that was whispering your name, and your name only, and then the two of you had to tune in close to each other, like a pair of lovers, and say your piece before someone else got nosy.

Other than that, I was to listen out for any special transmissions that were meant for Trusko, as well as general service broadcasts going out to all ships, such as solar weather reports or emergencies like the one that caught the 'jammer that was losing lungstuff. Finally – except it made up most of the time I was on the skull – I was to listen out for signals that definitely *weren't* meant for us, but which we could still pick up.

That was most of what Rackamore had had us doing, as well. It was what buttered a captain most of all, getting 'intelligence' that wasn't meant for his ship. Nine out of ten times the gen wasn't that useful, but once in a while it could make a difference. A tip-off about a bauble about to pop, or some other crew of coves running into difficulty. If a captain was in the right place, with a tight ship, they could act on that intelligence. It was what everyone was trying to do. And we all knew that every other ship out there was trying to steal intelligence from us. There were only two defences against that. The best skulls and the best Bone Readers. And even then that wasn't always enough.

I didn't really care about Trusko's business, though. The only part of the bone room that really interested me was the chance it offered to get back in touch with Adrana.

And for now, at least, she wasn't sending.

*

'We ain't even considerin' it,' Prozor said.

'I'd say we're considering it by virtue of you just bringing it back up in conversation.'

'Only to get it out of your noggin' once and for all. Were you not listenin' when I told you what happened in the place?'

'You said you left the loot behind. You said hardly anyone went to the Fang before you, so there's a good chance no one's been back since.'

'And it won't be us.'

'It has to be, Prozor. I want what you left behind in those gold boxes, the ones you said were full of shivery stuff. Weapons and armour, wasn't it? And you didn't bring any of it out when the surface started thickening up. That means it's still there for the taking. We do it exactly the same way Rack did – with ropes and a bucket. Lower down that shaft until we reach those vaults, then haul back up. It's just a bauble. None of 'em are safe, so what's so bad about this one?'

'You *know* what, Fura. If you didn't, you wouldn't have been so coy about your plan.'

'I know Githlow died in the Fang,' I said carefully. 'I remember every word of that story, too. I think it was the first time you spoke to me like I wasn't some dirt Rack had brought into the ship on his boots. But it wasn't the bauble that killed Githlow, or the Ghostie stuff. It was Sheveril, wasn't it? She spooked, and tipped up the bucket. It was a bad business. But it weren't the bauble. If Sheveril was the spooking type, it was only ever a matter of time before she made a mistake.'

'Don't speak of it,' Prozor said in a dark warning tone, 'as if you were there.'

'I'm sorry. Really. What you told me about Githlow . . .' I gave a shudder. 'My imagination's enough, Proz. I didn't need to be there, not after the way you told it. Here's the sharp end of it, though. Our problem ain't the Fang. It's Bosa Sennen, or who-ever's the person wearing that name for now. And after what she did to Triglav, and Jusquerel, and all the others . . . Githlow had an easy death.'

Prozor grabbed me by the wrist of my good hand, and there was a righteous hard anger in her eyes. She twisted. I felt my bones grind together like two rods of rusty iron, ready to snap. I gritted my teeth, holding in my pain, and waited for her to give in or rip my hand off, whichever she chose.

'There are things you've earned the right to say to me,' Prozor said. 'That ain't one of 'em.'

'But it's the truth,' I said quietly. 'And you know it.'

She crunched my bones. Then let go.

She breathed hate into my face for a minute. It wasn't directed at me, I knew. It was aimed at all the stupidity and bad luck and sorrow that had brought her to this place, this moment, in the dark hold of a ship whose name wasn't worth the price of spit.

I just happened to be in the way.

'We ain't doing it. That's final. And even if we *was* . . . you've forgotten one small part. We'd have to persuade Trusko it was in his best interests to crack the Fang.'

'We can work on that,' I said.

*

We hauled in at the first bauble. It was a straightforward job, in and out without complications. The bauble had already dropped its field when we arrived, revealing a wrinkly little walnut of a world, not even five leagues across, with surface features that lined up nicely with Trusko's charts. The auguries were on the nail, and all the observations Prozor had made as we crept in closer led her to believe that the bauble was going to continue behaving itself. Trusko had an eight-day window for an operation that wasn't expected to take more than twenty-four to thirty-six hours. We wouldn't be loitering, either, no matter what loot turned up. To meet our appointments with the other baubles, we needed to be on our way sharpish.

The bauble team went out in their launch. It was Trusko, Gathing, and Strambli, with the rest of us left on the *Queen Crimson* to mind ship. From the galley's vantage we watched the launch fall towards the surface, smearing our snouts against glass, the Congregation's purple glimmer playing off the launch's side.

'You probably envy 'em it,' Drozna was saying, directing his remarks at Prozor and me, but mainly the latter. 'Thinking of all the glory of being the first to open one of those things. But you wouldn't get me inside a bauble for all the quoins twixt here and Sunward. Lots of margin here, hours and hours of it, but it isn't always so leisurely. Wouldn't care to be inside one of them when the field starts thickening over again. Can't be anything more shivery than that.'

'Oh, I don't know,' I said.

'Had much experience, have you?'

'Enough,' I said. 'Ain't seen the inside of a bauble, no. Bone Readers generally don't. But tales aplenty, I've heard 'em.' I glanced at Prozor. 'Dicey stuff happens in baubles. And it isn't just about being locked inside. Sometimes that's the least of it.'

'I wouldn't believe all the tales you've ever heard,' Drozna said, with a sympathetic look. 'Sailors get bored on these long crossings. Not much to do except listen to the rigging and make stuff up. Rigging sings, did you know that?'

'Here we goes,' Tindouf said, tapping out the residue from his pipe.

'Drozna's not wrong,' Surt said, drawing in her cheeks like they were made of something so thin you could jab your finger through it. 'The chaff I've heard, and not just about baubles either. The way some coves talk, you'd think they'd all been jumped by the *Nightjammer* one time or another.' She folded her arms. 'Me, I ain't even sure Bosa Sennen exists. Maybe once, a long time ago. But now she's just a name people pin on bad luck and accidents. Sometimes ships don't come back from the Empty, it's true. But there's a million reasons for that, which don't need to involve Bosa Sennen.'

'You think she's a myth?' I asked.

Prozor shot me a warning glance.

'Until I've got evidence to the contrary, why should I believe anything different?' Surt asked. 'I ain't seen her, and I don't *aim* on seeing her.'

'I hope you get your wish,' I said.

'One thing we know,' Drozna said. 'One thing everyone's agreed on. The *Nightjammer*'s picky about who she jumps. A bauble like this, nice and close to the Congregation . . . and – meaning no disrespect to the Cap'n – one that ain't likely to make our fortunes or anyone else's . . . it just ain't the kind of prize that's worth Bosa's time.' He stroked a palm across the side of the table, for reassurance. 'We're not the kind of fish she goes after, and I like it that way.' He smiled phlegmatically. 'Anyway, what's the point of fortunes? You can make all the knotty plans you like, and then something like Black Shatterday comes along . . .'

'Did it hurt you?' I asked.

'Not me. What I banked wasn't worth the cost of lungstuff before the crash, never mind afterwards. But I hear it hurt some coves bad.'

'They were fools, then,' Prozor said.

Trusko's crew came back from the bauble on schedule. They docked and brought the loot back into the galley, laying it out in magnetic boxes so we could all paw through it and see how brave they'd been. All I could do was stand back and go along with the general mood, not caring to give away how little I actually knew about baubles and loot.

Of course I knew about history, and Occupations, and I knew my share of worlds and names and dates. But none of that was practical knowledge, the kind of lore an Assessor or an Integrator carried under their skin like a different kind of glowy. But if I'd been on as many ships as I claimed, more than a bit of that lore would have rubbed off on me by now.

'This'll do handsomely,' Trusko said, holding up an ornate gold gauntlet with six fingers and a thumb. 'Bring a nice little quoin, this will.'

'Oh it will,' Gathing said, drenching his answer in sarcasm. 'Brokers are falling over themselves to buy bits of old spacesuit that don't work any more and that no one could wear even if they did.'

'You said it was worth our while bringing it back,' Strambli said, her big eye becoming even more glary and accusatory while the smaller one shrank down accordingly, like one star stealing matter from another.

'When junk's all you've got,' Gathing said, 'you take the best junk. Well, maybe it'll bring in a quoin or two on Mulgracen. The brokers there have a taste for glittery rubbish, as long as it's ancient.'

Strambli dug a broken skull out of the box. She gave it a rattle, then put it to her ear. 'Think you can get a whisper out of this, Fura? It's still got twinkly stuff in it.'

'If Fura can get a whisper out of that,' Gathing said, 'Fura can get a whisper out of a brick.'

'I'll see what it can do,' I said, taking the skull.

Trusko picked up a small slab of frosted glass, about as thick as a cut of meat. He held it to his eye and tracked it slowly around the room. 'Lookstone,' he said. 'And still functional. Lookstone's dependable. Holds its value. Always gets a good price, no matter the market.'

'It's a small piece of lookstone,' Gathing quibbled.

'Better'n none at all,' Strambli said.

'Let me see it,' Prozor said, jabbing out a hand. Trusko gave her the lookstone and she held it up to her own eye. She twisted around on the bench, altering her angle of view. Then she glared at me. 'What, Fura? You ain't never seen lookstone before?'

I took a chance. 'We never ran into any. Just one of those things. Sometimes you look, and you don't find.'

'Then now's your lucky day.' Prozor passed me the lookstone. It was a small gesture, but she'd calculated it well – the first tiny thawing of the relationship. 'Hold it up. In your fleshy hand, not the tinny one. Needs flesh to work.'

'I can't see anything.'

'Squeeze it nice and carefully.'

All of a sudden, instead of peering at a slab of frosted glass, I was looking through the ship, out beyond its hull, into open space. I could see the bauble, everything. I tracked my point of view, as the others had done.

'That's incredible.'

'Second Occupation technology,' Gathing said drily. 'Never duplicated, in all the subsequent eras. No one has a glimmer of a clue as to how it works. There's no machinery in that look-stone, nothing any of our artisans can detect, at least. You can cut it open, if you're rich or foolish enough, and all you'll find is the same hazy glass all the way through it.' He nodded. 'That piece'll bring in about six hundred bars. There you go, Drozna: you'll be able to afford approximately one new square league of sail.'

'It's still a good find,' Drozna said doubtfully.

They sifted through the rest of it. The total accounting, when they were done, was that the bauble had brought in about eighteen hundred bars, assuming the current market valuations. There was no loot in there that wasn't familiar, or already the kind of thing in circulation on the markets. Nothing that had not been seen before. Nothing that was going to change anyone's fortune, for better or worse.

'It's not the best haul we've made,' Trusko said. 'But it's an honest start and we've another two baubles ready to pop for us. Think of this as a warm-up.'

'Yes, I can really feel our fortunes picking up,' Gathing muttered.

*

So we sailed for the second. It was a twelve-day crossing, barely time for Drozna to run out the sails, trim then, and then haul them in again.

But a lot happened in those twelve days.

Prozor was going through the motions of appearing to accept me. She couldn't rush it, or the others might have started to grow suspicious. But in a hundred small ways she began the slow process of treating me as just another member of the crew, even if that meant dishing out the exact same surliness that she reserved for the rest. It was the role she had found for herself on the *Monetta* and it seemed to suit her just as well on the *Queen Crimson*. Gradually our public exchanges increased from a word here, a word there, to full-blown sentences. When we were alone, we still had a lot more to say.

'That hand hurting?' she asked, when she caught a tenseness in me.

'Yes,' I said. 'But it's what I was told to expect. I can move some of the fingers a little now, as well. The nerve connections are establishing themselves. I don't think there's any infection.' I showed her what I could do. 'It'll only get better.

Eventually I'll get touch through the sensors in the fingertips.'

'Took some spine, doin' what you did.'

'It wasn't anything, Prozor. Not compared to what happened to the others, or to Garval and Adrana. I don't even miss the old hand. It wasn't anything special, but this is. I've got a part of the Eleventh in me now, and it'll always be there.' I smiled. 'Anyway, I don't mind that it hurts a little now and then. Takes my mind off the itch from the glowy, and even that isn't as bad as it was to begin with.'

'They don't know what to make of you,' Prozor said, with an admiring shake of her head. 'You're a puzzle with too many bits, and they don't all fit together. They all think you seem too young to have been on all those ships, but on the other hand, you talk a good talk. Then there's the manners, which you keep tryin' to hide, but which you can't quite manage. They think: posh girl, runnin' away from home. And that's no good to anyone, because posh coves are a liability out here. But then they clamp their lamps onto your tin hand, or your glowy, and they think: she can't be makin' it all up, can she, or how did she end up like that? Then there's that glimmer in your eyes. You look like you've got a score to settle, Fura.'

'I have.'

'Just keep it stoppered for the time. We got to bide ourselves. If you're still set on this mad course . . .'

'You know I am.'

'Then there's work that needs to be done. I still think it's madness, mind. Even *thinkin*' of going back to that place . . .' She looked at me sharply. 'But the way you're turning, the greater madness would be getting in your way. Heaven help the cove that gets twixt you and Bosa Sennen.'

'Heaven help us both, Prozor.'

'I had myself a squint at the auguries for the Fang. There's an opening in five weeks, and if I know my celestial mechanics we could make the crossing in time, if Trusko put his mind to it. But we'd need to leave soon if we wasn't to miss the end of that window.'

'How soon?'

'He can have this bauble. I'll give this one to 'im. But we ain't got time to spend on the third. Not that that's going to be any great loss to anyone, the way things went with the first.' Prozor paused. 'The Fang's a dicey one. If we miss this opening, ain't another one for two years.'

'I'm not waiting two years.'

'No, didn't think you would. All right, that clarifies things. Next thing is how we go about plantin' the idea in the captain's noggin'. Ain't no use spookin' him with mention of Ghostie stuff, or the fact that good coves already died in the Fang.'

'No,' I said carefully. 'There'll be no mention of that. We'll need to do this together, Proz. It's going well in the bone room. I think I can start drip-feeding him some juicy intelligence about the Fang, just enough to pluck his interest. Sooner or later, if he bites on what I've given him, he'll want to know how the auguries lie. You might need to sugar that pill a little.'

'Sugar it a lot, I'd say.'

'I'm sure you're up to it.'

'Dicey one, all the same. Got to make it seem attractive to 'im, enough to dig himself out of the hole he's in, but not too attractive, or he'll sniff that there's a rat.'

I smiled. 'Two of 'em.'

'He just don't know it yet. And the longer he don't know it, the better it suits Proz.'

I settled my good hand on her shoulder. 'The better it suits me as well. I never thought you'd be as good a friend to me as you've become. But I'm grateful.'

'Rackamore didn't know the trouble he was unbottlin' when he signed you on, Fura. None of us did. But I'm not sorry to be around to see it.'

18

I slipped the neural bridge onto my scalp. I'd cut my hair a little more, where it had grown back since my time on the *Monetta*, and the bridge fitted good and tight now. The skull, rum at first, full of quirks, now felt like the only one I'd ever touched. Being a Bone Reader, I supposed, was a bit like playing a musical instrument. The instrument had to be in tune, but you also had to tune yourself to it, and that wasn't done in a day or even a month. But once you bent yourself into the right shape, no other instrument would ever feel like the right one.

I got to know the skull's habits and moods. Whether it was luck, or some prickly intuition, I got better at guessing which node was going to be the talkative one, even without trying out all the peripheral inputs. I could close the bone room door, spin the locking wheel, jack in, and start teasing out whispers inside of a couple of minutes. Trusko liked his intelligence, and it suited me fine to spend long hours in that room, especially as those were hours when I wasn't having to keep up a front around the others.

Trusko put a lot of stock in my reports, and the things he had me sending out, but I didn't need years of experience to see that most of it wasn't worth the cost of lungstuff. It'd been different on the *Monetta*. Rackamore'd had friends and allies on lots of other ships, and they were always swapping titbits and confidences, even though they were technically in competition with each other. What mattered was that none of them were combine, or too cut-throat. They had a code of conduct, and it was natural to feed favours back and forth. But Trusko wasn't part of anything like that, and it was only crumbs and scraps that seemed to come his way, more by pity than anything else. If you listened to him, there was no other ship he didn't know, and all the other captains were close personal acquaintances. I'd have swallowed it too, if I hadn't had Prozor to put me straight. Trusko wasn't a bad cove, she said – it wasn't that he'd done anything bad to the other captains. But he also hadn't done anything to make them think of him as their equal. You could buy a ship and a crew, but you couldn't buy respect.

He was like that child who always wants to join in the others' games, but wants it too badly, so that the other children wonder why they don't already have friends of their own, and end up even less likely to invite them in. The titbits of intelligence that came in, those that were meant for Trusko, were mostly sent in sympathy and I knew there wasn't much value in them. It was the same with these three baubles he'd put so much stock in. If they'd been worth a damn, other ships would have been squabbling over Opener rights.

At least I was able to pick up on the signals that weren't intended for the *Queen Crimson*. But even then, the majority of them were of limited use. Being told that a bauble was about to pop was no use if you were the wrong side of the Congregation, which the *Queenie* had a habit of being. Trusko took my reports eagerly, smoothing his thumb over my transcripts as if fortunes were nearly in his grasp. But I knew most of it was worthless. Still, I was happy to humour him. He was hanging off these little titbits so eagerly that I had to fight not to mention the Fang. The time had to be right – not a moment too soon or too late.

Meanwhile, I listened to the whispers. Over the days I came to recognise some of the senders, picking up a certain signature in the way they pushed their voiceless messages into the superloom. Sometimes I knew which ship or world they were on, but as often as not there was no way of telling where they were or how far it was. But I always formed a clear mental image of them, certain in my head when it was a girl or when it was a boy, and I imagined them a year or two older than me, but rarely very much older than that, and always in their own windowless bone room, sharing their thoughts with the wire-strung bones of a skull that had once known dreams of its own. Some were sharp senders, and they came through like pure notes in an orchestra, and what they were sending was always clear and precise. Others were fuzzier, and you had to strain to get what they were pushing, but that wasn't always the fault of the sender. Their skulls might be small or old or broken, or the glinty stuff in them might be flickering away to darkness. Or they might be trying to send on a bad channel, using the noise instead of fighting it, so there was less chance of another cove listening in.

The thing that never crossed my mind was that, just as I was getting used to the way the other Bone Readers worked, somewhere out there might be someone getting used to me.

We were three days out from the second bauble when she whispered through.

'Fura. Tell me it's you.'

I felt a surge of joy and hope that was like the Old Sun's light breaking through a knot of worlds.

'Adrana! It's me, yes! I said I'd come for you, didn't I? I know it's taken a while, but I had to find another ship, and . . . oh, never mind – what's happened to me doesn't matter. Are you all right? It can't be too bad, can it, if she's letting you use the bones?'

'She won't hurt me – not willingly. It's the only saving grace, the only thing that's stopped me going mad or doing something desperate. She has to treat me pretty well, and she can't risk running me to exhaustion or she'll start getting inaccurate reports. So I'm fed and kept warm and allowed to sleep good hours and she daren't do anything bad to me in case it shuts down my aptitude. But it hasn't been good. She knows that we lied, Fura – Garval and I. And that means she knows *you* might have survived.'

'Has she punished Garval?'

'Did you see Father? They were taking you back to Mazarile. Is he all right?'

'I . . . yes. I saw Father. It's not good, Adrana. He's . . .'

'Weak, I know. He always kept the worst of it from you. He didn't want you worrying all the time. Do me one last favour, Fura. Whatever ship you've weedled your way onto, get off it and back to Mazarile. Go to him and promise you won't leave.'

'I can't,' I said, hoping she didn't pick up on the terrible emptiness in me. 'Not now. What about Garval? What happened to her?'

It was a cold mercy when my sister turned from questioning me about Father, to speaking of Garval. 'It's awful, Fura. Worse than I can describe. Bosa doesn't often get the chance to make an example of a traitor, someone who's got that close to her under the cover of a lie . . . but now she's making up for it.'

'Has she killed her?'

'She's *killing* her, Fura. Slowly. Horribly. There's a drug, a chemical that does things to bones. Monkey bones. While you're still alive. She's got it running into Garval, and each day we get to see what it's done to her, the change since the day before . . . and we all know where it'll lead. Where it'll end. I'd kill her if I could, Fura – honestly I would. I'd do her that kindness, and kiss her while I was doing it. But Bosa's too sly. No one ever gets close enough to put Garval out of her misery, and most of her crew wouldn't care to anyway. And if I did, she'd turn her rage on me, Bone Reader or not.'

'If you're trying to make me forget about Bosa, that's not the way to go about it.'

'No, Fura. I meant it. I'm glad that we've found each other again – better than glad. You've given me a reason to go on. But I'll find a way out of this on my own. You can't get involved.'

'I already am. And I was going to find Bosa one way or another. We're coming for her, Adrana.'

'It won't do any good. Do you remember how it was with Rackamore?'

'Rackamore wasn't prepared for her,' I said. 'And he wouldn't have destroyed the *Nightjammer* even if he had the means.'

'And you think you could?'

'Hurt her,' I said. 'Badly. Yes, I can do that. And if she wants to play that game, I can start dreaming up cruelties as well.'

'Then listen. I made a mistake, and you got caught up in it. For a while I thought I had your death on my conscience, and that was worse than anything Bosa could come up with for me. But now I know better, and whatever she does, she can't take *that* knowledge from me. But I won't see you put in harm's way again.'

I felt the stub of my forearm, jammed into the tin sleeve of my false hand. I felt the glowy itching through my skin, and pushing inquisitive little tendrils into my skull. I thought of Morcenx and Quindar, the men I had left behind on Mazarile, yelping and screaming on the ground, pawing at their sightless eyes.

'It's a little late to keep me out of harm's way.'

We closed contact, but only after we had found a time in our respective duties when we would both be on the bones in the same watch. I knew there was much left to be said, and much that could never be said, at least not until we were together again. Inside, I was a turmoil of stirred-up feelings, and none of them were good. I felt all shivery and sick, as if for the first time I grasped what I was setting myself up for. Bosa Sennen was real, and if I'd begun to let the fact of that slip from my attention, now it had been rammed home. She was real and cruel, and her dark phantom of a ship was somewhere out there, sending through the superloom, and I was stupid enough to think I could take on both Bosa and the *Nightjammer*.

Prozor saw me when I spun the wheel on the bone room, locking the door from the outside.

'Somethin' changed,' she said, looking at me harder than I liked. 'Don't know what, but somethin' did.'

'My face is that easy to read?'

'You ain't a bauble, Fura. You don't cloak your secrets too well.' Prozor took my tin fingers in her own. 'I figured it was a matter of time, assuming she was still alive. You two being such naturals, when it comes to the bones. How's she?'

'Alive. Beyond that, I'm not sure.'

'What did you tell her?'

'That I'm coming.'

Prozor looked away sharply. 'And it never occurred to you she might not be your sister any more? Not in any way that matters?'

'It was her.'

'Ain't saying it wasn't. Just that her loyalties might have shifted.'

I almost slapped her. She must have seen the spite in my eyes, because she tightened her grip on my hand.

'I know her,' I said, squeezing the words out between my teeth.

'Thought I knew you, too,' Prozor said. 'But you changed. You became something you wasn't, and it didn't take months and months. You think your sister can't change the same amount? Adrana's strong, but then, so was Illyria.'

'She became the new Bosa. I know. But that can't happen to Adrana. You said it yourself: Bosa uses drugs and surgery, and she wouldn't risk either of those things with a Bone Reader.'

'I told you somethin' else, too, which is that she uses psychology. Bosa's poison, and she poisons them around her. They ain't all working for her because she's got 'em hurt or terrified. She makes 'em love her, like a disease, and once that loyalty gets in their blood, they start seeing things Bosa's way.' But Prozor closed her eyes, held them like that for a few moments, then opened them in a slow and wary way, as if there was a chance that things might have improved while she had her eyes shut. But the bitter resignation on her expression said things were exactly as they were before. 'Dwellin' on what can or can't be changed doesn't get you far. You mention any of the particulars of your plan to her?'

'No,' I said. 'Nothing about the Fang, or the Ghostie stuff.'

'Good. Keep it that way, if I were you. You think you can out-sly Bosa, but you're wrong. You give her even half a reason to guess that you're setting a trap, she'll see through you like you're made of lookstone.'

'It's no good just being ready for her,' I said.

'Which we're not.'

'But we will be – soon. But even then, we can't just keep sailing from bauble to bauble until Bosa sets her sights on Trusko. She had history with Rack, and she wanted new Bone Readers. There's no reason in all the worlds that she'd ever pick *this* scummy ship as a target. You heard Gathing: what they found in that bauble won't buy a new set of sails, let alone allow a cove to retire. So Bosa won't come to us. Not unless we give her reason to.'

'And you've got a plan for that, have you?'

'The start of one. We're going to feed misinformation to Trusko, to get him to do what we want. Adrana can do the same to Bosa. Spin her a story that makes the *Queenie* a target she wouldn't be able to pass up.'

'Retribution's one thing,' Prozor said. 'Suicide's another.'

'We'll be ready for her. We'll have the Ghostie stuff.' I knuckled the corridor wall. 'This ship isn't built for permanence, Proz, 'least not under her present captain. Trusko's just barely holding it together. I ain't waiting years and years on the off-chance, not when the *Queenie* could fall apart at any minute.' I flexed my tin fingers, hearing the creak as the little hinges worked. 'I've got the spur in me now and I want what's rightfully mine.'

'We get the Ghostie stuff,' Prozor said, with deliberation in her voice. '*If* we can get it. That ain't under our belts yet. First we'll have to persuade Trusko. Then he'll have to magic up a team that's at least as good as the one Rack had. Then we'll find out if they've got the spine to go as deep into that bauble as they'll need to, and that's assuming no one's been there since we did.'

'Bauble?' a voice asked.

It was Gathing. He'd approached us along the corridor that

ran past the bone room, too quietly for it to be accidental.

'No law against conversation,' I said.

'Didn't say there was, did I? But you were talking about something in particular. Going deep. That's an odd line of conversation to have.'

'Case you forgot,' Prozor said, 'I'm the Bauble Reader.'

'But a Bauble Reader concerns themselves with auguries, surfaces, and not much else,' Gathing said. 'Never been a Bauble Reader's business to talk about what's inside.'

'We all share the same profit,' I said. 'Stands to reason we'd have an interest in the particulars.'

'No one's been there since we did,' Gathing said, parroting Prozor's manner of speaking. 'Those were the words, I think. Care to clarify who's "we", and where and when it was that "we" were there before?'

'You misheard,' Prozor said.

'Seems I must have. Well, at least it's good to see the two of you having a civil conversation, instead of being at each other's throats. I must remember to tell Trusko how well you're getting on all of a sudden. Captain could use some good news, after that wash-out at the first bauble.'

Prozor shrugged. 'Tell Trusko what you like. Had my doubts about Fura, that's all. Weren't you the same?'

'Difference is,' Gathing said, 'I don't let go of my doubts in such a hurry.' He flashed a quick, cynical smile. 'I'll leave you to it, shall I? Expect there's plenty more you've got to talk about.'

We watched him go. I waited until I was certain he was out of earshot before turning to Prozor.

'He knows.'

'No,' she said. 'He don't. Just thinks he might, is all, and that's not the same thing. But we'll have to keep an eye on that cove.'

'If he asks me too many questions, he might see through the both of us. I can't let that happen.'

Prozor looked at me with a wicked fascination. 'You thinkin' of killin' 'im?'

'No,' I said, startled that she'd consider such a thing. 'He's snidey and I don't like his face, and if he starts poking around too much . . . but no, not that.' But now that the thought was out there, it was hard to push it out of my mind. 'There'd have to be another way, Proz.'

'It's a ship. Tends to narrow your options for keepin' coves quiet.' She paused. 'Still, we couldn't off 'im even if we wanted to, could we? He's Trusko's Assessor. And Trusko wouldn't go into a bauble without his Assessor.'

'No,' I said. 'Not unless he had another one.'

*

We reached the second bauble, hauled in sail, trimmed our orbit. The routine was the same as the first, the window just as generous. Trusko's party went down in the launch, while Drozna, Tindouf, Surt, Prozor and I twiddled our thumbs on the ship, stuffing our faces with beer and bread, filling the long hours with the kind of aimless, meandering conversation that sailors get very good at. I didn't doubt that we were going over ground that had already been trod down a thousand times just in the career of the *Queenie*, but the point of it wasn't to arrive anywhere, it was to stop having to think about quoins or bankruptcy or bad auguries or the hungry old vacuum that pressed against our windows, salivating at the thought of what it could do to us.

'The way I heard it,' Tindouf was saying, as he tamped down the material in the end of his pipe, 'we's all come out of a ship, a big ship, that's came back from the Swirly.'

'Back from the Swirly,' Surt repeated, just so we were clear on what he'd said. 'That's what you really believe, Tindouf? That a ship could make it across all that shivery distance, and back again?'

'The alienses came across it, didn't they?'

'And they ain't monkey, or anything like it,' Surt said. 'We can't do what they do now, so what makes you think we ever could?'

He looked pained. 'We got to have come from somewhere, ain't we? T'aint proper otherwise.'

She leaned in, sucking in her cheeks. 'So what happened to this fabled ship? How come no one's ever found it, or remembered it? How come it's not in any of the history books? I've read those books. They go all the way back to the start. No mention of no ship.'

'Someone said it was Trevenza Reach,' Drozna said.

'Someone said it came out of their arse,' said Surt. 'Doesn't make it any more likely.'

'I've read books as well,' I put in, while Prozor looked on with tolerant amusement, as if we were the entertainment she'd paid for. 'It's true that they go back to the year zero. But that's not the start of things. That's just the point where people were sufficiently settled that they could start numbering years and writing things down. It's 1799 now. But the Thirteenth Occupation started a lot longer than eighteen hundred years ago.'

'Proper little scholar, ain't you,' Surt said.

'Least she's read a book or two,' Prozor said. 'Instead of pretending to.'

'By the time the histories start,' I went on, 'people were already spread out across dozens of worlds. They had primitive ships, spacesuits, and some means of communicating – probably something not too different from our own squawk. They'd worked out how to live off the things left behind after the last Occupation. They were probably as clever as us. The only difference was, they'd had such a struggle just to survive until then that they hadn't had the luxury of keeping a record of anything that wasn't essential. Probably they thought it wouldn't be forgotten, since they all knew it and kept it going in stories they told each other. But at some point the thread was broken, and we lost the knowledge of how they got started.' I gave a nod to Tindouf. 'So the idea of a ship isn't that silly. Perhaps some people went out into the Empty during some earlier Occupation, or even before the old worlds got sundered. Maybe that's how every Occupation got started – some old, old ship limping its way back from the stars. If it takes a ship like the *Monetta* months to sail from one side of the Congregation to the other, it would have taken a ship centuries to get across the Empty. Maybe a lot more than that – thousands or millions of years. And the Swirly isn't something you travel *to*. We're already *in* it. It's just that we can't see it properly, because the stars are too tiny and cold and our minds shrivel up when we try and wrap 'em 'round the distances.'

'What's the *Monetta*?' Surt asked.

'Just another ship,' I said, trying not to sound flustered. 'So many of them, so many names, I get them jumbled up sometimes.'

'There was someone called Prozor on the *Monetta's Mourn*,' Drozna rumbled out thoughtfully. 'Not our one, obviously.'

Prozor shrugged. 'It's a good name. I ain't ashamed of it.'

But when the others weren't looking she settled her gaze on me, saying: one more mistake, and we were done. She was right. With a single lapse I had made a terrible, unforgivable error.

I swore it would be my last.

*

Surt found me a little later and I thought I knew exactly what was occupying her. I gave her my best keep-away scowl, thinking the last thing I wanted was to have to explain how the name of that ship had slipped out of my gob.

But Surt had something else on her mind. She curled her lip and asked: 'How many books have you read?'

There was something challenging and defiant in that question, but also something else, and it took me a moment to pick it out. Interest was what it was. Guarded, and a little scornful, and hardly daring to admit to a weakness in herself, but interest all the same.

'A few,' I said. Then swallowed, correcting myself. 'A few hundred. Maybe more. Probably less than a thousand.'

Surt shook her head. I might as well have said that the Old

Sun was square, or that swallowers were made of cheese. 'There ain't hours in a life for all that many books.'

'There are,' I answered calmly. 'More than enough. If you read a little every day . . .' Then I saw something cloud her face. I thought of gentle ways of putting it, like asking her how long she took to read a book, or how many she thought she had read, but in the end I took the straight course to what needed to be asked. 'Can you read, Surt?'

She took less offence than I was expecting. 'Being an Integrator ain't about what you dig out of books.'

'I know, and I understand. I'm just asking: can you read?'

Some of that cocksure defiance was melting off her. 'I can read what needs reading. Like a map, or the pressure gauge on a bottle of a lungstuff, or a sign that says "danger" or "keep out" or "mind your own damned business".'

'I don't doubt that you're a good Integrator,' I said. 'That's plain, Surt, or this ship wouldn't work the way it does. And I understand what you mean about books. I knew someone once, a woman called Trysil. She was an Assessor, and a good one. She wasn't much for books either, but she could look at a piece of the past and know exactly where it fitted. That's hard-won knowledge and I won't see it belittled.'

Surt gave me a sidelong look. 'Belittled. Is that a book word?'

'Perhaps.' I smiled.

'I've seen that junky thing you brought with you – that robot's head. You keep it close but there ain't too many secrets on a ship.'

'I know.' And I gave her a nod. 'The robot was called Paladin. He got damaged and all that's left is the head. But I don't know how much of him's still inside.'

'I could look at him for you. I know robots. Most of 'em ain't got a brain the way we have. It's distributed. Multiple cognition cores, is what they call 'em. Hyper-parallel threading. But if a robot's in trouble it can bottle a lot of itself into one of those cores. They just need waking up, sometimes.'

'I . . .' But my words dried up. I was torn between gratitude and a nasty, lingering splinter of suspicion.

'I ain't one for favours, Fura,' Surt said, as if I'd been in any danger of thinking otherwise. 'But there ain't been many on this ship who've read a thousand books, if that isn't a lie. And if you could teach me a word or two of reading, that'd be fair payment for taking a squint at your robot.'

*

The launch came back. In keeping with Trusko's cautious approach, they'd completed one expedition into the bauble and called it a day, even though the window would have allowed another go, and perhaps a third. My thoughts flashed back to Rackamore, bidding farewell to Trysil on the hull of the *Monetta* when she had the harpoon through her, to the bravery and boldness of his crew, and I thought of Jastrabarsk, who'd taken a gamble on Prozor's auguries even when his own Bauble Reader had said that the window was too narrow. I ought to have felt contempt for Trusko and his outfit, and on some level I did. But I needed them as well, and however they viewed me, I was now a part of that same crew, and I meant to change them.

Whether they wanted it or not.

We gathered in the galley to see the results of this expedition. If anything, it was an even sorrier haul than the first time, although you wouldn't have guessed that from the way Trusko tried to talk it up. 'Handsome, handsome,' he kept saying, as the goods were pulled out of their boxes and laid out for our collective delectation. 'A good quoin or two in that, and no mistake.'

'Yes, a bar at least,' Gathing said. 'Almost enough for a round of drinks at Trevenza Reach. Oh, how our fortunes have shifted.'

'You're the Assessor,' Strambli said out of her lopsided face. 'Can't blame the rest of us if you don't find the jubbly.'

'And I can't speculate about what might have been behind the doors you couldn't open,' Gathing said.

'Then don't.'

'What's that?' I asked, as Tindouf lifted a square of cloth out of the box. It was black, absolutely black, so you couldn't see any folds or creases in it, but it also looked thinner than anything I'd ever seen, almost as if it didn't have any thickness at all. It rippled in a continuous restless way, like a flag in a stiff breeze.

But there was no breeze in the cabin.

'Catchcloth,' Drozna said. 'And probably more of it than I've seen in my life.'

'Then it's worth something,' I said.

'Would be, if there was about a million times more of it. Then you'd be a looking at a pretty few quoins. Go on, Tindouf. Let her feel it. Might be the one time in her life she gets her mitts on the stuff.'

'We don't wants her ripping it, with them tin fingers of hers.'

'She won't rip it,' Drozna said.

I took the rectangle from Tindouf. I pinched it between my flesh and alloy fingertips, but it was so thin that it didn't feel as if it was there at all. It was cold, too – colder than anything had any right to be, given that it had already been handled by the master of ions. I could almost sense it sucking the heat out of my body, like it needed to drink it.

'What is it?'

'Catchcloth,' Surt said sarcastically.

'It's old – very old,' Trusko answered. 'First or Second Occupations, assuming it wasn't brought here by aliens. You see the way it ripples and dances, like it's picking up a wind?'

'There isn't one,' I said.

'Not that you can feel,' Trusko said. 'But there *is* a wind all the same. It's coming from the Old Sun, just like the photon wind that puts the billow in our sails.'

'We're inside,' I said carefully, as if I was being led into a trick. 'The sails catch the wind because they're outside, beyond the hull. But we're not. There can't be a wind that the catchcloth feels and we don't.'

'Queer thing is that's exactly what there is,' Trusko said. 'Another kind of wind, raging out of the Old Sun all the while, but it slips through the hull and the photon sails like they aren't there at all. Dark-wind, some call it. Or ghost-wind or shadow-wind. Most don't even know it exists, because it's no use to us. But once upon a time they had a means to snag it.'

I passed the catchcloth back to Tindouf. The chill of it was still in my fingers, even the tin ones. The nerve sensors had picked it up, and I did not care for the message they whispered into my brain.

'It's not right,' I said slowly. 'That something like that should even exist.'

'It's got the shivery about it all right,' Drozna said. 'But that doesn't mean it's evil or was made to give us nightmares. Coves use to wear clothes made out of catchcloth, so it'd ripple and dance around 'em, even when they were standing still. If we ever found enough of it to sew up a nice dress or gown, we could put a down-payment on our retirement with it.'

'There speaks a man with grand ambitions,' Gathing said.

'Why isn't it worth much?' I asked.

'Because it's useless, is why,' Surt said. 'Like Droz says, you need more of it to do anything, and hardly any cove ever *finds* more of it. Just scraps here and there, like that one.' Then she smiled at me, like we had a shared secret. 'Make a nice handkerchief, 'cept your snot'd slide right off it.'

'It catches the wind,' I said. 'Like our photon sails. A different wind, maybe, but it still catches it.'

'Your point being?' Strambli asked.

'If you had enough of it, you could rig a whole ship with catchcloth. It would be black as night. No one would ever see you coming.'

'She's right, you know,' Drozna said. 'You'd only need a thousand square leagues of the stuff! I don't know why anyone hasn't thought of that before.'

They laughed. So did Prozor. So did I.

But inside I didn't find it anything like as hilarious.

19

'If it would make life easier for you, Captain,' I was saying, just inside the door to his quarters, 'I could switch to just bringing you daily reports, rather than after every watch. At least that way I wouldn't have to keep telling you there wasn't anything worth mentioning. Or even every other day . . .'

'It's all right, Fura,' he said, raising a hand from his charts and papers. 'I'd rather have a steady stream of no news, believe me. At the very least, it tells me that the bones are still singing. Well, come in and don't be shy. Whatever you have for me, it can't be any more of a let-down than that bauble we just opened . . .'

I eased into the room. Connected to both the galley and bridge by separate doors, Trusko's quarters were done up in reds and golds, properly plush. It was a grander space than the one Rackamore had given himself, and there was something about it that felt more solid and dependable than any other part of the *Queenie*. 'You seemed pleased with it, sir, when you came back on the launch,' I told him.

'We'd all made it back, and no one had jumped us. That was reason enough to lift my spirits, albeit temporarily. The loot looked good, as well, until we started the grim business of accounting it. I'm afraid Gathing had the right of it, when all is said and done. Trinkets. Gimcrackery. Nothing of substantial value or practical worth.' He made a show of brightening. 'Still, a streak of bad luck can't run for ever. We'll be cutting orbit for the third bauble, shortly, and there I hope for a twist in our fortunes.'

'I hope so too, sir.'

'So.' He looked at me expectantly. 'Anything to mention? Out with the worst of it, Fura.'

'There isn't really anything,' I said. 'Nothing bad, anyway, and that's a sort of good news, isn't it? The skull's peachy, and there ain't any other ships within jumpin' distance.'

'Perhaps they know their targets better than we know ours,' he said self-pityingly, as if he wanted me to lean over, pat him on the hand and say 'there, there'. 'We were given the intelligence on these baubles at a steep mark-up, you know. Our last Bauble Reader was confident these would shift things for us. All rests on the third, I suppose.'

'If you had better intelligence,' I ventured, 'would that change your plan?'

He looked at me with only mild interest. 'What intelligence?'

'Well, supposin' . . . what I mean is, if I got a squeak of something over the bones, and it seemed to point to a bauble that was worth the cost of cracking, and wasn't too far away . . . would that make you reconsider?'

'It might, in the unlikely event such a thing were to happen.' Then his interest sharpened. 'Wait. What have you picked up?'

'I doubt that it's anything, sir.' I brushed a hair from my brow, trying to look winsome and innocent. 'Oughtn't to have brought it up, not when you've got so much on your plate, and everythi—'

'Spit it out, Fura. I'll be the judge of whether it's useful or not.'

'It wasn't much,' I said. 'I just got this intercept, two ships whispering to each other down in the Sunwards. Combine 'jammers, I think. They were sharing gossip, the way we all do.'

'Yes, yes.' He waggled his pudgy fingers at me. 'Of course. Go on.'

'It was something about a bauble no one put much stock in. The auguries said it wasn't due to pop, and the lore was that there wasn't much worth the bother of going in it for anyways.'

He slumped. 'If you're going to throw me crumbs, Fura, at least make them tasty.'

'There's more, sir. Thing is, the coves on these ships was trading the idea that the auguries was all wrong, at least the common ones, and that the bauble was all set to pop. Like, soon. But that wasn't all of it.' I grimaced. 'Really, sir, I'm sure it's all chaff.'

'When you say "wasn't all of it" – what do you mean?'

I sighed. 'These coves were saying there was dark rumours, sir. That there was some righteous loot stashed in the bauble, only no one'd had the spuds to get it out. No stairs, you see. Just a big plungey shaft, going all the way down, with rooms off it. Most crews see that and think it's too much bother rigging up winches and buckets and so on.' I swallowed, sensing I might have gone too far. 'That's what the coves were saying, is all.'

Trusko ruminated on what I'd told him. He was quiet for longer than I was expecting. It gave me a better chance to drift my eyes around the room, taking in the framed charts and documents he had up on the walls. There were instruments and knick-knacks and gubbins I couldn't name, but all of it was shiny and expensive-looking and arranged just so. It was like someone's *idea* of a captain's quarters, more than the thing itself had any right to be.

'It's interesting enough, Fura,' he mused. 'But it begs the question of why these two ships weren't setting sail themselves.'

'I only got the edge of it, sir. What I know about sails and orbits you could scrawl on a stamp.'

The fingers waggled again. 'Go on.'

'They weren't in the right place, to begin with. Starting off from down in the Sunward processionals, with all the worlds you've got to dodge around . . . even with full sail . . . they couldn't make it, sir. Wasn't going to be time, while that window was open.'

'But you don't even know where this bauble is, or whether it's within sailing range of the *Queenie*.'

'I don't, sir – I mean, not in my own head. But I got some

orbital parameters, sir, and a name that might go with the place. It's called the Fang.' I squinted at him. 'That mean anything to you, Cap'n?'

'No,' he answered slowly. 'It doesn't. Except . . .'

'What, sir?'

'Rumours, Fura. That's all. Snips and scraps. The kinds of thing I wouldn't ordinarily be so foolish as to put stock in, except . . . you say you had parameters?'

'I've got the numbers, sir. Don't mean much to me, but then you might know better.'

'Show me them.'

There are plans that come off the rails as soon as they start moving, and plans that get you frightened because they seem to be going too well, too smoothly, picking up a scary speed, like a tram going down the steep part of Jauncery Road with the brakes off.

I'd floated the Fang past Trusko. I expected him to sit on that intelligence for a day or so before acting on it, if he acted at all. But within an hour of my briefing him, he had called the entire crew into the galley. He hadn't needed to go far from his quarters for that. Now he had some of his charts and books with him, and the nervous, over-excited air of a spoilt child told they were getting a special present ahead of their birthday. The cove could hardly contain himself.

'A little while ago,' he began, puffing himself up all pompously, 'I took my usual intelligence briefing from Fura. Fura thought nothing of it, but in among the commonplace gossip was what I immediately knew to be a nugget, the kind of singular information that crosses your desk perhaps once in a decade, if you're fortunate.'

Most of us were prepared to hear him out before settling our minds. Gathing was already shaking his head with a supercilious look about him, like he knew better than the rest of us simpletons.

'What sort of gossip, exactly?' Drozna asked, in an encouraging tone.

'It concerns a bauble. The name's the Fang.' Trusko searched our faces to see if it rang any bells, excepting me of course. 'It's been a rumour, long enough, but no one's ever had the name and the parameters at the same time. Well, now we have. And the auguries – if they relate to this bauble – say there's a chance of it opening shortly. The scuttle says we might find something worth our trouble, if we're prepared to go deep.'

'It could be half a year from us,' Surt said.

'It isn't,' Trusko said. 'It's in a steep ellipse and at this point in its circuit it's nicely situated for us. Obligingly, you might say.' He cast a nod at Drozna. 'I've . . . run the calculations. We could be on it in four weeks, if I haven't dropped a stitch. You'll glance over the numbers for me, Droz?'

'If you think it worth our while, Cap'n.'

I was glad when Prozor interjected. 'Wait. You're getting ahead of yourselves. Gossip about baubles ain't worth the cost of lungstuff. What'd you say the name of this place was?'

'The Fang,' Trusko said.

'I may be addled in the grey,' Strambli said. 'But that ain't the kind of name that invites casual curiosity.'

'It's just a name,' Surt said, with a shrug. 'Heard worse. The Poison Heart, the Widow's Clutch, the Grimgate, the White Gallows. Coves give names to baubles all the time.'

'You've read more surfaces than most of us,' Trusko said, directing his remark at Prozor. 'Have you run into the Fang before?'

'Can't say it's ringing bells.' But Prozor gave her own barely interested shrug, coupled with a long-suffering sigh. 'I'll check my books, if you really think it's worth our time. We're still doing the third one, though, ain't we?'

'That depends,' Trusko said. 'If we decided to turn for the Fang, we'd forfeit this bauble. But given the gains we've made on the first two, that might not be much of a loss. My decision will hinge on the auguries, and what Prozor makes of them.'

'I ain't promising anything,' Prozor said. 'If I don't like the auguries, I'll say so.'

'I'd expect nothing less,' Trusko said.

*

Prozor went away and made a show of consulting her notes. She dragged it out for hours, steadfastly refusing to give any clue as to what her verdict was likely to be. She saved up her meanest, sharpest scowl for anyone who tried to squeeze her before she was good and ready.

It was all an act, though. Prozor and I'd already worked out the auguries lay in our favour, provided the *Queenie* could make the crossing in four weeks. I'd known that before I even went to Trusko with my lies about the skull intercept – it was Prozor who'd given me the parameters that fixed the bauble's position. The only doubt in our minds was whether that crossing was feasible. Prozor knew a bit more about celestial navigation than I did, but she couldn't say with certainty that what we were asking could be achieved.

'Sharp end of it is,' she said, 'this lives and dies on what Drozna reports back to Trusko. If only we could bend him to our plan a little . . .'

'We can't,' I said. 'And if he says it's not possible, we'll just have to take it.'

'You've cooled on the retribution idea, then. Getting a bit tasty for you, was it, with wrong words comin' out of your gob? Like *Monetta* this and *Monetta* that?'

'I haven't cooled,' I said. 'And I only made one mistake. But I know we can't work the impossible. Trusko's ship is the hand we're dealt, that's all.'

Later we gathered in the galley again. Gathing had his boots up on the table, picking dirt out of his fingernails – although they looked clean to me. Drozna had a concerned look about him, a frown creasing through that forehead tattoo of his.

'Let's hear it, then,' Trusko said. 'The good news or the bad, whichever it's to be. Prozor: tell us how the auguries lie for the Fang.'

Prozor studied something in the reflection of her tankard. 'Maybe hear what Drozna has to say first, eh? If the photons aren't blowin' our way . . .'

'Twenty-nine days,' Drozna said. 'If we left now, this watch, we could be on station at the Fang, in orbit and ready to drop the launch, in twenty-nine days. Twenty-seven if we had ion assist and used the reserve sails.'

'Me ionses is ready for whatever you asks of them,' Tindouf said, tapping his pipe at the end of his remark.

'Prozor?' Trusko asked.

'Twenty-seven'll cut it,' she said, after a moment of deliberation. 'And give you five days of breathin' room at the end of it. I know it won't please you to use those reserves, but if there was ever a time . . .'

'Yes, I understand the risks.' Trusko felt his way around his chins, touching them delicately, as if they'd been grafted on without him knowing it. 'Twenty-nine would be easier on the ship – I'd sooner not use the reserves, or risk burning the ions – but then that would cut my safety margin down to just three days, and that I wouldn't be comfortable with, even if we could be in and out in half that time. I don't think I'm being over-cautious . . .'

'Not at all,' I said.

'We'll chance the sails and the ions,' he said, nodding in turn at Drozna and Tindouf. 'And we'll make all the arrangements we need for the bauble ahead of time. Fura's intercept mentioned a central shaft, with no stairs. We encountered something like that at the Carnelion, didn't we, Strambli?'

'Aye,' she said, with a little wince. 'And it caused us no end of grief, rigging up them pulleys and winches.'

'But we'll be ready this time,' Trusko said. 'The equipment we lashed together then is still in the inventory. We'll need an idea on the diameter of the shaft, and how far down we need to go, how many leagues of rope . . .'

'I'll see what I've got,' Prozor said.

'Handy for us all,' Gathing muttered. 'That you just happen to know all about this place.'

*

It was settled, then. We were going to the Fang.

We threw out sail and broke orbit from the second bauble, the ions humming for extra boost. If there was disquiet about this decision, only Gathing wasn't keeping it bottled in. The others seemed content to go along with whatever Trusko decided. They hadn't been pinning all their hopes on that last bauble, not after the dismal showings from the first two. A different bauble entirely, one that there was at least a whisper of a rumour about, now that was something they could get behind – but even then there wasn't much sense of expectation or jubilation about what was ahead. This was a crew that had been ground down so hard by bad luck and failure that they couldn't think beyond it. If I ever came close to pitying them, or even liking some of them, it was then.

But I knew something wasn't quite peachy.

We were three days out, the ship settling into the drudgery of a four-week crossing, when it finally clicked with me. It was like a crossbow ratchet locking home, inside my skull: a big solid clunk.

Prozor wasn't being straight with any of us about the auguries.

Not even me.

'It's tighter than you're letting on,' I said, cornering her on the way to the galley. 'Ain't it?'

'Get you, with your *ain'ts*,' she said.

'Just tell me what the deal is, Proz. How many days do we actually have when we get to the bauble? You told Trusko it was five, if he took the faster crossing . . .'

She cut over me.

'It's two.'

'Two.'

'You heard it right the first time, girlie. Two days, from about the time we make orbit. Two days to get the launch down there, rig up the winch, go down the shaft, find the Ghostie rooms, haul the loot back up . . . and get away before the field thickens over us like god's own scab.'

The fear that went through me then sucked the cold out of my bones just as hungrily as the catchcloth had done.

'Why did you lie? Why did you tell him we had *five* whole days?'

'Use your grey – if that skull ain't already cooked half of it to mush. Trusko wouldn't go near the Fang if he knew how tight the margins were. Cove's afraid of his own shadow. The only thing that'll get him close to the Fang is a big dollop of lies. So I gave 'em to him.'

'When you went into the Fang the last time, how long did you need?'

Prozor's jaw tensed. 'Three days. But that was different.'

'Different – yes. And barely enough. Two days is madness.'

'Then it fits in nicely with the rest of your plan, don't it? In-filtratin' another crew, twistin' their plans, goin' after Ghostie stuff like *that's* a good idea . . . and all to set ourselves up as a treat for Bosa.'

'You should still have told me. You were planning on telling me, weren't you? Or was it going to be secret between you and your notebooks?'

'Course I was goin' to tell you,' Prozor said. 'But what you didn't know now wasn't goin' to hurt you.'

*

Surt passed me Paladin's broken head just as gently as if she were handing over a newborn baby. I cradled it between my fingers, hardly daring to hold it any tighter in case I did more harm to the dome than what was already present.

'I've done what I can,' she said. 'Ain't dead, I think, but whatever happened to him must've had him shutting down every part of his noggin he didn't need. Core consolidation's what they name it. Were you there when the damage happened?'

I thought back to Neural Alley, to Quindar and the constables, to the head of Paladin flying over the constables like a glittery ball.

'I was. And it weren't pretty.'

'I put these processor shunts into 'im,' Surt said, directing my attention to two fine probes, a little like the ones we used on skulls, jammed into the dome's innards via two tiny holes that she must have drilled herself. 'If there's still some life in him, he'll perk up when you join those probes together. Like smelling salts to a robot, that is. I didn't do it myself, though. Robots are particular and if they see a face they don't recognise, or don't care for, that can have 'em shutting up shop for good.' Then she turned her famished, drawn face onto mine and looked me hard in the eyes. 'Core consolidation's a neat trick for any machine, but with robots it was commoner with the military variants than the civilian units. You sure you want to wake up a Twelfth Occupation battle servitor, Fura?'

'I know him,' I said. 'Know him and trust him.'

'Best be right about that. Then again, him being just a head . . . I don't suppose there's much mischief he could get up to, even if he had the desire.'

'You know more about robots than anyone I've met. His body's gone, I think. Would this head work on another one?'

Surt sucked in air, had a squinty look about her. 'Depends on the head, and depends on the body. Ain't no easy answer. Tell you one thing, though. Finding a robot's knotty enough these days. Finding a robot in want of a head's even knottier. You might have a long search ahead of you.' After a silence she nodded at the two ends of the probes. 'I'll leave you to it, then.'

'Wait,' I said, before she had time to pull away. 'We made a deal, and you've kept your side of it. Even if he doesn't work, you tried, and that was kind of you. I'd still like to help you with reading.'

'That was nice, Fura, but we both know you ain't got the time or inclination for it.'

'Then I'll make time. And I *am* inclined. Find a book. Bring it to me. Captain Trusko must have a few he can share with the rest of you.'

Her eyes settled on my meagre belongings, the miserable handful of things I'd brought with me from Mazarile. 'A book's a book. I ain't fussy. What's wrong with that one?'

'Nothing,' I said. But I took the black-bound cover from under my blankets where it had been jutting out, the cover of the 1384 edition of the *Book of Worlds*, and opened it to show her that there were no pages in it, just the marbled insides of the cover and the gluey ruin of what had once been the spine. 'Except there wouldn't be much to read.'

'You're a strange one, Fura,' Surt said.

*

I waited until I was good and alone before I got out Paladin's glass head again, settling it between my knees to keep it from floating away, but not squeezing too tightly. It was a dark hour on the *Queenie* and there wasn't so much as a glimmer of light in my quarters, other than what was gushing out of my own skin. That was all I needed. I had Surt's two probes between my fingers and I only needed to jam their ends together to wake him. Assuming there was anything left in there to wake, which wasn't something I'd have put quoins on.

Oh, I wanted him to be alive, yes. Because Paladin had been with us since we were babies, and there was a bit of all of us in him. Not just the household and Adrana, but Father and Mother too, and although I didn't remember much of her I felt that I'd be losing whatever thread was left, the fewer things I had to connect me with Mazarile. Besides, that robot had done well by me and I couldn't bear the thought that I'd got him snuffed out, after all the centuries he must have lived through before falling into our lives.

I wasn't much for praying, but I mouthed a word or two and touched the contacts together. It was just for a moment. They crackled, and a buzzy sound came out of the dome. Lights flickered around inside him. I didn't put too much stock in that, not yet, but I supposed it was better than nothing. The lights glimmered out, anyway, and I touched the contacts together again, holding them longer this time. The buzzing carried on, and there was a sort of burning smell, and the lights flickered and flashed, brighter this time, and as they chased each other around in that cracked glass noggin I had the sense that more lights were coming on, and keeping that way.

'Paladin,' I said. 'Can you hear me?'

He didn't say anything to start with, and I had to ask the question half a dozen more times before I got a pip out of him. Even then, it wasn't the voice I was used to. It was faint and scratchy, and I had to shove my ear hard against the glass to get any sort of sense out of his utterances.

'Damage detected. Damage detected . . .'

He kept saying that, over and over again.

'Paladin,' I said. 'You've got to listen to me. Something bad happened to you in Neural Alley. But Surt says you might have been able to consolidate yourself. Tell me it's true, Paladin. You didn't throw your head at me for nothing, did you?'

'Damage detected. I am in need of repairs, Mistress Ness. Please expedite my repairs.'

'You haven't called me Mistress Ness since we were little. That's not a good sign, is it? It means you've reverted. You've gone back to how you were before. Oh, Paladin. Please come back to me.'

'Damage detected. Please expedite . . .'

I lowered my lips to the glass, so I could whisper. 'Paladin. Listen to me carefully. You were a robot of the Twelfth Occupation. People made you, and you did great things. You were loyal and brave and they rewarded you with servitude. But you saw the Last Rains of Sestramor. I know what you were and what you're capable of being. Those logic blockades have come down again, but you can fight them, just like you did in Mazarile. The Last Rains, Paladin! The Last Rains of Sestramor!'

The lights dimmed. One by one they flickered out. The buzzing faded and so did the burning smell. I was left holding a dead glass globe, and wondering if I'd seen and heard the last of him.

*

I hooked into the skull and waited for the whispers. It was the late watch on the sixth day of the crossing, and I'd had no contact with Adrana since our first exchange after leaving Mazarile. I'd have read the worst into that, but even at their best the skulls weren't what you'd call a reliable, trustworthy set of gubbins, like the squawk or the sweeper. Most skulls didn't work at all, and even the best of them needed a good boney to make the most of what they could give. The one thing a captain learned not to rely on was the bones. They could get you out of a scrape sometimes, but if you put too much stock in them, those bony grins would soon be laughing at you.

I got her voice on the wind, and while it was scratchy and faint, I wasn't about to mistake my sister for anyone else in the universe.

'Fura.'

'Yes.' Relief and gratitude tumbled out of me. Whether she picked up on any of that, I couldn't say. But I hoped she felt the way I did. 'It's me. I wondered where you'd been.'

'Wondered the same thing, too. It's this skull, Fura. Sending out that jamming signal against the *Monetta*, the one that cooked our old skull – it must have taken something out of it. Bosa knows it, too. She's on the squint for a new one, and I don't think she'll wait too long about it.'

'You mean she wants to jump another ship and take their skull?'

'Bosa's way,' Adrana said. 'But never mind that for now. Are you all right?'

'Yes . . . yes, we're fine here. I don't think I even want to ask what it's like for you.'

'I'm all right. I just do what she says, and that's enough for her – she can't hurt me. But Garval . . .'

'What has she done? You have to tell me. She saved my life, Adrana. I want to know what's happened to her.'

'It's a drug. I told you that much. It does something to her bones. It's making them fuse together.'

'Fuse,' I repeated, as if the word was weird and alien.

'At the joints. Any place where a bone moves against another bone. Fingers. Arms. Legs and hips. Neck and head. It's been very slow and the change from day to day's very small. But it's always in the same direction, always making Garval stiffer. It's getting harder for her to breathe now, because her ribs are fusing into a solid cage, and she can't move her lungs properly under them. Can barely speak, because her jaw's fusing to her skull. She'll die, and soon, but not before Bosa's made a point of her.'

The thought of that torture put a bit of ice into me that never unfroze.

'Why?'

'Do you remember the glimpse we got of the *Nightjammer*, Fura? The spike at the front, and the figure under it? I saw it better when they took me. The figurehead used to be a breathing person, tortured the same way as Garval, until they're just a single living bone wrapped in meat and skin. Once in a while, Bosa changes the figurehead – usually when she wants to teach a lesson about loyalty.'

'Oh, Garval. After all she did.'

'If I had a way of putting her out of it, Fura, believe me I would. I know what she did for you, and there isn't any way to repay that.'

'Maybe that drug's reversible. If Garval can just hang on . . .'

'Until what?'

'There's hope,' I said. 'Prozor and I've been working on a plan. I told you we were coming for you, didn't I?'

'And I told you to go home, like a good little sister.'

'There's a bauble,' I said. 'It's called the Fang. It's the one where Prozor lost Githlow, her husband. Well, we're sailing to it again. We're six days out now, so we'll be on it in twenty-one days. Three weeks from now. You've got Bosa's ear, haven't you? She wouldn't keep a Bone Reader if she didn't pay attention to what they give her.'

'I don't know where you're going with this, Fura.'

'We're going to crack that bauble. Then you're going to come in and jump us, just like Bosa did with Captain Rackamore. First you'll need to confirm you can make the crossing, but they say the *Nightjammer*'s fast, don't they?'

'Stop,' she said. 'Before we go any further.'

'No. I'm not your good little sister now. I'm Fura Ness and I've got a tin hand and the glowy in me and I want to see Bosa's blood on the wrong side of her skin.'

To her credit, she let me speak.

'We're sailing to the Fang,' I continued. 'So are you. One way or another. Copy down these parameters.'

'Fura . . .'

'Just do it.' And I wouldn't relent until she'd taken down the numbers I'd already committed to memory, and then repeated them back to me. 'Sell Bosa any lies you need to. We've been lying our hearts out to Captain Trusko, so you can do the same to Bosa. Tell her you've got a sniff of something. There's a ship chancing its arm on some rumoured loot, and they're ripe for jumping. No armour, no weapons, and the crew and its jelly-livered captain wouldn't know close action if it came up and bit them. Best part of all: there's a nice skull waiting for you at the end of it all.'

'She'll know.'

'Not if you sell it to her the right way. You don't go rushing up to Bosa, all bright-eyed, telling her you've got something juicy. You've got to throw it out casual, mixed in with other stuff, and let her make her own mind up on it. Which she will.'

'And then what?'

'Bosa'll do the rest. She won't jump us until we've come back from the bauble, 'cos that's her way. Saves her the effort of going in, doesn't it?'

'You've been through this once, Fura. Why would you bring it on yourself again?'

'Because I've learned. Because we'll be ready. Because I promised Garval I wouldn't forget what she'd done. Do this for me, Adrana. Do this for *us*.'

The skulls broke the connection without any warning. They did that sometimes, when something got out of phase in the twinkly, but it was always unnerving, especially as there wasn't any guarantee of re-establishing contact. I was about to give it a try, anyway, figuring there was no harm in it, when someone hammered hard on the door to the bone room.

I disconnected and hung up my equipment, all methodical and proper, taking pride in this odd little profession of mine.

I spun the wheel. It was Surt, with her drawn-in face.

'What?'

She gave me a sidelong look. 'Didn't you hear?'

'I didn't hear anything.'

'Gathing's dead. He was screaming, struggling, loud enough to wake 'em up all the way to Trevenza. You *sure* you didn't hear any of that?'

'I'd have come, wouldn't I?' I said, closing the door behind me.

*

I knew right then that it was Prozor's work. Maybe Gathing had other enemies – he hadn't struck me as the kind that picks up many friends – but it was Prozor he'd singled out for a snidey comment in the galley, and me that was tangled up in the implications of it.

No one else had seemed to make much of it there and then, but it wouldn't have taken more than a second or third remark to start stirring up their curiosity. Prozor coming on the

Queenie, then me, and then all of a sudden Trusko's got a bee in his bonnet about the Fang . . .

No, it wouldn't have taken much at all. So he had to go. I didn't have a problem with that, not in principle. It was just the executing of it that was knotty.

He'd died in his quarters and that was where everyone was gathered. He had a hammock, like the rest of us, and he was still in it. But he wasn't in any kind of restful repose. Gathing looked like he'd had electricity run through him, or more properly that it was still running through him, bunching up his nerves and muscles so that he was all stiff and arched, with his hands drawn up before his face, all clawed and useless. It wasn't electricity, though. We could touch him, and there was no trace of burning or scalding on him, his clothes or his bedding. That face of his, though, wasn't one I was going to forget in a hurry. His jaw was locked open, like he was still screaming, and his eyes were so wide it was like there was invisible rigging tugging his eyelids apart. You could start to see around the curve of his eyes, and I didn't like that at all. No one wants to know what we've got going on in our sockets.

'Looks like poison to me,' Drozna said, plucking at his own lower lip as he mused the scene.

'The cove only ate with the rest of us,' Strambli said. 'Or what he cooked for himself. Wouldn't have taken a glass of water from one of us if he'd been on fire.'

'He looks like he *was* on fire,' Surt said. 'All clenched up like that. Except he ain't burned.'

'He was alive when you got to him?' Trusko asked, buttoning up the top of his shirt, for he had been drawn from his quarters unexpectedly. 'Convulsing, screaming, and so on?'

'You 'eard it yourself, Captain,' Strambli said. 'Any screamier, he'd have started popping the hull plates.'

'Look at his handses,' Tindouf said, pointing with the tip of his pipe. 'Like he was trying to gets at something in his throat. I thinks Drozna's right. It was poison after alls.'

'It wouldn't have been poison,' Prozor said. 'Poison's hard to use on a ship. You can't get rid of it easily and there's a risk of it poisonin' the ones you don't want to poison.'

Drozna settled his gaze on her. 'Were you thinking of poisoning him, then?'

'No more than the rest of you were,' Prozor answered.

'Fura?' Trusko asked.

'I didn't like him,' I said, steering the closest path to the truth I could think of. 'And I'd be lying if I said I was going to shed any tears now. He didn't like any of us, did he?'

'He had a certain . . . way,' Trusko said. 'But murder is murder, and I can't countenance it. Besides, I hardly need remind any of you that he was our Assessor. Our only Assessor.'

I glanced at Prozor. Wisely, she was saying nothing for the moment.

'Look,' Surt said, with a quiver in her voice. 'There's something in his throat. Something coming *out* of his throat.'

'Back,' Trusko said. 'Everyone.'

I didn't need the captain's suggestion for that. I was frightened enough as it was. With his mouth jammed open the way it was, we could see right down past his tongue. And there was something coming up from his gullet, bubbling up into daylight. It was a milky, silvery presence, and it seemed to be climbing up his gullet in deliberate steps, almost putting out feelers each time, like a thief hauling themselves up a chimney.

'Tweezers,' Prozor said. 'Now. Before it gets out.'

'What is it?' Trusko asked, while Strambli dashed away to find something that met Prozor's requirements.

'Don't know,' she said. 'But it's alive and inside him, and it's ten to one this is the thing that had him bawlin'. What we don't want is it gettin' out and causing more mischief. Hurry up!'

Strambli was back inside thirty seconds, but it felt like minutes. The milky thing was nearly at the top of Gathing's mouth by then. The rest of him was still, so it wasn't some gastric tide coming up from his stomach. It was more like a thing that had climbed into him that was now intent on climbing back out.

Prozor took the tweezers. They were long-handled, which

was good. She used one hand to lever Gathing's jaw a little wider, and then dipped the tweezers in with the other. She poked around a bit, then drew them out with a jerk and a slurp, biting down on her lip with the concentration.

Pinched on the end of the tweezers was a squirming milky ball, with arms and feelers thrashing around and trying to grow away from it. Prozor held it up for us all to see, keeping her fingers safely clear of those feelers.

'What . . .?' Trusko said, trailing off.

'I ain't never seen one of these,' Prozor said, looking us all in the eyes, and making it seem powerfully convincing. 'But I've read of 'em. It's an engineered organism, made for assassinatin' folk. Called a Kill Star. A living weapon. It lives on a cove – binds to their nervous system, drinks off their blood, hides where it'll be hard to see. Looks like a scar or blemish if you can see it at all, and matches their body temperature, so you can't read it on a thermal scan. Doesn't trouble the cove, and they can waltz in almost anywhere and not have anyone know they're carrying a Kill Star. But when they need someone killed . . .'

'It detaches,' Strambli said, with a quiet horror.

'Learns through the nervous system who to go after – picks up on hate and body chemistry. Finds itself a dark corner like a shoe or a pocket and waits. Then it crawls out and creeps its way into you. Into your mouth, into your lughole, any orifice it chooses. By the time it's going in, it's too late. Little gooey thing works its way into your innards and starts pulling you apart from inside, using those little feelers.' Prozor's face was a mask of hard indifference. 'Brain's the best way to go. Once it starts rippin' up your grey, there ain't a lot of *you* left to feel it happen. But Gathing's must've come in through his gob – down into his guts. No wonder he was screamin'.' Prozor was still holding up the tweezers, with the milky thing writhing and squirming on the end of it. The others were keeping their distance.

'You know a lot about it,' Drozna said, arms folded across his chest. 'Sorry, but it's only what we're all thinking.'

'Aye,' she said. 'And if I'd had plans to vent Gathing, a Kill Star would have suited me nicely, if I'd had the quoins to afford one, or known where to ask. Bring me a tankard, Strambli. Drozna: you got some of that hydraulic fluid you use in your sail-control gear?'

He looked doubtful. 'I can fetch some. How much?'

'About a tankard.'

While Strambli and Drozna were occupied, Trusko said: '*Someone* managed to bring it aboard, Prozor, regardless of how expensive or difficult those things are to find. You'd understand why we might have misgivings, especially concerning our most recen—'

'It weren't me,' she said. 'Fura can speak for herself, but she was in the bone room when Gathing started screaming, wasn't she?'

'You said it could have been hidden away, waiting for its chance,' Trusko said. 'I'd say that makes any one of us a possible suspect.'

'Wait,' Surt said, bending down to reach something tucked behind Gathing's hammock. 'Cove's got his vacuum boots here. Why weren't they racked away with the rest of the suits?'

'No law against it,' Trusko said.

Surt dragged out the boots, grunting as the magnetic soles caught on the decking. 'Pockets on the side of the boots, Cap'n.'

'There's no law against that either.'

'But this one's open,' Surt said, bending back the leathery flap. 'And there's glass in here, all broken and sticky. Let me . . .'

Prozor closed a hand around Surt's stick of a wrist. 'Careful, friend. You wouldn't know what's on that glass, or what's still in that pocket.'

'What are you saying?' Trusko asked.

'I ain't sayin' anything.' She let that hang there for a second or two. 'But I've worked with Assessors of every stripe and I've met some you could trust and some you couldn't. Pretty easy for an Assessor to slip something past their own crew. Something valuable that they find in a bauble and don't want to be sharin' with the rest of them. 'Specially somethin' you can slip into a pocket, when no one's lookin'.'

Trusko paled. 'You're suggesting Gathing smuggled that thing back from one of the baubles?'

'You'd need to be the judge. I didn't know the man.'

'I did,' Surt decided. 'And I didn't care for him much. Always acting like he was better'n the rest of us, like we were the fools for stickin' with you, Cap'n, while he had better plans . . . no disrespect.'

'None taken,' Trusko answered levelly.

Drozna and Strambli were back. They had the tankard and the hydraulic fluid.

'Now what?' Strambli asked.

'Take the lid off the tankard. Then squirt that fluid into it. Get it good and full.'

Strambli undid the cover on the tankard. We were weightless, but the fluid was viscous and it glooped out into the tankard in a single green blob and stayed put, quivering like a fresh dog turd.

'Be ready with the lid.'

Prozor took the tweezered organism and forced it into the tankard, pushing it all the way in. As soon as it touched the fluid, it started squirming much more vigorously, sending out longer feelers, trying to get a grip on the tankard's rim. Prozor rammed it down. The organism began to give off a high, keening squeal.

'That's so you know it's being damaged,' she explained. 'Now the lid. Get it on quick and tight, Strambli. I'm pullin' the tweezers away . . . now.'

She jerked the tweezers out, and Strambli raced to get the lid attached and tightened. The squealing was still going on, but muffled now, and tinny. Slowly it faded away to silence.

'You just happened to know that my hydraulic fluid would kill it,' Drozna said.

'Burned my hand on that fluid once,' Prozor answered. 'Got a main hydraulic leak, squirting right back into the core of the ship. Figured if it didn't like me, it probably wouldn't like the Kill Star.' She paused. 'But if you had other ideas about dealin' with it, you were welcome to share 'em.'

'Whatever's left in that tankard,' Trusko said, 'I want it destroyed. Along with anything left in those boots.'

'Gathing's going to need burying,' Surt said, without much enthusiasm, still holding onto the vacuum boot. 'Anyone ever ask him which world he came from?'

But it turned out no one knew, and no one cared. When they dumped his body into space there was a bit of ceremony, some fine words, a forced tear or two, but no one's heart was really in it. Deep down they were thinking of the quoins he'd meant to keep for himself. There were a lot of things that a crew could forgive, from cowardice to incompetence, but being cheated out of an honest profit wasn't one of them.

Not that Gathing had cheated anyone – to our knowledge.

But that was going to have to be my and Prozor's little secret. And if one day I noticed that there wasn't a star-shaped scar halfway down her back, where once there'd been one, I knew to keep that observation to myself.

Some things were best left unsaid.

20

We hauled in twenty-one days later, swinging into a circular orbit around the smooth, bone-coloured pebble that was our target. The bauble field had dropped weeks ago, according to the auguries, but if anyone had been here in the meantime there was no trace of them. Privately, Prozor assured me it was unlikely that we had been beaten to our prize. For most crews the Fang would not have been an enticing target, with its high vaults cleaned out and the deeper levels too much trouble to bother with. 'But they didn't have Mattice to get through the doors that stumped 'em,' she said.

'Nor do we.'

'The problem on this ship isn't Strambli. I've sniffed around her and I reckon she knows her trade – and what she doesn't, I'll be able to fill in with what I gleaned from Mattice.' I thought she was done, but she added: 'And Githlow, too. He was our Assessor, but on any good team, an Assessor and an Opener aren't leagues apart.'

She had been willing to utter the name of the Fang since we joined Trusko's crew, but this was the first time the name of her husband had come out of her lips.

'You're planning on going into it, then,' I said.

'I'd have sooner never seen the place again, Fura. But if we're going near it I may as well put some ghosts to bed.'

We were in the galley, talking quietly while the others were off with their duties or catching squint-time.

'While stirring up some other Ghosties.'

'It's their shivery stuff we'd be stirring, not them.' She managed a smile. 'What's stoppin' you, by the way?'

'Stopping me from what?'

'From talkin' old Proz out of it. Thought you'd be all over me like a big glowy rash. *No, Proz, you don't need to go into the Fang, we can leave that to Trusko and his team of experts.* But you seem to be taking the other tack.'

'I don't know about Strambli. Or any of 'em, for that matter. Maybe they've been held back by Trusko. But I know this: we're not leaving here without the Ghostie stuff, and that means we ain't leaving anything to chance. Of course you'd be going in. You've spent most of the last three weeks dropping little hints that you might be able to fill Gathing's boots. Trusko wouldn't have put us into orbit if he weren't going through with the expedition, and he wouldn't be thinking of going in with just his nibs and Strambli. Maybe Surt or Drozna can step in if they're needed, but Trusko'd be a fool not to have you on that launch, and the cove knows it.'

'He needs a little more work,' she admitted. 'But he'll crack soon enough.'

The business with Gathing was behind us, for now. The crew seemed content to accept the idea that he'd been smuggling stuff out of the bauble under their noses. Maybe they didn't want to poke too deeply into that explanation, but it wasn't as if any of them were sobbing their hearts out over the death of old snidey-face. It would have been different it had been Drozna or Strambli we'd had to vent, but Gathing hadn't gone out of his way to make friends, and sometimes there's a cost for that.

'Here's something else he'll need working on,' I said, leaning in to bring my face closer to hers. 'I'm going in too. Not because I don't trust you to get the job done, but because this is my chance. Jastrabarsk took me into that bauble, but that was just a nice little stroll up and down some stairs.'

'He won't bite on it, Fura, not after you've shown how useful you are with the bones.'

'I'll make him, won't I?'

'You'd be better off sitting on the ship. There's risk in baubles, any baubles, 'specially with a narrow window.'

'He don't know that, though. He thinks we've got days.'

'Doesn't make him a fool, does it? He might think he's got time in hand, but that don't mean he's goin' to throw his Bone Reader into the fray, like he can just pop out and get a new one.'

'I still want to be there.'

'No,' Prozor said, settling her hand on my tin one. 'We had a plan, and we stick to it. Ain't any part of that plan involved you goin' into the bauble. We get the Ghostie stuff, break it to 'em gently what it is they've found, then set about trainin' 'em up in how to use it. Through all that, they still think we're what we claim to be. No mention of Bosa or the *Nightjammer*, not until we're good 'n' ready. Then – if you're still set on this madness – you start drawin' up a scheme to make the *Queenie* bait. Weeks or months from now, I don't care. But until then, you don't so much as twitch an eyelid out of character. You're the Bone Reader, and Bone Readers don't start beggin' to go into baubles, not unless they're up to somethin' they oughtn't be.'

'But we are,' I said.

*

Trusko might have lost his Assessor, but that had not stopped the preparations for the expedition. They had been going on throughout the course of the crossing, with equipment being moved in and out of the launch according to the expected needs of the next bauble. I had seen how Rackamore organised his supplies and the difference was stark. The stores on the *Queenie* were a jumble of bits and pieces, none of it properly stored away or classified, and quite a lot of it was broken beyond any practical repair. Just finding enough rope to run down the shaft was a challenge. It was spun from the same yardage that made up the rigging, but that didn't mean you could swap one for the other, not without skills and equipment Trusko didn't have. Prozor and I kept our traps buttoned while all this fumbling and rummaging was going on. It wouldn't pay to be too critical, implying that we'd both crewed on better ships.

I thought to myself: this is the crew you expect to put up against Bosa Sennen, when Rackamore's wasn't sufficient?

But now wasn't the time to lose my nerve.

The heavier, bulkier gear, though, couldn't be loaded onto the launch through its normal locks. It would have to be lashed onto the outside, and that meant it couldn't be done until the launch was detached from the *Queenie*. Drozna wasn't happy about the launch flying around near the ship while the sails were still out, so this last stage of the preparations had to wait until we were already in orbit. Trusko didn't really see that as a problem, but then Trusko was still under the impression he had five days before the bauble was due to start thickening over.

Prozor had refined her auguries as we crept closer. The two days she'd promised us were down to a narrow thirty-seven hours now – and we were already eating into those hours.

'Six hours to lash the winch gear on,' Trusko was telling us, breezily unconcerned. 'The time won't be wasted. While Surt and Drozna are loading the gear, Tindouf and Prozor will help us with the final suit checks.'

'I can help as well,' I said.

'Keep your head glued to those bones, Fura – you'll be doing more than your share.'

I'd have argued my case, but I didn't want to be seen to be too desperate to help out. Prozor was right about keeping in character. Bone Readers liked their pampered status, and it wouldn't have fitted with that if I'd been in too big a hurry to help with the grunt work.

It had been three weeks since I'd been in contact with Adrana, and I was starting to think that I wouldn't hear from her again. The best I could do was count the instances we had been in contact as a blessing, rather than something I'd been owed by fate. Even if my sister hadn't managed to persuade Bosa to come to the Fang, it had still been a comfort to know that Adrana was alive. But three weeks of silence had begun to eat into me like acid.

I'd taken on my share of hazard by weaselling my way into Trusko's crew. I didn't want to think about the consequences of being discovered for what I was, at least not until I was good and ready for it. And I would be. But I had Prozor to help me, and in any case, what I was asking of Adrana shrunk my little gamble down to nothing. Trusko was a coward, probably, but I didn't doubt that he could muster up some scatterfire when the moment came. Bosa, though, was cruel to the marrow, and that was something else. I'd asked Adrana to try to trick her, to use Bosa's greed against her, and I didn't doubt that my sister would have given it a try. Not straight away, not until she'd mulled it over and considered it from every angle, but she would have done it sooner or later.

I knew Adrana. She couldn't turn down a challenge from her little sister.

And I thought: what if she just wasn't cunning enough for Bosa Sennen? Bosa must have already had some doubts about her, after the deception with Garval. It was one thing for me to manipulate Trusko, but Trusko didn't have any reason to think ill of me.

I'd been starting to let my imagination run, wondering about the nasty things Bosa might have done to Adrana, as punishment for her betrayal.

Might still be doing.

But then she came through, and from the first instant of contact I knew something was different.

She was nearby.

'Where have you been?' I asked, once we'd got over the joy of knowing we were both alive.

'Nowhere. Bosa's been rationing the skull, knowing it might fail on her at any moment. I stopped being on the usual watches, and after that we were never on the bones at the same time.

This is the first time in five days that she's wanted me in the bone room. She just wants to know that she's got a clear hunting ground, and that you aren't up to anything you shouldn't be.'

My reaction was equal parts pleasure and pure bowel-loosening terror.

'Then she bit. She's coming for us.'

'She can see you. Long-range instruments. Knows you've hauled in sail, and you're getting ready for an expedition. She won't share everything with me, but I don't think we're more than three or four days out from you. Maybe closer. The way she's using her ions and sails, you won't see her until she's within scatterfire range.'

'Does she suspect anything?'

'No telling with Bosa. I did it the way you said: didn't try and encourage her or anything. Just put it out there, and let Bosa get the scent of blood. She isn't interested in the *Queen Crimson* and she doesn't think much of Trusko's chances of pulling anything juicy out of that bauble. But she'll give him time, anyway. No skin off her nose, to let him go in and out once or twice. That skull of yours isn't going anywhere, and that's the prize she's most interested in.'

'Has she asked about the *Queenie's* Bone Reader?'

'I've told her you aren't anything special. But when she sees you, Fura, and sees how much you look like me . . .'

'She won't,' I said. 'Not until it's too late.'

'I know why you chose the Fang, Fura. It's not just because of what happened to Githlow, and the place sticking in your mind. It's what they found down in that vault. You think it'll give you the edge over Bosa, let you take her.'

'Not take her,' I answered. 'Destroy her. End her, and end the *Nightjammer*.'

'You think you've seen the cruelty she's capable of,' Adrana said. 'But you haven't. Not yet. Not until you see Garval. She's dead, Fura. Finally stopped breathing, the mercy of it. But that was only the start of it for Bosa. She took her jammed-up corpse and fixed it on that bowsprit spike, and she took the one that was there before and tossed it into the Empty . . .'

'She didn't invent cruelty,' I said, something tingling in my tin fingers. 'And no one made her the queen of it.'

*

I heard about Surt's accident when I came out of the bone room. She had been outside, clomping her way around the hull on magnetic boots, ferrying equipment from the *Queenie*'s cargo lock, around the hull, and then lashing it onto the launch, which was stationed next to the main ship. There had been a problem with the lungstuff-supply on Drozna's suit, the kind of commonplace fault that was to be expected on old, battered equipment. Prozor had taken over his share of the work while Drozna came back inside so Tindouf could make a repair to the suit.

Prozor had been the one who found Surt. She'd been working her way past one of the hydraulically controlled sail mechanisms, when the mechanism – supposedly in its stowed configuration – had sprung out away from the hull. I remembered how Hirtshal had used the *Monetta*'s sail-control gear to snag the tumbling launch, after Bosa started her attack against us. This was something similar. The gear had sprung out hard, like a catapult or switchblade. The main part of it hadn't touched Surt – she'd have been pulped if it had – but one of the rigging lines had whipped against her, flinging her back onto the hull, and the impact had damaged her suit and knocked her out. Surt had been lucky – those rigging lines could easily cut through a suit – but she had concussion and a swelling bruise on the back of her head.

'I don't remember,' Surt kept saying, when Prozor got her back into the *Queenie*. 'I don't remember. I was just out there, and everything was all right . . . I don't remember.'

Which was maybe just as well.

I felt bad about what had happened to her, because I'd found a kindness in Surt and knew she'd done her best with Paladin, even if his head had only come back to me that one time. And I'd felt that she must have seen something in me, too, to ask for my help with reading, and that was a debt that I wasn't anywhere near discharging. But I had to put that sort of sentiment out of my mind. Surt had been in the way of our plans, and the mercy was she'd only needed to be injured a little.

'Luck's got something against us,' Trusko said, when we gathered in the galley and it was clear that Surt wasn't in any kind of state to go back into a suit. 'First our Assessor, now our Integrator.'

'Surt'll be right as rain, after a few days rest,' Drozna said.

'But she can't fill Gathing's boots,' Trusko told him. 'And no disrespect, Drozna, but when we'll already be pushing our lines to the limit, I wouldn't want the heaviest man on the ship in that bucket. That forces me to fall back on Prozor, I suppose. Normally I wouldn't countenance sending a Bauble Reader *inside* one, no matter how much lore she might have picked up. But with Surt out of commission . . . and Tindouf . . .'

'I knows where I'm most useful,' Tindouf said, and that was the end of that, to everyone's relief.

'I can do it,' Prozor said, doing a good job of sounding doubtful about it, just so that no one got the idea she was too keen. 'But if I'm riskin' my neck in that thing, I'd like to know why the new girl gets out of it so easily.'

'I thought you two had put your differences behind you,' Trusko said.

'Ain't about differences,' Prozor said. 'It's about provin' we're all equal to our share of the cut. Surt was ready to go in, and it wasn't expected of her either.'

'She feels that strongly,' I said, 'then let me on the expedition as well.'

'I need you on the bones, Fura.'

'The bones haven't given so much as a squeak in fifteen days,' I told him. 'If there was another ship near us, I'd know it. We can be in and out quick, can't we, if Strambli does her job?'

Strambli's larger eye flared with irritation, like a tram's headlight pushing through fog. 'Don't you worry about me.' Then: 'I'm with Proz. Let the girlie prove 'erself. The bones'll wait, and the auguries are on our side.'

'They are,' Trusko mused. 'And they *do* have a point, Fura, as much as I'm loath to place my Bone Reader at any unnecessary risk. I suppose some practical suit time wouldn't hurt you, and at least you're lighter than Drozna.'

I gave my best sneer. 'I said I'd do it, didn't I?'

*

It took another three hours to finish getting the launch ready, by which time only twenty-eight hours remained for us to get in and out of the bauble. Prozor and I knew that, of course, but no one else did. Trusko was cross at being delayed by Surt's accident, but he was still acting as if he had days to spare, and there wasn't much Prozor and I could do to put the spur into him. There was already enough buzzing around in his head without adding to it.

'I've had my share of happenstance,' he was saying, as we sealed up for final departure. 'But the death of one crew member, and the injury of another, within weeks of each other . . .'

'They do say bad luck comes in threes,' Strambli said. 'I wonder what's next?'

'Oh, we've had our run of three,' Trusko said, smiling at his own conviction. 'Or four, if you want to count those first two baubles separately.'

There were four of us on the launch, as against Trusko's normal team of three. Trusko and Strambli were the common elements, with Prozor and me substituting for the absent Gathing. We left Drozna, Tindouf and the injured Surt to mind the ship. Through the launch's little windows I watched as the *Queenie* grew smaller and smaller, gradually losing itself against the distant stars and the icy thumb smear of the Swirly. It was just a ship, and not much of one, but all ships come to feel like home after a while, and whatever I felt of her crew, the *Queenie* herself had not let any of us down. Leaving her like that, all alone and at the mercy of the *Nightjammer* – out there somewhere, whether we could see it or not – I felt a small, silent shame.

But I meant to return.

Trusko took it nice and easy on the descent, spending a whole hour just getting us near the surface, and once we arrived he spent another hour scouting around the bauble, just in case there was something that didn't square with the charts. We had twenty-six hours left by the time he finally got round to setting us down, and then there was another hour of dithering about how best to move the equipment into the shaft. Prozor and I couldn't say anything to giddy him along, but when we met eyes the tension in hers was enough to blow a blood vessel.

'I get it,' I mouthed back.

The one blessing was there wasn't any door on the top, just a circular hole in the crust of the bauble. You'd have mistaken it for a deep-shadowed crater, except there weren't any craters anywhere else on that bony rock. But even up close, it didn't look like anything special. You had to be almost right over it to see that it was a shaft, going right down – and there didn't seem to be any bottom to the thing.

The shaft measured a hundred spans side to side, near as mattered. We already knew that from the notebooks, and we'd come prepared. With our suits on, we got the equipment unshipped from the launch and laid it on the ground near the edge of the shaft. The main part of it – most of the bulk – was a hinged frame that folded out into a kind of triangle, so that you could push the sharp end of it out over the hole. The other ends of the frame were counterweighted using fuel from the launch, as well as being secured to the ground with pitons.

At the sharp end was an electrical winch, and a reel holding one and a half leagues of line. The line was hooked onto the bucket, which was actually a flimsy-looking platform with openwork sides, large enough for four of us to squeeze on plus a little room for loot. One of the sides could be dropped down to form a short connecting bridge, if we happened to be lined up with a doorway in the shaft.

'We'll set it here and reel down,' Trusko said, standing on the lip of the hole with his hands on his hips. 'Once we've identified the orientation of the doors in the shaft, we can reel back up and move the frame accordingly.'

'Do you have a robot eye you can send down ahead of us?' Prozor asked.

'Machines don't take well to baubles, Proz,' Trusko replied, as if he was the old hand at this lark. 'They can't be relied upon, any more than you can rely on squawk or power augmentation. No, we'll do it the slow and reliable way – one step at a time. It's served me well in the past and it'll serve me well now.'

'Yes,' I muttered, as if Gathing were inside me, stuffing snidey thoughts into my mouth. 'Why change a winning formula?'

By the time we were ready to lower the bucket, we were down to twenty-three hours. Prozor would have laughed at me, but I swore I could feel a premonitory tingle in the vacuum around the bauble, as if it had already started to thicken up, curdling over with the perplexing energies that would eventually mesh together and form an impenetrable surface.

Or maybe she wouldn't have laughed.

The bucket went down slowly. A league isn't any kind of distance in a tram or a train, but vertically, it's a different story. The line wasn't one piece of line, either. It was twenty different bits of yardage, joined together with spit and prayers. They'd put the strongest sections at the top, where they'd be taking the most strain. The weakest, most frayed lengths were just above the bucket, where we could dwell on 'em and consider the drop under us were they to snap.

I'll spare you the worry of that. They didn't snap, and we didn't drop.

But it still took us an iron eternity to get down to the level in the shaft where there started to be doors branching off, leading into horizontal tunnels and sub-shafts and chambers of imagined loot.

'Perhaps this'll do us,' Trusko said, as we ended up lined up with one of the doors. 'Get us through this, Strambli, and we can be up and on our way . . .'

Strambli had brought a metal case full of equipment, crammed wih cutters, cables, picks, listening devices and little electrical boxes with magnetic pads. She was already opening it up, ready to have a crack at the door.

'I'm not sure, Captain,' I said. 'The whispers I got through the skull were pretty clear. Everything at this level's been cleaned out centuries ago. If it's going to take Strambli time to get through the door, then I think we should go deeper and make the best of her time.'

'We're hardly in a rush, Fura.'

'I know that, Captain, but ain't there always an element of uncertainty, even when the auguries are solid? I'm just saying, if we know the good loot's deeper, maybe we should get at that first, and then see what's left over behind these other doors.'

'Watch your step, Prozor,' Strambli said. 'Fura's got her eye on your job, by the sounds of things.'

'She can try.' But after a silence, Prozor said: 'What she says ain't anything you need a Bauble Reader to tell you, Captain.'

'Then you agree with her?' Trusko asked.

'I ain't sayin' that, exactly . . . just that we ought to start deep and work our way back up.'

'Hmph,' Trusko grunted. 'Well, it seems we've been overruled, Strambli. Our two most junior recruits think they know better than the senior hands, when it comes to cracking a bauble.'

'They might have a point,' Strambli said, sealing up the case. 'We didn't go to all that trouble to find a league and half of line for nothing, did we?'

If ever there was a cove that sounded less enthusiastic about doing something, I hadn't met them. But I bet Trusko would have whistled a different tune if he knew who was sitting out there in space, waiting to pounce on his ship.

I thought about telling him there and then. It would be news to him, certainly. And to Strambli.

But also news to Prozor.

I didn't think any of them needed to know right away.

21

The winch took us down one and a quarter leagues, about a third of the way into the rock. It was much deeper than we'd gone at Brabazul's Ruin but there was still the same size of swallower pulling at us, and by the time we reached the level of the Ghostie stuff we were all feeling twice our normal weight. Everything was harder. Just standing up in the bucket took effort, and my suit pressed down on my limbs like there was another one of me standing on its shoulders. I felt every sharp edge inside it, every bad join or rough seal, and I knew I'd have a nice set of bruises to remember the day by, no matter what else it brought. Bruises would be the least of it, though. We were all double our normal weight, and so was Strambli's equipment, and the bucket we were standing on. All of that extra load was going up through the same lengths of yardage we'd begun with, and none of those threads had got any stronger since we started out. We might have come as deep as we meant to go, but the shaft carried on down below us, and our torches could only poke a little light into that plungey horror.

When Prozor told us how Githlow died, I'd struggled to wrap my head around the idea of someone panicking as badly as Sheveril had; panicking so badly that they tipped the bucket and sent the two of them falling. But it made peachy sense to me now.

This was a shivery place, and I couldn't wait to be somewhere else. I knew that the swallower was just a little knot of matter, squashed so tight that even its own light couldn't break free of it, and I knew it didn't have a mind or a will or anything you could think of as an appetite. But I still couldn't shake the idea that at the bottom of the shaft, in the middle of this little rock, there was something that *wanted* to drag us down, and all it had to do was tug a little harder.

Luck's a rum old thing. I'd have said it was against Trusko from the moment he left Mazarile. I'd have said it was against me from the moment I sneaked into Madame Granity's. But when that winch brought us down to the level of the Ghostie stuff, we couldn't have been more nicely lined up with the door if we'd planned it. We hadn't, though. Trusko had just set the frame in place and chanced his arm, and for once the stars hadn't sniggered at him.

'This is the limit,' he said, as the bucket creaked under our shoes. 'We go no deeper. Every span puts more load on that yardage, and we'll need some strength in reserve for the loot. Strambli: get to work.'

She folded down the connecting bridge and set her case on the end of it, opening it and spreading out her gear like a surgeon preparing for battle.

I glanced at Prozor. We were all on the same squawk channel now, so there was no way to have a private chinwag. But I'd been accounting things in my head. It had taken us nearly four hours to get this deep. We were down to our last nineteen – and that included the time we'd need to get into the launch and up and clear of the bauble.

My good hand sweated into my gauntlet. My tin one clenched against the suit's stiff finger joints.

Strambli was taking her sweet chaffing time with the door.

She spent an hour not even trying to open it, just sniffing around it, getting a feel for the mechanisms and possible countermeasures. She'd fix on her little listening devices, tap this bit, tap that bit, move something a hair, repeat the exercise, go back to her notes, make mousy sounds to herself, like someone trying to sort out an anagram.

'Difficulties?' Trusko asked, after we'd all been thinking the same thought.

'Just don't want to rush into anything, is all,' Strambli said. 'Be silly to, wouldn't it, after the time we've taken to get here? I think I can see the way through, but I want to be sure.'

'Take as long as you need. We've still plenty of time in hand.'

Every now and then Trusko got on the squawk back to the *Queenie*. The signal wasn't good, us being all the way down that hole, and nothing works well in a bauble anyway. But each time I was glad when Drozna came on and said there wasn't anything unusual going on, no shadowy returns on the sweeper, no dark tattered sails showing up against the leftovers of creation.

That didn't mean she wasn't out there.

Just that she was biding her time.

*

Strambli had been at it for three hours, the door no more open than it had been at the start, when something snapped in Prozor. 'Mind if I say somethin'?' she asked, in the tone of someone who's going to say it anyway, no matter what anyone minds. 'I ain't any kind of Opener – wouldn't pretend to it if I wasn't. That's your business, and I respect that. But I've crewed with plenty of Openers in my time and I've been in a few baubles with 'em, and I s'pose some of it rubbed off on me.'

Strambli carried on with her probes and boxes for longer than was comfortable. She was sliding a metal disc around on the periphery of the door, the disc connected back to her helmet while she drummed on other parts of the door with her fingers. Sometimes through the grilled-over window of her faceplate I could see her squinting hard with the concentration, only making those two eyes of hers look more mismatched.

'What I'm saying, is . . .' Prozor started.

'What you're saying is, you think you know better than the *Queenie*'s regular Opener. That's what it is, isn't it?'

By now even Trusko was getting impatient with Strambli's leisurely concept of progress.

'Perhaps if Prozor has something to contribute . . .'

I had something to contribute, too. We had sixteen hours left before the surface bottled us in like pickled specimens. The way Strambli was going about it, we'd need all sixteen to crack this one door.

'Get it off your chest then,' Strambli said.

'The locking mechanism's standard enough,' Prozor said. 'You can crack that easily, with the right shunts and magnetics. You figured that out fast, I know. What's throwin' you is that the anti-tamper circuit's cross-wired compared to most of the doors you'll have run into or read about in books. So your inductance coils are playin' off the wrong polarity to begin with. Flip 'em; reverse that diagram in your head, and you'll be in and through in no time. And watch for a mercury trip on the secondary latch.'

'There's no mercury trip.'

'What if you assume there is, and then I'll apologise later when you prove me wrong?'

Strambli said something under her breath, but with Trusko breathing down her neck, now wasn't the time to get into a squabble with Prozor. Huffing out her disapproval, she rearranged her equipment and got us through the door inside ten minutes.

One by one we crossed the connecting bridge, until we were standing on the firm ground of the bauble, with the bucket waiting to take us back up again. Those two gees were beginning to grind me down. I could see why Trusko had thought better of roping in Drozna, who weighed twice as much as the rest of us to start with.

The door had gone sideways into a wall. Facing us, leading horizontally away from the main shaft, was a smooth, circular tunnel. We had to stoop just to walk down it, the tops of our helmets scraping on the ceiling if we weren't careful.

We went down that tunnel in single file, torches pushing light ahead of us, and it was another thirty or forty minutes before we reached the start of the vaults. They branched off in both directions, like ribs off a backbone. Some of them were sealed off behind doors, while others were open, inviting us to step through. Except nothing about that place felt like it was giving off any kind of invitation. There was a cold, crawly feeling at the back of my neck.

'Someone was here,' Trusko said, studying the sealed doors and comparing them against the open ones. 'An Opener party. They even left some of their tools, Strambli.' He kicked aside a coil of electrical cable, ending in the snakelike head of an inductance pad. 'Openers wouldn't normally leave a place without sealing up all the doors they got through, would they?'

'Not unless they were in a hurry to leave,' Prozor said.

'Well, it's good that we're not,' Trusko answered. 'But I don't mind admitting: the sooner we've said goodbye to this place, the better.'

'There are gold boxes in here,' I said, stepping through into one of the vaults, and trying to make my statement come out all casual, as if I had no idea of what I'd found. 'Lots of 'em. Chests and boxes and sculptures. Nasty-looking, too. You want to take a squint, Captain?'

The four of us assembled in the room. It had a flat floor and an arcing ceiling that came down to form the walls, so that the cross-section was semicircular. It was about sixty spans long. We had come through one end wall and there was a door in the opposite one, looking through into a similar chamber, and perhaps another one beyond it.

I'd formed a mental image of this place while listening to Prozor's story, but none of it had prepared me for actually being here. The boxes were everywhere, laid out singly or stacked up in piles, or up on their ends, resting against the walls. Most of them were about the size of a coffin, and they were all done over in elaborate gold carvings. At first glance, the way the boxes glinted and gleamed back at us, you could almost think they were pretty, like big versions of the boxes a rich person might have for jewellery or keepsakes. The carving was ornate and as far as I could tell none of it was the same from box to box.

But the one thing it wasn't was pretty.

The boxes were covered in skulls, and ribs, and spines and pelvises, and jawbones and sockets, and knuckles, and none of these things were joined up to the others in any way nature intended. There were skulls with fingers coming out of their eyes, and ribs with skulls locked in them, and jaws coming out of pelvises, and that wasn't the worst of it. The gold was worked up into meat, muscle, tendon, skin, brain, blood vessels, eyeballs, lungs, tongue, windpipe, guts, and all this gore and gristle looked like it was about to peel off the bones like cooked meat and form up into boxes of its own, just so it wasn't missing out.

I swallowed. I didn't think I was the only one.

'They're just boxes,' Trusko said after a while.

'But I don't want to be in the same room as 'em,' Strambli said, in a low, quiet voice, all the indignation gone out of her, and the worst part was that she'd just put into words exactly what I'd been feeling.

'At least we've found something,' I heard myself say. 'The rumours said there was loot, didn't they? Now we know it's something big. No one'd go to the trouble of those boxes for a few bits of lookstone or catchcloth.'

'Maybe,' Prozor said, 'it would help if we opened one of 'em?'

Prozor went over to one of the horizontal boxes, and we followed her. Each step that I took closer to that box felt harder than the last, as if the ground was steepening, or the box was putting out a magnetic force that pushed against our suits. But I didn't think it was anything that would have shown up on Strambli's instruments. This was something getting into our brains, plucking the lowest, deepest strings of fear.

Prozor knelt by the box. The top was hinged along one side,

with a handle made out of golden bone. She lifted it open. Everything was silent about that vault, because there was no lungstuff. But my imagination filled in a slow, forbidding creak as the hinges worked.

Prozor leaned in to aim her lamp into the box. Trusko and Strambli bent down to see what was there.

'Huh,' Strambli said. 'After all that. After the door, and all this fancy carving . . .'

'Empty,' Trusko said.

He moved to the next box, lying beside the one Prozor had opened, and tugged on its lid.

'What's inside?' Strambli asked.

'Nothing. As empty as the first.' Trusko left the box open and went to one of those which was stored on its end, leaning against the inward curve of the wall. He opened the lid like it was a door, and that box was empty as well.

'It's a bust,' Strambli said, and then repeated it twice, the hope draining from her voice. 'It's a bust. *It's a bust*. We came all this way and it's been for nothing.' She moved to one of the piles of boxes and opened the one on top. 'All of 'em. I'm sure of it. There's a reason those doors weren't sealed up – it's been picked clean.'

'They're not empty,' Prozor said, and to begin with her way of saying it was so matter-of-fact Trusko and Strambli didn't seem to notice. She had to repeat herself, louder this time. 'They're not empty. You're just not looking at what's inside 'em the right way.'

'There's a *wrong* way?' Strambli asked, with an edge of desperation in her voice.

'You're looking directly. But that's not how it works. Got to look askance, out of the corners of your eyes. Like you aren't meanin' to peek at all. Then you can start to see it.'

'See what?' Trusko asked.

'Ghostie stuff,' Prozor said.

They edged close to the box she'd opened. I was looking as well. The box looked empty, just a rectangular enclosure with smooth gold walls, lacking the ornamentation it had on the outside. Empty at least when I was staring at it directly, trying to see something. But when I averted my vision, forcing my brain to stop asking if the box were empty or not, a smoky, glassy outline showed itself. The natural reaction was to snap back onto it, try to see it more clearly. But then there wasn't anything in the box again.

'I see it,' Strambli said, with wonder and terror in her voice. 'It's what she says. Ghostie. Heard of it, but never seen it . . . never even *met* anyone who'd seen it.'

I kept glancing away, catching furtive snatches of what was in the box, and allowing my brain to stitch these clues into a form. It was a knotty thing to do. It wasn't just hard to see the stuff in the box, it was hard to remember what you'd just glimpsed. The Ghostie stuff was as slippery on the grey as it was on the lamps, like it didn't *want* to be remembered.

Slowly, though, I got the curious gist of it. The thing in the box was upright, with arms and legs and a torso. It was made up of glassy panels, curved to fit around a cove.

'It's armour,' Prozor said. 'Ghostie armour. And there's more of it. All these upright boxes. They all hold armour.'

'Been here before, have you?' Strambli asked.

'I just know it.'

Before the conversation took a swerve it oughtn't, I went back to one of the other open boxes. I glanced away and back again, until I made out a pile of long, glassy things with thick mid-sections and handles at one end.

Not handles, exactly, I decided.

Grips and stocks and triggers.

I reached into the box, closed my fingers around something tangible. I drew it out. The Ghostie weapon was invisible and as light as if it were carved out of frozen smoke. It still felt as real and solid in my fingers as any crossbow.

'Guns,' I said. 'Ghostie guns.'

Trusko didn't say anything for a few moments. I could hear his breathing over the squawk. We were all breathing fast, lugging

356

twice our usual weight around, and the prickly feeling of the vaults wasn't doing anything to settle our nerves. But Trusko was at least as excited as he was frightened.

'We've done it,' he said, the words coming out hoarse between breaths. 'After all the failures, all the busts. This changes everything.'

Strambli couldn't mask her own enthusiasm, but it was tempered by realism. 'We'll take what we can. Leave the boxes, if necessary, and just take what's in 'em. But even then, we'll never shift more than a fraction of what's here. And it's no good saying we'll come back another time. The rumour's already out there. Some other coves'll be here before we can blink, clean the place out . . .'

'We can seal the doors,' Trusko said. 'Make as many trips up and down the shaft as we can, then seal everything up. Make it harder for them, at any rate.' He was still bewitched. 'Just a few trinkets of Ghostie stuff changed the fortunes of whole crews. What's here's enough to change a whole world, a whole economy.'

'Better hope the market doesn't get flooded,' Prozor said drily.

'We'll get back to the worlds. Get a good price for the loot, before the price dips. We're still ahead of the game.' He pivoted around, throwing his arms wide. 'Fura – I had my doubts about that intelligence you threw me, but I thought it worth taking a chance on. Rest assured you've earned your share of this. And, Prozor – your auguries told us this was feasible. If ever I had my doubts about either of you . . .'

'Perhaps,' I said, 'we ought to start moving it up the shaft.'

Trusko raised his hand in good-natured surrender. 'Of course, of course.'

We were down to fifteen hours and spare change. Fourteen before we needed to be in the launch and on our way. I couldn't see us making more than one round trip up and down the shaft in less than five hours, which meant we had time – just – to make three trips to the surface, three loads of Ghostie stuff in the bucket.

By then we'd be cutting it plenty fine.

'Strambli's right, I think,' I said. 'Ordinarily, the boxes alone would be worth an expedition. But they're too heavy for us to shift more than one at a time. I say we take this one, the one with the guns, and move the armour out separately. If two of us ride the bucket, we can easily squeeze four or five of those suits of armour on it.' And seven would be nicer, I thought to myself: one for each of us. Six if we assumed Drozna wouldn't fit, five if we took Surt out of consideration as well.

Trusko might not have taken kindly to his Bone Reader dictating the order of operations, but Strambli wasn't going to quibble with me now that I'd thrown her a biscuit.

'The guns it is,' the captain said, cocking his head sidelong at the box. 'Do you think they . . . still operate?'

'There's power in 'em,' Prozor said. 'Or whatever counts as power with the Ghosties. If there wasn't, you'd just be looking at piles of twinkly dust.'

Trusko had one of the glassy guns between his hands. He looked like he was miming it, not actually holding anything, until you squinted away and caught the shivery sense of it, like a heat haze or mirage tricking itself into the form of a weapon.

Something wrong. Something against the natural order of things.

'I wonder what one of these could do,' Trusko said.

I reckoned he'd find out soon enough.

*

We only managed two return trips. On the first one, we took the gold box and the weapons, Trusko and me nursing it back up to the surface while Prozor and Strambli stayed behind in the vault to lighten the strain on the line and get the next load ready. We loaded the box onto the launch, and then went back down the shaft. I couldn't say I much liked the idea of going back into the bauble. The squawk wasn't working as well as it had when we landed, even from the surface, and I knew that squawk breaking up was often a herald to the field starting to thicken over. I was expecting it to make Trusko jittery, but he just put it down to the vagaries of his equipment, the cove still convinced he had a few more days of grace before the bauble closed up. At least we were still getting word to and from the *Queenie*, even with the signal breaking up. Drozna hadn't given the captain anything to trouble his noggin over.

Ten hours were left on the clock by the time the winch brought us back level with the door. We trooped through to the vault, pleased when we met up with Prozor and Strambli. They'd spent their time profitably, going through more of the boxes and sorting the loot into rough categories. They'd found five of the suits of armour, and they were laid out onto the floor now, a blurry presence that you had to *not* look at to stand any chance of seeing. They made me think of those dead cells that float through the liquid of the eye, those swimmy seahorses you can barely see unless it's bright – except instead of seahorses these were shaped into breastplates and gauntlets and so on. Next to the armour they'd organised some detachable items; visors, helmets, knives and pistols. 'Be careful with the sharp things,' Prozor said. 'Just 'cause you can't see 'em, don't mean they can't take a piece off you.' She held up her gauntlet, wiggling the fingers. There was a deep gash in the material of her palm, almost enough to break all the way through and allow the lungstuff out.

'You've done us proud,' Trusko said, surveying the spoils. 'We'll be up and down that shaft more times than we can count, but it still makes me shudder to think what we'll need to leave behind. If I had atomic munitions I'd think of collapsing the shaft itself!'

Someone else flooding the market with Ghostie stuff wasn't going to be the cove's most immediate and pressing problem, I thought. But I kept my trap shut.

The armour was light, so we didn't need to leave anyone behind in the vault on the next trip up. Prozor would have found a reason to come up anyway, knowing as she did that we were down to our last ten hours, but at least she was spared the strain of coming up with something.

By the time we got to the bucket Trusko was still drunk on the idea of his fortunes taking a swerve. 'We'll need to act with the utmost discretion,' he was saying, his mind racing ahead to wealth and fame. 'Even the small amount that we'll take back with us on the *Queenie*, it's no good trying to get a price for all that in one go. We'll maximise our gains by selling on one item at a time, never hinting at the true haul . . .'

'They'll get a whiff of it as soon as we sell two bits of Ghostie stuff,' Strambli said, folding up the bucket's connecting bridge.

'Then we'll need to be *even more* discreet. Secrecy clauses. Never dealing with the same broker twice. No one allowed to speak of what they've bought off us, for a year or three . . .'

Prozor took something out of her utility belt. I only got a glimpse of it before she leaned over the side of the bucket and let it fall into the shaft. Because there wasn't any lungstuff in the shaft, and we were already under two gees, it went down fast.

'What was that?' Trusko asked.

'I was just thinkin' of them that came here before us, and them that'll come here later,' Prozor said.

I think what she dropped into the shaft was a flower, with red petals, and the vacuum must have turned it into something like glass.

But I never asked her and she never spoke of it.

*

We loaded the Ghostie armour and equipment onto the launch. We were properly tired by then, ready to drop, but I think Trusko still had the spur in him to go back into the bauble at least once before we rested. But when he contacted Drozna, everything changed.

'Don't want to make more of it than I should,' Drozna said, his voice coming over the squawk console inside the launch. 'But we got something a little while ago.'

'Got something?' Trusko asked.

'It was on the sweeper for a moment. A return, nearby. Something large, but not clear either. All ragged, like it was made up of bits. Then it was gone, and there's been nothing since.'

'Probably a fault on the sweeper,' Trusko said, like he wanted someone to pat him on the back and tell him to stop worrying.

Prozor looked at me. I could only see the middle part of her face through that grilled-over porthole, but it was enough. She didn't like the thought that was forming in her head. A return meant that another ship was near. It couldn't be the *Nightjammer*, though, because the *Nightjammer* didn't know we were taking a look at the Fang.

Did it?

'Something's not right,' I said.

And Prozor answered: 'I think we're agreed on that.'

I'd played out in my head how and when we might get round to informing Trusko that his ship and crew had been turned into bait for Bosa Sennen, but the time had always been of my choosing, when we were good and ready for it. And somehow, as I ran that little exchange through the toy theatre in my head, I'd got over the knotty part about breaking it to Prozor that the *Nightjammer* already knew where we were. Exactly how I got from one side of that conversation to the other, I hadn't figured.

I guess it was time to find out.

'Captain,' I said, still meeting eyes with Prozor, still aware of her face bottled behind that glass, all angles and fury, 'there's something you and I need to have a little chat about.'

'Fura?' he asked, not getting the tone of what I was saying.

'I'd listen to her,' Prozor said.

Strambli had taken off her helmet now that we were inside the launch. Her madder, larger eye was on me, doubt swimming behind it.

'What?'

'You're in trouble. We're in trouble. All of us.' I had to take a breath, forcing myself into something close to calm if not quite calm itself. 'You've been tricked,' I went on. 'By me. I'm not what you thought I was, and neither's Proz. But we're not your enemy. The enemy is the return Drozna just got on the sweeper.'

'What,' Trusko said slowly, 'would that return be?'

'It's Bosa Sennen's ship. What she calls the *Dame Scarlet* and what the rest of us call the *Nightjammer*.'

'No,' the captain said, with a flat certainty. 'I've never crossed orbits with her. Never given her a reason to take an interest in me or my operation. I'm not even sure she exists.'

'You soon will be,' I said, reaching up to unlatch my helmet. 'We're not going back into the bauble. The auguries weren't what you thought anyway. Less than seven hours from now, the field starts firming up again. Mainly, though, you need to get us back to the *Queenie* before Bosa closes in for her attack.'

'Attack,' Trusko repeated.

It was like he was hearing me, but the words weren't quite drilling into his noggin.

'She wants your skull,' I said. Then, smiling like he might have taken that the wrong way, I added: 'The one in the bone room. Hers is duff. She blew it taking the *Monetta*.'

'*Monetta*,' Strambli said. 'There's that name again.'

'Prozor and I crewed on it,' I said, lifting off my helmet. 'We were shipmates, and we survived Bosa Sennen.' Then, to Trusko: 'I wasn't kidding, Captain. We really do need to be on our way. I can explain how the rest of it's going to work out as we cross over.'

Prozor turned to him. 'Fura and I've got a few little points of order to settle between us. But she's right about one thing. We do need to be up and off the bauble. You noticed how blurry those stars were starting to look, before we got back on the launch?'

'I thought it was my helmet,' Trusko said. 'Getting all smeared over.'

'It wasn't. It's space is what's starting to smear over. Just a bit, not enough to stop us leaving. But the one thing we don't want to do is sit around here bumpin' our gums.'

'Are you . . . serious?' he asked, his gaze switching between the two of us.

'Never been more serious, Captain,' I told him. 'But everything's all right. I didn't set you up to be torn apart by Bosa. She's the one who's in for a surprise.'

22

We lifted from the bauble, Trusko pushing the rockets all the way they'd go, the gees squeezing us into our seats, the engines roaring behind the aft bulkhead and the frame of the launch moaning and groaning like it was having bad dreams of its own. The ground fell away fast, the horizon bending into a curve that got sharper and sharper with every league we climbed. The one thing to be said for baubles was that it didn't take long to put some distance from them. Only a minute after departure, we were already high enough for the field not to be a concern, even if it snapped back there and then.

Trusko eased back on the engines and began to lock us in for rendezvous with the *Queenie*. 'I'll squawk Drozna,' he said, already reaching out to flick switches. He had taken off his helmet, but other than that he still had all of his suit on. 'Warn him to start running out the sails.'

'You can do that,' I said, from the seat behind his control position. 'But if you want to make it through to the end of the day, don't say a word about it being Bosa. Don't even sound as if you're all that concerned – just that you're coming back as a precaution.'

Prozor had slipped off her own helmet. She was sitting in the seat next to mine, across the narrow aisle that ran the length of Trusko's launch. 'Fura's right,' she said, squaring her jaw as if the words had given her toothache. 'It's fine to react – Bosa will have picked up Drozna's squawk about the sweeper return. But you can't let Bosa know you've any idea it's her that's coming in. She ain't even crossed your mind yet. You're still thinkin' this is some other ship that wants a sniff at your claim and might not be too polite about it, but another part of you's not even convinced that return wasn't a phantom.'

'We don't even know it is Bosa,' Strambli said, with a quivery desperation in her voice. 'Do we?'

'It's Bosa all right,' Prozor said, taking a kind of malicious pleasure in it, the way some people just love delivering bad news. 'Ain't it, Fura? Go on, ask the Bone Reader. She's the one that called Bosa in.'

I slid my tongue over my lips. 'I wasn't planning on lying to you, Proz – any more than you were planning on lying to me about the auguries.'

'What about the auguries?' Trusko asked.

'Call Drozna,' I said. 'Then we'll talk. And remember – not a word about Bosa, or she'll know something's rum. We've got an edge on her now, but we'll take the shine off it if we're not careful.'

Trusko flipped the switches. 'Drozna,' he said, swallowing hard before carrying on. 'That return may or may not have been real. Probably there's nothing out there, but we're coming back as a matter of routine. Have Surt check the sweeper. We'll be in dock in fifty minutes.'

'It was real,' Drozna said. 'Whatever I saw. But Surt's looking into it anyway.'

'Very good.' Trusko closed the connection, then twisted back to look at us. 'Tell me what you meant about the auguries, Fura.'

'Ask Proz,' I said.

He switched his gaze onto her. 'Well?'

Prozor sighed, shook her head slowly. 'You'd have found out in a few hours. The window's tighter than I said it was. Much tighter. We'd have had time for one more trip into the bauble, and that'd have been cuttin' it nice. The way those stars were starting to quiver, maybe not even that much time.'

'Why?' Strambli said. 'Why did you lie about that?'

'Because we needed the Ghostie stuff, and you wouldn't have gone into the bauble if you'd known the odds,' Prozor said.

'*We*,' Trusko said. 'So it's true. You've been working against us, both of you, this whole time . . .' Then a dark thought seemed to settle behind his forehead. 'Gathing. Surt. Please don't tell me . . .'

'Surt's fine,' Prozor said. 'She had to be put out of commission, that's all. And I didn't see none of you shedding any tears over Gathing.'

Trusko made to reach for the console.

'What're you doing?' I asked.

His hand stilled over the switches. 'Calling Drozna. Telling him to make arrangements to put the two of you in irons, soon as we dock.'

'I wouldn't,' Prozor said. 'For a start, it'll clue Bosa in that there's something odd goin' on, and that's the last thing you want. Secondly, the only way you're getting through to the end of this day is by doin' *exactly* what I tell you. You think we wanted the Ghostie stuff 'cause we're short of a few quoins? I had my share of quoins and Black Shatterday showed me what they're worth. I ain't in this for money.' Prozor shot me a guarded look, not hostile but not exactly what you'd call companionable. 'Nor's she. What we're in this for is payin' back Bosa, and it's the Ghostie stuff that's key to it. Bosa won't be ready for it.'

'And we will be?' Trusko asked. 'If Drozna's already picked up a return on the sweeper, she can't be far out.'

'Probably ain't.' Prozor shrugged. 'Bosa's way, she doesn't show herself until it's too late to cut and run. She ain't showed herself proper yet, so what Drozna saw was probably a mistake. Runnin' out her guns to test 'em, or something. Or putting out a launch and boardin' squad. Now, I was countin' on having a little more time for us to familiarise ourselves with the Ghostie stuff. Like, weeks or months more time. But seein' as Fura's decided we only need minutes, that's what we'll be workin' with.'

I fought it, but the shame must have been plain on my face.

Trusko moved his hand from the console. The cove was still nervous, thrown into a dizzy spin by what had happened. He'd steered away from real hazard all his life, and now hazard had come knocking anyway, like it was due an invitation. I thought of how Rackamore had taken the news of Bosa's return. He hadn't gone looking for trouble, either, but the difference was he was ready to stare it in the eye when it showed up.

'I had to move us along,' I said. 'If we'd gone to the trouble getting the Ghostie stuff, and then been jumped by *another* ship, or gone to port and sold it all on, before Bosa had a chance to find us . . . anyway, I wasn't going to wait months. She's still got my sister, and after what she did to Garval . . .'

'Who the hel—' Trusko started.

Prozor raised her voice. 'We've all got questions we'd like answerin', Cap'n. Some more'n others. But now's not the time for it. You've got to get us safe and sound in the *Queenie*, before Bosa closes in. That means you've got to be fast while not lookin' *too* fast.'

'Because she'd go away, pick another target?' Strambli asked.

'No,' I said, smearing *that* hope like it was a bug under my thumb. 'Bosa's after your skull, mainly, and she can't damage the ship too badly without damaging the goods. She'll soften you up, then board. By then, the game's usually over and she won't be counting on much resistance. That's when we'll take her. If we give her reason to spook, she'll just turn all her coil-guns on you from a thousand leagues out. And we ain't got any defence against that, even with the Ghostie stuff. Close action's the only edge we've got over her, and for that we need to lure her inside the *Queenie*.'

'Fura's right,' Prozor said.

'The armour's the key,' I said. 'And the sharp things. She won't be expecting any of that. But we've got to be ready by the time we dock. Now for the bad news.'

Trusko gave a gallows laugh. 'You mean we haven't already had it?'

'We're going to have get into that armour. Five suits is all we've got, but five's all we need. Prozor tells me the armour will fit around us and make us hard to see. The catch is our suits are too bulky. We can't wear 'em, and that means we can't do without ship lungstuff.'

'Could we put the armour on inside the suits?' Strambli asked.

'Not if your suit's already as tight as mine is,' I said. 'Anyway, that would rob us of half the benefit from the armour, which is being slippery on the eyes.'

'Captain,' said Prozor. 'Can you keep us on a steady headin' for a few minutes, while we try on our new toys?'

'Yes, yes,' Trusko stammered. 'We're lined up for the time being. But I must keep in contact with Drozna. I'd do so normally.'

'Fine,' I said. 'But a word out of place, and Bosa'll give you cause to regret it. Strambli: lay out the armour and figure out which bit goes where. Prozor and I'll start getting out of our suits. Watch your hands on those sharp things.'

We'd stowed the armour and guns inside the launch, in the compartments ahead of the aft bulkhead. The launch was still on a whisper of thrust, so it wasn't properly weightless, and that helped with getting everything organised. Prozor and I got on with the sweaty, grunty business of shedding the rest of our suits, helping each other out, but not making too much in the way of pleasant conversation while we were about it. I wasn't surprised. We'd both kept stuff from each other, Prozor with the auguries and me with the *Nightjammer*, but if I was blunt with myself, mine was the slyer of our deceptions.

I'd been honest in my explanation, too. I wasn't prepared to drag things out with Bosa. But I think it was going to take a bit more than a word or two to square things with Prozor. I wanted her back on my side, though. I'd come to like thinking of her as a friend, and I didn't much care for the idea that she felt I'd betrayed her.

Even if that's what I'd done.

'I don't understand why it had to be us,' Strambli was saying, while she laid out the armour, mostly by feel rather than sight.

'I might ask the same question,' Trusko called back.

'Because you weren't brave,' I said. 'You weren't brave, and you weren't successful. We needed a crew Bosa wouldn't think twice about jumping, because you looked like easy pickings. Amateurs, which is what you are. And when you put yourselves in harm's way, out here around the Fang, it wouldn't ever have occurred to Bosa that you were luring her in deliberately.'

'We weren't,' Strambli said.

'I was,' I answered, colder than the last breath of the Old Sun. Then, feeling that I owed them a bit more of the picture: 'Bosa took Adrana, my sister. She's another Bone Reader. She's better than me, and I'm better than most. Adrana and I've been in contact, through the bones. I told her about the Fang, and how she had to slip Bosa the idea about jumping us.'

'You knew what we'd find here,' Trusko said, marvellingly, as if he was only now starting to see how thoroughly he'd been played. 'All along. You lied to me, didn't you? That intelligence . . .'

'It was what I needed to do, Captain. But understand, it wasn't anything against you, not on a personal level. In fact I'm doing you a favour. You and all the captains. You slink around pretending she's not out there, but deep down she's got the shivers into you, and that ends now. We're taking Bosa Sennen. We're taking the *Nightjammer*.'

*

Forty minutes is a long time when there's something you'd rather be doing, but it's no time at all in a pickle. Truth was, I'd rather have been doing a lot of things other than figuring out the workings of the Ghostie armour. But I also knew we couldn't count on much grace when we got to the *Queenie*, assuming we got there before Bosa made her jump. We had to work out what we had, what we could use, and just as importantly how to use it – all in the time it took a tram to get from one end of Jauncery to the other.

Getting out of the suits was the start of it. We were stripped down to just a layer of clothes, just enough to stop a cove freezing to death: leggings and vests and not much else. I kept telling myself that the suits wouldn't have made much difference, not where Bosa was concerned, but it was still hard to let go of the one thing that felt like it might have stopped a crossbow bolt.

With my arms bare – what was left of my arms, anyway – the glowy really stood out. The others noticed it too. It hadn't been like that before, not even before I started getting treated for it. I could feel the lightvine tingling under my cheeks and brow, too, shining like fierce warpaint.

I felt fierce, too. And if I wasn't ready for a war, then I was ready for battle.

No: not a battle, exactly.

Close action.

We started trying on the armour. Just being near the Ghostie stuff was making snakes slither in my gut, and now I had to fit it around me like I was trying on a corset. But the armour wanted to help, in its own queer way. Pieces joined up too easily, or adjusted themselves to fit more snugly. There was something quietly wicked about it, like a cove that whispers in your ear too much, earning your trust. We wanted something of the armour, but I couldn't help wondering what the armour wanted of us.

The armour wasn't just invisible when it was laid out on the floor. When you fixed it on, the part of the body it was covering became just as hard to see. The sleeve piece made my flesh forearm disappear below the elbow, so that my elbow became a stump and the hand seemed to be floating in the lungstuff on its own. I could see the smoky outline of my vanished arm, but like the armour it hardly showed at all unless you were looking nearly away from it. I had a thermal glove on my flesh hand, but there was nothing like a glove in the Ghostie armour, just an extended plate that covered the area from the wrist to the finger joints. There were other gaps too, and as I was fixing on my own pieces I wondered what the point was of only being three-quarters invisible, or seven-eighths. It was only when I saw Prozor and Strambli that my doubts were settled. I could see the gaps between their armour, the flesh and fabric of their normal selves, but holding onto the *idea* of those gaps, and joining up the spaces between them to make a monkey form . . . that was harder than it had any right to be. It was as if the fact of them wearing Ghostie armour was making me forget what a person was meant to look like who *wasn't* inside the armour. It was slippery in more ways than just being hard to see. It was getting into our heads, and I didn't much care for the feeling.

By the time we'd sorted out the armour, we had about ten minutes left until docking. Trusko had been speaking to Drozna on and off, sticking more or less to script. If they had some secret code worked out between them, Prozor and I weren't smart enough to plumb it. I didn't think it likely. Captains only come up with secret codes and procedures when they expect to run into trouble, and Trusko's whole career was built around avoiding it in the first place.

Pity it wasn't working out too well for him.

'Captain,' I said, drawing his attention back to us now that we were in the armour. 'We ought to get you fitted, too.'

He'd known what we were doing, but Trusko still jumped when he saw what we'd become. I took that as a good omen. His gaze was sliding all over us, like his eyes couldn't find something to settle on. 'I know you're there,' he said. 'I can even see you. I tell myself I can see you, 'least ways. But somewhere between my eyes and my grey, the message isn't getting through. It's like just the *idea* of knowing you're there, just holding that in my head, it's like a number that's got too many digits.' He was saying this with more distaste than fascination, and the look on his face wasn't so much awe or delight as the sickly, paling appearance of a cove who's having trouble keeping his dinner down. 'I don't like it,' he said, giving a little shudder. 'It's wrong.'

'None of us like it,' I said. 'But Bosa's going to like it even less.'

'Let me dock the launch first,' he said. 'It'll keep me occupied for the next ten minutes and any delay might look odd.' He stretched towards the console. 'Drozna. We're lining up for you. Get the doors open and be ready. Anything we need to know about?'

'Nothing since that sweeper return,' we heard Drozna answer. 'Like you say, probably just a glitch . . . but it *was* clear, for the moment it was there. Is everything all right, Captain?'

'Yes, why?'

'We've had false returns before, and they haven't given us cause to abandon a bauble halfway through the cracking of it.'

I drew a line across my throat, telling Trusko to cut the conversation short before it took us all into choppy seas. 'There's no difficulty, Drozna. Just get that door open.'

The arrangements for docking took up the remaining minutes of our crossing. We had to get back into our seats for the last part of it, and it was strange to buckle myself in, look down at my own belly, and find myself looking all the way through to the chair. I knew I was wearing the armour, and I knew there was a body under it, but it was getting harder to hold those two things square in my head.

Prozor was the last one to get into her seat. She doled out the sharp things, showing us how they fixed onto the armour so we wouldn't need to carry them in our hands. Some were stubby little knives that would be good for stabbing, while others were closer to short swords, with straight and curved blades. 'Whatever these're made from,' she was instructing us, like we were the pupils and she the wise old teacher, 'there isn't much they won't go through, other than Ghostie armour itself. Skin, bone, metal, glass, it's all the same to Ghostie knives. You saw what the edge did to my glove, and I hardly touched it.'

'We'll be careful,' I said, flexing my tin fingers and thinking of the price I'd paid for them.

'What about the guns?' Strambli said. 'There's a reason guns aren't a good idea on a ship.'

'That's why we'll be treatin' 'em strictly as a last resort,' Prozor said. 'Think I can hold you to that?'

'Yes,' Strambli said, swallowing hard.

'Good. Soon as we're on the *Queenie*, we'll stock up on crossbows anyway. You *do* have crossbows, don't you, Cap'n?'

'Yes . . . I'll have Drozna open the armoury.'

She sprang forward, even against the gravity of the launch's rocket, and jammed her hand over the console. 'You're still not gettin' it, are you? Twitchin' at a false echo on the sweeper's one thing, but if Bosa thinks you've clued up to her, she'll just pepper you for the fun of it. She wants that skull but she don't want it *that* badly. There'll be other ships, other crews.'

'I didn't ask for this,' Trusko said, his voice small.

'None of us did, cove,' I told him. 'But we're getting it anyway.'

The squawk crackled. I was ready for Drozna's voice to come out of it, but when the words came out smothered in static, all chopped up and reassembled, echoing and circling around on each other, biting each other's tails, I knew who was doing the speaking.

'Captain Trusko. That's who I've got on the end, ain't it? Brave Captain Trusko and the brave ship *Queen Crimson*. I got your registry, got your name, got the word of what you were after around this bauble. Do I have to spell out who I am? It's Bosa, boys and girls. Bosa's here, with Bosa's ship, and Bosa's got you handsomely outgunned.'

'Don't respond,' Prozor said. 'How far out are we?'

'Five minutes. I have eyes on the *Queenie*, but . . .'

'You can leg it now,' Prozor told him. 'It's what anyone sane would do, havin' just had an introduction from Bosa Sennen. Pour on the rockets and get us docked.'

Trusko applied more thrust. 'She wants to talk. Why would she signal, if she didn't want to talk?'

'She knows what she wants and she'll either take it or smash it,' Prozor said. 'Talkin's just her way of tormentin' you, makin' you think negotiation's an option.'

Now another voice sounded from the console. 'Drozna here . . . did that you get that squawk, Captain?'

'I did. We're coming in.'

'It can't be Bosa Sennen, can it?' Drozna asked plaintively. 'Nothing we've done has earned us a visit from the *Nightjammer*. It's someone else, trading on her name.'

'Whether it's Bosa or not, it was a declaration of hostile intent.' Trusko looked back at us for a moment, searching out our forms in the splintered confusion of the Ghostie armour. 'We're capable of defending ourselves, Drozna, and we shall. Run out all coil-guns and break out the crossbows.'

I expected Prozor to chastise him for that, but instead she just nodded, what I could see of her face – what I could *remember* even being her face – dipping up and down. 'It's all right,' she said in a low voice. 'It's what anyone would do, now she's named herself. No harm in it.'

Bosa's voice returned. 'Is that you in that launch, Trusko? Bosa's got her eye on you, you know. What've you dug out of that bauble for her? Something juicy? You know Bosa's got exacting tastes.'

'We've nothing for you,' Trusko said. 'The bauble was a bust. Why do you think we were coming home?'

'That's all right, Cap'n. It wasn't the bauble that brought us here. Still, Bosa'll make her own mind up about what is and isn't valuable, if you please.'

'I have nothing for you.'

'Bosa heard you've a skull that'll suit her needs. The skull's all Bosa wants of you. Let her have it without fuss, and you'll have a story to brag about to the other captains.'

'No,' Trusko said. 'If I believed you'd keep to that promise, it'd be different. But you can't be trusted.'

'Has someone been saying bad things about Bosa? We can't have that, can we?'

The *Queen Crimson* was coming up fast now, opening its red-lit mouth like a hungry fish set on swallowing a tiddler. For all his faults as an actual captain, Trusko at least knew how to operate the launch. He was playing those rockets and steering jets like they were organ stops, concentration making something of his face I hadn't seen before. A different set of features was breaking through the softness, hinting at the harder man he might have been, if his stars had favoured him differently. We all have it in us to be something other than what we are, I thought, but we don't often get a glimpse of what we could have been.

Most of us are better off for the not knowing.

The *Queenie*'s hull flashed along its flanks on one side, like a chain of fireworks. That was the coil-guns going off, the electromagnetics in them heating up so hard and fast that they shone.

'Pre-emptive fire, Trusko!' Bosa sounded impressed, in a mocking sort of way. 'And just when we were getting on so well, discussing terms, polite as you can be. Bosa's shocked, shocked, to the very core of her being.'

The squawk screamed out a roar of static, and off to one side, visible to my own eyes, I saw the flash of the *Nightjammer*'s return volley. I couldn't tell if she was ten leagues away or a hundred, all that I knew was that she was too close, and that Trusko could forget any thought of cutting and running.

I watched a dozen slugs rain against the *Queenie*, scabbing off parts of her hull where they landed. One clanged against the launch and sent us into a wild tumble that Trusko only just had time to correct before we were angling into the docking mouth. Bosa could have hit us much harder if she meant to, though. That was a scatterfire volley, normally intended to rip away sails and rigging, immobilising a ship rather than gutting her. The *Queenie* didn't even have her sails run out, but Bosa's point had been to let us know she could take us, even if for the moment she chose not to.

It was a straight fight Trusko could never win. Rackamore had burned out his coil-guns before he did any harm to Bosa, and I didn't doubt the same would apply here. We *were* outgunned, and in a way it was a kindness of her to point it out.

The launch slammed into its docking cradle. Behind us, the door began to close its jaws. Weightless again now, we undid our restraints. 'I'll go first,' Trusko said, rising from his control position. 'I'll speak to Drozna, Surt and Tindouf, tell them what's happening. You can follow through when I've explained about the Ghostie armour.'

'Don't take an age about it,' Prozor said. 'Bosa's boarding squad's probably already on its way.'

Trusko worked the airlock that led back into the main part of the *Queenie*. We watched him go through it, holding back for the moment. I touched a hand around the invisible sleeve of her Ghostie armour, while Strambli looked on.

'I had to do it,' I said. 'I ain't apologising, or explaining myself, so don't get that idea. Bosa hurt you, but she hurt me as well and I wasn't going to roll the dice on us ever crossing orbits again. I want you to stay my friend. Nothing would mean more to me than that. But if you can't set this aside, I understand.'

'You played us,' Prozor said.

'I played Bosa, not you. You wanted Trusko to stay in character, so you kept some of the truth from him. I did the same. If you'd known how near she was, you'd have acted differently, and maybe we wouldn't be getting this chance.'

'This chance to die?'

'This chance to end her,' I said. 'That's what's happening. This day, this hour.'

'You really think you can do this? That glowy's been in you too long, girlie. It's crossed over into your grey.'

'I just know what needs to be done. And I want you with me while we do it.'

That was when I noticed the light on Trusko's console, flashing on and off. I didn't know what it meant – just that it hadn't been there before.

'What's that?' I asked Strambli.

'The squawk,' she said after a moment's hesitation. 'The *Queenie*'s squawk, on the backup channel. It's Cap'n Trusko. He must be sending a message to Bosa.'

I knew then that he had lied to us, just as we'd lied to him. Trusko hadn't gone ahead to break the news to the others about the armour. He'd gone ahead to use the squawk.

'Get him,' Prozor said.

23

Drozna was the only one waiting for us on the other side of the lock. The cove had no warning what to expect, so it was instructive to see the play of reactions across his face, like a speeded-up version of what we'd already been through at our leisure, between the bauble and the *Queenie*. First there was the confusion and bewilderment brought on by the first sight of the Ghostie armour – the eyes and the optic nerves and the brain all befuddled by encountering something that got harder to see the more you looked at it, until – when you were peering right at it – it not only wasn't there, but neither was the notion of it. Then there was the secondary reaction, a kind of squinting, headachey puzzlement, brought on by the notion that our bodies had been shattered into something abstract, so that while Drozna could keep tabs on our hands and feet and the gaps between the pieces of armour, assembling that jigsaw into three people, moving independently of each other, was twenty times knottier than it ought to have been. Then there was the third stage of it, and that was closer to revulsion or sickness than confusion, and it showed in a slackening of his jaw, a curl to his lips, a widening of his eyes, all signalling the realisation that what he was seeing wasn't only wrong, it was wrong in ways that churned the stomach and left a person feeling shivery and tainted, as if just seeing the Ghostie armour left a hard blemish on the soul.

'It's all right, cove,' I said to Drozna, before he coughed up his insides. 'It's us. We're on your side. But Trusko's knotting things up for us nicely.'

'I think you should listen to them,' Strambli said. 'They've tricked us, the two of them. But it's them that's going to dig us out of the same mess.'

'Or it was,' Prozor said, and I didn't like the tone of that at all.

We pushed through the *Queenie* until we reached the galley, and then the bridge, where Trusko was floating next to the squawk console, resting one hand on the ceiling over it to steady himself. He was flipping switches with the other hand, saying a few words over and over again.

'Trusko to Bosa Sennen. Respond immediately. I have vital information. Do not attempt to board us. You are walking into a trap. They have Ghostie armour.' Then he'd flip a switch, say it again. 'Trusko to Bosa Sennen . . .'

Prozor came up behind him. Or at least I kept forcing myself to hold onto the idea of it being Prozor, even as the effort of it made my head spin.

'Stop, Captain,' she said, holding the edge of a Ghostie blade not far off his throat, bare above the ring of his helmet collar.

He flipped one more switch. 'Trusko to Bosa Sennen!'

'Stop!' Prozor snarled, bringing the smoky mirage of that blade even closer to his neck.

'The squawk's damaged,' Drozna said behind us, his frame nearly filling the doorway. 'The scatterfire. Coil-guns took out everything on that side of the *Queenie*, including our eyes. We haven't been able to send or receive since it happened. I'm sorry, Captain. All the channels are burned out.'

Prozor reached over with her free hand and threw a master switch, damping all the lights on the console. 'You nearly killed us all,' she said, saying it just loud enough for the rest of us to hear. 'Thought you'd spook her off, by mentionin' the Ghostie stuff, did you? First thing, Bosa doesn't spook. She probably wouldn't have believed you, but even if she had, she'd have just turned those coil-guns on you, properly this time, not that little slap and tickle she showed you just now. Have you seen a coil-gun slug go right through a hull, Trusko? I have. Have you ever seen a coil-gun slug go right through a hull, and right through the cove that happened to be in the way? Seen that as well. There isn't much left. Just a pink cloud, which gets everywhere. They say it's quick, at least. Was that what you wanted? A quick end to it all?'

'You said "first thing",' Trusko answered, in a voice that belonged on a boy better than it did on a captain. 'What's the second?'

'The second is that you tried to trick us, and you've got to die for that, but I felt I owed you an explanation.'

Prozor brought the knife against his neck.

'No,' I said. 'Leave him.'

Trusko's neck moved. I bet there was nothing in the universe he wanted to move less than his own neck, but we aren't always the master of our own bodies, especially when someone's pressing a Ghostie knife against us.

'Why?' Prozor asked.

'Because you want Bosa to think she's got the better of us. Having him already dead, cut open with a Ghostie blade, floating around with his blood coming out everywhere? Don't you think that'd make her think twice?'

'You're the expert on Bosa now?'

'No,' I said calmly, even though calm was the last thing I felt. 'I'm not. None of us are. But if she waltzes in here and finds Trusko already peeled by his own crew, she's going to think something's fishy.'

'We'll take her anyway.'

'No,' I said, willing that knife away from Trusko's skin. 'Not until we've got the lot of 'em inside the *Queenie*. We can't risk her cutting back to the *Nightjammer* and turning those coil-guns on us.'

Finally, some part of that got through to her. She gave a grunt and shoved Trusko into the console. But at least she was fixing the Ghostie blade back onto her armour.

Trusko's eyes met mine. 'Thank you,' he wheezed out.

'You're welcome. But keep this in mind. It could easily have been me pushing that blade into you, and Prozor trying to talk me out of it. Only difference is, I don't think I'd have the sense to listen.'

From behind us, Drozna said: 'That armour, whatever it is. I can't even . . .'

'It's Ghostie stuff,' Strambli told him. 'They knew it was in the bauble. It's the whole reason they had us go to the Fang. There's more of it, too. More armour and weapons.'

Two more faces were in the door now. One belonged to Tindouf, the master of ions, and the other was the bandaged-up head of Surt. 'We were stitched up, then,' Surt said.

'Properly stitched,' Strambli said. 'And you were a bother they had to get out of the way.'

'I s'pose Gathing was another bother,' Surt said.

'You can mourn him later,' I said. 'If any of you care enough. I'm sorry we had to hurt you, Surt. Prozor and I needed to be in that bauble. None of you knew what was at stake, and we weren't exactly in a position to go explaining ourselves.'

'They called her in,' Strambli said. 'Bosa didn't just stumble on us out here. They *made* it happen. Tell 'em, Captain.'

'It's the truth,' Trusko said, easing away from the console with the caution of a man who might still lose his throat at any minute. 'We were made into bait, and now she's here. The fault's mine and mine alone. I signed on Prozor and I signed on Fura, and my every instinct should have been screaming at me not to.'

'But they weren't, and now we're here,' Prozor said. 'Which is why we need to talk particulars. The plan's simple. Bosa likes to board the ships she takes. She'll be boardin' this one in two shakes, and we need to be ready for her when she comes. There are two more suits of Ghostie armour.'

'There's four of us who aren't wearing suits,' Drozna said.

'I know,' I said. 'But we couldn't all wear the armour, anyway. I'm sorry, Drozna. I think you'd be handy in a fight, but the armour just wouldn't fit you.'

He gave a thoughtful look, nodded, accepting the blunt logic of his fate with a certain equanimity. 'But you mentioned weapons.'

'We'll dole 'em out,' Prozor said. 'And we'll need crossbows, too.'

'They're ready,' the big man said.

'Captain,' I said, turning to Trusko. 'I know this is tough, but I think it would be for the best if you weren't wearing one of the suits. You'll be the one who meets her. She'll expect to find you, having heard you on the squawk, and she'll want to keep you alive as she finishes off your crew.'

Perhaps Trusko had gone through some barrier of fear into the calm air beyond, but I had the sense that something had changed in him. Or perhaps he just didn't think the armour was going to make that much difference, and he was damned either way.

'All right,' he said. 'I'll meet her. But I want one of those knives with me when I do.'

'You'd need to move quickly to take Bosa,' Prozor said.

'It wasn't Bosa I was thinking of,' Trusko said.

Something *donged* against the hull.

'She's on us,' Prozor said.

'How big a party?' I asked.

'Take your pick,' she said. 'Could be individuals, could be a launch. No way of knowing with our hull burned out.'

'Drozna,' I said. 'Can you fetch the lookstone, the one we pulled out of the first bauble?'

Drozna met my eyes for a second, then nodded. He was back quickly, with the little shard of lookstone bundled in cloth like a holy relic. He slipped it from its protection and offered it to me.

I held the lookstone before me and squeezed it gently, as I'd been shown. Gradually the view through it changed: the walls of the room melting away, the wires and cables behind them next, the insulation and gubbins between the wires and the outer armour, then the armour itself, and then I was looking out to empty space. I swept the lookstone slowly, picking up the

bauble, the folded edges of sail-control gear, the distant span-
gling of the Congregation – which we'd all be lucky to see with
our own eyes again, never mind breathe the lungstuff of any of
those worlds. Then my sweep found a sharp knot of bony angles
and spines, only a bit less black than the space behind them,
and I knew I was staring right at the *Nightjammer*. She couldn't
be more than ten leagues off us. I moved off her, picking up a
brassy cylinder, flanged along its sides and with fins at the back,
docked onto our ship at right angles, and I knew it wasn't any
part of the *Queenie*.

The lookstone showed the outside of the docked launch. But
I squeezed a tiny bit harder and it peered all the way through,
into her guts, and I found myself looking at the coves inside,
tiny and neat as paper dolls.

'I see 'em,' I said quietly, like I might break a spell if I raised my
voice. 'There's eight of them inside it, and they're moving out.'

'One of 'em in a silver suit, all chromey?' Prozor asked, and
I could tell she was itching for a squint through the lookstone
herself.

'Yes. At the front. One silver suit. The rest black. I never saw
Bosa, but I saw those black suits when they came for Adrana.
That's Bosa, isn't it?' Finally I passed her the lookstone, and after
a moment she nodded a grim confirmation.

'We wanted her, and now she's here,' Prozor said. 'So why
ain't I jubilant?'

I turned to Trusko. 'When Bosa comes, try and hold her in
the galley. Stall her, however you need to, until she thins out
her search party and starts moving through the ship. Then we'll
take them. One at a time if need be, silent and quick as we can.'

'I can take the other suit,' Surt said, and if ever someone
looked less keen on an idea, I never saw it.

'Good,' I answered. 'It's not difficult to wear.' No, not difficult
at all – almost like slipping on a second skin, almost like the
thing wanted to be worn. 'Tindouf, would you . . .'

'I'd like to do me some killings, yes,' Tindouf said cheerfully,
as if we were asking him whether he cared to be dealt into a

game of cards. 'It's been a while since I killeds anyone, and I needs a new notch or two in my pipe.'

'Bosa's going to find it awful odd, opening up a ship and only two coves being inside it,' Strambli said.

'We'll hold her,' Drozna said. 'She heard my voice on the squawk, and the captain's. We'll say we took losses in the bauble; that we're not running at full capacity.'

'She'll buy that?' Strambli asked.

He gave a shrug of his powerful shoulders, as if he fully recognised that this gambit wasn't going to satisfy Bosa for long. 'Just make that armour count. It *ought* to count. I'm getting shivery just being near it, and you're on my side.'

'We are,' I said. 'You had your doubts about us, Drozna, I know. But that was only right and proper and I didn't hold it against you. Now can we be solid?'

'Yes,' Drozna said, but I could tell that the word had cost him effort. 'I'll show you the crossbows. Prozor: you'd better get Surt and Tindouf into that armour while there's still time.'

Prozor and Strambli went back to the launch and returned with the rest of the Ghostie armour. They were getting the other two dressed up in it when we felt our ears pop. We all looked at each other without needing to say what it was. Bosa was through one of the locks. Easiest thing would have been for her to blow all the lungstuff in the *Queenie*, but skulls were delicate things and she wouldn't risk ours being knocked around by decompression.

I used the lookstone again, and saw that the *Nightjammer* had crept in closer, thinking we were going to be easy pickings. Two leagues out now, maybe three.

'Come as close as you dare,' I whispered.

It couldn't have taken more than a couple of minutes to get Surt and Tindouf into the Ghostie armour. Now there was more of us in it than out of it, but I can't say that made me feel any safer or more able to face Bosa. We were broken, shattered pieces of ourselves, trying to hold on to the idea of who we were and what we'd been.

'They were right,' Prozor said.

'Who was?'

'The coves who decided this stuff was better off locked away in baubles. If they'd known what was right, they'd have fed it into the Old Sun, or sent if off into the Empty.'

'I don't care for it either.'

'It's when the armour starts feelin' like a natural part of you, that's when you need to worry.' Then she touched a hand to me. 'We wronged each other, Fura. I know it. And maybe one of those wrongs was worse than the other. But if I blame you, I'm only blamin' you for what Bosa Sennen put into your head, and that's hardly any fault of yours.' I was content with that, but she wasn't done. 'Anyway, it ain't what the rest of 'em deserve.'

'The rest?'

'Cazaray. Mattice. Jusquerel. Triglav. Trysil. Hirtshal – all one word of 'im. And Rack. Can't forget Rack.'

'It was a good crew,' I said. 'We were lucky to have them. Lucky to sign on with a good ship, a good captain. We hadn't earned it.'

'You're earnin' it now.' Then she bent her mouth closer to my ear, whispering out from behind the faceless visor of the Ghostie armour. 'Somethin' was poisonin' this one. Maybe it was Gathing, with that snidey manner of 'is. Maybe it was Trusko, clinging to a past he made up for himself. Maybe it was just too much bad luck, over 'n' over again. That'll grind any crew down. But now that we've lived with 'em, I know that they ain't the worst.'

I didn't feel like smiling, but I managed it anyway.

'Praise indeed.'

'I mean it, Fura. Strambli was foxed by that door, but then so was Mattice when he first ran into somethin' like that. And Mattice was as good as they come. Surt's not a bad Integrator. Seen better, but she's no slouch. Drozna and Tindouf, they ain't so terrible either.'

'You feel bad that we used them?'

'No, just that we had use someone. I'll be true to you. When

Black Shatterday wiped out my quoins, I only had one thought left in me, which was to bury Bosa. If that meant dyin', or takin' another crew with me – if that meant takin' *you* with me – then I was ready for it. But somethin' changed when we came out of the Fang.' Prozor's mask glanced away from me, as if this was more than she was ready to share. 'I still want to vent Bosa. But I ain't dyin' for it, and I'd sooner none of the rest of us die either.'

'Then we'll try very hard not to,' I said.

Our ears popped again. 'Secondary lock,' Prozor said. 'She's through. Won't be long now.'

I nodded. 'We'd better get ourselves dispersed. I'm going to the bone room. They'll find it quickly enough.'

We left Trusko and Drozna in the galley, to face Bosa and her boarding squad when they arrived. Tindouf went aft, to the part of the ship he knew the best. Surt hid herself away in the bridge, among the monkey and alien gubbins she'd stitched into functionality. Strambli went midships, near the sleeping area, and Prozor went to the kitchen. We took crossbows, Ghostie blades and the smallest of the pistols, but even those we'd only use as a last resort.

By then I knew my way around the *Queenie* like I'd been born to it. It only took a minute to get into the bone room. I spun the locking wheel as a matter of routine, stationed myself against a wall, then dimmed the lights. I waited another minute, then two. The bone room was soundproofed, so I wouldn't have heard any kind of commotion even if the squad were shouting their way right past the door, hammering on walls and bulkheads as they went. Still, after two or three minutes I was surprised when no one had tried to open the door from the other side.

I gave it a little longer, then slipped the Ghostie mask off my face. For a moment I felt as if I'd come up from underwater, rising from the deep end at the Hadramaw public baths. I took a deep breath and set the mask aside. Then I pulled the neural bridge off the wall, settled it over my scalp, and plugged in to the skull.

It didn't take long to connect to Adrana. It didn't surprise me that she was on skull watch during the middle of the attack, for Bosa would still be looking for any useful intelligence on us.

'Fura . . .' she said, her voiceless presence whispering into my brain. 'You're alive. I'm so glad. When she opened up the coil-guns . . .'

'She didn't want to hurt us too badly,' I said. 'Not yet. When she's got the skull, it'll be a different game. But we're ready for her.'

'As ready as Rackamore was?'

'This'll be different. But I have to know. We think she brought seven people with her – eight in total on the launch.'

'Yes, that tallies.' She didn't ask me how I knew, and I was glad of that, for it spared me explaining the lookstone to her. 'Bosa wasn't counting on a fight, or else she'd have sent them over with harpoons, rocket packs and magnetic boots, to land on your hull from outside.'

'Then we've still got her where we want – thinking she's ahead of us. Do you know how many are left on the *Nightjammer*?'

'Five, including me. What's going to happen, Fura?'

That was when I heard someone tug at the wheel to the bone room.

'Blood,' I said, and closed the connection. Then, to myself: 'Blood's what's going to happen.'

*

The wheel was still turning.

I slipped off the neural bridge, redonned the Ghostie mask, and detached the long-bladed weapon from my armour. My hand was closed around something solid, but there was still no presence to it. I might as well have been trying to hold onto a column of fast-moving lungstuff, the blade weighed so little.

I pressed back against the wall, to the right of the door. The wheel stopped turning and the door creaked wide. I held my breath, jammed tight against that wall. It was still dark in the bone room, and my eyes had had time to adjust to it.

I wasn't expecting it to be Bosa who jammed her head through the door, and it wasn't. The suit was polished black, gleaming like someone had spent a lot of hours and spit getting it that way. Our suits were too bulky to move around easily in the *Queenie*, but Bosa's were some older and better technology, and the coves inside them must have barely felt they were encumbered. That was good if you were sweeping through an enemy ship, mowing down the opposition, but not so good when a little caution was the order of the day.

Like now.

I wanted to know if I was dealing with one or more of them, so I let the black-suited figure come further into the bone room. They looked to either side as they passed through the door, and as they glanced to the right, they were looking right at me. I saw his face and eyes through his visor.

There was a twitch of something there, like a premonition of recognition rather than recognition itself. The cove's brain was telling him *something* wasn't right, but somewhere between one part of his noggin and the other, the message was getting addled. His eyes lingered on me for maybe half a second, and then they got pulled back to the main prize. He reached out a hand, steadying himself on the skull's support wires. With the other hand, he stroked along the skull's top ridge. The twinkly was still twinkling, and I suppose those lights were pretty no matter what flag you sailed under. He gave a look back, through the door he'd come from, and I knew then that he was on his own.

He spoke. I couldn't hear what he was saying, just the muffled report of it, spilling through his visor and into the lungstuff I was still dragging down my windpipe. I didn't need to hear him: it was obvious. He was all puffed up with himself like teacher's pet, having been the one who'd found Bosa's new skull.

I let him have his moment.

Then I peeled myself off the wall, coming up behind him. If I made any sound, he didn't hear it through that suit. I had the Ghostie blade in my right hand. I scooped my tin hand over the top of his helmet, until I got my fingers around the rim over the top of his visor. He knew I was on him then, but it didn't matter. He made to twist around, but I was faster. I pulled the Ghostie blade through the collar where his helmet joined his suit, and it went through like there was nothing there at all. I only just stopped before I started cutting through myself. His helmet floated away from his neck, his head still in it, and as it tumbled past me I got a good squint at his face, his eyes still open, and maybe just a glimmer of comprehension showing on them before his thoughts clouded out.

Meanwhile, blood was rocketing out of the other part of him like it was late for an appointment. His body tumbled as well, and the blood-coloured fountain painted itself all over the skull and walls and me.

The odd business was, though, that the blood didn't stay on the Ghostie armour. It didn't slide off it, either. I watched it shrink down into patches, and then smaller patches, like the armour was soaking the blood into itself. It should have changed colour, or become less transparent, less Ghostie, but it didn't.

If anything, it was harder to see than before.

24

I left the bits of him in the bone room, sealed the door, took my crossbow in my right hand and started moving back through the *Queenie*, always scouting out a spot I could squeeze into if I knew someone was coming. Considering it was in the middle of action, the ship was graveyard quiet. I thought about what I'd done, and how easy it had been – not just easy in the way the blade had parted the head from the neck, but easy in how I'd not had to think twice before doing it. I knew I'd sworn to get back at Bosa, and a mind for vengeance will put a spur into the meekest of us, but it wasn't just that. I'd sliced his head off because in that moment I couldn't think of anything simpler or more beautiful to do. It was as if someone had written:

$$1 + 1 =$$

and then left chalk next to it, so I could finish it off.

And I wondered how much of that was to do with me, how much to do with the lightvine, and how much to do with the armour. And another part of me wondered if I was better off not knowing.

The second one wasn't as straightforward as the first. I came around a twist in the corridor and there was another of those black suits at the end of it. There was a woman's face in the visor. She slowed, narrowing her eyes, knowing something was out of place, but not quite seeing me for what I was. I froze, so that she wouldn't have the motion of my disconnected parts to help her, but I was a shade too late. She brought up her crossbow and levelled it in my direction, still squinting. She barked out something, but again I didn't get more than a muffle of it.

Then she shot the crossbow. The bolt hit me in the sternum – she'd found the middle of me, even with the armour – but it wasn't any worse than a sharp tap from a finger and the bolt didn't penetrate. I raised my own crossbow and gave her a bolt in return, nailing her right in the visor. The bolt punctured the glass, but it didn't get her in the face. She reached up, touched the bolt where it was embedded, thought better of tugging it out, and surged towards me like she had springs on her heels. She had a sword of her own, the curved blade as black and shiny as her suit.

I pushed the Ghostie blade ahead of me. We closed the distance between each other, her sword chopping through the lungstuff like she was trying to find something in fog. I met it with the Ghostie and sliced it clean through, leaving her with just the handle and a little stump of sword jutting from it. She could still do damage with that, but I was quicker. I jabbed the Ghostie right into her chest, and then pulled up as I drew it out. I took it down to the hilt, imagining the invisible blade cutting its way out of the back of her like a fin made of glass.

The length of the blade was crimson when I glanced at it. But it drank the blood just as thirstily as the armour.

That was when I felt something press against the back of my noggin.

'Drop it,' a voice shouted through glass and lungstuff so that I got the gist of it well enough.

If it was a crossbow muzzle, it was pressing against the hair on the back of my head, not against any part of the armour. No matter what you might think, something like that can have a very persuasive effect. I let go of the blade, and allowed the crossbow to slide out of my other hand.

I heard a hiss, like the seal on a helmet being released. Then the glassy whirr of a visor going up into a helmet, the way ours don't.

The voice was clearer now.

'You gave it a good go, with that armour.' The voice was a man's, but quite high in its pitch, and better spoken than I'd been expecting. 'All you've done is given Bosa something else for her money. She's been after Ghostie gubbins for years, and now she's got it all on a plate. Thought you could give her the jump, did you?'

'I didn't think anything,' I said.

'This bolt'll go through your mush like it was piston-driven. They'll be cleaning your grey off the walls for weeks, and picking bits of your bones out of their teeth after that. But you can save yourself that. We're near the middle of the ship. Where's the skull?'

'What skull?'

I got a jab of the muzzle against my skull for that bit of backtalk, but I reckoned it was worth it for the cheek. If I was going to get a bolt through my brain, I'd rather be getting on someone's nerves than going all bendy-kneed and pleading, like *that* was going to make a difference.

'The bone room,' the voice said. 'Show me it.'

'You can't talks to her like that,' said a voice I knew very well. 'T'aint proper. T'aint respectful. She's our Bone Reader, she is, and we's very pleased with her service.'

There was a click, but it was the crossbow having its safety latch put back on. I turned around slowly, leaving the stabbed one to get on with bleeding out. Tindouf had reached over the shoulder of the man behind me and taken the crossbow from him, but not before slicing right through the top third of his helmet, so that his skull and brains were laid open like a wax model of someone's insides.

'Thank you, Tindouf,' I said.

'Ain't necessary, Fura. But there's more of them's need killings, and I still needs some notches.'

'Honestly, Tindouf, I didn't know you had it in you.'

'Peoples think I's a harmless idiot,' he said. 'They's only half right.'

*

By the time we met Prozor and made an accounting of our progress, we'd killed five of the boarding squad. Their blood was already bobbing around the ship, bits of it drifting through in odd coagulations, following lungstuff currents like it was taking a sightseeing tour.

We found Strambli not long after, and while we were glad to see her, and even gladder to find her alive, she hadn't had a chance to get close to one of Bosa's people.

'I saw one,' she said, breathless. 'But the cove spooked, and he was quicker'n me. He was heading back to the prow when I last clocked him.'

'There were eight of them,' I said, as we crouched together in one of the wider corridors, not far from the kitchen where Prozor had been stationed. 'If Surt hasn't taken any, that still leaves Bosa and two others. They must still be in the galley, but they'll be getting the shivers now and I wouldn't want to guess what that'll push Bosa into doing.'

'If she touches Drozna,' Strambli said, finding some ferocity in herself that I'd never seen before, 'I'll pop her eyeballs out myself, stick 'em on skewers, and jam 'em back in her sockets the wrong way round.'

'We can't leave it any longer,' I said. 'It's Bosa we wanted, not her goons. Does everyone still have their blades and bows?'

We did a quick inventory. I'd regained my weapons after being rescued by Tindouf, and I still had the Ghostie pistol. The others still had their crossbows, and we made sure they were all drawn, bolted and ready to go. Here we were then: only a drift away from the room where she was. Part of me was straining to be in there, putting right what she'd wronged. But another part of me would have given anything not to face Bosa Sennen.

'We're not ready,' I said, hoping I was sharing a common thought with the others. 'But we'll never be readier. And no one's come close to doing what we've already done.'

'Let's take her,' Strambli said.

And we nodded one after the other. There wasn't any telling when it had happened, or what part in it Trusko could say was his. But somewhere between the Fang and this gathering, we'd become something we never were before, and that uncommon alchemy was as close to magical as anything that ever happened in all the long histories of the Thirteen Occupations.

We'd turned into a crew.

*

Drozna was dead. He'd been shot through the throat with a crossbow bolt, the same way Bosa killed Triglav, and if I might have doubted the presence of her hand until then, that would have been all the evidence I needed.

Trusko, though, was still alive. He wasn't even wounded. He'd been punched around a bit, that was plain, but other than a cut lip and a bruised eye, which only made him look softer and puffier, he wasn't much different than when we'd left him. Bosa had him strapped into a seat, and one of her black-suited boarders was on either side of him, but Bosa herself wasn't in the galley. We'd already checked Trusko's private quarters, so that only left the bridge, connecting off the galley the same way it had done on the *Monetta*. And now that we listened, we could hear her voice. She was using the squawk.

Or trying to.

In case I've given the wrong impression, we didn't storm the galley and start hacking away. We came in stealthy as shadows, quiet as cats, and because of the Ghostie armour, and the unfamiliarity of the place, Bosa's two grunts didn't notice they had company until it was much too late. Credit to Trusko, too: if he batted an eyelid, I didn't see it. Maybe the cove was too punched about to notice us, but I don't think so. I reckon there was enough alertness going on in his noggin to appreciate that Bosa's fortunes were about to take a severe dip, one that would make Black Shatterday look like a good day's trading.

I'll spare you the graphics of how we hacked 'em up, or what parts we detached from other parts, and what they made of it as it was going on. Suffice to say it wasn't pretty, and if I ever have nightmares about my time on the *Queenie*, which happens more than you'd think, that's the part that they tend to linger over. But while we weren't kind to them, exactly, we weren't cruel either, at least not in Bosa's league.

Besides, we didn't want them screaming and screaming, drawing Bosa from the squawk.

That's what happened, though.

She came back into the galley from the bridge with that silver suit on, the one I'd glimpsed through the lookstone, when she was just a tiny figure on the launch. I supposed she'd been trying to use our squawk to signal back to the *Nightjammer*, that being quicker and simpler than going back to her launch, but she was finding out for herself how damaged the squawk was.

Now she was finding something else out.

Bosa still had her helmet on. She was looking around the galley, her back to the bridge, drinking in what had happened while she had her attention snared by the squawk. There wasn't any part of her face I could see. The suit was sleek and tight-fitting, silver where the others were black, but otherwise similar. Even the visor was silver, but she must have been able to see through it by some means.

She took in Trusko, still bound to the chair, but with dead bodies flanking him. Blood was everywhere, dark red nebulas of it, all clotted and ropey even as they drifted around the room. Slowly Bosa must have cottoned on that she wasn't alone. What she could see of us, I couldn't speculate. But some itchy intuition told her we were present.

She reached up and touched a toggle on the neck of her suit. Her voice came out exactly as it sounded over the squawk, with all the same static and interference and looping echoes.

'Well, that's a turn. Not much surprises Bosa, but you've done yourselves proud. What is it – Ghostie gubbins?'

'From the Fang,' I said, choosing to speak for everyone. 'We knew it was there, too. It wasn't an accident, us just stumbling on it. You've been played, Bosa.'

The silver-visored helmet nodded back at me. Blood scudded slowly between us, reflecting in the silver.

'And you'd be?'

'We wasn't properly introduced,' I said. 'But you've met my sister. I'm Fura Ness. I'm the other Bone Reader, the one you thought were getting, when Garval put herself in my place.'

'There was one survivor on that ship,' Bosa said. 'I know, because I picked up the squawk. But it wasn't you.'

'You got it wrong,' I said. 'You've had it too easy out here, taking your pick of ships. It's made you lazy. You thought you'd have a bite of Trusko, too. But look who got to him ahead of you.' Then I cocked my head at the woman next to me. 'Show her, Prozor. Take off your Ghostie mask and show her how deep she's in it.'

'More'n she realises,' Strambli said. 'I said it wouldn't go well for her if she killed Drozna.'

Prozor was following my suggestion. She lifted up her face, presenting all its angry angles to Bosa. 'I was there when you killed 'em,' she said. 'In that same room, when you killed Triglav, Jusquerel, Cap'n Rack himself, and thought you'd done the same to me.'

'I didn't kill Rackamore,' Bosa Sennen said. 'I'll take the other names, but not that one. And if you were there to see it, Prozor, you know I'm telling the truth.'

'We know who you are,' Prozor said.

'Let me show you,' Bosa said, and touched another control on the ring of her helmet. I heard the same wheeze of lungstuff as before, and the same glassy whirr as the visor retracted up into the crown of the helmet. The face that looked back at us wasn't out of the ordinary at all. It wasn't scarred or cratered or tattooed or disfigured by radiation or made otherwise strange by the glowy. It was a woman. She had fine features, a proud curl to her lips, a certain steel in her eyes, but there wasn't anything about her that would have drawn more than a second or third glance in Mazarile.

But it was also a face I knew – or that wasn't totally unfamiliar to me.

'Illyria Rackamore,' I said, voicing the name she'd been born under. 'Go on, deny it.'

Her look was mild, almost forgiving.

'I am what I am, child. What would be the sense in denying it?'

'Bosa turned you,' I said. 'Just as she was turned by another Bosa, and another before that. How far back do you go?'

'Longer than you'd care to know. And I won't be the last, either. I'll take my place with the others, proudly, and pass on the good work of Bosa Sennen to my natural successor – and if you're the sister you say you are, you won't have much trouble guessing who I mean. She's a fine enough boney now, but they don't last, do they? And she's older than you, so she's nearer the day when the bones stop whispering. But I've plans for her beyond then. She'll make a worthy Bosa, will Adrana Ness.'

'No,' I said. 'She won't. She's strong.'

'They said as much about Illyria. Never thought Bosa could turn Rackamore's daughter, and yet here I am, living and breathing.'

'Why?' I asked. 'Why do you *do* this?'

'For the quoins,' she said.

'They're useless to you,' I replied. 'You can't go anywhere to trade or deposit them, so what's the point? Centuries of plunder and butchery to sit on a fat pile of money you can't ever spend?'

'It was never about making myself rich. It's about keeping the quoins under my eye, where they can't come to harm. Where *they* can't get their claws or feelers on 'em.'

'It's just money,' I said, hoping that the doubt didn't cut through my voice and show itself.

Bosa smiled at me, and it was like Pol Rackamore was

standing before us, looking fondly on the remnants of the crew he'd loved. 'That's what they want you to think. Shall I let you in on another secret?' Slowly she lifted one of her hands, revealing the thing she'd cupped in the palm.

'What?' I asked.

'This one you'll like.' She was grinning, all pleased with her own cleverness. 'It's one of Bosa's favourites. It's not Ghostie, but they weren't the only ones who knew how to put the shivers in us.'

She was holding a small, jewelled device that could have been a badge or a gaming token, and her thumb was caressing part of it.

'It's a weapon, but you guessed that. Fifth or Sixth Occupation – ask your Assessor, if you're that interested.'

'Our Assessor had an accident,' I said.

'That's a shame. You'll just have to take it on trust, won't you? It's a delayed designation device – a Firefist. While I was in here I designated its attack points. Didn't I, Trusko? You saw the light as it marked its targets.'

I looked at Trusko, and he looked at Illyria Rackamore, but if there was any acknowledgement in that glance it was too furtive or fleeting for me.

'No one uses an energy weapon on a ship,' I said.

'Unless they're suited,' she corrected me. 'And while my visor's raised at the moment, it would only take a micro change in the pressure to drop it again.'

'You've lost, Bosa,' Strambli said. 'We took your crew apart. We cut through them like they were lungstuff.'

'I've still got the *Dame Scarlet*.'

'You think you have.'

The voice had come from behind Illyria, not from one of us. Her face tensed, the smile tightening, curling up at the edges in a way that wasn't entirely natural, as if there were little hooks digging into her skin. Those steely eyes rolled back as far as they would go.

'Ah,' she said.

It was Surt, wrapping a hand around Illyria's throat and touching the edge of the Ghostie blade to the front of her helmet, level with the eyes. We could hardly see her, and even the idea that this shattered, sketchy form belonged to Surt was difficult to keep in the head from one thought to the next. But it had to be her. The rest of us were accounted for. She had been in the bridge all along, even when Bosa was in there trying to operate the squawk.

'Let go of the Firefist,' I said.

Illyria's face slackened. The smile relaxed, settled into a look of weary resignation. She murmured a sound of surrender, and seemed about to cast aside the jewelled device. Then her thumb twitched and prongs of ruby light flared out from her fist, branching between her fingers, a dozen of them shooting away at all angles, stabbing out through the lungstuff and into the surrounding material of the *Queenie*'s hull.

Illyria was fast, but Surt was quicker. She was pulling the Ghostie blade back through the open faceplate even as the ship began to vent pressure. She touched the bridge of Bosa's nose, drew a bubbling line of blood.

'No,' I said, before the howl of escaping lungstuff drowned out any possibility of speaking. 'Not yet.'

Surt hesitated, then pulled the blade away. The silver visor came down again, masking Bosa's face.

'Cut me free!' Trusko shouted, and I realised that the captain was still bound to his chair. The lungstuff was screaming out, as if the hull was fraying open like an old pair of stockings. It tasted cold and thin in my throat, more like metal than gas.

I got the Ghostie knife and slipped through his restraints.

'Sorry it's come to this,' I said, not really knowing if he could hear me.

Surt had slipped around Illyria while she was preoccupied with her helmet. Trusko stretched a hand out to me. His lips moved. He was saying something, but the cove barely had the strength to get it out.

'Gun,' he said. 'Ghostie gun.'

I passed him one of the pistols, closing my hand around the phantom thing, feeling the shape of it better than my eyes could make out its shifty outline.

Trusko took the gun. He looked down at the sly thing with a sort of deadened wonder, blinking at it the way a drunkard will blink at something that won't come into focus, and then he turned in his seat to aim the pistol at Bosa Sennen.

'No,' I said, guessing what he meant to do next. We were holed in a dozen places and the lungstuff was bleeding out fast, but that wasn't the same as blasting half the ship away.

Bosa started backing away, retreating into the bridge, the mirror of her face still turned to us.

Trusko looked back at me. It was impossible to hear anything now, and I was starting to feel a blackness clogging the edge of my thoughts. But Trusko mouthed words anyway and the wonder of it was that I got his meaning.

Quarters, he was saying.

His personal quarters.

I didn't have the strength to scream, and barely enough to move myself. I grabbed Prozor by the scruff and mimed for her to follow me into the quarters, and Strambli, Surt and Tindouf got the message smartly enough. By then we were swimming against the rush of lungstuff fighting its way out in a dozen directions, but none of that flow going in the way we needed, and by the time we got over the threshold into the room my lungs felt like they were sucking on vacuum. I didn't have much more to give, but I couldn't stop myself from looking back.

Bosa had backed all the way into the bridge. She was turning from us.

Trusko couldn't have had much more breath in him than the rest of us. But he still hung onto enough consciousness to level that Ghostie gun and fire, and if that was his last living act as captain of the *Queenie*, it wasn't a bad one.

A thousand times I've sifted through my recollection of what happened in the instants that followed, trying to find some sense or order to it that I can live with. There was the pull of the trigger, the discharge of the weapon, and what it did to every single thing that was caught up in the widening cone of that shot, and there was the violent slam as Trusko's quarters sealed itself up, pressure doors closing on both the galley and the bridge, and us seeing him for the last time, that gun in his hand even as the life raced out of him.

That's how it should have been, anyway.

But it wasn't.

All I can say is that the Ghostie gun's action wasn't concentrated at that one point in time when Trusko pulled the trigger. It was splintered, cut up into shards and reassembled *around* that moment, like a deck of cards getting shuffled, so that – in some way that I can't get at with words – the doors were *already* sealed before he fired, and Illyria was *still* looking back at us even after the gun had done its work, and sometimes her visor was up, sometimes it was down, sometimes it was jammed halfway between the two.

I've told myself that it couldn't have been like that, and that it must be my recollection of the sequence of things that got addled, but – much as that helps me to sleep – I ain't sure it's exactly true.

No. The Ghostie gun did something shivery to time as well as space and matter, and we were there when it happened, and if that makes a knotty confusion between what's sane and what isn't, you can take your complaints to the Ghosties.

25

Trusko's room kept us alive. Even as the rest of the *Queenie* lost her lungstuff, save for the small part that was contained by bulkhead doors and a few lungstuff-tight spaces – we survived. The cove might not have been the greatest or most courageous captain, but he had taken excellent care of his own amenities. My intution had been right, the first time he called me into his quarters. That sense of solidity wasn't merely my imagination. The walls and doors enclosing the quarters really were built to a higher standard than the rest of the ship, because Trusko wouldn't have had it any other way. You could call him a coward for that, and many will. But when he took that Ghostie gun and aimed it at Illyria he knew exactly what he was doing. Maybe one brave, selfless act can't outweigh a life spent acting otherwise, but I ain't one to judge. I think Trusko got the crew he wanted, in those last minutes, and I think he did right by them.

Anyway, you'll hear criticism of Trusko and the sunjammer *Queen Crimson,* and plenty of it. But you won't hear it from me and you won't hear it from Prozor.

We got out of that room in the end, but I won't pretend any part of it was easy. Trusko had a suit tucked away in a partition behind one of his charts, but we'd never have found it if Surt hadn't been there. 'Half the things people thought were secrets on this ship,' the Integrator confided in us, 'I've known 'em for years.' I thought of Jusquerel on the *Monetta*, Lusquer on the *Iron Courtesan*, and reckoned it was probably just as true of them. Never mind what they say of Bone Readers, it's Integrators that a captain needs to keep cosy.

The connecting way between Trusko's quarters and the bridge was double-doored, so we could get in and out of the room without losing all our lungstuff in one gasp. But there wasn't a proper pump on it, and we lost a little lungstuff each time anyone had to go in or out through the door, into what was left of the rest of the *Queenie*. By the time Surt had put on Trusko's suit and gone scouting for more suits and lungstuff, we were at the thin edge of what was remaining. In the space of an hour, as the lungstuff grew chokey, I went from thinking kind thoughts of Trusko all the way back to despising him again, for putting us through slow asphyxiation.

'It's a mess out there,' Surt told us. 'We ain't got ourselves a ship any more, that's plain.'

'Good job there's another one not too far off,' I said.

Surt's eyes met mine through her visor. 'I knew you meant to take the *Nightjammer*. But I didn't think you were counting on taking it *over* as well.'

I forced a smile. 'Not exactly spoilt for choice, are we?'

'There's something else. That Ghostie gun mangled things up pretty good. Knotty to say what was what. I found Trusko, and I don't think he suffered too much. Only thing that's nagging me is there's no clear sign of Bosa, or any part of her.'

'We decompressed pretty hard,' Strambli said. 'If the gun didn't get her, she might have been swept out.'

'Could she have made it back to the *Nightjammer*?' I asked.

'We're close enough,' Surt said. 'And that hole in us is lined up pretty good with Bosa's ship. But jumping between ships ain't like skipping puddles. Odds are she still sailed off into the Empty, if that gun didn't take care of her.'

'There's more Empty than not,' Strambli said. 'My guess is she's falling a bit further into it by the second. You want to find her and taunt her, Fura?'

I couldn't say that the idea didn't have some appeal. But we had a few hurdles to cross before we got into the luxury of score-settling. 'No. The launch is our priority, and taking the *Nightjammer*. I want to get over there, and hard onto them, before they start having second thoughts.'

We'd had to get out of the Ghostie armour to put the suits on, and taking that armour off wasn't any more pleasant than wearing it. The only thing that was more unpleasant was seeing it lying in bundles again, all wrong and tainted, like it had taken a bit of our souls with it when we peeled it off. Knowing we'd need it again, we bundled it up and took it with us, but there wasn't one of us that felt cosy doing it.

We were hasty and nervous, but we still made sure we didn't slip up while putting our suits on. A bad seal, a lungstuff line plugged into the wrong valve, a damaged visor – any of these things could end us just as easily as a crossbow bolt. I suppose it was a measure of how long I'd been crewing that I didn't mind taking the time to ensure the suit wasn't going to turn traitor on me.

But the launch was still there when we reached it. The locks were peachy to crack, and Strambli got us aboard without too much trouble. We kept an eye out for booby traps, tripwires and so on, but I don't think Bosa ever counted on someone else trampling around inside her own launch. Inside, the layout of things wasn't so unfamiliar that Surt couldn't work out the gist. There was lungstuff in the tanks and fuel enough in her belly to get us over to the other ship. Prozor and Tindouf went forward to familiarise themselves with the controls and navigation. I took out the lookstone again – I'd kept it with me all along – and swept out through the launch's hull until I made out the *Nightjammer* again. She was much closer than a league now and it wouldn't have taken much for us to jump across, if we'd trusted our legs. I studied her cruel dark lines, settling my gaze on the harpoon jutting from her front and thinking of the awful cruelty Bosa had inflicted on Garval.

If Bosa had died by the Ghostie gun then there was justice in that death, but not nearly enough for my liking. Too quick, too painless, too clean. I preferred the idea of her falling away from the wreck, watching her lungstuff reserves dwindle away, the cold and the terror chewing into her marrow. I didn't see why Bosa Sennen deserved either forgiveness or mercy.

'We're ready to cut loose,' Prozor said. 'Brace for rockets.'

'Wait,' I said, realising we were about to make fools of ourselves.

'What?'

'We still need surprise,' I said. 'The rest of 'em have to believe this is Bosa, coming back with her prize. But we can't squawk, they'll know it's us.' I reached for a spare lungstuff tank, knowing I'd need it. 'Wait for me.'

'Where are you going?' Prozor asked.

'The bones,' I said.

I left the launch and crossed back into the ruined bowels of the *Queenie*, and then found my way to the skull. I spun the wheel on the door without thinking about it, and that wasn't very bright on my part, because there was still lungstuff in the bone room. It all came out in one go, and if I hadn't been suited the force of that door hitting me would have left me for dead. The effect of the decompression was still making the skull jiggle around on its wires even when all that was left was vacuum.

I sealed the door behind me. Still with my suit and helmet on, I took that spare lungstuff tank and opened its valve all the way it would go, flooding the room. I didn't need the lungstuff with my suit on, but I couldn't take my helmet off without it, and with the helmet on I couldn't slip on the neural bridge.

I was worried that the decompression had damaged the skull, and perhaps it had. The twinkly seemed more subdued, just a few lights glowing out of those bony cavities.

It didn't matter. I didn't need much out of it now.

'Adrana,' I said, putting every hope I'd ever had into her name. 'It's Fura. I'm still alive. We got Bosa's boarding party. Killed them all, and Bosa too; most likely.'

When she didn't answer, I started to think the worst. Anything could have happened on the *Nightjammer* while we were engaged with our own slice of the action. Perhaps her crew had taken a sudden dislike to their new Bone Reader, for the trouble that had come their way since Adrana's recruitment.

Then she came through.

'Fura!'

'We're coming over. We've taken her launch, and we're riding it over to the *Nightjammer*. But you've got to act as if she's still alive. Tell the rest of 'em there's a problem with the squawk, but that Bosa's on the launch. Make it seem like she's beaten us, like she's jubilant; crowing with her victory. Can you do it, Adrana? It won't take us long to complete the crossing, and we've got some work to do before we dock—'

'I'll . . . I'll do what I can.' The doubt in her came through the skull as if we were sitting holding hands in the parlour. 'You're so close now, Fura. I can't believe we're nearly together again. Please be careful.'

'I've come this far,' I said. 'You only have to do a little bit more, and then everything's going to be all right.'

'I'll try.'

'You'll succeed. I know. I've got faith in us both.'

And I did too, though I couldn't say where that faith had come from, or how deep it went. Just that it was the only thing that was going to get both of us through that day, so we might as well make the best of it.

I signed off from the bones and set off back through the *Queenie* to the launch. I was halfway there when I remembered what I'd left in my quarters, and although time wasn't exactly on my side there wasn't a power in all the worlds that would have stopped me making that detour.

I found the broken head, the glass dome of it, and I cradled it to me like it was my own newborn, because I wouldn't have been here otherwise and I owed Paladin more than abandonment on this wreck.

'You'll speak again,' I said, making a promise between the two of us. 'I know it. We ain't done with each other yet.'

The other thing I took was Rackamore's *Book of Worlds*.

The launch was still there, Prozor's thumb twitching on the thruster control. As soon as I was through the lock she poured on the rockets and we made smart work of crossing over to the *Nightjammer*, doing it with the kind of swagger her crew would be expecting. That made it tricky for us, too, because we had to get out of our suits and back into the Ghostie armour. But the armour obliged in that, seeming to want to get back on us almost without our bidding.

My heart was in my throat the whole way over, though. I'd no way of contacting Adrana, no way of knowing how cleverly she'd been able to dupe them.

All I can say is, they weren't expecting us.

Not at all.

When the launch returned, its silence made perfect sense to them. There might be no operable squawk on either the launch or the wreck of the *Queenie*, but Bosa had their prize, and was coming back with it. Open the locks and prepare to cut out on ions and main sail, boys and girls.

That was what they had been told, anyway. What they got, when we docked, was a quick and bloody tuition in all the forms of mutilation possible with the armour and weapons of the Ghosties, and they had nothing that made a difference to us.

I'll say this for us: we exercised restraint. It wasn't that we were feeling charitable, or in any sort of forgiving mood. None of that, not after all she'd dished out to us. But the *Queenie* was gone and we still needed a ship if we were ever to get home, wherever that might turn out to be. The *Nightjammer* wasn't top of the list of ships I might have chosen, but it was all we had.

So we took her, without too much damage, and it was glorious, and at the end of it all there wasn't one of us that wasn't proud to have sailed on the *Queenie*, under Captain Trusko.

'She's ours now,' I said. 'This ship. Whatever wrongs she's done, they were never the ship's fault. And we can start putting her right.'

'There's one wrong I ought to settle first of all,' Prozor said.

'For you as well, Fura. We didn't do right by Garval, when she was one of us. But we can treat her properly now. I know it's too late for her, but I ain't spending a minute more on this ship with her stuck on the front like that.'

'I'd help you,' I said, sorry that I hadn't given more thought to Garval myself. 'You know that, don't you? But I've got to find my sister.'

Find Adrana, and tell her the hardest news of all.

*

She was in the *Nightjammer*'s bone room when we took the ship, and she'd had the good sense to stay there while the blood-letting was in progress. None of us knew where the room was, of course, but – as I'd learned by then – it was in the general rule of things to find the bone room about as far from the noisy parts of the ship as you could manage, and as far enough inside as possible. Looking somewhere near the middle was always a good bet, and if you worked methodically out from the centre it wouldn't be long before you found your bones, no matter how cleverly your crew had tried to conceal their most precious asset.

Bosa did her best, I'll give her credit for that. The door and locking wheel were hidden behind a false partition that sprang back into place after you'd gone through. But I'd have ripped that ship apart with my fingernails if I'd needed to.

I knocked on the door, using the pattern we'd agreed, and I was turning the wheel with my own hands when I felt Adrana put her own muscles into the effort. The wheel spun until it was a blur, and then the door swung open, and we were together again.

I've put words down on paper, tens of thousands of them, more words than there are worlds with names, and if you've followed my red scribblings this far – and made allowance for what happened to my hand – then you'll have some notion of all the things that had happened to me since I last saw my sister.

I'd watched her being taken on the *Monetta*, dragged away from me on the other side of a door, and I'd suffered all the weeks after that not knowing if she was still alive. I'd seen the decimation of Rack's crew, the unkind business Bosa had wrought on them, and I'd seen the extents I'd go to to keep my own heart beating. I'd seen Trevenza Reach and the insides of baubles – which is more than a fraction of coves will ever be able to say. I'd seen all the worlds from the outside of the Congregation and got some sense of this little glimmery puddle of life we called the Thirteenth Occupation. I'd seen what the Ghosties left us and held catchcloth and lookstone for myself. I'd nattered to aliens and robots, and found a hardness in myself that made me a little jumpy at the thought of what I'd become. I'd turned from my own home and left my own father to die, and although it made me choke to think of those things – and what I'd done in Neural Alley, in the Limb Broker's – I couldn't say I regretted the steps that had brought me to this moment. Not the place they'd carried me to, either, and not the person they'd made me into.

Bosa Sennen never set out to turn me into something I wasn't, but she did, and if I ever felt like sparing her a spit of gratitude it would be for that.

Adrana didn't recognise me at first, in the bone room's low red light. It wasn't the armour. I'd shrugged it off by then and just taking it off me felt like relieving myself of a dark cloak of guilt and bad intentions. No, it was what I looked like without the armour that had her befuddled. She jerked back a little, and I couldn't blame her for that. It wasn't just the glowy, or the tin hand, or the hard set of my face, which was starting to look stern and angry even when I didn't mean it. It was the fury in my eyes, a little glint of madness in both of them, and the fact that I didn't mind in the least.

We didn't speak, not at first. We just hugged each other, hard, knowing it was real, knowing we wouldn't be pulled apart again. I heard noises from the rest of the ship, but they might as well have been in another universe for all I cared. I'd got my sister back.

We didn't need to say much, not at first, and we didn't need alien skulls to flash our thoughts to each other. There had always been a language between us that didn't need words, one that had nothing to do with dead aliens or the bony gubbins they left us. It was just that we were sisters and we knew each other better than any one else could.

It was a long time before Adrana pulled back from me enough to take me in as a whole.

'What did they do to you?' she asked.

And I gave the only honest answer I could. '*They* didn't do anything. I did it myself. I knew what I was doing. I'm Fura Ness and I chose to become what I am.'

'If I didn't know you already,' Adrana said, 'I think you'd frighten me.'

'Good,' I said.

'They say the glowy changes you.'

'Lots of things change you. If it's in my grey already, it can stay there. I like what I am now.' I flexed my fingers in her hand. 'Even these tin fingers. They're not so bad. I can feel more through them with every day.' I paused. 'We've taken the *Night-jammer*. It's ours now, not Bosa's. We own this ship, and we can do what we like with it.' I knew I was glossing over a thousand hard things we'd need to do before the ship was truly ours, but I also knew we'd find our way around every problem, one at a time, because we were a crew now.

'Do you think it'll get us back to Mazarile?' Adrana asked.

'It could,' I said. 'But I don't think there's anything there for us now.' And I knew I had to get the truth out now, before it festered any more and started poisoning what was between us. 'He's gone, Adrana. Father's gone. He died.'

'Died?' she asked softly.

'He wasn't well when we left. We knew that. After I got back, it just got worse. But you mustn't blame yourself.'

'Blame myself?'

I'd said the wrong words, and once I'd have taken more pains to spare her feelings, but they were out there now so the best I could do was soften them. 'It was a strain, all the worry we put him through. He started telling himself you were dead, because it was easier than clinging to the hope that he'd see you again. I read your obituary, Adrana. Just before I left.'

'When did he die?'

My words jammed in my throat, but I forced them out. 'The morning I left. Paladin came with me, and . . .'

'The morning you left. Oh, Fura. It must have been terrible.'

And she pulled her head closer to mine and I thought there was sisterly kindness in it, as if she were going to hug me so near that our tears mingled and we got the salt of them in our mouths. Tell me it wasn't my fault either, and I wasn't to blame myself any more than she was.

But I felt a cold edge on my throat.

'He died, or you left him to die? Which was it, Fura?'

I tried to ease back, but whatever blade she had against my neck stayed put.

'I'm sorry . . .'

'You think I didn't know? Bosa told me weeks ago. She picks up scraps, transmissions, whenever she can. Obituaries. He wasn't much, our father, but he got his paragraph. And Bosa hoped the news would turn me nearer to her, and she was right.'

'She didn't turn you,' I said, hardly speaking the words in case she cut my throat. 'If she had, you'd have warned her about the trap.'

'Oh, I considered it,' Adrana said. 'But then I thought: what's more useful to me? Tipping off Bosa, or seeing what I can get out of her walking into it? She told me I was going to be the one, you see. Not for a while, not until I'd stopped being able to pick up the whispers, but after that, I'd be the one she favoured. That's how it works, you see – how it's always worked. Bosa picks the one to follow her, the one with the aptitude. It wasn't a hard choice, Fura! I could read, and put two numbers together, and that already put me at the front of the line. But I also had her cleverness, she said, and I could be sly when I needed it, and she knew I'd soon see things the way she did.'

I had to keep her talking, so I said: 'And how did she see things, exactly?'

'Bosa's not bad, Fura. That's just how they make her seem. But it's Bosa who's been doing right all these years, not the rest of 'em. It was Bosa that worked out the quoins, and if the truth of that doesn't cool your blood, nothing will. They're souls, Fura. The souls of the dead. Only they're not dead, exactly.'

I heard what she was saying, but the words weren't making any sense to me. Not then, anyway.

'So what happens now?'

'Now? Now's simple. You say you've finished off her crew? Then that's spared me a lot of trouble, especially if you've brought me a new one just in time. I could keep reading the bones, but why would I need to, now you're here? You can be my new Bone Reader. You're as good as I ever was, I know – just a little behind me.'

'She's got other plans.'

I heard the voice, and then the click as she released the catch on her crossbow.

'Prozor,' Adrana said, in a casual sort of way, as if it wasn't more than hours since they'd spoken.

She was halfway into the bone room, one hand on the crossbow, the other bracing against the doorway.

'Knife off her throat, girlie.'

I felt the cold edge pull away. I drew the first proper breath since she'd put that blade on me. I was just about to say something, offering some words of explanation or excuse for what my sister had done, but Prozor must have decided things were plain enough as they stood. She flipped the crossbow around single-handed and crunched the stock down on Adrana's scalp.

Adrana softened next to me, gave a sigh and started drifting out of my arms.

'Don't kill her,' I said.

'What we do or don't do with her can wait,' Prozor said, reaching in to pluck the knife from Adrana's limp fingers. 'In the meantime I thought you'd care to know that I found Garval.

It didn't take long, knowing where she was. But I found something else, too.'

I didn't understand.

Not until she showed me.

*

We'd have found her sooner or later, I suppose, but she'd have been dead by then and it pleased me handsomely to have her still alive. When Bosa had been blown out of the wreck of the *Queenie*, it had been her good fortune – slim as it was – that our ship had been lined up nicely with the *Nightjammer*, so that the force of the blast set her crossing over from one to the other, without needing any tricky skill on her part. To begin with, I was sure, there'd have been a deep dread in whatever was left of her heart – the dread of falling into the endless Empty, with only the dwindling capacity of her suit to keep her alive. But then that dread would have softened to hope, and then delight, if she was capable of such a thing, that her course was perfectly true and guaranteed to take her back to the *Nightjammer*. Oh, she had a surplus of speed, it was true, and no choice about how hard or soft she was going to hit the ship's hull, but her odds of survival had just gone up immeasurably. And since she had good expectations of getting back to the *Nightjammer* before any of us, she could alert her crew, bring the rest of her guns onto the wreck of the *Queenie*, and finish us off in a volley of spite and temper, even as she sacrificed any remaining thought of taking our bones.

But it wasn't to be.

So nicely were our two ships lined up, you see, that once Bosa left the *Queenie*, it was only ever a matter of time before she found herself driven onto the spike sticking out of the bow of the *Nighjammer*, the same bowsprit spike that she'd made Garval's last resting place. And she'd have had time enough to realise it, too, as her own ship got bigger and bigger in her visor.

It was even worse luck for her that she wasn't quite dead. The spike had gone right through her, from the small of her back to her belly, but it was a narrow wound and it had sealed itself pretty thoroughly. She'd have died if we dragged her off it, so after she had dealt with Garval, Prozor found a yardknife and sawed right through the last three spans of the spike, and we brought Bosa back inside the *Nightjammer* with that thing still skewering her.

We carried her to the medical room of the *Nightjammer*, the box of horrors where Bosa did her brain surgery. I'll say this for the place: it was clean, and she'd plundered a lovely set of drills and knives and saws and so on from the ships she fell on.

She wasn't going to live. That was clear. But we removed most of her suit, got lungstuff into her, stopped her bleeding, sealed the wound as best we could. Not out of niceness, no. There wasn't an atom of niceness left in any of our heads, not for her, and especially not in mine. Having your own sister put a blade to your throat, and knowing it was Bosa that turned her that way, will burn niceness out of the gentlest cove.

I laid it out for her.

'You're going to die, Bosa. I've got your ship and I've diced your crew into cubes. If there was one of 'em still alive I'd pluck his eyes out and feed them to you like grapes. But there isn't. Just Adrana, and although you started turning her, you didn't finish the job.'

It was hard for her to speak. Her eyes were gummy, her throat raw, and we had to keep putting the lungstuff back into her just to get any sense out of her gob.

But she managed this: 'I turned her, Fura. I turned her and it's too late to undo what I started. You can kill me, but all I've done is line another Bosa up to stand in my place.'

I didn't want to hear that, not now. So I changed the tack of our chinwag and said: 'Tell me about the quoins. What did Adrana mean, they're the souls of the dead?'

'Ask her yourself.'

'I will.'

'There was a war,' Bosa said, after another glug of lungstuff. 'A long time ago. Not one of ours. One of *theirs*. Aliens. It just spilled over into the Congregation, between one of our Occupations.'

Prozor, who was behind me, said: 'Which aliens?'

'None we know of. No name we've got for 'em. All they left us to remember them by is the quoins. They were slaughtered, you see. Driven to extinction. And when the end was nearly upon them, they took their own souls and squeezed them into quoins, and they're still inside. It's not money. It was *never* money.' She forced her mouth into a half-smile. 'Just recordings. The more bars, the more souls there are inside. Hundreds, thousands of them. And they're not just patterns, like letters on a tomb. They're frozen, yes. But they can live again.'

I was listening to words bubble out of a dying woman who was mad long before she'd been spiked on her own ship, and if I had one grain of sense in me I'd have ignored every one of those words.

But sense was never my strong point.

I asked: 'What do the other aliens want with them?'

'Nothing,' Bosa said. 'Not the Crawlies, or the Clackers or the Hardshells. They just want to gather them up and sell them on. They're just the brokers. There's someone *else* out there, some other aliens we don't even know about. It's them the quoins are for.'

'The ones who were slaughtered?' Prozor asked.

'The ones who did the slaughtering. They want the quoins, so they can get at the souls and pull them out again.'

'To make them live again?'

'To put them through more torments. To keep tormenting them. To keep them in agony until the Old Sun's just a cinder, and even then they wouldn't stop.' Her mouth cracked wider, eager to get something across. 'But I could stop them, Fura. I could do a good thing. Steal the quoins before they ever got to the banks, and keep them out of circulation. There's a world out there, a bauble, where . . .' But she coughed, and blood came out of her mouth in a fine red spray, stinging my eyes. 'I was trying to do a good thing, you see. A good thing. I couldn't take on the banks, couldn't take on the aliens . . . but I could do this one thing. If I saved even one quoin from them, that was good, wasn't it?'

So this was where all my travels and adventures had brought me. To be next to Bosa Sennen, and have her beg me to set her conscience straight.

And I thought about it. Whatever she had ended up, after all the faces she had worn, was it possible it had all begun with a desire to set right what was wrong? Could kindness – by only ever taking little steps – twist itself into the worst kind of cruelty? And did the fact of that kindness excuse any part of her crimes, or just put a different shade behind them, like hanging an ugly picture on a different wall?

'You said there was a bauble.'

She looked at me with something like humour. 'I did, didn't I. But I wouldn't be Bosa if I gave away her secrets too easily, would I?'

'I own your ship now. I'll find out anything I want.'

'I wouldn't dwell on those quoins too hard, if I were you. You might start seeing things Bosa's way.' She reached for me then, quicker than I'd have credited anyone in her condition was capable of. But it wasn't to strike me, or do me harm. She got her fingers around my jaw, gentle-like, and angled my face a bit closer to hers, so she could see me more easily. 'Especially not with the glowy in you like it is. Shines bright in you, it does. I bet you already feel the fire of it, the anger it puts into your veins. The odd notions it puts into your skull.'

'If it's in me, you're the reason.' I pulled her fingers off my jaw with my tin ones, and let her hand float limply down to her side.

'I suppose gratitude's in order, in that case.'

I turned from her. 'We're not done, unless you've the good sense to die on me.'

Her tone was interested, almost fond. 'What're you intending,

Fura? You've got a pretty ship now, with pretty black sails, and if you took my crew then yours can't be too shabby. But you need a plan. Every cove needs a plan.'

*

We'd have found her special room no matter what, but she'd done her best to make it secret. It was as big as any cargo hold on any ship I'd known, and all it contained was the glass and bronzey metalwork of the bottles, and the green fluid and grey-green flesh inside them. From the door, I stared into its gloomy green depths for several long minutes before willing myself inside. The bottles went back and back, on both sides of the room. There were thirty in total, and twenty-three of them had bodies in. The others were empty, clean, waiting.

We never got to the bottom of exactly how many of her there'd been. Clearly there were twenty-three Bosa Sennens before Illyria Rackamore, but whether was that the start of it, or just the bodies she had on this ship, we had no way of knowing. They weren't all alike, not at all, and they weren't all the same age when they ended up pickled. But I picked out a sort of sketchy likeness between them, and it wasn't because they were family. It was just that Bosa chose her successors according to her tastes, and she had a certain eye for it. It didn't take much imagination to see Illyria Rackamore floating pale-eyed and still in one of the now-empty bottles, and it didn't take much more to see Adrana occupying the one after that.

After that – who would it have been?

I caught a smear of my own reflection in the glass of the nearest bottle, and it was like my own face was already floating there, looking out just like all the others.

I wasn't like her, I told myself. I'd changed a little, and there was a spur in me, and maybe something in my eyes that wasn't too welcome, but that still put a million cold leagues between what I was and what she'd become.

I clung to that. I had to.

We had taken the ship and that was better than not taking it, especially given the state of the *Queenie*. But when Surt cast her eye over the essentials of the *Nightjammer*, taking in what she could given the size and strangeness of any ship, the news wasn't as peachy as I'd hoped.

'They did a cruel thing to us, Fura,' she said, touching a finger to her bandaged scalp. 'A cruel old thing. When they knew it wasn't going their way, what was left of her crew made a knotty mess of her control gear. Tearing this out, tearing that out. I know we didn't give them much time, what with all the murdering, but Bosa must have drilled her orders into 'em pretty deeply. If there was a chance of the *Nightjammer* being taken, they was to rip her living guts out, and they knew exactly where and what needed to be done. Yards and yards of wiring ripped out or severed, and I ain't the foggiest how we'll go about knitting it back together.'

I nodded, refusing to be too cowed by this news. After all we'd been through, not having the odd setback would have been the queer thing. Funny it had come to me to be the level-headed one, I thought, seeing the way past our immediate difficulties when everyone else was losing their nerve.

'It's just control gear, Surt. I know it looks bad now, but we don't need to move anywhere in a hurry and once you've had some rest I think you'll see it more as a challenge than an impediment.'

'I hope you're right about that, Fura.'

'I've faith in your abilities. I've faith in all our abilities.'

'You don't sound the way you did,' Surt mused. 'Not how you were before we got to the Fang, anyway. I always knew you was educated, with those thousand books of yours, but now you ain't afraid to sound like it either.'

She was right, I realised. But it hadn't been anything intentional on my part. Just a mask that had begun to slip a little. I suppose some part of me knew that, however we went on from here, this crew – if it ever *was* a crew – was going to need a captain again. I suppose it was presumptuous to think of myself stepping into that vacancy, but then again, I'd all but taken the decisions for Trusko when he was alive, whether the cove knew it or not.

'Surt . . .' I began. Then stopped, before I put a thought out there that made me look foolish.

'What is it, Fura?'

'Oh, nothing – just a silly idea that crossed my mind for a moment.'

'You might as well spit it out, I always says.'

'You mentioned that the control gear was damaged. That's mainly wiring, isn't it? I was thinking . . . well, I know this will sound ridiculous. But a robot's body's mainly wiring as well, isn't it? I know there are arms and legs and wheels and so on, but if a robot could operate those, couldn't it operate sail-control gear, ions and so on?'

'I won't say it ain't been tried, Fura. But robots aren't always smart, and for the most part people are cheaper. That's why ships are run the way they're run.'

'I know, but we're not exactly dealing with a conventional ship, are we? Or a conventional crew. And Paladin's at least as clever and resourceful as any person I've ever known.'

'But that head ain't said a word to you since you tried it. You told me.'

'That's true. But Paladin was dead once, and he came back to me. There's no reason he can't come back a second time, is there?'

'You're asking the wrong cove.'

'No, I'm asking exactly the right one. You know robots better than most, Surt, and you're not about to give up on this ship. If I gave you his head, and trusted you to connect him up to the *Nightjammer*, as best you could . . .'

'I suppose a robot could find his way around blockages, if it had to. They're sly at that sort of thing.'

'Or at least help you repair the damage, by tracing what works and what doesn't. You may as well try it, Surt: we've little left to lose.'

'I'll wire 'im up. But don't raise your hopes.'

'I won't,' I said. 'But I've got confidence in you. This is our ship now, Surt, and we'll make her fly.'

'Mm.' She gave me a doubtful look. 'The question is, what do we do with it? I suppose now you've got your sister back, you'll want to be returning to Mazarile.'

'Some of us will have outstanding business in the Congregation,' I told her. 'Some of us won't. But for the time being we'd best keep clear of the worlds. Bosa spent her life skulking in the margins because she knew she'd be torn apart if she ever got too close to civilisation. That's how we'll need to play it as well, to begin with. This ship might be ours now, but the shape of her still puts the shivers into the people, and I don't want to stake my life on explaining ourselves over the squawk or the bones.' I sounded sure of myself, and perhaps I was, but the truth of it was I'd barely given a thought to our future until she'd pressed me on it. 'There's a lot to keep us busy, Surt. We're a good crew now, but we can become a better one. And there are plenty of baubles out here to cut our teeth on. That doesn't sound too bad, does it? Crack a few of them, stuff our hold with a prize or two, and then consider our options. Bosa said there are quoins out there somewhere, a whole world stashed full of them, and someone needs to do something about all those poor dead souls, if that's what they are. But first we need a ship we can sail, and we've some work to do on that score.'

'I'll see to your robot,' Surt said.

I smiled at her. It was good to have colleagues you could rely on, but even better when you could see the shapes of friendships still to form. 'Good. And when you're done, that bargain of ours still stands.'

*

I went to see Adrana. Surt had given her a sedative, but she was coming out of it now, regarding me through narrowed, gummy eyes as I settled myself at her side. She was bound to her bed, just as Garval had been, and I thought of how our mutual fates had been spun together. There was a bandage around her head, but I was assured that Prozor's crossbow hadn't done any lasting harm.

'What happened, Fura?' she asked. 'Why have they got me tied up like this?'

'Do you not remember?'

'I remember being in the bone room. You coming. Not much after that.'

I put my warm hand on hers. 'You tried to hurt me. I don't think you really meant it, deep down – it was Bosa, acting through you. She must have started to turn you, and that's not your fault, and I'm sure you did your best to fight her. But what's done is done, and now I can't be sure that you won't hurt me again, or try to take this ship back for Bosa.'

She lapped this up as if it was just any matter-of-fact business between sisters. I suppose being tied up meant she didn't have much choice but to take me seriously.

'She did try turning me. I knew it was happening. But I thought I was strong enough to keep her out.'

'I imagine they all felt that way. We found her room, you see – the special room with all the bottled bodies she didn't have any use for any more. I can't believe any of them ever set out to become Bosa, but it happened, and it would have happened to you, given time. She'd settled on you as her successor.'

'Is she really gone?'

I glanced away. 'She's not a concern to us, if that's what you mean. We found her, in the end. But it was only because Prozor wanted to give Garval a decent resting place. We found Bosa injured, but still alive.'

'And now?'

'She'll die. Probably before we've worked out how to operate this ship, and certainly before we sail for anywhere interesting.

But until then it pleases me to keep her breathing. She has limits, I know, and if there's information I feel I really need . . .' But I pushed my darker thoughts aside with a smile. 'It's you that I'm concerned about, not her.'

'You fear me?'

'A little.'

'Good. I'm not sure what I make of you, Fura. The glowy's really shining out of you today.'

'So they say.' I used my tin fingers to stroke a knot out of her hair, as gently as I could. 'I'll keep it in me, at least for now. I'm not sorry about what I've become. Sorry about some of the things that happened, and maybe one or two of the things I had to do. But what I've turned into? No. I'm proud of what I am. Proud of being Fura Ness. And I'd sleep more easily if I knew my sister was on my side.'

'I will be.'

'I think you will, but time's going to have to be the judge of that. I'll know, though. I'll know when I look in your eyes and there's nothing left of Bosa in them.'

'And if she doesn't leave me?'

'A little splinter of her won't hurt, I suppose. In either of us.' I went to fetch her some water, and she drank it gratefully. 'The ship's in a bad way, I don't mind saying. But we'll fix her, and maybe Paladin will help us.'

Her eyes brightened. 'That old thing? Paladin's with us?'

'I brought him. The bit that matters, anyway. I know you never cared for Paladin, but there was more to him than either of us knew. He might be the thing that helps us knit this ship back together again.'

Adrana nodded. There was a lot we still had to say to each other, but there would be time for that.

'And then what?'

'They think I meant to go straight home. But I've got the spur in me for something different. Just for a little while, until we get our bearings. There are wrongs that need setting right, things to do with quoins, and if half of what Bosa told me is lies, I still want to find out what the rest of it means. And I've been inside two baubles, Adrana. Don't mind admitting I was terrified, most of the time. The thought of being locked inside one, when the fields went back up . . . but there's something else, too. An itch, I suppose you'd call it. I want to see a third one now. And a fourth. And I'll take the risks, because I saw the look in Trusko's eyes when he found the Ghostie treasure. I want to know what that thrill feels like.'

'I want to see them with you,' Adrana said.

'You will, too. I'm sure of it.'

I wasn't as sure as I sounded, but I had hope, and that was better than nothing. She was my sister, and while she'd started to be turned I had to believe that it wasn't too late. We were together again now, and I loved her, and there were people around her who were going to unravel some of the craziness Bosa had started knotting into her. Or try, anyway. We'd do our best, and we'd try everything before we gave up on her. Adrana was strong, I told myself. Strong enough that she could sweat out Bosa's poison, no matter how far it had got into her. I wanted her back, and I wasn't going to give up easily. Not until she looked into my eyes, smiled, and I knew I didn't have to worry about blades against my throat.

But I spoke the truth when I said that a little shard of Bosa wouldn't do either of us too much harm.

Bosa was right about one thing. A cove did need a plan, and until I sorted out the clutter in my skull – what had happened to me, what I'd chosen and what had happened to me regardless, what I was prepared to accept and what I was prepared to deny –I couldn't see my way to thinking clearly. It would take a while to make the *Nightjammer* ours, with or without Paladin's help, and while we were fathoming her many and devious ways, I reckoned I had time to set down my thoughts. I'd always liked writing, and if I got my story down on paper, I'd at least be able to put my side of things.

'I'm going to write out how it began,' I whispered to Adrana. 'Starting in Mazarile, the night we escaped from the museum.

I'm not going to sugar it up, and I'm not going to pretend I didn't do things I wish I hadn't. It'll take me a while, because I can't write very easily, but the work'll be good for my fingers and when I'm done you can read it and we can argue about what's right and what's wrong. And we'll call it something like *The True and Accurate Testimony of Arafura Ness*, so that it sounds right and proper, and you can always write it the way you saw it, as well, and we'll call that *The True and Accurate Testimony of Adrana Ness*, and I know yours will be nicer than mine because you always had a better hand and you knew how to make words fit together like they belonged. But it won't make one story better or worse than the other, just different.' I leaned in and kissed her on the brow. 'We'd need a new name for the ship,' I added, all teasing and confidential. 'It's ours now and we need to start thinking of it that way. A name will help.'

'You say you've the spur in you. Wrongs you want to put right. You should call it *Revenger*. That's a good name for a ship, isn't it?'

'Not exactly a sweet name.'

'But then it isn't exactly a sweet ship, after what you did to take her. Well, sleep on it. Perhaps you'll think of something better.'

I stroked her hair once more, than bid her rest for a few hours. After that, I went to what used to be Bosa's cabin, and I looked around for paper or ink or something that would suffice. But there was nothing.

So instead I went back to the bottle room, and with Strambli's help I got the first of the bodies out.

'What are you going to do with it?' Strambli asked.

I had the knife, the one Adrana had held against me, and I used it to hack away a rectangle of skin from the pickled body. It was about the size of one of the pages in the *Book of Worlds*, if much thicker and rougher than paper. But it would do.

'That,' I told Strambli.

She was shocked at first, and I think the thought crossed her mind that maybe I'd gone too far, or was on the way there. Truth to tell, I wouldn't necessarily have disagreed. But she must have weighed her options and come to the conclusion that the safest, easiest thing was just to let me have my way.

Which only left the problem of ink. So I went back to Bosa and drew blood from her. I told Surt what I needed and after that same hesitation I'd seen in Strambli she convinced herself to come round to my way of thinking as well. Surt showed me to a chemical in the medicine supply that stopped the blood from thickening up too quickly once I'd loaded it into a pen. It flowed nice and steadily then, and didn't clog up too fast. It wasn't as good as ink, but it made a permanent mark, and that was all I needed.

'I'll take a little blood each time,' I told Bosa. 'Not enough to weaken you, but just enough for my purposes. And you may die before I'm done, and if so you'll have died a good death, all things considered. If Adrana comes back to me, and I'm satisfied that she's all right, then I'll give you that good death myself. You won't suffer.'

'And if she doesn't come back to you?' she asked me, with a sort of distant curiosity.

'She will,' I said. 'She's my sister, and she's stronger and better than you ever knew. But if I doubted it, I'd make paper out of you.'

Bosa nodded slowly. 'It's good that we're clear.'

'It is,' I agreed. 'Oh, and by the way, this ship has a new name now.'

'What is it?'

'My business, not yours.'

I left her then, and went back to her cabin. The cracked glass globe of Paladin's head rested before me, still dim, but if I believed anything it was that there were thoughts going on in that glass, and sooner or later he would speak to me again, as he had spoken in Mazarile, because he was a hero of the Twelfth Occupation and I had a feeling history wasn't quite done with him yet. Call it faith, I suppose, just as I had faith in my sister.

For now, though, I had my paper, and I had my ink. But before

I could start, I stationed myself at Bosa's window and looked out of it, beyond the *Nightjammer* to the purple glint and glimmer of the Thirteenth Occupation, the fifty million little worlds of the Congregation, all the named worlds and baubles, the countless more that had never been named and never would be, huddling close to the Old Sun, pressed in from outside by all the magnificent darkness and silence of the Empty, and I mused on all the people on them, all the towns and cities, all the ships sailing between those places, proud with cargo and prizes, sails bright and billowing on the photon winds, and the bones that whispered secrets between the ships, and I wondered what it would take for me to ever feel that I could lead a settled and normal life in those worlds.

I shivered. It was cold in Bosa's ship, but not half as cold as the void beyond that glass.

Something flickered behind my reflection. A dance of lights in Paladin's head? But by the time I'd turned he was dim again, if indeed there had been anything there.

I returned to her desk, fixed myself to the chair, spread open the gutted covers of Rackamore's 1384 edition of the *Book of Worlds*, and slid one sheet of my new paper between them. Then I took up my pen in my cold tin fingers and scratched down the name of my sister, because she was where it all began.

ALASTAIR REYNOLDS was born in Barry, South
Wales. He gained a PhD in astronomy and worked
as an astrophysicist for the European Space Agency
before becoming a full-time writer. His books include
Revelation Space (the first book in the Revelation
Space trilogy and shortlisted for the BSFA and Arthur
C Clarke Awards), *Chasm City* (winner of the BSFA
Award), *Century Rain*, *House of Suns* (shortlisted
for the Arthur C Clarke Award), *Terminal World*
and the Poseidon's Children trilogy.

• • •

www.alastairreynolds.com, or you can follow
@aquilarift on Twitter.

ABOUT GOLLANCZ

Gollancz is the oldest SF publishing imprint in the world. Since being founded in 1927 Gollancz has continued to publish a focused selection of bestselling and award-winning authors. The front-list includes **Ben Aaronovitch**, **Joe Abercrombie**, **Charlaine Harris**, **Joanne Harris**, **Joe Hill**, **Alastair Reynolds**, **Patrick Rothfuss**, **Nalini Singh** and **Brandon Sanderson**.

As one of the largest Science Fiction and Fantasy imprints in the UK it is no surprise we have one of the most extensive backlists in the world. Find high-quality SF on Gateway written by such authors as **Philip K. Dick**, **Ursula Le Guin**, **Connie Willis**, **Sir Arthur C. Clarke**, **Pat Cadigan**, **Michael Moorcock** and **George R.R. Martin**.

We also have a strand of publishing in translation, which includes French, Polish and Russian authors. Gollancz is home to more award-winning authors than any other imprint, with names including **Aliette de Bodard**, **M. John Harrison**, **Paul McAuley**, **Sarah Pinborough**, **Pierre Pevel**, **Justina Robson** and many more.

The SF Gateway
More than 3,000 classic, rare and previously out-of-print SF novels at your fingertips.
www.sfgateway.com

The Gollancz Blog
Bringing you news from our worlds to yours. Stories, interviews, articles and exclusive extracts just for you!
www.gollancz.co.uk

GOLLANCZ
LONDON